Unpunished

A Novel By
William Peter Grasso

Novels by William Peter Grasso:

Moon Brothers WW2 Adventure Series
Moon Above, Moon Below, *Book 1*
Fortress Falling, *Book 2*
Our Ally, Our Enemy, *Book 3*

Jock Miles WW2 Adventure Series
Long Walk to the Sun, *Book 1*
Operation Long Jump, *Book 2*
Operation Easy Street, *Book 3*
Operation Blind Spot, *Book 4*
Operation Fishwrapper, *Book 5*

Unpunished

East Wind Returns

Cover design by Alyson Aversa

Dedication

To everyone whose life has been saved by love,
and to Peg, who saved me

PART I

IN THE AIR

Chapter One

Sweet Jesus, make this stop! No atheists in foxholes, eh? How about no atheists in bombers, either? Just us guys stupid enough to volunteer for this shit. That Kraut fighter just hit us somewhere. I felt it...cannon shell, I think. I'm breathing so hard I'm going to blow this oxygen mask right off my face, and my ears are ringing like the Bells of St. Mary's. Me and Larry...probably Eddie, too...just pumped about a thousand rounds of 50 cal at him and it didn't matter a bit. Probably never scored a hit. But he sure as hell scored one on us, somewhere. Survive thirty-five missions like this? You've got to be kidding me. And this is only number three. There's just too many ways to die up here... flak, fighters, weather, your own mistakes. Please, God, don't let me piss myself.

Where are those damned escort fighters? If this is the best they can do keeping the Krauts off us, we're in deep shit.

The Lady is still flying, though, still in her place in the formation, her engines making their droning noise just like normal. That Kraut came straight at us from 12 o'clock high...he must have been aiming for the cockpit. Goes from a tiny dot in the distance to right on top of you in a second or two. I hear Captain Pilcher in my headphones, so he and Freddy must be okay. Pilcher's screaming for damage reports. Nothing to report up here in the nose. Me and Larry are okay. Tail gunner says he's okay. So does the top turret and ball turret, too. Something wrong at the waist guns, though. Linker says Lapinski's gone...got blown out his gun window, no chute. Big hole in the roof of their compartment. So that's where we got hit? Flying Fortress, my ass. Oughta call it Flying Target...or Flying Coffin.

Now Pilcher's screaming for somebody to check Moscone, the radioman. He didn't report in. Hell...I'll do it. Unplug and grab me a walkaround oxygen bottle...anything to get out of the nose, this cramped, plexiglass fishbowl. Not like the rest of this plane is any safer. I'm just the navigator...not even the lead navigator in this formation. About ten more planes gotta die before that honor falls to me. I just do my position confirmation checks and play follow the leader. Hell, I can do the navigation in my sleep...I'm a mathematician, for cryin' out loud! But my skills only become crucial if we straggle out of formation. Until then, I'm just another gunner on this crate. What the hell am I doing here? I've got a wife. I could have had that war work deferment at the Institute. What a dope!

Crawl up into the cockpit, my gear snagging on stuff like crazy in these tight quarters. Freddy, the co-pilot, has the controls. He keeps looking over at Pilcher, who doesn't seem to be doing a damned thing...just sitting there with his hands in his lap, staring straight ahead. Some aircraft commander, that Pilcher! Wonder what they're saying? The oxygen masks hide everything but the eyes, and Freddy's look like they're shooting daggers at Pilcher. Freddy looks back at me, probably says something into the interphone but I can't hear. I'm not plugged in.

As I slide past Eddie Morris's top turret, he's

letting loose with his 50 cals. Hit him, Eddie! Kill him! Please!

The firing stops. Nothing changes. Just more spent cartridges piled up on the deck and the stench of cordite getting stronger.

Tony Moscone, the radioman, is lying on the floor of his compartment. David Linker, that smart-mouthed Jewish kid with an answer for everything, is hunched over him, bandaging his head. The first aid kit is scattered everywhere. Moscone pulls off his oxygen mask, screaming like a terrified child, "I don't wanna die, I don't wanna die," over and over again. No shit, fella. Save your breath before it freezes all over your face. And put your goddamn mask back on.

The Lady's guns fire again and I start to duck, like there's someplace to hide. Dumb shit!

Linker pulls off his own mask and yells to me, "He'll be okay. Just got banged up a little...Get him to calm down, will you, Lieutenant? I've got to get back to my gun."

Then he adds, "Lapinski bought it, Lieutenant Joe. He's just gone...fell right out of the airplane."

The tears Linker tries...and fails...to fight back freeze as soon as they drip away, just like the radioman's blood. Moscone curls into a ball on the floor, rocking gently. This kid's gone...shell shock...combat fatigue. I'm not in such hot shape myself, after only three missions. Only thirty-two more to go...

I get Moscone back into his seat and strap him in. One look in his eyes tells you he's someplace else. Even with his mask on, I can tell he's mumbling something. I unplug his microphone...nobody needs to listen to his crazy shit right now. He stares blankly through his radio console to God knows where...anyplace but here, on this B-17, where the rest of us wait to get blown to bits or fall

*to the earth in flames. Ship's guns start firing
again...another Kraut is coming. Will he be the one that
kills us? In an instant, we'll know...*

*Nothing. We're still flying. We're not dead yet.
Our guns fall silent...until the next one.*

*Squeezing back to the cockpit...I brush Morris's
foot as I pass beneath his turret. He glances down from
his domed perch atop the airplane, unrecognizable in
leather helmet, oxygen mask, and sunglasses. He gives
me a thumbs up...I'm glad he thinks so, the stupid
bastard.*

*I get to the cockpit and crouch behind the
pedestal, between the two pilots: Captain Leonard
Pilcher and Lieutenant Freddy O'Hara. I pull off my
mask and shout the news about Moscone. Pilcher, who's
been sitting there like he's in some kind of trance,
suddenly turns to me and says the words that knock me
for a loop:*

*"Gelardi, give me a course for Trelleborg,
Sweden. The Lady's shot up and we've got to get our
injured man medical help ASAP. Keep us out over the
water, away from the Danish coast."*

*Freddy O'Hara pulls off his mask and explodes:
"Sweden! You're outta your fucking mind! We take
casualties and you want to desert? Sit out the war? No
fucking way! Just bail him out and let the Germans take
care of him if you're so fucking worried. Sweden and
Switzerland...that's where all the yellow bastards go.
There's nothing wrong with this airplane. She can still do
the mission."*

*"You forget who's in charge here, Lieutenant,"
Pilcher replies. "I decide what this ship does. I've got to
look out for my men."*

*"Bullshit...you're just yellow. You get wounded
up here, it's tough shit, that's all. I ain't no deserter."*

"*Suit yourself, O'Hara. Feel free to bail out over Germany, the Baltic...I don't give a shit.*"

Freddy turns to me. "*Three missions with this clown and now he pulls this Section 8 bullshit! We get jumped, and first he acts like he's in a fucking coma, then he decides he's the boss again. Joey, are you going along with this high-brow scumbag? You know what it would mean...for the rest of your life?*"

All I can manage to say is, "*I...I guess...I'll do what I'm ordered.*"

"*Great, two fucking deserters,*" Freddy spits through clenched teeth. I'm amazed I can hear him at all over the drone of the engines and the clatter of the guns. Now Freddy's shouting again. "*Tell you what, Captain. I'm tellin' the rest of the crew what's goin' on here and give them the choice you just gave me.*"

"*I don't need to remind you of the penalty for mutiny, do I, Lieutenant?*" Pilcher shouts back.

"*Fuck that! Mutiny against a deserter! That's rich! I'll take my chances with the enemy, you chickenshit coward. Typical fucking rich boy...*"

Freddy O'Hara is through talking.

In a minute, the tally is done. Sergeants Ed Morris, David Linker and Frank Hughes—the tail gunner—elect to stay. Morris is torn. He has no interest sitting out the war as an internee in Sweden, but he's the flight engineer: *The Lady M's* airworthiness is his responsibility. Plain and simple, he loves her. He won't leave her.

Frank Hughes is more afraid of parachuting than staying on board.

Tony Moscone is incapable of making choices and Linker won't leave him. After unlucky Harry Lapinski, Tony is David Linker's best buddy. And like I said, Linker is Jewish. Jumping into Nazi Germany by choice *probably doesn't seem like much of an option to him, with that big J stamped into his dog tags. We've all heard the stories...Jews fleeing for their lives all over Europe. We were all skeptical of those stories, too. All except Captain Pilcher. Linker says he overheard Pilcher once, spewing with all the certainty of willful ignorance, "Sure Hitler's gotta kill off the sheenies. That's the only way he'll get control of the banks."*

And me, Joe Gelardi...I'm going to stay, too. But I've got a problem right off the bat. "Captain," I say, "I don't have a chart for airfields in Sweden."

Without a word, he reaches into his flight jacket and produces a folded map.

Shaking his head in disbelief, Freddy cries, "You fucking bastard! You've been planning this! Count me the fuck out!"

I unfold the map and stare at it in disbelief. This is a damned road map...like some tourist would use! How the hell am I supposed to navigate off this? What are we going to do? Read signs?

Still, I'm going to stay with the ship. With the Captain.

Pilcher grabs his control wheel and announces, "My airplane." Freddy relinquishes the controls in disgust. Pilcher retards the throttles, and The Lady M begins her descent, dropping out of the bottom of the formation.

Besides Freddy O'Hara, Lieutenant Larry Harkin—the bombardier—and Sergeant Lou DiNapoli— the ball turret gunner—want no part of Pilcher's plan. They bail out somewhere over northwest Germany, close to the Danish border.

Before he leaves the airplane, Freddy O'Hara confronts Captain Leonard Pilcher one last time:

"I promise you, Pilcher...if I ever see you again,

I'm gonna kill you, you useless bastard."

He takes one more deep breath from the oxygen mask. Then, the last of the three, he jumps.

PART II

TO THE GROUND

Chapter Two

Miraculously, no German fighters bothered *The Lady M* as she made her way, alone, north across the Baltic Sea. Two fighters had passed close by but did not engage, even though her gunners had let loose a few useless bursts at them. Probably low on fuel and out of ammunition, they were desperate to get home before prowling American fighters feasted on them. But there had been no American fighters, either.

Just as well, Captain Pilcher thought. *I've only got three gunners left.* Ed Morris would handle the top turret, if necessary, but for now, he was helping Pilcher fly, operating the systems Lieutenant O'Hara, the co-pilot turned parachutist, usually handled. Tony Moscone was nothing more than a passenger; physically present, mentally elsewhere. *The Lady M's* bomb load—and the top secret Norden bombsight—were jettisoned harmlessly into the Baltic on Captain Pilcher's orders.

Then he gave the order to jettison the machine gun ammunition.

Ed Morris pulled off his oxygen mask to register a personal protest: "Why, Captain? What if we get jumped? You know the stories of the guys who started cleaning their guns over the Channel…and got shot down?"

Pilcher responded into the interphone for the whole crew to hear. "No Germans around here…This is neutral Swedish airspace now. We don't want to seem like we're posing any threat. Take the hand-operated guns off their mounts and stow them. Point the top turret guns full up, all the others full down."

As he listened to Captain Pilcher's orders, a

thought popped into David Linker's head: *Is this guy reading from "The Deserter's Handbook" or something?*

This all seemed too strange to Joe Gelardi, like they were suddenly over a different planet, one that was not consumed in a war. *What the hell are we doing? A little battle damage to the ship, one gunner gone, and the radioman out of commission...That's a reason to divert? Ships have been shot up a lot worse and still finished their mission. Pilcher's the boss...but why does following his orders feel so much like...disgrace?*

The Lady M had descended below 10,000 feet; they no longer needed oxygen. Gelardi had given Pilcher a rough course to fly, but without current wind and weather information—or an aviation chart—there was little he could do to provide drift corrections. Just wait for the landfall and try to figure out where they were visually.

Little was said onboard *The Lady M,* the silence a testament that events were now completely beyond their control. The crew assembled in the cockpit; there was no point staying at their weaponless battle stations. A coast came into view. Joe Gelardi tried to reconcile what he could see on the ground with the ridiculous map Pilcher had given him. "Should we turn east or west?" Pilcher asked his navigator.

Joe Gelardi replied, "I have no earthly idea yet, Captain."

Pilcher inquired about fuel reserves. Morris, the flight engineer, snapped his reply: "We've got plenty...we had enough to get back to England, remember?"

Pilcher ignored the barb, looking instead to Gelardi for confirmation of the engineer's assessment. The navigator nodded in agreement; they had enough fuel to stay airborne for at least three more hours. But they needed a place to land in Sweden. No other non-hostile nation was in reach; too far to the west, you were in German-held Norway. Too far to the east, you were in Finland, still a co-belligerent with Germany but at war only with Russia. Gelardi felt pretty sure the land below them was Sweden, but that was about all. *Wouldn't it be hot shit,* he thought, *to come all this way, just to land in occupied territory anyway?*

Airborne specks in the distance grew large quickly. Two fighters, wearing Swedish national markings, now bracketed *The Lady M.* The Swedish pilots were used to this sort of intrusion; it was their only connection to the war that raged in all directions around their neutral country. Stray aircraft from both sides— some lost, some badly damaged, some full of able-bodied crewmen just looking to sit out the war—appeared with regularity: over 300 aircraft since the war began four years ago. The Swedish pilots had their instructions: only engage if hostile intent was displayed. Otherwise, if they seemed determined to land, guide them to an airfield designated to accept internees. None of the intruding aircraft had ever displayed hostile intent, and *The Lady M* was no exception. Pilcher saluted the Swedish pilot who had given the "follow me" hand signal and turned the big bomber to trail its new escorts.

"Where do you think they're taking us, Lieutenant?" David Linker asked.

"Beats the hell out of me," Joe Gelardi replied. "We turned west, so I guess we could be heading to Trelleborg, maybe Malmö," he continued, moving a finger along the map. "We'll find out soon enough."

Within 15 minutes, they were over a small city with an airfield on its eastern outskirts. A narrow strait separated the city from a land mass to the west. The escort fighters lowered their landing gear. Leonard Pilcher began his landing preparations.

Joe Gelardi felt certain now: *This must be Malmö. That's occupied Denmark across the strait.*

"The left gear's not down! Still got a cross-hatch!" Pilcher cried.

"Not surprised," Morris replied. "We took some hits around there. Give me a minute…I'll try to get her down and locked…Tire's probably shot up, though…Maybe no brakes, either."

"NO! Never mind!" Pilcher commanded. "Bring the right gear back up…I'll belly her in."

"Wait, Captain!" Morris pleaded. "I think I can get it down. Let me try…Don't belly her!"

"I said *no*, Sergeant. I'm not going to risk landing on one gear and cartwheeling. Pick up the right gear."

Morris was begging now. "But this will only take a minute, sir!" The thought of a needless belly landing in this indifferent place—which would reduce this slightly damaged, yet perfectly flyable aircraft to nothing more than scrap metal—seemed foolish and irresponsible to the young sergeant.

"NOW, Sergeant!"

"Yessir," Morris sighed as the indicator signaled the right gear was retracting. "Gear up."

Pilcher aligned *The Lady M* with the grass field adjacent the paved runway. The descent was gentle, steady—but poorly executed nonetheless. He was too high and would land too far down the grass strip; even sliding on its belly, the heavy bomber probably would not stop before crashing into some of the hangars encircling the airfield. He should have gone around and tried again. But he pushed the nose over, increasing the sink rate and airspeed, pulling out at the last moment to meet the ground where he originally planned, but going much too fast.

Oddly enough, to the crew of *The Lady M*, strapped in for dear life, the initial impact with the ground felt like bouncing off a mattress. The second impact was far more severe. Numerous pieces of onboard equipment broke loose and flew forward as the aircraft dug in and rapidly decelerated. The four propellers—and the engines that drove them—stopped abruptly as their blades impacted the ground and folded as if made of rubber. The sound of rending metal filled the crew's ears. Gasoline from ruptured fuel tanks spilled from the wings and pooled below the now stationary bomber. Within seconds, the fuel ignited and *The Lady M* was consumed in fire. Her six crewmen barely escaped through the gaping hole in the nose where the bombardier's plexiglass bubble used to be. Any other escape route would have led them to a fiery death. Ed Morris's fears for his aircraft—this machine that he loved—had been fully realized.

"You should have let me get the gear down, Captain," Morris said softly, fighting back tears as the crew milled around without purpose at a safe distance from the blaze. He could not recall another time he wanted to strike someone so badly. But he did not dare.

Tony Moscone wandered around the crash site perimeter, still like a dazed child, his physical wounds anything but life-threatening—but his mental wounds life-altering.

Pilcher, with all the arrogance of one who refused to admit mistakes, offered this rationalization: "See? If we hadn't dumped the bombs and ammo, it would be cooking off like crazy right now. And look around...we're in good company." His arm made a grand, sweeping gesture.

A dozen American bombers—B-17s and B-24s—

were parked on the airfield's periphery, their guns removed, their insignia painted over. Three British bombers were among them. A few of the planes sported combat damage so severe it was obvious, even viewed from a distance, their flying days were over. The rest looked perfectly airworthy. And looking across the field, the crewmen of *The Lady M* were disturbed to notice something else: two Luftwaffe aircraft, unmistakable, their markings still clearly visible.

A police car drove up, its occupants satisfied by the crew's proximity to the inferno that there was no danger of the aircraft blowing up. Two constables emerged from the car and politely demanded that the crew surrender their sidearms immediately. Several fire trucks arrived and began, ineffectively, to combat the blaze. After a few fruitless minutes, they focused on preventing the spread of the flames across the grass until the wreck burned out.

Frank Hughes, the tail gunner, was grateful to be on the ground in one piece. He dropped to his knees and ran his hands through his close-cropped blond hair, bewildered by the sight of the flaming wreck from which they had just escaped. But silently, he wondered: *What can of worms did we open by coming here?*

A different thought filled David Linker's head: *We should have just done the damned mission and gone home.*

And yet another occupied Joe Gelardi's: *I should have jumped with Freddy.*

Chapter Three

The pain in Fred O'Hara's left ankle made walking an imposing proposition; just standing proved difficult enough. He had come down in a wooded area and tangled with a tree just before reaching the ground. It had stopped his descent enough to deflate his parachute canopy; then a tree limb had broken with a sickening crack, sending him plummeting 30 feet to the ground, slowed only by impacts with several more tree limbs. He was lucky, he supposed, to only have the sprained ankle—and the assorted bumps and bruises. He'd have to learn to deal with the pain. After all, this was just another scrap, like countless others growing up poor in a turbulent Pennsylvania mill town. Brickbats, knives, guns—he had faced them all before. But he wished he had been dealt a better hand this time.

His parachute canopy remained high in the tree, flapping like a big white flag of surrender in the late morning breeze. His impaired mobility had doomed his efforts to bring it down. He had no choice but to try and distance himself from it.

He had expected to be met on the ground by German troops, or at least angry civilians. Three parachutes dropping out of the clear morning sky were hard to miss. Surely someone had seen their arrival.

He got his bearings. He'd seen the other two land before him. Lou DiNapoli, the ball turret gunner, was a bit to the north; Larry Harkin, the bombardier, a bit to the west. Either man could not be more than a few hundred yards away.

He suspected they were near the German city of

Flensburg, not far from the Danish border; he was sure he recognized the outlines of the city to the north as he drifted down in his parachute. No matter—the American and British lines were hundreds of miles to the southwest. They did not have a snowball's chance in hell of getting there. If they were not killed outright, they would live out the rest of the war in some prison camp. But the odds did not bother Fred O'Hara very much.

At least nobody can call me a deserter. Not after Pilcher's little stunt.

He limped painfully toward Larry Harkin's likely landing place. He had to cross a narrow road; he would have much preferred to sprint across it—less chance of being seen—but his ankle put that out of the question. He hoped DiNapoli would not be wandering along the road—in plain sight—in search of his co-pilot and bombardier. But O'Hara was pessimistic: *DiNapoli's dumb enough to ride the ball turret, so he just might be dumb enough not to hide, too.*

As O'Hara struggled along, he was struck by the peacefulness of his surroundings: the woods quiet, only the sound of birds chirping; the bright blue sky above the tree tops; tall grass and wildflowers in the open fields bowing to a light breeze. A peaceful summer morning. Just minutes ago and miles above, he had faced violent death while preparing to deal violent death. The tangled, white contrails left by that airborne mayhem were dispersing, like so many wispy, windblown clouds. The contrast disoriented him; surely this beautiful setting could not be part of a world at war? The jarring pain in his ankle dragged him back to reality.

The heavy flying suit—so necessary to keep warm at high altitude—was causing O'Hara to be drenched in sweat here on the ground. He pulled off the leather jacket and flying helmet and tucked them under his arm. The ankle was killing him; his slow progress made him wonder what chance he had of escaping capture. Maybe he should just tell the other two to strike off without him. Assuming, of course, they were not injured, too.

But Larry Harkin was injured, far worse than O'Hara. He, too, had tangled with a tree, and his left leg was fractured. It was twisted unnaturally beneath him as he lay on the ground; the jagged end of the broken femur protruded from the torn leg of his flying suit. Blood spurted from the severed femoral artery, turning the dark brown soil black. And his parachute, too, remained suspended in the tree that had caught it, a second white flag for all to see.

Another harsh contrast plagued Fred O'Hara. Just last night, while visiting a pub in the little village near their English base, he had been furious with Larry Harkin, ready to come to blows. *Damn Midwestern farm boy, with his tall, blond good looks...*the girl O'Hara had been trying to chat up ditched him to make a play for Harkin's attentions. She was not even polite about it; he had overheard a comment she made to another girl, calling him a "bloody Irish thug." O'Hara had proceeded to get nasty drunk, and only Joe Gelardi's intervention had prevented the inevitable fight between the co-pilot and bombardier. At least he had gotten back to the billet early and gotten a few hours' sleep before the 3 a.m. wake-up, something most of the other crew members lacked. They had used those same hours attempting to coax young English ladies out of their knickers. But who really cared about sleep? You lived on coffee and adrenaline—and you stood a pretty good chance of your young life ending very soon.

"Freddy...I think I'm fucked," was all Larry Harkin managed to say before slipping into shock.

Fred O'Hara flopped to the ground, next to Harkin. He tried to fashion a tourniquet from his belt but it was no use; Larry had lost too much blood already. Fred watched his crewmate's face turn ashen as his life slipped away.

Suddenly, a sound of thrashing footsteps; Lou DiNapoli appeared. He did not seem injured from the jump at all. *Damn eighteen year olds can take all kinds of punishment...us old men of twenty have it real tough,* O'Hara thought.

"Ahh shit, Lieutenant!" DiNapoli cried as he saw Harkin's broken body. When, a second later, he realized that O'Hara could hardly walk on his injured ankle, he mumbled, "Oh, brother...what are we gonna do, Lieutenant?"

"First, get Larry's and my chutes out of the trees. They're a dead giveaway to where we are. Where's your chute, Louie?"

"I hid it under some bushes."

"Okay, good. Pull this one down, then go do mine...it's about a hundred fifty yards that way. Unfortunately, you can't miss it," he said, pointing east. "Then come back here. Maybe I'll have an idea what to do next by then."

It took Lou DiNapoli several minutes to free Harkin's parachute from its tree. He rolled it up, set it down next to O'Hara, and said, "Here...use it for a cushion or something." Then he reached into the pockets of his flying suit and pulled out two chocolate bars. After flipping one to O'Hara, he tore open the other.

"How many bars you got?" O'Hara asked. He knew DiNapoli never went anywhere without an ample supply of chocolate.

"Enough to last us a coupla days."

Then DiNapoli set out to take down the last chute,

intently munching on the chocolate bar.

O'Hara lay back on the soft silk of the parachute and waited. *This DiNapoli kid seems to be a lot like me...grew up poor in a tough neighborhood, a little guy scrapping for every crumb. And he's brave enough—or crazy enough—to ride the ball turret.* The ball turret gunner hung beneath the aircraft in his plexiglass fishbowl, curled into a most uncomfortable position, his head stuck between two big machine guns. The worst part was that with his feet as high as his head, he seemed to be presenting his genitals to the enemy. Literally asking to get his testicles shot off. O'Hara managed a fleeting smile: *Maybe that's why they call it the "ball" turret.* Small guys like Louie DiNapoli seemed to have the least trouble working in that cramped, contorted hell. Claustrophobics need not apply.

Harkin's breathing became a shallow rattle. He was unconscious now. The flow from the severed artery was slowing. He could not have much longer. Suddenly there was a new sound—vehicles on the road nearby. They stopped, and in a few moments, German soldiers were walking toward Fred O'Hara and Larry Harkin. Fred stopped counting them at 10. Most had what seemed to be American chocolate bars sticking out of their tunic pockets. An officer, with pistol drawn, led the way.

Lou DiNapoli was in the center of the group, his hands on his head, his sidearm holster empty. O'Hara thought about drawing his own sidearm but found his body would make no such movement, like his subconscious had already passed judgment on the pointlessness of the act.

"I didn't tell 'em shit, Lieutenant!" DiNapoli yelled, then was knocked to his knees by a rifle butt across the upper back.

"I know you didn't, Louie," O'Hara replied. "Just

be quiet. Only name, rank..."

Waving his pistol at O'Hara, the German officer said, in thickly accented English, "You would do well to follow your own advice...be quiet. Are you injured, airman?"

"Yeah. My ankle."

"I am so sorry. Parachuting can be quite dangerous, no? And your comrade?" the German asked, pointing his pistol toward Harkin.

"What do you think, Fritz? He look okay to you?"

The German sighed. "We used to have a very fine hospital near here, but your *jabos* attacked it a few days ago. Most of the medical staff were killed. So unfortunate."

Jabos...short for *Jadgbomber.* Ground attack aircraft.

O'Hara was transfixed by the German officer's face. On each cheek there was a small, dark circle with several lines radiating from it, like a star—or a spider.

"You are looking at my face, my friend. A most interesting wound, no? Courtesy of a Russian sniper with very good aim...but very bad luck. His bullet passed through my open mouth. I didn't realize I had been shot until I spat blood and bits of teeth."

Fucking fascinating, O'Hara thought, wishing the sniper better luck next time.

Then the German raised his pistol and fired one round into Larry Harkin's head. The pink mist—brain tissue and blood spurting from the bullet hole—settled on a startled, deafened Fred O'Hara. The noise of the pistol shot, the muzzle so close to O'Hara's head, might just as well have been a cannon shot.

"I do him a favor, no?" the German asked as the shot's echoes dwindled, not expecting an answer. Then he summoned two of his men to pick up Fred O'Hara and carry him to one of the vehicles. A stoic Lou DiNapoli was marched to a different vehicle, where he was placed along with Larry Harkin's tarp-shrouded body.

Lying on the floor of the truck, surrounded by German soldiers and still covered with his crewmate's brains and blood, Fred O'Hara silently renewed his vow: he would kill Captain Leonard Pilcher.

Chapter Four

Oskar Steenslund was an impatient man. He had grown weary of this whole process. Another American aircrew had arrived, to be accommodated as internees. Worse, this crew's insolent young commander was now sitting before him, asking—no, demanding—special privileges. This captain spoke in obscure parables, alluding to some exalted lineage, high social status and the entitlements thereof. Yet, he became surly when you failed to understand and questioned his meaning.

"You are aware, Captain Pilcher, we have quite a few American and British aircrews in Sweden," Steenslund said. "But you are the first, I believe, to ever request specific housing accommodations, apparently based on your social status. Several of your fellow internees are sons of American government officials. A few of the Brits are titled nobility. None have ever thought to place such demands on their hosts. We appreciate the fact that your father is 'the noted industrialist Max Pilcher,' as you say, and his firm has done much business with this nation, but quite frankly, my good Captain, you are all unexpected and unwelcome guests. You will be treated with decency and kindness, nevertheless."

Steenslund had expected the young captain across the table to become dismayed and defensive when tagged as an "unwelcome" guest. All the officers he had interviewed before had done so. They would carry on passionately how they had no choice: their plane was too badly damaged, or they had severely injured crewmembers, or they had become lost, separated from their formation. But their troubles mattered little to Oskar Steenslund. He was a civilian official of the Swedish Ministry of Defence, and his government had no interest in getting involved in this war in any military capacity. Sweden was officially neutral: holding and tending to wayward airmen from any of the belligerent nations until hostilities ceased or an equitable arrangement for their return negotiated was a function of that neutrality, no matter how those airmen came to be in Sweden. This had proved to be a great and costly bother, one for which the Swedes could expect little compensation and no profit other than a collection of warplanes for which they had little use. Judging whether an airman was a true casualty of war or just an opportunistic deserter was not something that officially concerned him or his government.

No, this airman—Captain Leonard Pilcher, US Army Air Force—had merely smirked at Steenslund's remarks, as if he knew better than this fat old civil servant. Then he renewed his request for lodging in a specific hotel in Stockholm—a very posh hotel, which he claimed to know well. Actually, he had never been to Sweden before; he had just heard the stories his daddy's friends told.

Steenslund glanced across the large table to his assistant, Pola MacLeish, and shrugged. Pola knew the shrug meant *I am finished with this idiot. He is your problem now.* Then Oskar Steenslund left the room, his gait a mid-paced waddle born of corpulence.

Pilcher eyed this woman with whom he was now alone, sizing her up. She had yet to say a word. He thought her mousy, perhaps—her white-blonde hair tied into a bun; pale blue eyes behind wire-rimmed eyeglasses; a prim skirt and blouse, buttoned all the way up. He could not see her shoes, but he had heard their sound as she walked into the room. They sounded like oxfords, practical and unfeminine. Definitely not heels. It was a shame, he thought. *She probably has a nice figure under those dowdy clothes. Hard to tell her age, though. She looks young, maybe early twenties...maybe a little more.* Steenslund, that fat old man, had been a bureaucratic bore; Pilcher was glad to be rid of him. It should not be any problem manipulating this unimposing frump. After all, she was just a woman.

"MacLeish...that's an interesting name for a Swede. You are Swedish, aren't you?"

"Yes, Captain, I am Swedish. My full name is Pola Nilsson-MacLeish. I am married to a British Army officer...a Scot...who is currently fighting the Japanese in Burma."

That bit of information surprised Pilcher and he schemed how to use it to advantage. He decided it best to feign interest. "How about that! How'd you two ever get together?"

"We were both students at London School of Economics, before the war. Postgraduate studies. When Reginald left for India in 1941, I returned here, to Malmö, to stay with my family."

Okay...Grad student. Definitely in her mid-twenties. Bookish...probably never been laid good in her life. Not by no Scotsman, anyway...they're all queers, just like the Brits...I'd fuck her in a pinch.

"And you haven't seen him in three years?"

"That's correct, Captain. A much-delayed letter now and then, since mail with England was re-established two years ago, but like everything in wartime, it is undependable. I can only assume...and hope...that he is well. We all suffer somehow, Captain. Even those of us in neutral countries...but I bore you with my problems. Now I must ask you some questions."

Start by asking me if I fucking care, lady.

But Pilcher responded: "Go ahead, I'm all ears," still feigning interest, still confident that this lonely young woman could be bent to his will.

"All ears...that's a very curious expression." Her English—impeccable but featuring a thick Scottish accent—was befuddling but charming: "Verrry cuooooriouuus." The word "internee" quickly became Pilcher's favorite. When she said it, it came out "intu-ooornee."

He smirked, enjoying a private joke: *At least that husband managed to inject her with a Scottish accent.*

"Captain Pilcher, you arrived with a crew of six. We are used to many more in an American bomber crew. Can you explain?"

"What does it matter to you?" he snarled, his friendly charade suddenly over.

"It matters, sir, because we must accurately inform your government of the serial number of the aircraft in which you arrived as well as the name, rank, identification number, and physical condition of each of its crew. We must confirm the roster you provided...and we must be specific as to each crew member's whereabouts. Any missing personnel must be listed as such."

Dismissively, Pilcher replied, "Well, I'm not sure what happened to the other four."

"I find that hard to believe, Captain."

"I don't care what you believe, miss. That's the way it is."

"As I mentioned a moment ago, Captain, it's missus. Please remember you are a guest in this country and hardly in a position to set conditions, as Professor Steenslund took great pains to explain to you."

"Well, we'll just have to see about that, miss. And

that stuffy old guy was a professor? Of what?"

"Economics. We are economists at the Ministry of Defence."

"That's funny...economists processing 'intu-ooornees.' I would think we would be more of a political issue for your government, with a special agency to deal with us."

"Oh, no, Captain. That is where you are wrong. The politics was decided long ago. We are neutral. We favor neither side. Accommodating aircrews of belligerent nations has become strictly an economic issue. And a burden for us. You're not supposed to be here. There is no organization created for the specific purpose of catering to your needs."

"Well, then...just give me what I want and I won't burden you any more," Pilcher offered, sounding more like a spoiled child than a grown man. He took great pains to mock her accent, pronouncing "burden" as "buooorden."

"Out of the question, sir. You and your crew...or what's left of it...will be accommodated here in the city of Malmö, at this police barracks, until further notice. I will be responsible for seeing that your basic needs are fulfilled."

Pilcher glowered from across the table. This plain-Jane brainy bitch was not budging. But she would see...They would all see. He had no intention of staying in this dumpy barracks, no matter how much freedom of movement he was accorded. Once the word got out the son of Max Pilcher was here, he'd be getting the royal treatment. All the money Daddy made for these frozen blond clowns would do its own talking. He decided to change tack.

"Neutral, eh? How come I saw Luftwaffe airplanes with their markings intact? You painted over all the markings on the Allied aircraft."

Pola MacLeish sighed and leaned back in her chair. She tapped the fountain pen on the table a few times, then replied, "Captain, German airmen can get just as lost and frightened as Allied airmen. Those aircraft you refer to only recently arrived, just as you did, and will be processed in due course."

"You think we're here because we were 'lost and frightened?'" Pilcher shouted. "I had to nurse that plane all the way...so shot up that the landing was nothing but crash and burn! I'm a goddamn hero! My crew can thank me, and only me, for still being alive."

Pola just nodded, making notes on the forms before her. Then, without looking up, she asked: "Even the crew members who are not here? Are they thanking you, too?"

"I told you...I don't know what happened to the other four, and I don't care if they're thanking me or not. They left the airplane...that's all I know. Anybody who says anything different is a liar."

"Left the airplane, you say. They parachuted?" Pola probed.

"That's a safe assumption, miss. Except for Lapinski...He got blown from the plane when the fighters got us."

"Is it also a safe assumption that they parachuted...or fell...over Germany? Or perhaps Denmark?"

"What makes you so sure our mission was up that way?" Pilcher asked, confident this was one question for which she would not have an answer.

"Because if it hadn't been, you'd be talking to a Swiss official right now."

Pilcher stared away, sulking. He was still losing this game. His response was soft and distracted: "I suppose Germany."

"What part of Germany?"

"Does it matter?"

"Yes, Captain, it matters greatly to your government. Can you name a city or region over which they parachuted?"

"I think we were near Flensburg. Why don't you ask my navigator, Gelardi?"

"In due course, Captain. Now I can complete this report and forward it to your government. No doubt your loved ones will be glad to know that at least six of you are safe and sound. That wasn't so hard, was it?"

Actually, that should be five, Pola thought. Sergeant Moscone might be safe, but he seemed anything but sound.

There was still something on Pilcher's mind. "I've got a question," he said. "Those Germans...how many are there? I don't know, but it sure looks like you're giving them special privileges."

"Less than a hundred. There are far more Americans scattered around Sweden...over one thousand. And about four hundred Brits. Slightly more than one hundred American aircraft have landed here...many in perfect condition."

"Are you saying we're all deserters?" Pilcher shot back, angry and defensive.

"That is not for me...or my government...to determine, Captain. But as you say...your aircraft was severely damaged, was it not? In fact, now destroyed...and for your information, Captain, we frown on the aircraft of any belligerent nation entering our airspace without permission...for any reason."

Pilcher was beginning to sound shrill. "And where are all these Germans?"

"They live among the general population of

Sweden, just as you will."

This was definitely not what he expected to hear. "Is that such a hot idea? Couldn't Germans and Americans come in contact with each other?"

"Of course, Captain, but fraternization would be unlikely. You have all been disarmed, and you will find it a daunting challenge to obtain any sort of weapon in this country. It has been our experience that most crews who arrive here no longer exhibit much of a will to fight. Feel free, though, to strangle each other with your bare hands all you like."

"You're joking, aren't you?" Pilcher asked.

Pola Nilsson-MacLeish just smiled, shook her head, and left the room.

Max Pilcher flung the telegram onto the huge desk and spun his chair to face the penthouse office window. This had been the second telegram from the War Department in two weeks. The first announced his son's aircraft had failed to return from a mission, declaring him "missing in action." The current one told of his son's internment in Sweden "for the duration."

Max Pilcher frowned. At least that foolish boy was alive and well. But still he thought: *That idiot son of mine better have a damn good reason to be in Sweden. His plane better have been shot to hell.*

He turned to the enormous intercom on his desk and beckoned to his secretary: "Dorothy, ring up General Marshall." Settling back into the plush, high-backed chair, he lit a cigar and waited for the call, still pondering the situation.

A few minutes later, Dorothy's voice spilled from the intercom speaker. "General Marshall on the line, sir."

"George, how the hell are you?" Max Pilcher bellowed at the Army Chief of Staff. Brief pleasantries aside, the industrialist and the general got down to serious business.

"George, my boy Lennie's gotten himself...and me...in a bit of a pickle. Seems he and his bomber have ended up in Sweden...I'm told he's okay...No, I don't know anything about battle damage...Yeah, I've heard those stories, too, but desertion? No son of mine would ever pull something like that, George!" Max Pilcher hoped the laugh that accompanied that last sentence would not sound forced. He knew full well that his son was capable of all sorts of irresponsible foolishness. Fortunately, Marshall did not know his son personally.

"Anyway, you know I've got that patent fight with the Swedes over that precision milling process. Lots of money riding on that one...lots they'll owe me if they lose. I don't need them putting me over a barrel by holding him hostage...I know he's not a POW, George, but isn't it pretty much up to them when he can leave? I don't need them using him as some goddamn bargaining chip. Getting him out of there might do us both some good...Surely they can't deny a request from the US Government, can they? You've done this sort of thing before, haven't you?"

Max Pilcher listened silently for a moment, then spoke: "I appreciate your help, George. Give my best to Katherine."

Chapter Five

The train was heading south, deeper into Germany. Fred O'Hara sat in the small coach car along with a dozen other POW airmen—ten American, two British. He had been able to use the hands of his wristwatch as a compass, just like he was taught in flight school:

In the northern hemisphere, point the hour hand in the direction of the sun. Halfway between the hour hand and the 12 is south.

The five Wehrmacht guards seemed like a ragtag collection of teenagers and old men. Their big, bolt-action field rifles seemed unsuited for guard duty in quarters so confined as this railway car. They could hardly point the weapons without hitting something—or somebody—with the barrels. Small automatic machine pistols would have been much more practical. No wonder they all seemed so nervous.

Thirteen of us POWs in all...a real lucky number.

Lou DiNapoli was in the seat in front of O'Hara. The officer who captured them—the man with the bizarre facial wounds—had assured them POW officers and enlisted men would remain segregated. This motley crew now watching over them—as they were being transported to Stalag Luft Who-Knows-What—had not bothered with segregation. The train had at least five coach cars, as far as O'Hara could tell. The other four seemed to be full of civilians. This was just an ordinary passenger train, with a handful of very special guests.

At first, the POWs had not talked, a few out of fear, the rest just trying to size up their surroundings and their captors. After all, it was their sworn duty to try to escape. The specter of their less-than-formidable guards was raising some hope that escape from this train might actually be possible. A series of winks, nods, and sidelong glances among the captives was spreading this hope like wildfire.

The POWs began to talk amongst themselves, murmurs at first, then full-voice. It was clear that none of their guards spoke English; repeatedly, they shouted *Ruhe! Ruhe!* at their prisoners, these ignored demands for silence adding to the mutual miscomprehension, raising the volume level and tension in the car. The guards sensed their control slipping away quickly. They backed against the walls of the car as trembling fingers tightened around triggers.

Lou DiNapoli turned to Fred O'Hara and asked, "Whaddya think, Lieutenant...should I make a go at this kid?" as he eyed the nearest guard, a smallish, pimple-faced boy who seemed barely 16. "I'll grab his rifle...you other guys jump the rest, right? It'll be all over in a second. Then we hop off this damn train and take our chances in the woods again. You think your ankle can handle it?"

"What ankle?" was O'Hara's cocky reply. He liked the odds. So did every other POW in earshot. If nothing else, they'd be a thorn in the side to the Germans for a while longer. He did not kid himself; even if he escaped this time, eventually he would wind up a POW for the duration. Or he would be dead, buried like Larry Harkin in a POW graveyard while the people back home lived in the false hope of his MIA classification.

But before anyone could make a move, the wooden roof of the rail car exploded in a shower of splinters, smoke, and dust. Some of the windows, so clean a moment ago, were now splattered with blood and human tissue. A few of the seats were shattered, along with their occupants. Then came the unmistakable roar of aircraft engines flashing by low overhead.

"We've been strafed by our own guys!" an American lieutenant cried, as he clutched the remnants of his severed left arm. He had been a fighter pilot until he was shot down by ground fire two days ago, doing the same thing that his fellow pilot had just done to them: shooting up any target he could find. He said nothing more; he slipped into shock and would bleed to death quickly.

Fred O'Hara and Lou DiNapoli seized their chance. Two of the guards had been killed outright, a third was mortally injured. Jumping over debris and human carnage, they rushed through the eerie shafts of dusty sunlight the bullet holes in the roof now projected to the floor. Each quickly overpowered one of the remaining two guards.

Another POW yelled encouragement: "Kill the Kraut sons of bitches!"

That sounded just fine to Lou DiNapoli, who leveled the rifle he now possessed and squeezed the trigger.

Nothing happened.

The two guards wordlessly decided that perhaps this was not the time to explain the workings of the rifle's safety mechanism. They wheeled and leapt from the train, their tumbling bodies quickly vanishing into the vegetation that bordered the track.

O'Hara realized the train was braking, slowing to a stop. More than this car had been devastated, no doubt. And no telling how many more German soldiers might be on board.

"It's now or never, boys!" he bellowed as he hobbled to the doorway. DiNapoli was right behind him, the useless rifle thrown away. O'Hara's injured ankle, forgotten in the heat of action a moment ago, was making itself felt again.

With DiNapoli's help, O'Hara lowered himself from the rail car to the ground. Then the two of them set off into the woods, heading west.

They never looked back to see if any of the other POWs followed.

Chapter Six

Some quiet and solitude at last...

At the police barracks, Pola finally had the small room that made do as an office to herself. Professor Steenslund had gone home for the day. She was finished, for the moment, with the odd, incomplete crew of *The Lady M.* Civilian clothes had been purchased and issued. Uniforms collected and stored. Medical examinations completed. Billets assigned. Subsistence money handed out; the monetary system explained. Guidelines for the expected behavior of internees spelled out. *Enough for today...just give me a minute to rest before I trudge home to my empty little flat, eat some supper, and spend another of countless bloody nights with my face buried in research for my thesis, wondering if I'm still a married woman. Reginald...I can hardly remember your face. Our brief time together in London and Edinburgh now seems lost in all that has happened since. I'm not sure I even know you anymore...or if I ever did.*

Her mind returned to those strange young Americans that had consumed her day. She and the professor had a dozen other crews under their supervision, all American but for two British—and one German. When each of the other crews had arrived, it had been obvious by their words and faces the calamity or conspiracy that had brought them to seek collective refuge in Sweden. But not this time. None of these boys gave a clear indication why they were here.

She felt nothing but contempt for that insolent dullard Pilcher. The circumstances of *Lady M's* arrival in Sweden—and her destruction on landing—seemed to support his assertion that she had, indeed, been crippled. And he did have a severely impaired crew member and several that were somehow absent. As Pilcher had put it, he made a command decision to bring his damaged airplane to the nearest safe haven and save his crew, or what was left of it. The correct decision, he insisted. But the story sounded like blatant lies coming from his lips. His words seemed contrived and defensive, full of false bravado, so unlike the other crewmen of severely damaged aircraft, whose naked fear of the imminent death they had just faced bonded them like family and was evident long after they had safely returned to earth. They were simply too terrified not to be telling the truth.

Yet, Pilcher's demeanor seemed equally unlike the sullen and reclusive aura projected by those crewmen who had conspired to desert in perfectly airworthy machines. She had one such crew under her supervision. They shunned their fellow airmen from other crews, as if contact with those who had actually faced the fears they had fled would turn the rationalizations for their actions to dust. She had thought it wise to house them in a remote facility—a boarding house outside of town—far away from other crews. Pilcher, she felt sure, was something altogether different: a shirker masquerading as a hero, hiding behind a wall of arrogance and privilege, completely indifferent to those under his command.

He even had the bloody gall to mock her English; she who could speak five languages fluently. He seemed barely fluent in his own. He would be trouble, she was sure—this upper crust twit who insisted on privilege when he deserved none.

The other crew members seemed far less convinced of the wisdom of their commander's decision. Understandably, they did not want to talk much—at least not at first—and she had no interest, officially, in the details of their mission.

Case in point: Staff Sergeant Edwin T. Morris, the flight engineer, who would only repeat his name, rank, and serial number over and over again, no matter what she asked. Her questions never involved anything about mission or objective other than to confirm they had not been participating in military action against Sweden. Not much of an issue with the Allied aircrews, who usually responded to that question with incredulous laughter; the Germans also answered the question in the negative but with ominous seriousness, as if such military action was actually in the realm of possibilities. She just asked personal questions to ensure the internee's needs would be met, like confirmation of pay grade (*Yes, you'll be paid accordingly while you are here*), clothing sizes, special medical needs, religious preference, dietary restrictions, smoking habits (*All but one does*); those sort of things. It had taken some doing, with the help of the crew's two officers, to convince Morris he was not a POW; he was in a neutral country and would keep his personal freedom within that country. He just could not leave. He had struggled to grasp the difference.

Ultimately, the 21-year-old had apologized for being uncooperative. Then he asked if there was any work for a mechanic available, since his job—his plane—was no more. She patiently explained he was a guest; he did not need to earn his keep. He rambled on about how he needed to stay busy, to work with his hands. Thanks to his captain, those hands were now idle. "It shouldn'ta been like that, ma'am…it just wasn't right. He killed The Lady." She told him it might be possible to work something out. Swedish Air Force personnel had enough to do looking after their own planes. If Sergeant Morris wanted to help maintain the interned American planes, that could be arranged.

Sergeant Frank Hughes, the gaunt tail gunner, hardly spoke at all. When he did speak, it was about home: halting, tormented words about a farm in the American Midwest, a place called Nebraska. A girl waiting for him there, in that land that was like heaven in his young mind. He was not sure why he was here, why his plane had left the formation and flown, alone, to Sweden. It was not their first mission, he said; they had taken fire before. "Threw away the bombs and bullets, like we were surrendering. It just don't make no sense, ma'am...but I gotta do what the man says, don't I? And I'm scared to jump...especially out of a perfectly good airplane."

Sergeant Anthony J. Moscone. *Poor Tony:* that's what they all called him. He said nothing at first, just stared vacantly into space. There was little point in conducting an interview. As she summoned a policeman to escort this shattered boy to the doctor, he finally spoke: *Are we home? Are we home yet, Dave? Tell me, Dave...Hey, where's Harry?*

Dave. Sergeant David Linker: waist gunner, Moscone's buddy and the missing Harry Lapinski's buddy, as well. The most talkative of the enlisted men. The youngest at 18 and the only crewmember who did not smoke or drink. *Keen mind. And a very smart mouth sometimes.*

I'll bet he asked me more bloody questions than I asked him:

What about Sweden's neutrality: did life really go on as before, even with the rest of the world around you at war? *(Of course not. How could it?)*

Was it true that Sweden continued to trade with Nazi Germany? *(Yes, but we would still be trading with Britain and the US, as well, if not for blockade of the North Sea by Germany. Half of our merchant fleet now sails with Allied convoys across the Atlantic.)*

Why weren't they in the custody of the armed forces? *(Actually, you are, but our military is far too busy with border security to play at being innkeepers to a few, sporadically arriving aircrew. You'll have to settle for civilian officials of the Ministry of Defence. Besides, we in the Ministry speak better English.)*

Will we be under guard? *(Technically, yes, but I believe you will find, at most, one soldier or policeman assigned to you; and his attentions will, no doubt, be perfunctory.)*

Where was the nearest synagogue? *(Directions were given.)*

Could I wear a yarmulke on the Sabbath? *(Yes, or any other day you choose, like the tens of thousands of Jewish refugees from occupied Scandinavian countries now living in Sweden.)*

Were they really to remain in Sweden for the duration of the war? *(Probably.)* What if we try to escape? *(Where would you go? You're surrounded by Germans or nations friendly to them.)* No, really...What would happen if we escaped? *(If we catch you, we'll have to throw you in the nick for a wee bit. If you succeed, good luck to you.)*

What happens to us if Germany wins? *(I wish I knew.)*

Pola was sure that, as a child, David Linker would have preferred debating the merits of Roosevelt's New Deal or discussing the rise of fascism in Italy and Germany rather than play children's games.

Then he asked what medical treatment was available for Tony Moscone. *(The doctors would do their best.)* Quietly, he added: "He's not going to be put in some insane asylum, is he? Tony's the only reason I'm here...Maybe I should have jumped with Lieutenant

O'Hara and taken Tony with me. Ahh, who am I kidding...that would have never worked. Get us both killed trying."

Last, but by no means least, her thoughts turned to Lieutenant Joseph P. Gelardi. *Immediately likeable, a person with whom you felt instantly in league. Wedding ring. My age. A sharp intellect, quite like Linker's but without the verbosity. Mathematician from MIT. We had both started our doctoral studies before the war intervened. Trim, average height, wavy dark hair. Bloody handsome. A smile like the morning sun. Polite, considerate, probably not a devious bone in his body...quite unlike his boorish, condescending captain. Appreciative of my efforts on behalf of his crewmates (again, quite unlike that bloody wanker of a captain). An excellent listener. And a good storyteller, too. I couldn't help but laugh as he told of Pilcher's expecting him to navigate over Sweden using only a tourist's road map—and his pathetic attempt to comply. But then he had become subdued and said, "Pilcher's the boss...but for the life of me, I don't know why we came here...like his mind was made up in advance."*

Perhaps Joe is a bit naïve about people and their motivations. Or extremely generous of their flaws. But still bloody handsome.

They talked of the war in general and internment in detail. Joe had said, "I guess staying here until the end of the war isn't so bad...it's going to be over by Christmas, you know. That would be about the end of our tour, anyway...if we survived our 35 missions."

Pola had replied, "Over by Christmas, you say? And who will be the victor?"

Chapter Seven

"Is that a goddamn wolf...or the biggest fucking dog I ever seen?" Lou DiNapoli hissed as he drew back against the wall of the old barn. He was searching for a weapon among the tools and farm implements scattered within that rickety structure. Something with a long handle—to hold off that gigantic thing on four legs.

"Easy, Louie...no sudden moves," Fred O'Hara said, locking eyes with the snarling animal. He decided it was better just to stay seated on this pile of straw. He had no idea how his injured ankle would manage an attempt to stand, even after a night's rest. He might stumble, lurch—and that *thing* would take it as a threat, no doubt, and be on him in a heartbeat.

After the escape from the train, they had stumbled through the woods for hours, heading west, with DiNapoli playing human crutch to O'Hara's useless ankle. The woods had yielded to farmland, with few places to hide. This barn was the only refuge in sight. Mercifully, save an abundance of mice, it had been unoccupied; no animals to announce their arrival. Until now.

A weathered old man appeared in the doorway. He shouted commands to the animal in German and the big dog retreated, grumbling in protest all the while. Then more words, this time to the intruders. Words they could not understand.

"What do you think old Fritz is saying, Lieutenant?"

"Beats the hell out of me. Here...let me try this," O'Hara replied. He pointed to himself, then DiNapoli.

Then he pointed to the sky with one hand, patting the silver pilot's wings embossed on his flying jacket with the other for emphasis.

"I think I should beat both their brains in with an axe or something," Lou mumbled, his eyes still frantically searching for any weapon he could reach before that monster dog ripped them to shreds.

"Easy, Louie...let this play out. He ain't got a gun...and he coulda sicced big Wolfgang on us a long time ago."

"You think he understands what we're saying, Lieutenant?"

"No, I don't," O'Hara replied, repeating the skyward hand gesture.

Then the old man nodded, pointed to the sky. He understood. He made a gesture to the airmen that said *Wait...Stay...*and left the barn. The dog remained at the door, a growling, unhappy sentry.

He returned minutes later, carrying bread, sausage, and bottles of beer. He laid the food and drink on the ground in front of the airmen. Then he left once more, issuing another stern command to the dog, who paced in a tight circle, then lay down, still grumbling. Its eyes were locked on the food the intruders were devouring. A string of drool began to drip from its mouth.

Between mouthfuls, DiNapoli said, "Goddamn, this is fantastic! What is this? Bratwurst? Knackwurst?"

"Who gives a flying fuck? Clam up and eat."

"Yeah," DiNapoli replied. "Who knows...it could be our last meal."

"Always the fucking optimist, ain't ya, Louie? Let's do ourselves a favor...save a few scraps for that mutt."

Their feeding frenzy was over quickly. The dog

had gotten his scraps, too, thrown from a safe distance. It ceased its grumbling. But it still would not budge from the door.

"Is there any other way out of this dump?" DiNapoli wondered aloud, scanning the featureless walls all around them.

"What's the hurry, Louie? This may not be such a bad deal. I'm betting old Fritz don't call the cops on us. Maybe we should lie low here a few days. In this terrain, we'd only be able to travel at night and hide out by day...this farmland ain't much for cover and concealment."

"So you think we should just sit here...guarded by that fucking monster?"

"I'm just saying that maybe this ain't such a bad deal, Louie. Get my ankle healed up and figure out where the fuck we are. We can't be more than a few miles from where we bolted from that train. We were making pretty crappy time on three legs...I owe you my life, Louie."

"Don't sweat it. You would have done the same for me," DiNapoli replied, his body still aching from holding up his lieutenant all that way.

"Yeah, I guess so...We were real lucky the Krauts weren't chasing us, too."

"Amen to that, Lieutenant. But that can't last forever."

"No shit. But I've been thinking, Louie. We've got no prayer of getting to friendly territory on foot. But if we could get our hands on a plane..."

DiNapoli's response began harshly. "Steal a fucking *GERMAN* plane? And fly it over friendly lines? That has got to be the most..." Then he paused. His tone softened: "You know...why the fuck not? What other chance do we have? You could really fly a Kraut plane?"

"If you can fly a monster like the B-17, you can fly anything. It's worth a shot, no? I just need one favor, Louie. If you're gonna be in this with me, start calling me Fred."

"Anything you say, Freddy...I'm your man."

"Good. Now let's see if we can buy a few days from old Fritz and Wolfie...without getting our asses turned in."

"Or chewed up like hamburger," DiNapoli added, eyeing the dog warily. "Shaking the Krauts ain't bad enough, but a fucking dog, too?"

Chapter Eight

Frank Hughes was the first to say it out loud: "We're gonna get shot as deserters, ain't we?"

The other members of *The Lady M's* crew sat in distressed silence, all except Captain Leonard Pilcher. He was visibly becoming more annoyed by the minute. He hated these weekly meetings, but their Swedish hosts required them. He saw no further reason to associate with these men who used to be his crew. But he was still the commander of record and the Swedish government, represented by that insufferable blonde bitch Pola Nilsson-MacLeish, insisted that he help ensure the welfare and proper behavior of his men, whether he wanted to or not. *Some Scotsman's whore*, he called her, though not yet to her face. She was nothing but a royal pain in his ass.

Pola sat quietly, glaring at Pilcher through the uneasy silence born of Hughes's question. It was not her business to answer it; that was the Captain's job. She took a quick glance at Joe Gelardi. His troubled expression was no different than Linker's or Morris's as they pondered that question, which they had been avoiding ever since their arrival in Sweden three weeks ago: how would the United States government view their little excursion? Would they see it as an act of desertion or an act of necessity? Were they traitors or heroes? In their hearts, they all harbored the same thought: *Was this trip necessary? The Lady M was okay. This was all the captain's doing...we just followed his orders. But the guys who jumped—O'Hara, Harkin, and DiNapoli—what would they say...if they're still alive?*

Tony Moscone sat quietly next to David Linker. His facial expression was as blank as the day they arrived. He seemed to grasp nothing of what was happening.

Pola grew impatient with Pilcher's irritation…and his silence. "Captain," she said, "I believe the floor is yours."

Up your hole, bitch, he thought as he stood, one foot propelling the flimsy chair backwards. It hit the wall, then fell on its side, the cracking noise and skittering motion seeming unduly dramatic in the awkward tension of the drab room. Gelardi, Morris, Linker, and Hughes all flinched; Pola and Moscone did not.

"I'm gonna tell you morons for the last time," Pilcher began, "I did what I thought was necessary, and you followed my orders. If that makes you deserters, then fuck Eighth Air Force, fuck General Jimmy Doolittle, and fuck Franklin Delano Roosevelt. No court martial in the world would ever convict me. I didn't fly a perfectly good airplane here."

Bullshit, thought Ed Morris.

An agitated David Linker jumped up to speak. "But what about Lieutenant O'Hara and Lieutenant Harkin and Lou DiNapoli?"

"What about them, Sergeant?"

"They didn't see it that way. The *Lady* could have done the mission."

"I don't give a shit what they thought. I'm the boss here. They disobeyed orders…they're mutineers! They're the ones who'll get a court martial, if their stupid asses didn't get shot off jumping into Germany."

This is interesting, Pola thought. A bit different than *I don't know what happened to them,* as he had insisted in that first interview.

"We know about the map, Captain," Linker shot back.

"What map?"

"The map you had hidden...that you made Lieutenant Gelardi try to navigate in Sweden with."

"You've got a big mouth, Jew-boy, and you don't know shit," Pilcher shouted. "I don't have to listen to any more of this. You fuck-ups are on your own...don't expect any more help from me! Where's my fucking subsistence money, MacLeish?"

Calmly, Pola replied, "The allowances will be distributed when this meeting is over, as usual."

Pilcher knocked over a few more empty chairs as he stormed out of the day room.

Joe Gelardi rolled his eyes and laughed. "You hear that, boys? We're not getting any more help from him! Ain't that something?"

Moscone let out a hooting sound—perhaps it was his attempt at a laugh—in response to Gelardi's comment, while his vacant expression changed not at all.

Linker wanted to kick a few chairs of his own. "That son of a bitch had the nerve to call me 'Jew-boy!' Who the fuck does he think he is? He's a fascist, just like that robber baron father of his."

"He thinks he's better than us," Morris chimed in. "That's bullshit...and he calls us 'morons' and 'fuck-ups!' He's the fuck-up...he killed *The Lady*. He ain't nothing but a *Lady* killer."

Pola rose and walked toward Gelardi's chair: "Gentlemen, since Captain Pilcher cannot be with us, command passes to Lieutenant Joseph Gelardi. The meeting is yours, Joseph." Her hand brushed and perhaps lingered on his shoulder as she spoke. His hand rose to meet hers as if guided by a mind of its own. They touched for a brief second but then she withdrew, leaving Joe to rub his own shoulder self-consciously.

Moscone repeated the hooting sound. Linker and Morris were still riled up, spewing more vitriol about the captain. They never noticed Joe and Pola's first touch.

Hughes remained dejected, slumped in the corner. He had not noticed the touch, either, and the wild exchange that had just transpired had only heightened his malignant fears.

Chapter Nine

There was something in the doorway—and this time it surely was not a big dog.

It looked more like an angel, backlit by the bright morning sunlight so her face was in shadow. That same sunlight blazed through golden curls of windblown hair and sketched her thighs through the translucent fabric of her summer dress.

Fred O'Hara stared at the apparition through sleepy eyes. All night, he had heard that damn dog—Wolfgang, for lack of knowing its real name—snoring in that doorway, his perennial post. This was a damn sight better. Could he be dreaming?

Lou DiNapoli was still curled up on his pile of straw, sleeping fitfully.

"Hey, Louie," Fred called softly. "Wake up. You gotta see this."

"Whaddya mean, Ma? Let me sleep," DiNapoli mumbled. "I'll do it later."

"Louie, you're dreaming. Wake up."

"Shit, Lieutenant… that was a great dream, too. I could almost taste my Ma's cooking. I am so fucking hungry…and them lousy Krauts took all my fucking chocolate."

"Well, young man, I believe your prayers have been answered. Look at the door."

DiNapoli rolled over and sat up, rubbing his eyes. "What? Is the fucking dog dead?"

"Better."

She stepped closer, her features no longer obscured by the eclipse-like effect at the doorway. She seemed sweet and pleasant and could not have been more than 14, probably younger. Like the old man, she said nothing and carried a basket of food and drink for the airmen, setting it down in front of Lou DiNapoli, who was the closest. As she bent over, Lou was treated to a view of firm young breasts over the bodice of her dress.

"Holy shit!" DiNapoli mumbled, transfixed by the display before him.

"Did you order room service, Louie?"

"Oh, man!" DiNapoli moaned. "You think she speaks English?" His mind raced past food to a different kind of hunger.

"I don't think so. Take it easy, there, fella...she's jailbait, for sure."

"You think I care? With all the shit we're in, you think I care about that, Lieutenant?"

"Fred."

"Okay, Fred, you think I care? Some of the best tail I ever had was jailbait."

"And you've had lots of tail, I'm sure," O'Hara snickered. This city kid put on a great act of being worldly.

As he plunged his hands into the food basket, Lou said, "I get my share. What do you think her name is?"

"I don't think she's gonna tell us. Let's call her Heidi...and try not to slobber on her, okay?"

"No promises, sir," Lou responded as he brought the basket to Fred and sat down next to him.

Through all this banter, the girl said nothing. Once the airmen's mouths were full, she twirled toward the doorway, the motion flaring the skirt of her dress, giving both men a fleeting view of her trim thighs—and her panties—and causing them to nearly choke on their food.

With a bemused smile, she said, in slightly accented but perfect English, "My name is actually Helga, gentlemen. Enjoy your breakfast." She passed through the eclipse at the doorway once again—and was gone.

DiNapoli turned to O'Hara, the stunned look on his face made more comical by the chunks of bread and cheese protruding from his stuffed mouth. He uttered something unintelligible, more of a grunt than coherent speech.

Fred O'Hara was pretty sure Lou DiNapoli had just said, "Fuck me!"

Chapter Ten

Joe Gelardi had had enough of the wretched food from the kitchen of that damned police barracks. It was time they explored more of Malmö in search of decent chow and diversions to fill their time. It was a month since they crashed onto Swedish soil and they had not ventured more than a block or two from that cold, boring place that was their indefinite home. The government-issue Quonset Huts that were their quarters in England had held more charm. They had tried going to the movie house, but it was pointless: the films were all in Swedish with no subtitles. At least they had lots of stuff to read. Pola MacLeish had established a cache of English language books and magazines, for which they were most grateful. For Joe Gelardi, there was a box of mathematics texts for his amusement, from her personal library.

Leonard Pilcher had become a ghost, only appearing—as briefly as possible—at the weekly sessions to pick up his subsistence money. The rest of the time he was invisible, either gone to places unknown or holed up in his room at the barracks, the door bolted, avoiding any contact with the remaining members of his crew. The only conversation with him lately had been the angry exchange at the last crew meeting, with chairs and harsh words flying.

They did not miss Pilcher a bit. The boys now looked to Joe Gelardi and Pola MacLeish for guidance. Once, when Morris had wondered aloud where the captain was, Linker replied, for all to hear, "Who gives a shit?"

Tony Moscone was like a ghost, too, just one who was always present. At first, they had tried taking him on their walks through the cobblestone streets of Malmö, but it proved too difficult. Enduring Tony's swings between catatonia and manic outbursts in public was more than any of the crew could stand. There was no managing his moods; enduring was the only option. Better to leave him in the barracks with a pile of picture magazines. He actually flipped through them from time to time.

Out on the street, Ed Morris complained, "I just can't get used to these civvies."

"We've got no choice, Eddie," Joe Gelardi said. "The Swedes insist...no uniforms. No military presence in public. We don't want to scare the good people of Malmö, do we?"

"Why shouldn't they be scared," David Linker chimed in. "They've got Krauts twenty-five miles away in Copenhagen. Just across the water."

"What?" Frank Hughes cried. "We're only twenty-five miles from the German Army? That's bad...real bad."

"It's as good as a thousand miles now, Frank," Gelardi replied, trying to soothe the troubled youngster. He cast a scolding look at Linker: "If the Germans didn't march in here back when they had the chance, they never will. Now what do you say we give this café a try, fellas? Pola said the owner speaks English."

"Looks good to me," Morris said as he scanned the narrow, unfamiliar thoroughfare, finding nothing more promising.

"Whatever you say, Lieutenant," Hughes mumbled.

"Just so they serve kosher," David Linker said as he viewed the sign in the window. "Oh, great! They do! I guess Mrs. MacLeish wasn't kidding. There must be lots of us Jews around here."

"Well, there are now, thanks to good ol' Uncle Adolph," Joe Gelardi said, ushering the boys toward the café door. Their escort, an old policeman, waved to them as he window-shopped half a block away.

The droning of airplane engines rose above the street noises. The Americans stopped and looked wistfully skyward. Frank Hughes quickly returned to gazing at the ground sullenly. "Civilian...DC-3," Morris stated with certainty, even before it came into the narrow field of vision the buildings allowed. When the plane appeared, it proved him correct. It was indeed a civilian DC-3.

Irritated, David Linker demanded, "How the hell could you tell that?"

Dismissively, Morris answered, "Different engines on pre-war export models. Completely different sound," as if this bit of trivia should be common knowledge to any airman.

The café's patrons turned to stare at the Americans as they entered. It was obvious who these strangers were; they looked out of place, even in their Swedish-issued civvies. As the airmen moved to a free table, they offered uneasy smiles and nods to the other patrons. The nods were returned; the smiles were not.

"I sure don't feel real welcome here," Ed Morris whispered.

"For crying out loud! Don't worry about it," David Linker said. "At least nobody's going to shoot at us."

"They'll get used to us," Joe Gelardi added. "Probably."

Frank Hughes just stared into space. Then he began to whimper softly.

"Frank, what's the matter?" Gelardi asked, putting his hand on the boy's shoulder as he thought: *This is one moody kid...I think he's spent too much time alone at the tail guns.*

"I don't know, Lieutenant...I just don't want to be here. I just *can't* be here..."

"This restaurant...or Sweden?" David Linker sniped.

Annoyed, Joe Gelardi said, "Come on, David...cut us some slack here." Softening his tone, he turned to Hughes: "Look, Frank, we don't have a whole lot of choice in the matter right now. Don't tear yourself up over this."

"Captain Pilcher did us wrong," Hughes sobbed. "He shoulda never done this. We're trapped...and then we'll all get executed..."

"And that rich bastard Pilcher will walk away scot-free while we all face the firing squad," Linker offered casually.

Gelardi had had enough. "Oh, come on, you guys...Stop! Pilcher's the only one who's got to explain anything to the brass. Believe me!"

Hughes slumped back in his chair. "I wish I could, Lieutenant. I really do. I just wanna go home. I can't take much more...the missions, now this..." He wiped his eyes and said nothing more.

Skeptically, David Linker said, "We'll see, Lieutenant."

Ed Morris shook his head and said, "I don't care what anybody says...we ain't no deserters." He folded his arms and looked away. This conversation was over as far as he was concerned.

An old woman, with two young children in tow, rose from an adjacent table to leave. She stopped at the Americans' table. Joe Gelardi looked up at her and smiled, hoping this old woman would break the ice and usher them into the bosom of Swedish hospitality.

"Amerikan?" the old woman asked.

"Yes, ma'am...I mean *ja,*" Joe Gelardi replied as he rose in greeting.

"Yngkrygg," she spoke. Somehow, it did not sound like a welcoming word. More like she was clearing her throat.

"I'm sorry?" Joe responded, gesturing to indicate he did not understand.

"Yngkrygg. Överlöpare. Desertör."

A man at the next table turned to Joe and spoke hesitantly in English: "I mean no disrespect, sir. The lady just called you a coward...and a deserter."

Flustered, Joe replied, "Yeah, I got that last part." He watched glumly as the old woman led her charges out of the café.

Chapter Eleven

Pola was leaving the police barracks for the day, heading home to supper. She spied Joe Gelardi alone in the day room. He did not look very happy.

"How was your lunch? Did you try the place I told you about?" she asked.

"Not so good, I'm afraid," Joe replied. "We tried that place, but some old woman called us cowards and deserters right to our faces."

The sight of the dejected Joe Gelardi changed her mind about going home. She set down her battered leather briefcase and pulled up a chair next to him. "Joe, I'm sorry that happened to you. But it's inevitable that *some* people will think that of every American and Brit in this country right now. Most of us don't. You know that."

"It makes me mad, though, Pola. Please don't take this the wrong way, but in America, most people think the Swedes...and the Swiss...are chickens for not fighting Hitler."

"Chickens? Did you say chickens, Joe? What on earth does that mean?"

"I'm sorry," Joe continued with an uneasy laugh. "Chicken means coward."

"Cowards? For having the good sense to keep their country out of a war that would be ruinous for them? We are not a militaristic nation, but let me tell you something, Joseph...we Swedes would fight to the death to defend our land when necessary, but this time, it just wasn't."

"How's that, Pola? I think maybe you Swedes protest too much?"

"That's nonsense, Joseph. We're fortunate...all Hitler wants from us is steel and the occasional safe transit of German troops between Norway and Finland. Our iron ore is the finest in the world...everybody wants our steel...Britain and America, too. Germany figured out in 1940 that it's much cheaper just to keep buying it from us rather than invading and taking it and having to occupy Sweden. Poor Norway wasn't so lucky...Hitler wanted ice-free Atlantic ports for his surface warships to better challenge the British Navy. You can't buy them...and it's certainly not like we became co-belligerents with the Germans, like Romania, Hungary, Finland..."

"Of course, it helps that you're more than willing to sell it to them."

"Why wouldn't we be willing to sell it...to anybody?"

"Okay, but you're selling much more steel to the Germans than the Allies, no?"

"Of course, Joseph, but that's because the Germans blockade the North Sea. Opening that route up to maritime trade again would change everything. We still sell ball bearings to Britain, you know. Vast amounts, in fact. They send special aircraft to collect them, 'Mosquitos' I believe they're called. They're very fast...the Luftwaffe can't catch them."

"So this war is just a big business deal to you?" Joe sneered.

"Isn't that true for everyone? Just the means of closing the deal differs. It's strange, Joseph...in your country, big business gets you into wars. In mine, it keeps us out."

He had no answer for that one; he had never considered such a position. Served him right, he supposed, for trying to argue business with an economist.

He was trained—no, indoctrinated—to believe this war was about principles, about freedom. Obviously, not everyone saw it that way.

His scowl turned into a sheepish grin. He really did not want to argue with her, to seem ungrateful and combative; he felt indebted for all her help. "Okay, Pola. Point taken. You win."

"Oh, no, Joseph...that's the problem. Nobody wins," Pola said, her eyes downcast. After a moment, she added, "I have an idea...why don't you join me for supper?"

"Is that allowed?"

A devilish smile lit her face as she took his hand in hers. "Of course not! That will make it all the more fun!"

Supper was a simple affair: just some beef soup, bread, and a bottle of terribly dry red wine. But it looked and tasted wonderful to Joe Gelardi.

"Damn," he spoke between mouthfuls. "This is the best meal I've had since England. No offense, but the food at the police barracks is pretty awful."

"Ah, the gratitude of the uninvited guest!" Pola replied, not entirely joking.

"What do you mean? You invited me here, didn't you?"

"I mean in Sweden, laddie. You're an uninvited guest in Sweden. But you're a most welcome guest tonight."

"Well, thank you, ma'am," Joe replied, with a little, sweeping gesture, as if bowing to nobility. "Mind if I ask you something?"

"Not at all, Joseph."

"What does your job at the Ministry entail when you're not looking after us wayward airmen?"

"Unfortunately, my job now entails little else. You can be quite a handful."

"And where are all these other crews?" Joe pressed. "How come we haven't seen any of them?"

"We scatter you around. The first arrivals were placed in small camps, but your numbers grew. The camps filled up...it caused too many problems. Animosities surfaced between the crews who flew here out of necessity and those who did so by choice. A few times it got quite messy. Ironic, isn't it? Now, we just sprinkle you all over the country, in whatever lodging we can find...hotels, boarding houses, police barracks...Less headaches for us. And of course, we separate you from any German crews than might be here."

"Are there other crews...Allied and German...in Malmö?"

"Yes, of course."

"So where are they?"

Pola let out a laugh. "Sorry, Joseph, but I'm not going to tell you that. I can't have all of you ganging up on me!"

"Isn't there a chance we'll meet them on the street?"

"Yes, it's possible...but it really hasn't been much of a problem."

She decided not to mention the recent repatriation of several hundred American airmen. The American government had transferred ownership of 10 of the more serviceable interned bombers to Sweden, to be converted to airliners. It had settled for the airmen in return; what the US had really wanted—and did not receive—was bases in Sweden from which to bomb Germany, just a short flight away. It had been so much easier in the war's early days, when repatriation of the few Allied and German aircrews on a one-to-one basis was practical and reinforced the tenets of neutrality; then came 1943 and the Luftwaffe's wholesale decimation of the American daylight bombers. The flood of American crews to Sweden and Switzerland, for reasons real or concocted, began.

They fell silent as they finished the meal. Pola poured them both another glass of wine and suggested they move to the sitting room of the small apartment. Joe offered no resistance.

"Can you at least tell me something about the other crews?" Joe asked, lighting cigarettes for both of them. The wine was relaxing him, loosening his tongue again. But not enough to voice his real question: *Are they deserters?*

Pola, seated on the other end of the small couch, turned to him and tucked her legs under her, not caring how much her skirt hiked up and exposing a good bit of her thighs—and the tops of her stockings—in the process. "I suppose that would be okay," she replied in a hushed tone, as if conspiring to include him in some great secret. Her wire-rimmed glasses, which he had never seen her without, plunked onto the coffee table before them. Her hair, suddenly freed from its usual bun, spilled like so many strands of spun gold to her shoulders.

Suddenly, Joe found himself startled and uneasy. Not that he did not find her attractive—quite the opposite—but he was a married man and she a married woman. Maybe her behavior was just the wine talking. He tried to cast his gaze anywhere except up her skirt or on the lacy pattern her bra traced firmly on the thin fabric of her blouse as she leaned back and drew deeply on her cigarette.

A smile crossed Pola's face as she blew out the smoke. Joe's embarrassment at her immodest play was somehow sweet and surprising at the same time.

"Do you find me shocking, Joseph?"

Great... now she thinks I'm an immature idiot. Shit...maybe I am. What would Clark Gable do now?

Taking a deep drag on his own cigarette, Joe looked her straight in the eyes; a feeble stab at feigning the composure that was so obviously eluding him. "You were telling me about the other aircrews." *Somehow, that didn't come out like "Frankly my dear, I don't give a damn."*

Pola was starting to take pity on his discomfort. *So he pretends to play coy, eh? So beautiful, so silly, this laddie is.*

Her head back against the cushion, staring at the ceiling, Pola continued. "There is another American crew that lives not far from you...I won't tell you where...but they are a very strange lot. Perhaps stranger than you and your lads."

"How so?"

"They consider themselves religious refugees. Apparently, they collectively decided that war is against God's will...and they are doing God's work by refusing to fight anymore. Their commander considers himself some sort of messiah. He's even starting to look like Christ, with long hair and beard. Very strange bunch."

"And they're stranger than us, you say?"

"Oh, yes. Your Captain Pilcher is a self-centered, manipulative sod but definitely no messiah. Just an over-privileged wanker. Those of you that are here in Sweden were afraid to go against his orders, dishonest though they were. Those of your crew who aren't with us saw the lie beneath those orders."

Joe Gelardi could not think of a thing to say in defense or rebuttal. She was probably dead on the mark.

"But you were a surprise to me, Joseph Gelardi. You are obviously a man of great intelligence. But you consider deference to authority a duty. Otherwise, I don't think you'd be here. You would have parachuted with the other three."

"I prefer to call it patriotism, Pola."

"Aye. You would."

He tried to decide if what she had just said was a compliment or condemnation. She sensed his discomfort; she reached over and eagerly took his hand in hers, asking: "Tell me about your doctoral thesis, Joseph."

Joe could hardly conceal his surprise. *Here I am, convinced she's trying to seduce me... and she wants to talk academics! Am I reading her all wrong? Or is that what gets her hot and bothered? Is she just like Alice Pasternak, the MIT co-ed who would actually get aroused by anything to do with Quantum Mechanics? Her face would flush, her voice become breathless. One guy swore she actually achieved orgasm during a discussion of the Heisenberg Uncertainty Principle. Oh, what the hell...*

He began earnestly. "My thesis is on binary mathematics as applied to electronic data processing." He then eagerly threw himself into describing his life's work to a fellow academic. Such opportunities had become nonexistent once in uniform. It felt simply wonderful. He tried to push aside, without success, the thought that all this might be foreplay.

"Binary math," she gushed. Ones and zeroes."

"Yeah. You know about it?"

"Joseph, economists are quite well grounded in mathematics." Then she added, very matter-of-factly, any hint of arousal absent from her voice, "My thesis was on business models for a post-depression Europe. I guess I'll be revising it to *post-war* Europe once all this is over. Things have certainly changed a bit."

"How far were you from finishing your doctorate

when you left London, Pola?"

"About three years."

"That's about what I had left on mine when I joined up...maybe a little less. It's funny, but I could have gotten a deferment for the work we were doing at MIT."

"And you didn't take it! Like I said about deference to authority! But an MIT man! I am very impressed."

No, Joe thought, it was not about deference to authority. He just did not feel that sitting in Cambridge playing with binary logic was properly "doing his bit" for the war effort. He was a healthy, able-bodied male; he wanted to be in uniform, to see the war first-hand. *Have I seen all I needed to see? In just three missions?*

Joe continued the spirited explanation of his academic work: the possibilities of electronic data storage, computation, and decision making. How the information could be processed and transmitted in split seconds, inhibited at present only by the cumbersome hardware of the vacuum tube computer. Such devices were colossally expensive, filled whole buildings, and required huge cooling systems: thousands of vacuum tubes generated enormous amounts of heat. He predicted that someday smaller, more practical, computers would change the way we lived. He was soaring.

She followed his every word. It was not a bluff; she really understood the principles and the logic. The questions she occasionally interrupted with were intelligent and informed. They had inched closer to each other during this exchange. Their eyes were locked; he was sure they were on the verge of embrace. He felt the guilt, though dulled somewhat by the wine, begin to rise again.

"Pola...we're both married."

"Am I? Tell me, Joseph, where is my husband? I certainly don't know." Then she smiled and said, "Don't worry, I'll send you back to your wife in good order."

"But what about you, Pola? Your job? Your career? What if someone found out?"

"Joseph, I grew up in Malmö. This is a small town and I certainly know my way around. You realize this is not my apartment, don't you?"

"No! I just assumed..."

"You didn't notice me clattering around in the kitchen, trying to find things?"

"No..."

"You silly sod! So provincial! This apartment belongs to a friend...a journalist...who is temporarily in Stockholm. She and I went to university together. My apartment is too near to my family. Heaven forbid I get seen with some strange man...an American, yet!"

He had no chance to respond. She straddled him quickly and seized his mouth with hers. Exciting as her actions were, he did not want to do this for so many reasons—being able to look his wife in the eye when he got home was only the first. Despite her nonchalant attitude toward her own marital vows, was it not wrong— a sin against the Ninth Commandment, in fact—to sleep with another man's wife? No doubt, as the de facto commander of *Lady M's* crew, he would have to occasionally stand up to Pola as an advocate for his men. How would that work with a woman—a married woman—he was screwing? The boys would surely sense it. And if Pilcher found out—if he ever bothered to show his face—what devious use would he make of it?

But her kisses worked their chemical magic; his body now responded eagerly, totally. His opaque guilt was punctured in a thousand places, yielding the dimly lit rationalization that made their coupling inevitable: *She's just lonely. Hell, I'm lonely, too.*

One final protest rose in his throat. "I don't have any condoms."

"Yes, we do," she replied.

Chapter Twelve

Pola MacLeish was right: it was possible to encounter other interned air crewmen on the streets of Malmö. Leonard Pilcher was having just such an encounter while eating lunch, alone, in a small café. This clown did not look much like an American airman, though, Pilcher thought. More like Jesus Christ, badly in need of a haircut and a shave.

"Excuse me, brother...aren't you a G.I.?" the Christ figure asked, in an accent of the American South. Tennessee, maybe Georgia, Pilcher surmised.

"What's it to you, you fucking bum? You looking for a handout?"

The patrons who understood English turned briefly and scowled. These American airmen lounging in their country were all either ill-mannered or insane.

"No need for foul language, brother. You're from the Northeast? Pennsylvania, perhaps?"

"And you're a fucking redneck cracker."

Jesus gave a soft laugh: "Why must we label each other? We're all God's children."

"Look, pal, I don't know what your game is, and I don't fucking care. Nice meeting you. Now fuck off."

"But brother, we may have much in common. Did you come to be in Sweden because you saw the light...that warfare is a tool of the devil?"

"You mean am I a fucking yellow deserter, like you? They'll shoot you, you idiot. You'll need a better story than that."

"I am a soldier in the Lord's army now."

"Swell...I wish you luck. See you at your firing

squad, numbnuts."

"Fear not the vengeance of men."

"Oh, believe me, brother...I don't. Not for a goddamn minute. Now get the fuck out of here."

"Please, brother...tell me your name."

"If that will get rid of you, fine. Pilcher. Leonard. Captain. Serial number 33204617.

"I am called Brother Thomas. I hope we meet again."

The looney toon was gone. Pilcher returned to his coffee and cake, surmising that if the Army did not shoot Brother Thomas outright, they'd lock him up in the Section 8 bin forever.

His solitude was short-lived. Another man now towered over him. He spoke English, too, but with a thick German accent.

"Excuse me, sir, but did I understand you to say your name is Leonard Pilcher?"

Pilcher's surliness, so easily dispensed just a moment ago, evaporated. Apprehension flowed in its place. He glanced at the imposing figure hovering above him and answered, "Yeah...that's my name, pal. What about it?"

"Son of the American Max Pilcher?"

He was afraid to answer that question. Rich men like his father made lots of enemies, even on the other side of the world. Maybe this Aryan giant was looking for revenge for one of those crushing maneuvers that his father joked so easily about, maneuvers that eradicated someone's fortune or stole their dreams. He felt cornered, devoid—for the moment—of the control over others that accompanied wealth and power. But he put on an act of false bravado.

"Who the fuck wants to know?"

"My name is Johann Lichtblau. My family has

been doing business with your family for years...or at least until your country declared war on mine. We had the pleasure of your father's company at dinner, perhaps five years ago...when the world was much different. Your father spoke of you. I believe you were at university then."

"Yeah...Yale. Dad sure gets around, don't he?"

"What a delightful coincidence this is! Your father is, indeed, a great man. But we may have even more in common."

"How's that?"

"You are an airman, no?"

"I'm a pilot...an aircraft commander," Pilcher replied, his surly superiority returning for a moment.

"I, too, am a pilot. I am an *Oberst* in the Luftwaffe. Bad fortune...perhaps not unlike yours...has caused my temporary detainment in this country."

The last thing in the world Leonard Pilcher expected was to be passing time with a German military officer. The whole point of this exercise had been to get away from his superior officers, who were trying to get him killed, and the Germans, who were more than willing to do it. He felt the knot tightening in his stomach. His fork clattered to the table, as if holding it in his hands might be seen as a provocation.

"*Oberst*...that's like a colonel?" Pilcher mumbled.

"I believe that is correct. But you are uncomfortable. I assure you, there is no reason to be. We are not adversaries here. The Swedes enjoy their fantasy that they are not at war. Why should we not enjoy it, too? There is no reason two men like us...*men of means*...cannot enjoy each other's company."

Men of means. Leonard Pilcher liked the sound of that. Maybe this Lichtblau was okay after all, even if he was a fucking Kraut.

"May I join you?" Lichtblau asked. "Perhaps there is much we can discuss."

"Sure...why not?"

But to Leonard Pilcher's surprise, the German took the seat next to him rather than opposite at the small table. And he thought it a little strange when the Luftwaffe colonel wrapped one huge arm around his shoulders and stroked his thigh with the other, proclaiming, "We will be great friends, Leonard. *Ja?*"

Then the German leaned in and whispered, "I don't suppose you could lend me a few *kronor* until payday?"

Chapter Thirteen

The noise jarred Fred O'Hara from sleep. That rhythmic rustling sound, in the nighttime silence of the barn, was maddening. He had heard it every night they had slept in this barn; he could not ignore it anymore. It was not the wind; it was not some animal. It was coming from the pile of straw Lou DiNapoli used for his bed; it was getting louder and faster. Soon it would stop suddenly, just like all the times before.

Louie has got to be the most prolific masturbator on the planet, O'Hara surmised. The way he saw it, these wops had such a need to spill their seed—an almost clinical search for reassurance that their genitals still worked on a daily basis—it overpowered the shame and guilt that kept most other men from regularly playing with themselves.

That shame and guilt had definitely had its effect on Fred O'Hara. Like all little boys, he had tried it when those first stirrings of puberty arrived, but he could not shake the notion that the spirits of dead people—his grandparents, aunts, uncles, even his little sister who died at age three—were watching and judging harshly from some heavenly perch. God never came into it; he figured that if God knew everything, he'd know that little boys were too enthralled and too weak to resist these autoerotic urges. But his dead relatives—that was something different. They certainly were not all-knowing—or all-forgiving. He vividly remembered Uncle Seamus castigating a son for needing eyeglasses at the age of 11, a failing surely the result of self-abuse.

O'Hara could not imagine grown men, like his

father, masturbating. Hell, his father could not have possibly wasted any of his seed; it must have taken prodigious amounts to impregnate his mother 13 times. His poor mother—by the time she was 40, she looked 60. It seemed she was with child all of her adult life. He imagined her sitting at the enormous dining room table, rubbing her ever-swollen belly and staring blankly into space while she sipped a cup of whiskey-laced coffee and smoked a cigarette, too drained to face the world. Three of his siblings had actually entered this world on that battered and rickety table.

Tonight's performance came to its abrupt end. Louie's climax was silent as always, only evident by the sudden absence of the rhythmic rustling in the darkness. Fully awake now, Fred O'Hara spoke the question occupying his mind: "What do you think about when you're doing it, Louie?"

"Doing what?"

"You know…jerking off."

Lou was silent for a moment. He was not sure whether he felt embarrassed to be caught or annoyed his privacy was being invaded. Maybe a little of both. But he covered it with masculine bluster: "You gotta think about *one* girl…just fixate on that thing about her that sets you off. Maybe it's the way her ass looks in a tight skirt, or the curve of her tits under a silk blouse. You gotta focus…if you let your mind wander around, it don't work…you'll rub the skin right off your dick and never get no release."

"Who were you thinking about just now?"

"Who do you think? Helga! Can't get that teasing little tart out of my mind. Can you? I live for when she brings us our meals."

"No, I guess you're right. She does have a way about her, even though she's about ten years old."

"Get outta here! She's fifteen!"

"Yeah, right...twelve at most."

"Pretty good tits for a twelve-year-old, don't you think, Freddy?"

"I wouldn't know. I don't chase jailbait."

"Bullshit. She's got a pussy, you chase it."

Fred had to laugh at Louie's visceral outlook on life as he steered the conversation back to practical matters. "We're just lucky she was born in Milwaukee and speaks such good English. A lot easier than dealing with her grandfather or that fucking monster dog of his. I still can't understand her parents sending her back to the old country, though, to 'share in the glory of the Reich' or some bullshit. They must be some kind of fucked-up Nazis..."

"Or maybe they just couldn't afford kids anymore," DiNapoli offered. "The fucking Depression, you know."

"You think we can trust her, Lou? We sure could use a little help."

"I dunno, Freddy. You think she wouldn't flash her tits and ass at some *soldats*, too? Maybe she's working with them...just setting us up."

"Nah, I don't think so. All I know is we gotta make our move soon. Now that I can walk pretty good again."

"I don't know...you still limp. I'll bet you can't run very fast."

"I can move as fast as I need to. I think the time has come, my friend. Let's go for it, Louie."

Helga was ecstatic, clapping her hands and twirling like a ballerina. She was taking great delight in her newly appointed role as co-conspirator. Their plan to steal an airplane and fly to safety sounded so exciting, so bold, so *American*. She'd be glad to help them plan their escape, delightedly kissing O'Hara and DiNapoli on the cheek as she removed the remains of their breakfast and hurried to the farmhouse, promising to return soon with the map they so desperately needed. The Americans hoped a map was the only thing with which she would return. It would be a crying shame to survive all this time as fugitives in Nazi Germany, to be undone by misplaced faith in a seductive child. But it was a gamble they felt they had to take. They had no one else to trust.

Helga returned shortly with a road map. On it, she had noted the farm's location. Fred and Lou were startled to see that they were only a few miles from where they surmised they had bailed out of *The Lady M*, in the farm country to the south of Flensburg. Smack-dab in the middle of the *Bundesländer Schleswig-Holstein:* occupied Denmark to the north, the Baltic to the east, the North Sea to the west—and the rest of Germany to the south. Almost a month's time and all this motion, on foot, trucks, and trains; they must have been going in circles. They were still several hundred miles from the American and British lines to the southwest, even assuming that significant advances had been made by those armies in the past month.

"You know how to read a map?" O'Hara asked the girl skeptically.

"Of course. We bicycle everywhere, sometimes great distances. No petrol for automobiles, you see. You can't afford to make a wrong turn. Too much wasted time and effort."

"Can you show us where the airfields are, Helga?" O'Hara inquired as the three hunched over the map.

"Yes. There are at least four I have seen that are close to here. This one here"—she pointed to a spot on the map—"is quite large, with many *soldaten*. I don't think you want to go there. The others"—she pointed three times—"are smaller, with not so many *soldaten*."

"Are there lots of aircraft at the smaller ones?" DiNapoli inquired.

With a look that made Louie feel like he was the child here, Helga replied, "Of course, silly. That's why they call them *aerodromes*."

"Hey, be nice to him," O'Hara said. "Louie's got a little crush on you."

If looks could kill, Lou DiNapoli had just murdered Fred O'Hara.

Helga intercepted DiNapoli's deadly look and returned a look of her own, one that melted his heart. "That's so sweet," she said softly. Then she kissed him full on the lips. The kiss startled Lou momentarily. He reached for her but she backed away, leaving just a shy smile in her wake.

An impish smile crossed O'Hara's face as he said, "I guess you're gonna be extra noisy tonight."

"Shut the fuck up, Lieutenant."

Helga ignored their sparring. "So when do we leave?" she asked.

"What do you mean *we*, Helga? You can't come. It's too dangerous," O'Hara replied.

"It's not dangerous for me at all, Lieutenant. If we get caught, I'll tell them you kidnapped me…forced me to help you escape…probably raped me, too. I'll cry…make a big scene…thank them for saving me…"

"Whoa, little girl!" O'Hara laughed, although he found all this not very funny. "With friends like you, who needs enemies?"

"Let her come, Freddy. I'll bet she can be a big help."

"Well…okay," O'Hara replied, still not entirely

convinced. "But once we get to an airfield, you've gotta get lost, Helga. I don't want you getting killed on our account."

"*Danke*, Lieutenant. But back to my first question...when do we leave?"

"Tonight. Everybody okay with that?" O'Hara offered.

"No," Helga replied. "Tomorrow night."

"How come?" O'Hara quizzed.

"I can't tonight. There's something I must do here."

O'Hara thought on that a moment: if she was going to rat them out, she could have done it a long time ago. "Okay," he said, "tomorrow night. But can I ask you one more thing?"

"Of course."

"How old are you, anyway?"

Helga let out a laugh and headed for the barn door. Looking back over her shoulder, her long, blonde locks falling across her face like some Hollywood pin-up, she gave her answer: "Old enough to know better, Lieutenant O'Hara."

Fred O'Hara was finding it impossible to sleep. He would have much rather been making his escape right now. But tomorrow night was the appointed time.

A light rain was falling, its noise on the roof amplified by the barn's tunnel-like acoustics. To O'Hara, it sounded like the gods were pissing on him. When Louie DiNapoli started his nightly festival of self-abuse, he probably would not even hear it.

O'Hara did not hear the barn door squeak open. He just noticed the dim slit of moonlight suddenly appear, then disappear. Soft footsteps made their sure approach, then became less certain as they neared Louie's sleeping place. A child's voice whispered.

Lou DiNapoli had not noticed the door open or heard her approach. Her hand gently over his mouth was his first awareness, then her whispered words. He sat bolt upright; she eased him back down and lay beside him.

Lou took a minute to convince himself this was not a dream. His hand slowly explored her arm, her shoulder, her face—the mouth kissing his fingers as they passed; then it moved to her breasts, their nipples small but erect. No, there was really a girl lying next to him. A little wet from the rain, but who cared? He wondered: *Does Freddy know she's here?*

He could barely make out her face. His hands gave him all the information he needed. She was wearing just a simple nightgown and underpants. He explored the insides of her thighs, the soft pubic hair, her vulva. Hesitantly, he slid a finger inside her, then another; it barely fit. Growing bolder, he massaged the button above her vagina with the thumb of that same hand, just like that kindly neighborhood hooker in the Bronx had instructed him when he was 12 or so. Of course, with the hooker, he was sure his whole hand had fit inside. Helga made no sound, although her breathing had become deeper and more rapid.

Lou rose to his knees and positioned himself between her legs. He grasped the waistband of her underpants to slide them off. Her hands stopped him. "No," she whispered.

"Whaddya mean, 'no?'" he whined. "You some kind of cocktease?"

Helga pulled his face to hers and kissed him. She whispered once again: "Continue, please, but we must leave our underwear on."

"You mean you wanna grind? Dry hump?"

"I don't know what you call it, Louie. I just know

that I want to remember you in my heart, not in my belly. And it would hurt. Hurry…we don't have much time."

He'd take what he could get, even a jail-bait virgin. It took him a moment to get the motion right, to get just the right friction. In another moment, he stiffened and groaned as his motion abruptly stopped. He rolled off her onto his back; she curled up next to him, her head on his shoulder, her arm across his chest. He fell asleep.

Before the dawn, she kissed him once more and rose to leave.

"Where're you going?" Louie asked, still groggy.

"I've got to get back to the house, before Ludwig wakes up and finds me."

"Who the hell is Ludwig?"

"The dog, silly."

Once she was gone, Fred O'Hara's voice sliced through the darkness: "Hey, quick-pop…that was *sooo* touching!"

Chapter Fourteen

The week that followed that first lovemaking with Pola Nilsson-MacLeish was both magical and troubling to Joe Gelardi. They had been together every night but one, when she had gone to visit her parents across town. When around others, they tried very hard to hide the glow of newfound romance. They told themselves they were succeeding.

But Joe alone walked under the dark cloud of marital infidelity. Pola seemed exempt; her marriage was a distant memory, almost forgotten in the cataclysmic years of war, kept barely alive only by a crumpled legal document, a few photographs, and a gold ring—now dull and uncared for—long filed away in a jewelry box. Her husband, Reginald, was somebody she knew once, thought she loved once—and then faded away to the other side of the world. The few letters she had long ago received seemed like letters from some old acquaintance, devoid of longing and passion, which spoke not at all of a life together once this war was over. But Joe Gelardi was here—in the flesh—for whatever reason fate had brought him into her life. She marveled that the consummation had been every bit as exciting as the initial, inexplicable attraction.

Joe still believed himself deeply devoted to his wife, Mary, a girl he had known his entire life. But this devotion seemed to dissolve at the sight of Pola, only to return—along with crushing guilt—once their coupling was finished and he was alone again. Joe and Mary shared humble beginnings in that small town outside Boston, were high school sweethearts, and married while he was still an undergrad at MIT and she at Boston College. She had always been there for him and she was here even now—an unseeing and nonjudgmental entity—in this surreal world on the periphery of war. But their lives were intertwined more by circumstance, proximity, and history than passionate love. Whatever juvenile passion had sparked their high school and college years had devolved into a dreary obligation long before Joe had left for military service.

Nevertheless, he told himself, *Mary will never know of this.* It was more of a plea than a certainty.

Joe's sexual passion for Pola Nilsson-MacLeish left him dumbfounded. He had little carnal experience outside of his life with Mary, but with Pola, sex was a totally new and captivating experience, so unlike the frantic, brief, but uninspiring episodes in the missionary position he had shared with his wife. He was startled the first time Pola ministered to his genitalia with her mouth. He had thought such a practice was just the stuff of lurid pulp novels, never actually happening in real life.

Then she taught him that his own mouth could be used for more than kissing the face. Their many-faceted lovemaking seemed to go on for hours, and when the sessions were over, they collapsed into blissful sleep, naked, sweaty, exhausted, but completely satisfied. But then they would have to part as discreetly as they had arrived. And he would again make the deluded promise to himself: *That'll be the last time.*

Her latest request startled him, but he eagerly, if inexpertly, tried to comply: *Tie my hands above my head. Lash them to the bedpost.*

When he had finished that task to her satisfaction, Pola commanded, *Blindfold me.*

He retrieved her kerchief and did so.

Now fook me, Joseph.

A different sort of foreplay was happening between Leonard Pilcher and Johann Lichtblau, one to which Pilcher seemed completely oblivious. The big German had, throughout dinner, been rubbing Pilcher's shoulders and thighs with his massive hands. Pilcher dimly considered the physical contact merely punctuation marks for his German friend's expansive, boisterous monologues, nodding in agreement as he filled his face with food and drink.

Lichtblau began to fear that Leonard Pilcher was even more vacuous than he originally thought—and apparently devoid of homosexual interest. For several days he had hurled advance after advance at Pilcher, with no response whatsoever. Maybe the waggish stories Lichtblau's father had told about the homosexual proclivities of American prep school boys were not completely true; Father's stories of their self-centered dullness seemed fairly accurate, however. Nothing spilled from Leonard Pilcher's mouth but obnoxious tales of the many girls he had taken advantage of and the two he had impregnated—all without consequence to him due to the protection of wealth and position.

"Anybody else, it would have been rape...but we're *men of means,* right, Johann?"

Lichtblau hid his disgust and said nothing in response. *At least these ignorant Americans get paid obscene amounts of money for their military service, which the Swedes dutifully dole out. I might at least avail myself of this fine food and drink, courtesy of this vacant fool, while I can.*

"You never told me how you ended up in Sweden," Pilcher said, only half interested as he stuffed another dinner roll into his mouth.

Actually, I have, Lichtblau thought to himself.

You probably weren't paying attention, you stupid swine.
But he began the tale cheerfully once again. "I was flying
back to Germany from Norway after a liaison mission.
My radio operator, Feldwebel Weiner, that imbecilic
peasant, tuned the wrong DF station. The weather front
we should have been avoiding...well, we flew right into
it. I got good and lost at that point..."

"And the Swedish Air Force intercepted you,"
Pilcher interrupted.

"No. I landed on my own, without their help, at
the first airfield I saw."

"So how long do they keep you?" Pilcher asked.

"Not long, I am sure. Something will be worked
out between the governments."

At least he hoped so. To this point in his brief stay
in Sweden, Lichtblau had been unable to procure suitable
male companionship. Quite a change from the
Geschwader, where homoerotic encounters among men
of dignity and culture were not hard to find. The
Luftwaffe, the High Command, the Nazi Party in
general—all full of men who loved men. The Swedish
homosexuals he had blundered into since his arrival were
loathe to associate with Germans. This crude, ridiculous,
yet privileged American seated next to him, whose social
credentials had suggested easy plunder, was not panning
out, either. Lichtblau was running out of options—but
surely Pilcher was a malleable idiot. He would not give
up on him quite yet.

"How long do you think the Swedes will keep
you, Leonard?"

"Until the end of the war will be just fine with
me," Pilcher replied, his mouth full of salad. "And you
still haven't told me how to get laid around here."

"Perhaps I can arrange something," the big
German replied. "Could you advance me, say...500

kronor?"

Chapter Fifteen

Fred O'Hara and Lou DiNapoli stared into the pale moonlight, unable to make out much of anything amidst the dull gray shapes and shadows that unfolded before them: trees not quite ready to surrender their leaves to autumn. From their position in the adjacent woods, the German airfield looked like little more than a void from which the low rumble of machines, flashes of artificial light, and raised human voices occasionally emanated. If there were any aircraft present, their silhouettes were invisible; they must be concealed in the tree lines to prevent being spotted from the air in daylight. They could have never found this place—in the dark—without Helga's help. But maybe she was dead wrong about this being an airfield.

"I'm not wrong," Helga insisted, as she joined them after hiding her bicycle by the road. "That line of trees to the right...you'll find it full of airplanes." Per O'Hara's request, she had dressed in a dark sweater and trousers, her golden blonde hair tucked into a black beret. *Clandestine* was the word he had used; the sound of that word continued to send chills of excitement down Helga's spine.

Angrily, O'Hara whispered, "Keep your voice down, girl." Then he caught himself. Why was scolding the one person who had just handed them their only chance at escape? He started to apologize, but Helga cut him off with a wave of her hand.

"Just follow the tree line around. That will get you to the airplanes," she said, her voice barely above a whisper. "And best of luck to both of you."

She leaned forward and gave O'Hara a kiss on the cheek. Then she turned to Lou DiNapoli, wrapped her arms around his neck, and kissed him full on the mouth.

Lou found himself paralyzed. Sure, he wanted to get the hell out of Germany. But he did not want to leave her, either. There was something so pure, so honest, yet so wise about Helga. What he felt was just so different, like nothing before. *It don't matter that she's jailbait.*

He had considered himself a hardened citizen of the cruel world; overnight, this young girl had reduced him to a smitten adolescent. He would not release her when she tried to disengage from their embrace.

O'Hara grabbed DiNapoli by the shoulder. "C'mon, Louie...this ain't no time to be falling in love."

"Okay, okay. Gimme a minute," DiNapoli pleaded. Still with one arm around Helga, he reached into the pocket of his flight jacket for a pencil.

"Gimme your address so I can write to you after this war is all over," Louie whispered.

Helga was astonished. "Are you crazy, Louie? When you get caught with that, my grandpa and I are as good as dead!"

Undeterred, Louie continued, "Okay, I'll give you mine..."

"No, no, Louie! Don't you see that's just as bad for us?"

"Louie, it's time to get out of here!" O'Hara hissed, angry once more. "And I don't care much for the sound of *when you get caught...*"

"It's just a figure of speech, Lieutenant," Helga said. "If you don't trust me by now, I don't know what else I can do..."

She had a point. O'Hara scolded himself: *What do you want from this poor kid? She's bending over backwards to help you...maybe even risking her life...and you're giving her shit?* Even DiNapoli seemed to be turning against him, as if he had decided to stay here—with her—and forget all about escaping.

"What's it going to be, Louie?" O'Hara demanded. "The sun's gonna be up soon."

Louie refused to accept the finality of their parting. He removed the St. Christopher's medal from his neck with one hand and began to place it over her head. He would not relinquish his grip on her with the other arm.

"Wait...wait!" Helga whispered. She took the medal in her hands and tried to examine it in the darkness. "There's no writing on this, is there?"

"It just says 'St. Christopher, Protect Us.' You know...he's the patron saint of travelers. No harm in that, is there?"

"In English?" Helga asked, fearful of the answer.

"Yeah, what's the big deal? You were born in America, right?"

Helga considered that for a moment. "Well...I suppose it's okay."

With a final, abrupt squeeze, Louie gave into the impossibility of remaining and released her. Without another word, Helga turned and disappeared into the early morning darkness, leaving him motionless and deflated. He was overwhelmed by the feeling that he had just lost something precious, yet he knew full well it was something he could never possess. O'Hara grabbed Lou's arm and whispered, "Let's get this show on the road, Sergeant."

Slowly, Lou DiNapoli turned and followed his lieutenant into the darkness. He was glad it was dark for a new reason—Freddy would not see his tears.

Sure enough, there were airplanes. Most were

single-seat fighters, the kind they had done battle with in the sky not so long ago. It would be extremely difficult to squeeze both of them into one of those cockpits. Another problem: O'Hara recalled from training films that the engines on those fighters featured inertial starters that had to be cranked manually, like giant, deadly wind-up toys. That might prove a bit difficult to pull off, even under cover of darkness, as the noise and motion this process created would draw much attention. They could hear many voices around them—voices of mechanics servicing the aircraft—but as yet had not seen the shadowy figure of another human being, just the random flashes from the lanterns they carried. The aroma of breakfast cooking—ersatz coffee, sausage, eggs—floated on the soft breeze.

An aircraft engine suddenly sprung to life somewhere to their right. Definitely not a powerful fighter engine, more like one from a light aircraft, perhaps a courier or observation plane. Alive with anticipation and apprehension, they crept toward the sound.

Now they could see the airplane's shadowy outline: a Fieseler Storch. Simple, lightweight, easy to fly; high-winged and spindly, it seemed more an awkward descendant of flying insects than graceful birds. They saw the shapes of two mechanics moving around the aircraft, lanterns in hand, checking her over, then the mechanics disappearing into the darkness, leaving the aircraft—its propeller whirling at low throttle—tethered and alone.

No words between O'Hara and DiNapoli were necessary. They both knew this was their chance. Get off the ground in the pre-dawn darkness, fly west until the sun follows them into the sky—and try to get down behind the Allied lines without getting shot to pieces by

American or British gunners. They stumbled hastily through the darkness to the abandoned Storch, the purr of her engine masking the noise of their advance. O'Hara jumped into the cockpit and was relieved to see how simple the controls and instrumentation were; their operation was, for the most part, obvious, even with German markings. DiNapoli quickly undid the ropes securing the aircraft to its tie-downs and pulled the chocks from her wheels. He nearly forgot to avoid the whirling propeller as he passed around the front of the aircraft but quickly shook off that near-fatal lapse—*Gotta get my head out of my ass!* He jumped into the Storch's back seat as O'Hara's trembling hand pushed the throttle forward. With a lurch, the little plane taxied off.

Helga pedaled slowly through the pre-dawn darkness, following the pulsating spot of dim light the bicycle's headlight provided. She had been so proud of herself; how she had led O'Hara and the irresistible Lou DiNapoli to their glorious escape. But now, she felt only sorrow and remorse. How could their plan ever work? Surely, they would be quickly found out. Without a doubt, she had led them to their deaths.

She coasted to a stop, tears streaming down her cheeks. The bicycle's headlight extinguished as its wheel-driven generator fell still. Her fingers clasped the St. Christopher's medal dangling from her neck.

"Patron saint of travelers...that sweet boy needs this so much more than me," Helga whispered to the retreating night.

Fred O'Hara was desperately trying to get his bearings: *Fucking trees looming up everywhere! Where's that goddamn runway?* From that last vantage point with Helga, he was sure he could make out the narrow grass runway, but he could not seem to find it now; their wandering in the darkness on foot had disoriented him. He had to keep steering around bunkers of trees; his feet worked the differential brakes madly, the little craft pivoting around the braked wheel, its tail swinging about wildly. He knew he did not need much of a takeoff roll to get airborne in this ungainly-looking but light machine. But he could not seem to find that all-important patch of unobstructed turf. *Will I even recognize it,* he wondered, *if and when we get there?*

Light beams—sweeping up and down as if held in the hands of running German men—began to parallel the little airplane's path; at first just a few lights, then many. Surely, German bullets could not be far behind.

"They're chasing us, Freddy!" DiNapoli yelled from the back seat.

A dimly-lit valley appeared—like a soft, gray ribbon—between the dark, mountainous tree lines. *The runway! This must be it!* O'Hara swung the plane around once more and gunned the throttle. The little plane accelerated eagerly. They would be airborne in no time…

Then the engine coughed.

"Oh shit…No!" DiNapoli screamed from the back seat.

O'Hara's frantic ministrations to the engine controls had no effect. Coughing and surging alternated for a few seconds, until the engine fell silent. The stolen airplane rolled to a stop.

In seconds, a dozen or more men stood alongside the plane, shouting in German. Some had weapons at the ready.

The exhilaration of the escape attempt was the only thing that had flown away. Fred O'Hara shook his head sadly and said, "I think the game's over, Louie."

A German in coveralls—a mechanic—spoke in

halting English. "Thank you for draining the fuel for us, *kamerad*…we were almost finished doing that!"

Chapter Sixteen

A very agitated David Linker paced the day room floor, barely able to contain himself. Every time he reached a wall, he punched it, then turned about and stomped off in the opposite direction, like some pugilistic wind-up toy. The dull thud of his fist against the wall sounded like it should be very painful, but Linker was not deterred. Each time David spun around, his G.I. dog tags and Star of David, which shared the same neck chain, swung outside his unbuttoned shirt. Joe Gelardi looked on in dismay, his head following Linker's traversing of the room as if at a tennis match—he had yet to make sense of Linker's ranting. Tony Moscone sat mutely in a corner, seemingly oblivious to the commotion.

Linker finally came to a stop in the middle of the room and shouted, "I'm telling you, Lieutenant...that bastard Pilcher is running around with a Kraut! I saw him! Like they were asshole buddies...laughing, punching each other in the arm like it's all some big fucking joke. Touching each other like a couple of queers. He's worse than a deserter... he's a goddamn traitor!"

"How did you know he was German, David?" Gelardi asked.

"I know a German accent when I hear one, Lieutenant! All my relatives speak English like that. And he took out a cigarette case with a big fucking swastika on it!"

"Hmm...I see." Joe Gelardi had no idea what to say next.

"So are we going to turn him in?" Linker pressed.

"And who would we turn him in to, David?"

"I don't know...the police?"

"I'm not sure they'd really care, David. They're not taking sides, remember?"

"We've got to do something, Lieutenant! He's a fucking traitor!"

"Okay, David...okay. Just calm down." Joe pondered for a moment, then continued, "I'll take this up with Mrs. MacLeish. She'll do something. The Swedes won't tolerate fraternization like that."

Linker tossed Gelardi's proposed action over in his mind for a moment. It was not the instant firing squad he had envisioned—but it was at least a start. Anything to get back at that pathetic coward Pilcher. But before anyone could say another word, Ed Morris burst into the day room, a huge smile on his face, waving a piece of paper in his hand.

"I'm packing my gear, you guys," Morris said. "Just got the word I'm going up to Stockholm to do maintenance on our planes. Gonna be livin' in a fancy hotel and everything! You sure you don't want to volunteer, too, David?"

"Nah...somebody has to take care of Tony."

"Okay, suit yourself. It sure seems better than rotting in this burg, though. I tell you...that Mrs. MacLeish said she'd take care of it...and she did. She sure is good to her word," Morris said. He kissed the piece of paper in his hands.

You bet she is, Joe Gelardi thought.

Solemnly, David Linker said, "She'd better be." Then he got back to the original matter at hand. "And I'm sure that son-of-a-bitch Pilcher saw me watching him, too...and he didn't even seem to give a shit. Arrogant bastard!"

Ed Morris did not follow Linker's remark; he was

only interested in spreading his good news. "Where the hell is Hughes?" he asked. "I've been looking for him all day. It's not like him to go wandering off, all mopey like he is."

Tony Moscone let out another of those loud, hooting sounds they all believed was laughter. Then he surprised them all by actually speaking: "Frank Hughes...he went up the ladder."

Joe Gelardi was first up the ladder to the attic. At the top, he froze, causing the still-ascending David Linker's head to bang into his feet.

"What the hell, Lieutenant?" Linker blurted.

Joe could not speak. The sight of Frank Hughes's lifeless body hanging from the noose had sucked every word right out of him.

Ed Morris shouted from farther down the ladder. "C'mon! What's going on up there?"

With agonizing slowness, Gelardi cleared the ladder and climbed into the attic, allowing Linker the vantage point.

For a moment, David was speechless, too. Then he managed to speak just these words: "That poor, homesick bastard!"

Chapter Seventeen

Pola MacLeish threw the telegram from the American military attaché onto her desk with great disgust. She spun in the swivel chair to stare out the window of her dingy office. She needed the added burden of a suicide like a hole in the head. The note attached to Frank Hughes's shirt had simply said, in childlike handwriting: *I cannot be here anymore.*

"Your useless attaché in Stockholm has washed his hands of the whole affair, as usual," she said to Leonard Pilcher and Joe Gelardi, who sat facing her across the desk. "Typical bureaucratic nonsense. It's up to me to get Sergeant Hughes buried and notify your government of his grave location. Your general in Stockholm just doesn't seem to care...I'm surprised I don't have to notify his next of kin myself."

Pilcher slouched in his chair, totally disinterested in the matter of Frank Hughes. Staring at the ceiling, he muttered, "Gee, ain't that too goddamn bad?"

Joe felt his blood begin to boil. He posed an angry question to Pilcher: "Shouldn't you be writing a letter of condolence and explanation to his folks, Captain? He was under your command."

"Fuck that. The crazy boy wants to hang himself, that ain't my problem. Anyway, you and your lady friend here think you're calling the shots now, so why don't *you* write the fucking letter, *Joseph?* That is what she calls you, right? *Joseph?* Does she call you that in bed, too?"

Joe and Pola exchanged brief but frantic glances. They shared the same thought, screaming in their heads like a siren: *Have we really been found out that easily?*

By this idiot?

"What the hell are you talking about, Pilcher?" Joe demanded, hoping Pilcher might only be bluffing.

"That's '*Captain* Pilcher' to you, *Lieutenant*. I think I know what's going on between you two. You've been seen sneaking out of here, then meeting up later. Tell me, *Joseph*...is she a good fuck? What language does she scream in when you're banging her?"

Pola jumped from her chair and desperately wanted to shriek *No! Don't do it!* But she was too late— Joe Gelardi had already delivered the punch to the jaw that knocked Pilcher from his chair and sent him to the floor like a sack of potatoes. Joe loomed above the sprawled captain, fists still clenched, saying nothing—but his actions loudly confirming Pilcher's accusation.

Pola sank back into her chair. Softly, ruefully, she said: "Joseph, I really wish you hadn't done that." Her mind reeled for some way to get this cat back into the bag.

Pilcher propped himself up on one elbow and rubbed his bruised and swelling chin. A sardonic smile came to his face as he said, "Looks like *Joseph* just bought himself a court martial."

Defiantly, Joe replied, "Is this court martial going to be before or after you get the firing squad for desertion? Or maybe for fraternization with the enemy?"

Pola threw her hands up in exasperation. "Court martial? Do you two gobshites suppose I could get that useless attaché of yours interested in a court martial? Perhaps you should worry about that after you're all gone from here."

Ignoring Pola's remark, Pilcher ranted, "Now what the fuck are *you* talking about, Gelardi? Nobody's ever gonna charge me with desertion...you know that. Hell, if I'm a deserter, you're a deserter."

Joe stood his ground. "That's just full of shit, Pilcher, and you know it!"

"And just what the hell do you mean by 'fraternization,' *Joseph*?"

"We know about you and your German buddies, *Captain*. Pola's got something to tell you...it had to wait until after she dealt with Hughes...but you're going on a little trip. Seems you're getting a little too friendly with some Krauts here in town. Some people might call that treason."

Pilcher shot a hateful look at Pola MacLeish. "What the hell is he talking about, lady? What trip?"

"I'll be relocating you shortly, Captain Pilcher, to an internee compound. It seems I've found one that can take one more American. It won't be quite as free and easy as your stay in Malmö has been, I'm afraid. There'll be guards, wire fences, off-camp activities closely supervised..."

Pilcher swung his hateful glare to Joe. "So which one of my jerk-off crew ratted me out?"

"Gee...wouldn't you like to know!" Joe replied with a triumphant laugh.

Storming toward the office door, Pilcher said, "It had to be that Jew bastard, Linker. Right? I saw him following me...you can spot that big hook nose of his a mile away."

While she still had a chance, Pola thought about asking Pilcher one simple question: *Who ratted us out?* But she decided against it. Instead, as Pilcher stormed out the door to the street, she turned to Joe. In a voice laden with apprehension, she asked, "So tell me, Joseph...just how good a *fook* am I?"

Chapter Eighteen

The sun had risen but Fred O'Hara and Lou DiNapoli were still firmly on the ground in Germany. The Luftwaffe mechanics holding them captive were actually quite friendly, offering them cigarettes, ersatz coffee, even a small meal of bread and sausage. They seemed very impressed by the Americans' escape attempt, even if they had been unlucky enough to try it in a plane devoid of fuel. The few mechanics who could speak English plied them with good-natured questions, but the Americans would say little; they were POWs once again. Name, rank, and serial number only.

But O'Hara did offer these words: *Can't blame a guy for trying.*

The Germans who could understand him started to laugh heartily. One mechanic, older than the rest, gave O'Hara a good-natured slap on the back. Those who could not understand English decided this must be one hell of a joke on the Americans and decided to laugh, too.

Within the hour, Fred O'Hara and Lou DiNapoli were once again on a truck with a few other unlucky Allied airmen, heading to a Stalag Luft deep within Germany. Thoughts of escape made their obligatory appearance one more time; these periods of transit always provided the best opportunities. The guards, however, were not the motley collection of teenagers and old men they had encountered before. They were fit, hard, and alert, carrying short-barreled automatic weapons quite suitable to close-in work with prisoners. The American flyers did not realize the twin lightning bolts on their captors' collar insignia signified they were *Waffen SS* until they arrived at the prison camp. A sign—in English and German—at the heavily fortified gate made that uncomfortable fact quite clear.

As they were being hustled off the truck, a sad-eyed Louie DiNapoli turned to Fred O'Hara and said, "Anything for you, brother...always."

O'Hara replied. "Me, too, buddy. Take that to the bank."

The sound of a submachine gun being cocked silenced any further conversation.

Chapter Nineteen

Pola rose from the bed, careful not to wake Joe Gelardi. She shivered; the borrowed apartment was quite cold in this early morning hour. She pulled a robe over her naked flesh and stumbled toward the tiny kitchen to put up the kettle. She cursed as she slipped and almost fell on a discarded condom lying on the hardwood floor. It was one of several expended in the night's lovemaking, detritus of this unwise—yet enthralling—liaison that she believed, just a few short days ago, had surely brought her life to ruin.

Leonard Pilcher somehow knew of their affair. One word from him to her superiors of this forbidden fraternization with internees would get her sacked. The professional disgrace that followed would sink her career. Even if she finished her doctorate, the Ministry could blackball her forever. She would be lucky to get a job teaching primary school. Forget professorships or positions as a government minister. If her husband did ever return from this war, could she have made it any easier for him to divorce her? But a divorce from her distant and disinterested spouse seemed to be the least of her worries.

Frantically, she had plotted—and failed—to have Pilcher shipped to the internee camp even before it was ready to accept him. Some hold-up in the paperwork of a Brit being sent home was keeping the slot into which she so desperately wanted to dump him occupied. She rationalized her actions for the thousandth time: *He had this banishment coming, didn't he? Fraternizing with Germans was so much worse than a lonely woman and man seeking comfort in each other, was it not?* Once she shipped him off to the compound, it would be easy to dismiss his accusations as nothing more than attempts at revenge.

Seeking comfort. Pola laughed at that dignified description of their coupling. *Shagging like rabbits would be more accurate.*

She thought for sure the moment of truth had come when summoned to Professor Steenslund's office two mornings ago. The professor instructed her to appear with Captain Pilcher and Lieutenant Gelardi. She was barely able to croak the words *Yes, Professor* into the telephone; her throat felt like it was lined with sandpaper. Despite the autumn sun pouring through the window, her world had turned black.

Nothing was said as they drove to the Ministry: Pola, Joe, Pilcher, and their policeman driver. Joe and Pilcher looked surprisingly impassive as they entered the professor's office. Pola felt awash in perspiration. She hoped her heavy tweed suit jacket would hide the sopping stains to her blouse; she felt sure she was leaving a trail of sweat from beneath her skirt, down her stockings, into her thick-heeled pumps, squishing out to the floor as she walked. *This is what attending your own funeral feels like,* she told herself.

Professor Steenslund, impatient as always, waved them forward to waiting chairs without looking up. Holding up a file for all to see, he said, "There is a matter of interest to all of you that needs to be cleared up quickly."

Pola noticed the word <u>REPATRIATION</u> stamped ominously in large letters on the file. *So this is how it ends? I lose my career, my marriage, my Joseph...all at once?*

Steenslund continued, "Luckily for you, Captain

Pilcher, your reassignment to Smedsbo Internment Camp must be postponed indefinitely. The position is not available."

Pola felt herself sinking; the Professor's announcement was news to her. *Pilcher's not really going to be the winner, is he?*

Steenslund rattled on. "I must insist, however, that all fraternization with German internees cease immediately. Is that understood?"

"Yeah, sure. Whatever you say," Pilcher said with his usual contempt. None of this mattered to him. He was more amused by how the folds of skin under the bloated professor's chin hung over his tightly buttoned collar and the knot of his necktie. No matter: this fat Swede was just another irrelevant authority figure to be ignored and swept aside. Pilchers made their own rules.

The Professor ignored the insolence. "With the tragic death of Sergeant Hughes and the reassignment of Sergeant Morris, your numbers have dwindled further, Captain Pilcher. That leaves only yourself, Lieutenant Gelardi, Sergeant Linker, and the unfortunate Sergeant Moscone." He opened the file, lightly flipping through the sheets of paper within. "Your government has requested that you, Captain Pilcher, be returned to England as soon as possible. A flight is being arranged for you."

"I'm sorry, *Professor,* but that ain't gonna happen," Pilcher replied. *Government, my ass. This is my father's doing. The old son of a bitch just can't stop pulling strings, just like always. I'm not even safe from his clutches in this shithole.*

The professor seemed confused. "Excuse me, Captain?" he asked, an eyebrow quizzically raised. To his knowledge, nobody had ever balked at repatriation before.

"I said I ain't going. Send someone else in my place."

"That is a most altruistic gesture, Captain, but surely you realize it would be most difficult for my government not to honor this request?"

Pola and Joe exchanged knowing glances. They knew full well Pilcher had no intention of going anywhere as long as this war raged. And, of course, by offering to give up his repatriation slot, he was trying to make himself look like a hero—however falsely—once again. Just like the fairy tale of how he saved his crew from certain death in a mortally wounded airplane.

"Not your problem, *Professor*. Just tell them I'm gonna send some lucky boy home instead."

"Actually, the Malmö district has available *two* slots for repatriation," Steenslund added.

Pola's heart sank a little deeper. The odds were getting worse. She spoke up: "The district, you say, sir?"

"Yes, Pola. Two slots for the entire district. Actually, my dear, the decision how to fill these slots is yours. You are the administrator."

Sounds like I still have my job, anyway. Is this some kind of test or does the professor not know...or not care...about me and Joseph? Pola's brain began to coldly compute the reality of internment, repatriation—and her own desires. Two slots. Roughly 100 American airmen under her jurisdiction, one of them her lover and one who knows their secret—the secret that could devastate her life. The process was complete in an instant. Pola announced her decision: "We must honor the will of the American government, whatever Captain Pilcher's personal feelings on that matter might be. The choice is obvious...we will repatriate Captain Pilcher and Sergeant Moscone, who needs more care than we can offer him."

Joe Gelardi let out his breath but his face

remained expressionless. He was not unhappy at all with her decision.

Pilcher loosed a string of profanity that could be heard well down the hallway. Two policemen rushed in; the professor instructed them to place the captain in custody—forcibly if necessary—and hold him at his present quarters until repatriation arrangements were in place.

Leonard Pilcher put up quite a fuss, more of a blustery show than actual physical threat, but force was used to subdue him nonetheless. He was quickly handcuffed and dragged away by the policemen.

At the office door, Pilcher managed to stop the officers' progress for one moment, turned to Joe and Pola, and screamed, "I'll get the both of you…you whore bitch and you insubordinate guinea cocksucker! You forget who you're dealing with!"

The professor smiled warmly and waved to the raving man in handcuffs being propelled out the door by his police handlers. "Have a wonderful trip, Captain. It was our pleasure having you."

Steenslund then turned to Joe Gelardi. "Lieutenant, would you excuse us for a moment?"

When Joe had left the office, the professor gave Pola a fatherly look and said, "A wise choice, my dear…almost Solomon-like." He picked up another file from the desk, one labeled PILCHER, LEONARD, CAPTAIN, USAAF. He pulled a handwritten page—a letter—from the file.

"It seems our Captain Pilcher has made some very unseemly accusations against you and Lieutenant Gelardi."

Pola stood silent and rigid, bracing for the blow, her moment of triumph dissolving as quickly as it had emerged.

"Of course," the Professor continued, "who can believe anything that despicable young man has to say? I think we're all well rid of him, no?"

Just as the wave of relief began to wash over Pola, the professor leaned back in his chair with a sigh and added, "But be very careful, my dear girl..."

Her deepest fear realized: *The professor knew!*

Her only thought as she fled the professor's office was: *That's it! This thing with Joseph is over!* She brushed past Joe, who was waiting outside, and hurried down the hallway.

He sprinted after her. "Pola, what's wrong? What happened?"

She was unable to answer. It was too difficult fighting back the tears. She needed to get out of this building, to feel the cool, crisp air on her face, to take a breath again. The autumn air did the trick. Once on the street, she composed herself and turned to face Joe.

He looked at her helplessly as he wiped away the one tear that betrayed her: "Oh my God...you got fired...sacked, didn't you?"

Pola managed a nervous smile. "No, I still have my job. But it was a very close call... Let's not talk about it anymore."

Pola pulled the bathrobe tighter against the early morning chill as the tea steeped. There had been one more fear deep within her, one she dared not speak and tried with all her might to suppress: *Suppose Joseph wanted to leave, to be repatriated? Maybe this was one great roll in the hay while it lasted, but given the chance to leave...back to England...back to MIT...back to his wife...he'd jump at it without a second thought.* He always seemed strange—a bit withdrawn—when it was time for them to part. She had allowed herself to think it sadness that the rendezvous was over, never guilt for cheating on his wife or sleeping with another man's wife.

But nothing that happened in those two nights since the visit to the professor's office gave any credence to the thought that Joe Gelardi was unhappy to be staying in Sweden. She had rehearsed the things she would say to break off their affair the rest of that first day. It was the rational thing to do. But that night was anything but rational—nothing but an explosion of raw lust from the moment they came together. All the words she had mustered to protect herself and her career melted away in an instant: *It's just Pilcher's word against ours...and he's finished.*

Last night had taken a gentler course: a light dinner, small talk over a bottle of wine, followed by a passionate discussion of binary mapping techniques that ended with a quick but tender lovemaking on the couch while they were still fully clothed. Then, after a brief rest, they undressed each other and settled into bed, determined to continue their carnal explorations.

Pola carried her tea back to the bed and sat on its edge as Joe stirred. "Wake up, laddie. We've got to get out of here," she whispered, smoothing his hair with her free hand. "Sorry...there's no coffee."

"That's okay. I'll live." He threw off the covers, then grabbed them back and pulled them to his chin. "Damn! It's cold in here!"

"Oh, get up, silly boy!"

Joe reached up and grabbed her shoulders to pull her down. She struggled to place the brimming teacup on the night table before surrendering and collapsing on top of him. Their lips met in a long, deep kiss.

When the kiss was done, she began to play with the two dog tags that dangled from his neck on a thin chain. "May I have one of these?" she asked.

"We're supposed to have two. One's for Graves Registration…"

Her outburst of laughter interrupted his sentence. Opening the chain and removing one of the tags, she said, "Oh, Joseph, nobody's going to die here."

He smiled and pulled her mouth back to his. Between kisses, he murmured, "How about one more time?"

Reluctantly, she pulled away. "How about you get your clothes on and go home?"

She instantly wished she had not used the word "home." He did not seem struck by the literal meaning of what she had just said, however, and kept trying to pull her back. She squirmed from his embrace and stood alongside the bed, smiling down on him, his liberated dog tag clasped tightly in her hand.

"I've got a special treat planned for you tonight, Joseph."

Joe was puzzled: *More special than what we've been doing all these other nights?*

"I'm going to show you the most beautiful autumn sunset you've ever seen. The church across the street from the police barracks…meet me inside at 1700 hours."

Chapter Twenty

Leonard Pilcher paced the floor of his barracks room—the room that was now his prison cell. The guards were, for once, unbending; orders had come down from above that Pilcher was to remain in quarters and remain he would. *And these are the same clowns who usually don't give a rat's ass who comes and goes from this building...they don't even bother handing out passes anymore. Where were you going to go, anyway? Even if you disappeared for days on end, they knew you'd always be back for payday. Somebody really put a bug up their asses this time.*

He would have tried to bribe them, but he was broke; Lichtblau's high-living ways had bled him dry again. Payday was still a week away.

Lichtblau's probably wondering what happened to me. We were supposed to meet up for dinner...that crazy Nazi even said he'd try to scare up some pussy.

Pilcher stepped from his room into the hallway. The policeman usually sitting opposite his door—his personal guard—was gone. His chair stood empty, the pages of a newspaper scattered around it. A steaming cup of coffee sat on the floor next to the chair.

I guess he won't mind if I go up to the roof and have a smoke.

Joe arrived at the church at the appointed hour of 1700, just as Pola had directed. *Funny how these Europeans tell time like the military,* he thought, as he took a seat in a back pew. Pola was nowhere to be seen. Two old women moved slowly about, tending to cleaning chores in the spare interior of the church, eyeing him suspiciously. *So this is what a Lutheran church looks like...so different from the Catholic churches I'm used to...nothing fancy here. Just a bunch of pews, a pulpit, and a big cross on the front wall. Drab brick walls. No statues. The windows are just that...no stained glass with saints and martyrs. No holy water...Looks more like an auditorium than a place God is supposed to dwell...and those two old girls don't know what to make of me. I wish to hell Pola would show up...I feel kinda naked. Damn, it's chilly in here.*

As if on cue, Pola appeared, striding from a door next to the pulpit. She walked straight to the old women, who greeted her warmly, with hugs and kisses all around. There was a brief exchange in Swedish, of which Joe understood not a word. The old women gestured with concern toward him, but Pola said something that seemed to allay their fears, if only a little. The old women then passed through the door through which Pola had just entered. Neither Joe nor Pola noticed the suspicious looks the two old women were still shooting their way as they exited.

"You look a wee bit cold, Joseph...that jacket is not going to be warm enough. Didn't you get a winter coat for yourself?"

He liked the way she said that. It had a tone that suggested *permanence*.

"Funny...I got one for David and Tony but not me."

"So typical," Pola gushed as she kissed him. "Takes care of the lads first...Come on, we're alone now," she said, tugging on his sleeve. "We've got to lock up. I told the ladies I'd take care of it."

"You work here, too?"

"No, silly. My uncle is the pastor. He trusted me

with a set of keys years ago." She locked the front entry doors. "There. Anna and Ingrid...the two caretakers you saw...took care of the back door."

Joe was confused. "I've never heard of a church that locks its doors..."

"We didn't used to, but there was a wee problem with vandals a while back. Communists, supposedly."

"Wow...Communists, huh? Is nothing sacred?"

Pola replied with just a knowing smile, the one Joe had seen many times before and taken to mean *you silly American.*

"So what about this sunset you promised?"

She led him to another door. "We're going up the bell tower," she said as she turned the key in its lock. "It's a beautiful view over the rooftops. You can occupy that mathematical mind of yours calculating the number of steps in the spiral staircase."

"Okay...how high is the tower?"

"You can calculate that, too, if you like, clever boy!"

Pola and Joe had arrived at the top of the bell tower. Like the rest of the building, the tower was a simple brick and stone structure. The open bell deck was surrounded by waist-high fencing, with brickwork forming the posts and railing. Thick stone pillars in each of the four corners rose to support the tower's roof and the bell's trunnion. A few pigeons lined the railing, totally unconcerned at the presence of humans. The bells were still, their slack ropes swaying in the light breeze.

"Two hundred twenty-five steps," Joe said. "And I estimated two hundred thirty, right?"

"Close enough," Pola replied, playfully leaning over the fence rail. Abruptly, she pulled back and ducked behind a pillar, pulling Joe with her.

"What's wrong?" Joe asked, straining to get a view around the pillar of what had startled her.

She pulled him back again before he could see anything. "We're looking down at the roof of the barracks, Joseph! Pilcher is there...on the roof! Bloody hell!"

Joe shook free of her grasp and peeked around the pillar. He was alarmed by what he saw. "Oh, brother...you aren't going to believe this, Pola...but Linker and Moscone just popped up on the roof, too! Just what the hell is going on here?"

"That's all I bloody need...him seeing us," Pola said. In a crouch, she started for the stairway.

"Pola, wait! Take a look at this!"

Hunched down, they peered through the fence posts. It looked like a stand-off between Pilcher and Linker. Joe and Pola could not make out precisely what their voices were saying, but it was obvious those voices were raised. An occasional, clearly distinguishable expression floated up to their perch. Despite the distance, the speakers of those words were unmistakable. David Linker shouted *traitor* and *fucking queer.* Pilcher screamed *Jew bastard.*

The physical struggle ignited an instant later. Pilcher and Linker locked into a clinch, like two punch-drunk prizefighters, stumbling in a bizarre, silent dance across the barracks roof. In an instant they were at the edge—Pilcher gave one thrust with his entire body.

David Linker plummeted to the street four stories below.

The distance from the street to the bell tower caused an audio delay, like a brief suspension of reality; a second after Joe and Pola watched his body crumple and skull impact the cobblestones, they heard the dull *crump* of that impact.

In shock and disbelief, they looked back to the barracks roof. Pilcher had vanished. Tony Moscone remained—head down, hands in his pockets—standing near the ladder hatch, not having moved an inch since he first appeared.

The pigeons had disappeared, too; they could simply fly away when calamity struck. They left behind only a feather that fluttered slowly downward between Pola and Joe. It brushed across his face as it fell. His open hand swept it away angrily.

There was shouting from the street below. People rushed to the broken body, some trying to help, some with a need to feel a part of this horror, but most simply out of morbid curiosity. After a few moments, they all stepped back, for there was nothing they could do. A widening river of blood flowed from beneath David Linker's shattered skull. Policemen spilled from the barracks and took control of the scene. They all looked up toward the barracks roof, expecting to find the cause of this tragedy. They saw nothing but the darkening sky. Two policemen bolted from the street and appeared on the roof of the barracks a minute later. They found nothing but Tony Moscone.

Joe Gelardi and Pola MacLeish were frozen in horror, unable to move. They stayed—speechless and panic-stricken—squatting behind the pillar. It was Pola who finally shattered the silence, imploring in a whisper, "Joseph, what are we going to do?"

Chapter Twenty-One

They never saw the sunset. It was nearly dark by the time Joe and Pola descended the stairs from the bell tower, yet only 10 minutes had elapsed since David Linker's murder. On the stairs, Joe reached for her arm but she pulled away, as if his touch was anything but comforting. Once in the empty chapel, a trembling Pola repeated her question: "Joseph, what are we going to do?"

Joe paced nervously by the front pew. He stammered his plan. "I'm going...I'm going to say...to say that *I* witnessed the whole thing from the bell tower..."

Incredulous, she interrupted. "Wait...wait. You *alone* witnessed it?"

"Yeah...why not?"

Pola stood, open-mouthed, completely astonished by Joe's suggestion. She began an agitated, wordless rejection, shaking her head from side to side.

Joe tried to regroup his thoughts. *Okay, she doesn't buy that idea.* He seized on another: "Pola, suppose *you* tell them you witnessed the whole thing from the tower?"

Pola seemed to vibrate, signaling the eruption that was only an instant away. When it came, she shouted so loudly that Joe was sure she could be heard throughout the city: "ARE YOU TAKING THE PISS, JOSEPH? WHY THE BLOODY HELL WOULD YOU OR I BE UP IN A BLOODY BELL TOWER ALL ALONE? AND HOW THE BLOODY HELL WOULD YOU GET THERE WITHOUT ME? WHO'LL BELIEVE THAT,

YOU STUPID SOD? BESIDES, ANNA AND INGRID SAW US TOGETHER! DO YOU WANT THEM TO LIE, TOO?"

"Anna and Ingrid? Who the hell are they?"

"THE CHURCH CARETAKERS! THE TWO WHO THOUGHT YOU WERE SOME BLOODY CRIMINAL UNTIL I TOLD THEM WE WERE FRIENDS!"

She defiantly stood her ground—feet apart, her blue eyes glaring like beacons—dangling the required keys before his face. Joe felt like he had been knocked backwards by the force of her outburst. It seemed to take an eternity for her words to stop echoing in that vast, empty chamber.

Unnerved, he still could not fully grasp her opposition. He tried to reason with her: "What would be so unbelievable about *you* being there alone?"

Pola launched into another volcanic tirade: "BECAUSE NOBODY EVER GOES UP THERE! I HAVEN'T BEEN THERE SINCE I WAS FOURTEEN OR SO...AND EVEN THEN, I SNUCK UP WITH A BOY!"

He had no answer for that. Against all reason, her last outburst distracted him. It stung, arousing jealousy deep within him, as if youthful sex—even just kissing and petting—with other boys was suddenly a threat.

More calmly, Pola continued, "Joseph, don't you see I'm in deep shite here? There'll be a police inquiry...they'll dig into *everything*. *Any* suggestion that you and I have been together and my career...my life...is finished. I've already been warned."

"What do you mean you've been warned?"

"The professor...do you remember when I said I still had my job, but it was a very close call?"

"Oh, yeah," Joe mumbled, eyes downcast, as the

memory of that chaotic morning flooded back.

"He knew then...and he won't let it pass again. We say nothing, Joseph. I don't lie very well...neither do you."

The grim calculus of Pola's decision had become clear: she had no choice but to trade the truth of David Linker's death for her own life. But what of Joe's perspective? In his soul, the issue was simple: *It just wasn't right...Linker deserved justice; Pilcher deserved to be hung for murder.* Yet, he would trade his soul for Pola Nilsson-MacLeish. Resigned and downcast, it was his turn to ask, "So what do we do now?"

"First," she said softly, "we need to slip out of this church the back way. I'll go straight to the barracks...I need to make sure those bloody policemen don't terrorize poor Sergeant Moscone. You take your time getting there...so we don't show up together."

They parted without so much as an embrace.

Chapter Twenty-Two

Joe Gelardi spent the night of David Linker's murder in his police barracks room. It had been the first night in some time he actually spent there—and it was the first night in some time he had spent alone. Sleep proved impossible. His tormented mind replayed the events of the day over and over. He paced the floor of the dark room, yearning more for his lover than justice for David Linker.

After he and Pola left the church, he had walked a long, circuitous path through a darkened Malmö for over an hour. The more he walked, the stronger became the impossible urge to avoid this whole mess and never return to the barracks. Eventually, he gave in to the inevitable and arrived on that street, the one that still bore faint stains from David Linker's blood, visible even in the streetlights' dim glow.

He found Pola in the police commander's office with several gentlemen. Although she looked pale as a ghost, she greeted him matter-of-factly; they all did. He nervously scanned the men's faces: the commander, several uniformed police officers, two detectives, and Professor Steenslund. No one seemed to look at him as if thinking, *Ahh...MacLeish's lover has arrived,* not even Professor Steenslund. Changing from Swedish to heavily accented English, the commander invited him to stay. "Please take a seat, Lieutenant. We have some very bad news."

With a nod from the commander, a detective began to speak. His English sounded like it came from the American Midwest, perhaps Minnesota. "Sorry to inform you that at approximately 1715 hours, Sergeant David Linker, US Army Air Forces, currently interned in Sweden, fell to his death from the roof of this barracks..."

Joe tried to display the appropriate surprise and shock. His voice managed to sound appropriately distressed when he uttered, "Oh, no!"

What he really wished to say was *Fell, my ass!*

The detective had more to say. "We have classified Sergeant Linker's death as a suicide. There is no evidence to suggest accident or foul play. While we believe Sergeant Anthony Moscone was present on the roof at the time of death, Mrs. MacLeish vouches for the fact that his condition, and his dependence on Sergeant Linker, would make it impossible for him to cause...or prevent...such a tragedy. We concur with Mrs. MacLeish." Smugly, the detective added, "As you well know, Lieutenant, suicides are not uncommon among interned aircrews."

Joe was stunned by the finality of the detective's statement. *They've closed the book on this already. Hughes committed suicide, therefore Linker did, too. They're really not interested in looking any deeper.* He struggled to decide if he should be relieved—or outraged.

Joe could see Pola go rigid in her chair as he asked: "Where is Captain Pilcher, anyway?" She would not look at him. Then he added: "Shouldn't he be here?"

The detective's face reddened in obvious irritation. This internee did not seem to realize it was not his place to be questioning the authorities. He tapped a pen on his notebook several times before continuing. "Captain Pilcher is in his room, where he has been confined pending his repatriation tomorrow. He has been confined the past three days, as you well know..."

Pola's knuckles were gripping her chair tight

enough to turn them white. She would not look at Joe. She wished he would just be silent.

The detective gestured to Professor Steenslund, who shifted his considerable bulk in the chair to face Joe Gelardi and added these final details to the report: "Since Captain Pilcher and Sergeant Moscone will be leaving us tomorrow, that makes you, Lieutenant Gelardi, the ranking officer...and the only remaining member of your unfortunate crew at this facility. Therefore, Captain Pilcher has requested that you write the letter of condolence to Sergeant Linker's next of kin."

Leonard Pilcher figured he had gotten away with it: *Nobody saw anything...and Moscone, that vegetable, won't be telling no tales.* He had been able to flee the roof and get back to his room undetected; the chaos in the street outside had seen to that. The chair that should have been occupied by his guard was still empty, the coffee cup and newspaper beside it unmoved. Nobody had checked on him until 15 minutes after his return; a policeman in full stride had glanced into the room, then continued down the hall toward the shouting and commotion without saying a word.

He found it impossible to calm down. He paced the room, muttering rationalizations over and over again for the homicide he had just committed: *Who does that sheenie think he is, calling ME a traitor...and a queer! I was just trying to make him shut his big Jew mouth...It was an accident he tripped and fell over the edge...that's all, just an accident. Wasn't my fault at all. Stupid kike brought it on himself.*

A thought surfaced that finally calmed him a bit: *Maybe it's a good thing I'm getting shipped out tomorrow and taking that looney toon Moscone with me...It'll be like it never happened in no time.*

With newfound resolve, he began to pack his personal belongings, an act he had had no interest in accomplishing until now. He whistled *I'll be Home for Christmas* while he worked.

Chapter Twenty-Three

She's avoiding me...

It had been three days since David Linker's murder, and Joe Gelardi had managed only a few moments with Pola MacLeish, all within the confines of the police barracks. When he tried to arrange a rendezvous of any sort, she always had some excuse.

Pilcher and Moscone were gone, whisked away at dusk on the appointed day. They were placed on a bus with a small group of internees also to be repatriated and driven to the airfield on the outskirts of the city. A daylight flight to England would be too risky; too many German fighters still prowled the daytime skies between occupied Denmark and Norway. The RAF transport flying them out arrived and departed in darkness, never shutting its engines down during its brief turn-around. By daybreak, they were back on British soil.

As he was being helped onto the bus, Tony Moscone kept looking back and yelling, "Wait for Dave! Wait for Dave!" Joe Gelardi felt certain he could still hear Moscone's pleas as the bus drove off, until the drone of a civil aircraft overhead drowned them out.

But David Linker was gone, too. Joe missed him more than he thought possible: the vibrant intelligence, the biting sarcasm, the delicate way he had cared for Tony. David was truly an exceptional young man. But every thought of him degenerated to that last moment of his life, that sickening sound of body impacting pavement. Joe had nowhere to turn for refuge but to Pola—and she, too, was threatening to become a devastating memory.

And that son-of-a-bitch Pilcher stuck me with writing the condolence letter! Sure...what would he have written? Dear Mr. and Mrs. Linker, I'm so sorry I killed your son...

Joe Gelardi hoped Tony Moscone would finally get the psychological treatment he so badly needed. He wished Leonard Pilcher would go straight to hell. And he prayed David Linker would forgive him.

But it was Pola who dominated his thoughts. He longed for her touch, to feel her body respond to his, to see that splendid mane of flaxen hair splayed across the pillow as they made love. Her refusal to see him drove him to desperation. One morning, that desperation poured recklessly out as they passed in the hallway. "Pola," he whispered, "I'm going to go out of my mind if I can't be with you again."

At first, she turned away without saying a word. After a few steps, she turned back and said in a voice that seemed to possess all the control his quavering voice lacked, "All right. Come to the apartment at 1800. I'll make supper. Bring a loaf of bread."

He bounded up the staircase to the apartment several minutes early, a loaf of fresh bread from the corner bakery tucked under his arm. No one answered his knock. He slumped against the wall next to the door, praying that she actually intended to show her face.

After 10 minutes that had seemed to Joe like 10 hours, Pola ascended the staircase. "I'm sorry I'm late, Joseph," she said, not bothering to explain further. Once inside the apartment, she went directly to preparing the food, broiling fish fillets and preparing a salad.

Rummaging the cupboards, Joe asked, "Is there any wine?"

"No...no wine. Slice the bread...there's a good lad."

He could take no more of her indifference. He seized her from behind, his arms alternating entwining her waist and massaging her breasts as he kissed her neck, her hair, her ears. She spun in his grasp to face him, their bodies tight together. Tepidly, her mouth met his fervent kiss and then gently extinguished it.

"Later, Joseph. Let's eat first."

That promise was enough. He released her and did as he was told. They spoke little as they faced each other at the small table, moving to the couch in the tiny sitting room for coffee. *This is later*, Joe told himself and he pulled her to him once again. She submitted passively, without enthusiasm. His hands began a full exploration of that body he so desperately craved, plunging beneath the full skirt of her dress and unbuttoning the bodice above the belted waist.

He pushed her down so she was supine on the cushions, her breasts exposed. Feverishly, he pulled the pumps from her feet. He stopped, for a moment, to slather her face and breasts with kisses, then returned to her thighs to unhook her stockings. Roughly, he slid them down her legs one at a time, followed by the panties and garter belt. When he was done, he straddled her thighs, pinning her hands above her head against the armrest. With a studied motion, he bound her wrists with one stocking and secured them over the armrest to a foot of the couch with the other stocking.

He stood, gazing down at his captive, his lover. Her eyes were closed, her body tense but motionless, awaiting the coupling she had allowed. His pants and boxers fell to the floor. He returned to the couch, knelt between her parted legs, slipped on the prophylactic and entered her quickly. She made not a sound as she absorbed his passionate attempt to reclaim her.

When he was finished, lying motionless atop her, their bodies still linked, she finally spoke.

"Joseph, there is something I must tell you...two things, actually."

He pulled away slowly and sat between her feet at the opposite end of the couch. Nervously, he asked: "You're not pregnant, are you? You can't be..."

"Not that I'm aware," she replied, "but I have received word from my husband's parents in Scotland. Reginald was badly wounded in combat several months ago. He may even be en route to England at this moment for convalescent care. It appears his war is over."

"I see," Joe mumbled as shame poured over him like a drenching rain. *A soldier's wife...a wounded soldier's wife.* He jumped up to untie her.

"Thank you," Pola whispered as she rubbed the sore red marks encircling both wrists. "The professor and I are trying to arrange some sort of transport for me to England after Reginald arrives. It's quite a dodgy thing at the moment."

"Yeah, I'll bet it is," Joe answered softly. The rapid switch from sexual frenzy to crushing reality was making him lightheaded and sick to his stomach. "At least he's alive," he said, then immediately wished he had not offered such a ridiculous platitude.

"Yes, I suppose I should be grateful for that."

"You said there were two things you need to tell me?"

She hesitated before continuing. "Yes. I've decided to stop using the police barracks as a billet. You're being reassigned to Stockholm. You leave in two days' time."

There was little reaction from Joe, just a confused smile, slight and pitiful. The full weight of her words had not yet made its mark on him. Her tears began to flow. "I'm sorry, Joseph. Every time I see you, I see that poor lad being murdered…and I can't do anything about it…I should give him justice and I can't…and now poor Reginald! I'm so ashamed!" She collapsed into deep, wracking sobs.

Her words began to take their full effect, capsizing whatever hope Joe had managed to keep afloat. He reached out for a lifeline and tried to embrace her, but she pushed him away. Fighting his own tears, he said, "But Pola, I love you…We love each other!"

Her reply was a shriek: "DON'T SAY THAT! NOT NOW!" She jumped up from the couch, flinging herself into the armchair across the room, her legs tucked defensively beneath her, a hand holding the top of her dress closed.

So many thoughts began to swirl in Joe Gelardi's mind—images of their days and nights together, things they had said, things they had done—spinning faster and faster until the ensuing vortex threatened to suck them all away. He began to plead. "So we can't do anything about David. That was for you, wasn't it? But that doesn't mean…"

But she cut him off. "Just go, Joseph. Please…just go."

PART III

AMERICA 1960

Chapter Twenty-Four

The walls of the office were lined with photographs depicting mobs of angry men, sometimes hundreds, sometimes thousands. Common-looking men, dressed in workingman's clothes, carrying picket signs—a pictorial history of this last century of class warfare in America. In some pictures, the picket signs were being held aloft, like countless pages with identical text. In others, the signs had become weapons—clubs and spears—leveled against the better-armed mercenaries of the corporations. It mattered not at all if these mercenaries were company goons, private "detectives," state police, or federal soldiers; they all served the same enemy.

Tom Houlihan leaned back in the armchair and lit another of his fetid cigars. "You don't mind if I smoke in here, do you, Freddy?" It was not really a question, just a confirmation of privilege masquerading as one. After all, as president emeritus of the Amalgamated Steelworkers Union, this was *his* office; always has been, always would be, no matter who actually sat in that chair. Even this brand-new, hand-picked successor.

The putrid odor of cigar smoke was the least of Fred O'Hara's problems at the moment. Something stunk far worse than that; Tom Houlihan's pronouncement, just prior to lighting up, still hung in the air like a cloud of deadly gas. And it smelled far worse to Fred O'Hara than the noxious odor of steel mills that belched from every smokestack, permeating the Pittsburgh air.

"That's right, Freddy. Our union is going to endorse Congressman Leonard Pilcher for President of these United States." He was grinning from ear to ear as he took another puff on the cigar. "You know, my boy, I couldn't be happier with you at this moment. You are truly the right man at the right time; 1960 is going to be another Republican year, and we're going to help make it so. The fact that you two boys know each other...served together in the war, goddammit!...is gonna bring good things for all of us. Even with that damn fool Ike still running his mouth, first with that *Republicans are the party of business* stuff...Gee, no fooling, General! And then he throws in that crap about the *dangers of the military-industrial complex!* Shit, son, we live off that goddamned military-industrial complex! That Daddy Pilcher...old Mr. Military-Industrial Complex himself...bought his boy that congress seat and he'll buy him the White House, too. And when he does, we kick the United Steelworkers and their Democrat friends right in their commie asses. We'll be calling our own shots."

Fred O'Hara was on his feet now, pacing the well-worn carpet. "You're sure about this, Tom?"

"Absolutely, Freddy my boy. Absolutely."

"This union is going to support a *Republican* candidate for president? Since when?"

"There's a first time for everything, Freddy. Gotta go with the times."

"Do you really think Pilcher needs our endorsement? Or would his daddy just rub the USW's face in it?"

"It's a win for us either way, Freddy my boy."

The pictures on the wall—so many bloodied strikers, fighting daunting odds—suddenly seemed discordant, an inappropriate backdrop to the heresy Houlihan was spouting.

"Then I've...no, we've...got a problem, Tom."

Tom Houlihan's face—cigar and all—twisted into

an expression of disapproval.

"What kind of problem, son?"

"Yeah, I know Pilcher…all too well. I've told you before about how Captain Leonard Pilcher took a perfectly good airplane to Sweden while I twiddled my thumbs in the *Stalag Luft.*" He pounded a fist on the desk as he said, "He's a deserter…and a coward!"

"The war's over, Freddy."

"The fuck it is, Tom! Why should I have to shine shit for that shirking son of a bitch?"

"Because if he wins, this union wins. Big time. And that's all that matters, Freddy boy. Besides, we're all sons of bitches, ain't we?"

"Not like him, we ain't. We're sons of bitches for the right reasons."

Houlihan shifted his old bones uneasily in the plush chair, exuding disapproval without uttering a word. He had given his proclamation; he was not expecting any debate.

But O'Hara kept right on talking. "What makes you so sure he'll get the nod, anyway, Tom? What about Nixon?"

"That nutcase? He's crazier than a shithouse rat. Just because he's vice president don't mean nobody in their right mind's gonna nominate him. Who the fuck cares about VPs, anyway? Ain't no real money on him."

"I don't know, Tom…I think Nixon's got a great shot."

"Fuck Nixon! Don't know his ass from a hole in the ground. Besides, if the Dems put up that other little rich boy, Kennedy, we're gonna need to cancel out all his war hero bullshit."

"Pilcher ain't no war hero, Tom. Anything but. Surely you don't expect me to…"

"I expect you'll do as you're told, Freddy." There

was not a hint of a smile on Houlihan's face or in his voice.

O'Hara dropped back into his swivel chair, the knot in his stomach threatening to deposit the lunch he had just downed onto the solid oak desk. He dared not envision himself at some podium—bright lights blazing, cameras rolling, a phalanx of microphones before him—endorsing Leonard Pilcher. He would puke for sure, right there on national TV.

"Tom, the last time I saw Pilcher was right before I bailed out of that plane. I swore that if I ever saw him again, I'd kill him."

Houlihan slowly rose to his feet, smoothing the fall of his expensive silk suit jacket over his abundant belly in the process. He shuffled behind O'Hara's chair, massaged the younger man's shoulders gently, then gave him a playful, yet firm, tap on the head. "The passion of youth, my boy...that's all that was. You're a growed-up political animal now. We're all counting on you. You're gonna do the right thing."

Do the right thing. Those words kept echoing in Fred O'Hara's mind long after Houlihan had made his way out of the union hall, patting the backs and shaking the hands of thuggish functionaries that Fred knew damn well were still loyal to the old man. As Houlihan's chauffeured limo disappeared into the rush-hour traffic, the *right thing* was painfully clear to Fred O'Hara—put a bullet in Leonard Pilcher's brain at the earliest convenience. Do everyone a big favor. *I should have done it a long time ago.*

Hell...maybe a bullet would do ol' Tom Houlihan some good, too. With all his gambling debts, he's ripe for a bribe. Old Man Pilcher must have figured that one out and swooped in for the kill. But Houlihan's eighty-two, for Christ's sake! Can't the old bastard just do us all a favor and croak right now, before he sells us out any worse?

O'Hara's gut still reeled at the irony—after all these years of doing Tom Houlihan's violent bidding to reach the pinnacle of union leadership, his first official act on the national stage was slated to be the political endorsement of a man he despised, a man he had once vowed to kill.

Houlihan's gone soft. Conflict...ain't that what unions are about? None of these son-of-a-bitch mill owners ever gonna give you nothing for free...You gotta fight for it...even kill for it.

*Kill for it...*the memory crept back into Fred O'Hara's mind like a persistent stain. A blood stain. Scrub it as hard as you like; you think you have gotten rid of it. But when the rinse water dries, the stain—and the memory of Billy Murphy—is still there, maybe dulled a bit, but there nonetheless.

Billy Murphy and Fred O'Hara had been friends since childhood in Pittsburgh. As teenagers, they fought side by side against the rival neighborhood gangs. Sticks and stones broke their bones, but they gave as good as they got. Always.

Billy joined the Navy right after Pearl Harbor. A talented mechanic, he chose submarines, spending the next three years roaming the Pacific in the sweltering, airless hell that was a sub's engine room. After VJ Day, the Navy wanted him to stay, offering him petty officer's rank. He told them to shove their stripes—and their submariner's dolphins—up their asses. He had had enough of the sea. He was going back to Pittsburgh. Back to the steel mills.

Fred O'Hara was already home from the war, liberated from the Stalag Luft just before VE Day, when

Billy Murphy returned to Pittsburgh. They saw little of each other, though; Billy hired on as a plant mechanic at a mill right away. Fred signed on as a pilot for a fledgling airline that promptly failed, then half a dozen more that folded within months of opening for business. Surplus transport planes were cheap, war-experienced pilots even cheaper. But the business acumen needed to turn a profit from the sky in those post-war years was neither cheap nor abundant.

After little more than a year, Fred O'Hara came home to Pittsburgh with his new wife, gave up on his dream of commercial flying, and took a mill job. A veteran union organizer, a USW man by the name of Tom Houlihan, took a shine to this new face. He seemed a tad sharper, a bit more tenacious, and a whole lot more comfortable speaking his mind than the average new-hire. And he had to be tough as nails to have survived as a POW. Tom spent many hours listening—with rapt attention—as Fred told of evading capture in Germany. But he figured the part about the angelic blonde girl who tried to help them escape—and crawled into the sack with his buddy—had to be bullshit, just there to spice the tale up a bit.

The United Steelworkers bosses were not a particularly scrupulous bunch. They declared their own lackeys as winners in the recent shop steward elections, even though a pitiful few of the rank-and-file claimed to have voted for them. Tom Houlihan had been a loyal USW man, but even he smelled the corruption and decay. He was leading the disenfranchised membership in a fight for a new union, the Amalgamated Steelworkers, to kick the USW out of this plant and any other plant where they could garner enough support. Fred O'Hara quickly became one of his trusted lieutenants.

It did not take long before the two unions were

engaged in violent confrontations—*head-busting,* they called it. Armed conflict came too easily to men who, less than two years ago, were making war against Germany and Japan. It was not too difficult to turn on your own countrymen if you thought it might result in adding another 10 cents to your hourly wage. Heads were indeed busted and worse: bodies pierced with bullets and knives, even makeshift weapons like sharpened screwdrivers and blunt hammers came into frequent play.

Fred O'Hara adopted the practice of keeping a change of clothes in the shed behind his mother's row house. He did not want his mother or his wife, pregnant with their first child, to see his blood-spattered garments, to know just how close he was to all this mayhem the newspapers featured endlessly, complete with gory black-and-white photos of blood-soaked union men littering the streets. The shed served another purpose: he could hide his pistol there.

It was never meant to be a confrontation, just a few of Houlihan's men sauntering into a dark and smoky bar, well into their cups already. A table of equally inebriated men—United Steelworkers men—sat far in the corner, anonymous and unnoticed. Their loud, boisterous comments—ugly words against the Amalgamated Steelworkers—were ignored at first. But the repetition of those comments raised the temperature of the room rapidly. Soon, they were met with angry challenges from Houlihan's men. A chair was thrown, then a few punches. Someone cried, *Look out, Freddy! He's got a shiv!* A gunshot, then deafening silence, with all the actors frozen on their marks.

As he and his cohorts fled the bar, Fred O'Hara took one fleeting look at the face of the young man bleeding to death on the floor. Only then did he realize he had just shot Billy Murphy.

I killed my enemy...I killed my friend.

When the police finally arrived, none of the noncombatants in that bar would profess to having seen anything. Among the men Billy Murphy had been drinking with, none knew the identities of their assailants. The police ended their investigation right then and there.

Fred O'Hara stored the memory of that murder as his darkest secret, to be spoken just once. He confessed the secret to his good friend, war buddy and fellow POW Lou DiNapoli.

His secretary's voice snapped him back to the present. "Are you okay, Mr. O'Hara?" she asked. Lost in his awful memory, Fred had no idea how long she had been standing in the office doorway, watching him.

"Yeah, Marion, I'm fine. Just thinking about something."

"Gee, you seemed about a thousand miles away."

"That's about where I was...See you in the morning, Marion."

She closed the door behind her, unconvinced of his sanity but glad to be going home. O'Hara turned back to gaze at the pictures on the wall once again. Of this he was sure: he had not clawed his way to union leadership to wear expensive suits, live in a house with servants, or hobnob with industrialists and their pampered offspring. He had done it for one reason and one reason only: to make sure the have-nots retained the power to impose consequences on the haves.

Leonard Pilcher definitely had some consequences coming that were long overdue. If Tom Houlihan could not see that, well...maybe he would have to go, too.

No fucking way this union ever endorses that son

of a bitch.

He spun the rolodex. Sticking a pencil in the phone, he dialed "O." "Yeah, Operator," he said, "long distance. I'm calling New York City..."

Chapter Twenty-Five

The New England winter of 1959-1960 had been unusually warm, threatening to make spring's arrival nothing more than a turn of a calendar's page. The air in the classroom was thick and uncomfortable as the radiators continued to produce the heat a Cambridge winter usually required. The solitary co-ed, Meredith Salinger, had already complained the room was *stuffy*. Assistant Professor Joseph Gelardi busied himself opening the windows wide as his students—MIT freshmen—pondered another problem of the Calculus. A *pop quiz*, they called it.

As his students labored in silence, Joe Gelardi's mind drifted elsewhere, to another time, another place. A simple conclusion haunted him, one he had confessed to no one but himself a thousand times before:

I failed you, David Linker.

He was not sure what triggered the crushing guilt this time; he could never be sure. Was it the sound of Meredith Salinger's solitary female voice in a sea of male voices, much like Pola's voice had sounded amidst those of *The Lady M's* crew? Or was it the sounds the open windows allowed inside—the deep rumble of piston-engined airplanes as they plied their way to and from Logan Airport, their sound still far more prevalent than the ear-shattering whine of the new jet airliners?

Or was it seeing the face of Leonard Pilcher once again, smirking like some sadistic, grayscale demon from a black and white television screen, ripping open an unhealed wound?

Pilcher: that murderer. I could have stopped him

in Sweden a long time ago. The Swedish government would have been more than glad to repatriate an interned murderer to face a court martial...and maybe a firing squad. But I didn't. Protecting Pola seemed so much more important.

What perverse god smiles on a man such as Leonard Pilcher? How many lives have been ruined by his very being, yet his arc of privilege never seems to falter from its upward path? President of the United States: could it be possible that someone as despicable and undeserving as Leonard Pilcher could achieve that office?

Sure it was. Anything can be bought. Price was no obstacle to the Pilcher family.

Do I still feel that way about Pola? After all these years, having never again seen or spoken another word to her? Would she still hold that power over me were she suddenly to appear?

Then the shame of his inaction—and the injustice it had allowed—washed over him once again. He knew that there was nothing he could have done to prevent David Linker's murder, save some quirk of fate that would have placed him close enough to stop it, somewhere other than the grandstand seat he had shared with Pola. That was not the issue. It was simply this: driven solely by loyalty born of love and lust, he let the murderer walk away. Rare was the day that some random incident would not trigger memories of David. It never took much: a male student in energetic, intellectual discourse, another putting his arm around a friend in a display of comradeship, or—and this was the most horrific one—simply watching something fall.

A few weeks before, he had been on the street when the rope hoisting a piano to an upper floor had parted, sending the piano plummeting in silence downward until it struck the pavement and shrieked its final, chaotic discord. While in no danger from the accident, afterward it had taken Joe hours to pull himself together.

The sound of a student's pencil plunking down dragged Joe Gelardi back to the present. The student, finished with the quiz, stretched at his desk, arms over head, a look of relief on his face. The pop quiz—that unexpected challenge to the young man's mastery of the Calculus—had been faced down and bested once again.

Joe checked the clock on the classroom wall. "Five more minutes, people," he announced to the class, and slipped back to his reverie.

It had been nearly 16 years since that fateful autumn day of David Linker's murder. After Pola banished Joe from Malmö—and her life—he completed his internment in a military camp outside Stockholm. The bleakness of that bitter cold winter seemed an all-too-appropriate host for his guilt-ravaged soul. The loneliness of that camp, far from the city life and a lover's ministrations to which he had become accustomed, became unspeakable. The only vestige of life in Malmö that remained was the pain of David Linker's murder. Incapable of bonding with his fellow internees at the new camp, he withdrew into himself.

The other internees were suspicious of him for entirely the wrong reason, convinced as they were that anyone as closed-in and self-absorbed as Joe Gelardi must have come to Sweden through a thinly veiled act of desertion and was crumbling under that shame. This particular group had long ago decided they were righteous warriors, spoiling to get back into the fight, who had been bravely doing their duty but were forced to crash-land their devastated aircraft in this strange, indifferent land through no fault of their own. Joe's isolation became self-reinforcing and absolute. He could not reach out to them; they shunned him.

As that winter turned to spring, the Allied pincers squeezing on Germany from east and west made the eventual victors of the war a certainty. The maintenance of neutrality became an expensive and politically unnecessary inconvenience for the Swedish, and they began repatriating their interned Allied airmen in droves. By mid-April 1945, Lieutenant Joe Gelardi found himself back at Eighth Air Force Headquarters in England.

The debriefing on his return had been perfunctory, much to his surprise. Gelardi had expected a court of inquiry, a first-class grilling by a panel of flying officers as to why their bomber had absented herself from the war, why three of her crew had bailed out, how two more had come to unlikely deaths in Sweden. But the solitary officer conducting the debriefing, a balding, porcine lieutenant colonel, seemed bored with the whole affair as he plodded through routine questions in the semi-circular gloom of the Quonset Hut's arches, without so much as an enlisted man to assist him. He spoke no more than necessary, but when he did, it was in that annoying, muted twang—that perverted melding of dialects of the American Midwest and South—which had become the standard accent of those overly enamored with military life. That twang tended to emphasize the first syllable of a multi-syllable word whether or not that was the word's proper pronunciation. Worse, this colonel lacked aviator's wings. Gelardi was certain this groundling officer—too fat to fit in the cramped confines of a combat aircraft—could not possibly understand or appreciate the travails of those who risked their lives in the air, despite the Eighth Air Force patch sewn to his sleeve. He was just another clerk, important only to himself, assigned by chance to the part of the Army that flew rather than the part that slogged. This debriefing would be nothing more than tying up a few loose ends to satisfy some artificial requirements of the military bureaucracy. The questions had been programmed to avoid unpleasant, inconvenient answers, for the war would be over soon. It was time to sugarcoat the past and move on. American airmen would never shirk their duty; Eighth Air Force would get the statements to prove it, by God. Joe Gelardi was not even told to sit down.

Captain Leonard Pilcher had arrived in England many months earlier, only to be quickly shipped back to the States. The colonel produced Pilcher's repatriation debriefing statement with little fanfare. In Pilcher's words, *The Lady M received significant battle damage from fighter attacks over northern Germany on 17 August 1944, resulting in one crew member MIA—presumed KIA—and another badly wounded. The battle damage proved so severe that completing the mission, or returning to base in England, was not possible. In the ensuing confusion of combat, three members of the crew bailed out over northern Germany. A normal landing was too risky to the remaining crew members. The aircraft was destroyed by fire after I, as pilot in command, executed a successful belly landing on Swedish soil, which all remaining crew members survived without further injury.*

The colonel asked, in that irritating twang, "Does your REC-ollection of E-vents differ from Captain Pilcher's statement?"

For a moment, Joe questioned himself: *Had the battle damage really been severe?* But he was no surer now than then. He was only the navigator. He did not fly the old girl; he just did the math. Judgment as to the airworthiness of *The Lady M* was not his to make.

The urge to refute Pilcher's statement was strong.

The rationalization not to was stronger. *What does it matter? This is just a formality, anyway. That's what they want to hear.*

"My recollection of the events on that day does not differ from that of Captain Pilcher," Joe said.

The colonel droned on to his next question without so much as a glance at the uneasy lieutenant standing before him. "Do you A-ttest that your IN-ternment in Sweden was due to your aircraft's IN-ability to RE-turn to base?"

The colonel's articulation was like nails on a blackboard, sounding officious yet illiterate at the same time.

Joe Gelardi said, "Yes, I do."

He felt no further remorse for saying those words. As far as he was concerned, it was just the *severe battle damage* question all over again.

Finally, the colonel asked, in that grating, incorrect intonation: "Are you A-ware of any AC-tivity by any member of your crew during IN-ternment that would bring DIS-credit upon the government of the U-nited States or its armed forces?"

Someone in that arched little room answered, *No, I was aware of no such activity.* Joe was not sure that he had actually uttered those words; it was as if he was standing beside a man who looked and sounded quite like himself, watching him speak this blatant untruth.

He had experienced that feeling of watching himself once before, as he descended the steps from that Malmö apartment after Pola had allowed him to plunder her one last time before casting him out forever. His spectator-self imagined that this broken man stumbling toward the streets of Malmö was now perfectly free to reveal Pilcher as a murderer, Pola's life and career be damned. He had nothing left to lose. And it would be a fitting gesture of revenge against Pola for discarding him, would it not? But the cold night air became the slap in the face that pulled him back from his fantasies of justice and revenge. His spectator-self dissipated; his corporeal-self realized that such an accusation would be a fool's game. She would simply deny she had been with him—*ever*—or that she knew anything about David's death. She would say he was just trying to discredit her as revenge for being reassigned to that godawful camp in Stockholm. Pilcher, of course, would deny any wrongdoing. And nobody in the Army of the U-nited States would give a rat's ass about anything that had happened in Sweden, anyway, as the manner of this debriefing was amply demonstrating.

But in reality, despite Pola's rejection of him, he harbored no ill will toward her and had no interest at all in revenge, no matter how many delicious impulses the id might generate. Quite the opposite; he would sell his soul again if only she would take him back.

And Pilcher would still get away with murder.

The groundling colonel slid a document before him with ceremonial flourish. It listed the three questions he had just been asked, with a block to indicate his response and another to affix his signature after each question. The colonel impatiently tapped the document three times with the tip of his pen, once in each signature block. Joe Gelardi began to sign.

When he reached the third and final signature block—*Are you aware of any activity by any member of your crew during internment that would bring discredit...*—his hand trembled as if being shaken by God himself. Yet, he managed to affix a jittery scrawl that passed for his signature.

The colonel, fastidiously straightening stacks of

folders on the desk, had taken no notice of Joe's tremors. As far as he was concerned, these proceedings were already finished—and with outstanding military efficiency. It was time to move on to the next returnees, shuffling about outside, nervously awaiting their turn, still unaware that this interview they dreaded was little more than a rubber stamp affair.

Joe Gelardi felt physically sick. As he laid down the pen, he blanched as the burning discharge rose in his throat, threatening to hurl the remains of breakfast all over the neatly stacked folders on the fat colonel's desk. When dismissed a moment later, he quickly fled the Quonset Hut to gulp the cool, refreshing air of springtime in the English countryside. When one of the men waiting outside asked, with trepidation, what the debriefing had been like, Joe mumbled, "No big deal." Then he walked away, the briskness of his stride masking the fact that he was wandering with no destination in mind. He felt hollow inside, an empty shell draped in khaki. The lies he carried were eating away his very soul like so many maggots.

A great sliding of desks brought Joe Gelardi back to the present once again. Students were rising uncertainly, spindling their quiz booklets nervously and gathering their belongings, knowing full well the class had reached its scheduled end but not possessing the courage to walk out on their preoccupied—and quite possibly disturbed—professor.

Embarrassed, Joe said, "I'm sorry, people. I seem to have lost track of time." The students fled the classroom quickly. His only female student lingered, a curious smile on her bespectacled, ordinary face.

"Doctor Gelardi, are you feeling all right?" Meredith Salinger asked.

"I'm fine, Miss Salinger. I just...I just have something on my mind."

"Oh...I'll bet it's that talk you'll be giving at the AMS meeting later, isn't it? I can't wait! You're such an inspiration to all of us!"

The AMS: American Mathematical Society. He was scheduled to deliver an informal speech, detailing his work in the mathematics of data processing and its military/industrial applications, in a few hours. He had completely forgotten about it.

"Ahh, yes, Miss Salinger. I'll be there with bells on. How did you find the quiz?"

Her face broke into a beaming smile, delighted that he had played the straight man so perfectly. "Oh, it was easy to find. It was right on my desk!"

It took a moment for Joe to return the smile but when he did, it was as bright and genuine as Meredith's. In more than a decade of teaching at the college level, he rarely experienced humor from the terrified, overburdened first-year students. How refreshing that this brilliant young woman of 18, subject to the intense pressure of a highly competitive university—populated almost exclusively by males—could be relaxed enough to make a joke to her professor, no matter how childish that joke sounded. Her drive and keen intellect reminded Joe so much of his 13-year-old daughter, Diane.

"No, really," she continued, still beaming. "The quiz was no problem. I'll see you at the meeting!"

She breezed to the door, the rustling of her full skirt as it swayed making a sound most appealing and unfamiliar in these environs. Still relishing this opportunity to command his attention, she stopped to deliver her parting quip. "You may think I'm silly, Doctor Gelardi, but I'm still just a freshman. Next year, I'll be *sophomoric!*"

As the sound of her saddle shoes faded in the hallway, Joe Gelardi found himself chuckling. Not at Meredith Salinger's little joke but the basic truth her commanding presence had just exposed: he had always been a sucker for brainy girls. Never mind the empty-headed beauties; leave them to politicians and ballplayers. He'd take the determined, intelligent woman every time.

And in Joe Gelardi's life, there had never been a woman more determined or more intelligent than Pola Nilsson-MacLeish. Or one who had devastated him so thoroughly. But that was such a long, long time ago. All that remained of that relationship was the cruel memory of their cowardly collusion that let a murderer go free.

He gathered the quiz booklets into his briefcase and began the walk back to his office in another building across campus. The informal speech he was obligated to deliver in just a few hours would be no problem to put together over lunch. After all, how difficult is it to talk about your life's work? Especially to an audience who knows just enough to superficially understand what you are talking about but not well enough to challenge any of your assumptions or conclusions? Besides, he liked the young students and enjoyed mentoring them like a wise older brother, much like he had done when thrust into leading the boys of *The Lady M* after Leonard Pilcher had so willfully discarded that role. He would leave being the harsh taskmaster and academic gatekeeper to his faculty mates.

None of the students in attendance at the meeting would realize that this work of which he spoke—the mathematical foundations of electronic data processing—might well take him from MIT. There had been offers from private industry: IBM, Bell Labs, Honeywell, Sperry, and UNIVAC were all interested in employing

Joe Gelardi and offered much more money than the university ever could. But you would never get rich from pure mathematics or science, regardless of your employer. While the prospect and challenges of the private sector seemed exciting on the surface, they had one great failing: a scientist in private industry did not own his work; the corporation did. Only the world of academia allowed you to publicly possess your legacy. Your theories, discoveries, and applications belonged to you and you alone forever. Einstein's work was always his, never Princeton's; Berkeley was never credited with Robert Oppenheimer's work; and MIT could not take credit for the genius of Joe's schizophrenic colleague, John Forbes Nash.

MIT must have had some inkling of Joe Gelardi's imminent poaching. Just a few months ago—after a decade of the institute's equivocation, habitual moving of the bar, and frequent, indifferent silences—Joe Gelardi's name had finally been proposed for elevation to associate professor and tenure. The security and academic freedom that tenure would bring could not be ignored. No matter which path he chose, his career would, at long last, be moving forward again.

He had time to decide, though—until the end of the semester, still three months away. That decision would hinge on what was best for his daughter. She was his only personal consideration, for Joe Gelardi was a single parent.

Chapter Twenty-Six

He sat much like a woman would, his slender legs tightly crossed, the top leg swinging freely from the knee, as if unencumbered by attachment to bone and sinew. Like the two Pilcher men—father Max and son Leonard—verbally sparring before him, he wore an expensive three-piece suit, crisp white shirt, and striped school tie that announced his East Coast aristocratic breeding. His hair—dark blond, somewhat longer than what you might expect for a businessman—was carefully cut, combed, and smoothly plastered in place. One could visualize that the current boardroom styling of that long, sleek hair was only one possible arrangement. A more relaxed styling, without the copious application of hair tonic, could transform him from buttoned-down corporate moth to androgynous, liberated butterfly. But at the moment, this gaunt man, Tad Matthews, was hardly a butterfly. He was legal counsel, political advisor, and loyal company man to the Pilcher family.

The conversation to this point had confused Leonard Pilcher. He asked his father, "Who the fuck is Henry Cabot Lodge, anyway? An ambassador or something?"

Max Pilcher frowned, tossing the Wall Street Journal on to his dreadnought of a desk. Was there no limit to his son's arrogance...or his ignorance? He thought: *You can dress them up, buy them a place in a prestigious university, an Air Corps commission, even a seat in Congress, but even after 40 years on God's green earth, the boy was still nothing but a damn fool. But perhaps a useful one...for damn fools sometimes make convenient presidents.*

The elder Pilcher was in his 80s, yet he still cast that aura of total dominance and command. A captain of industry. Made of stone. Filthy rich. His every pronouncement infallible, expecting no challenge. In his icy stare, you felt your well-being in jeopardy should you displease him, maybe even your very life.

If Max Pilcher possessed any qualities of human compassion and forgiveness, he reserved them for his only son. Otherwise, you might suppose someone as impertinent and inauspicious as Leonard Pilcher—this unique example of American entitlement, this inadvertent parasite of his father's creation—would have perished in his father's glacial stare long ago.

"Pay attention, Lenny," the elder Pilcher said. "Cabot Lodge is the ambassador to the U.N."

Leonard Pilcher smirked at the mention of the U.N., as if that organization was hardly worth a moment of his thoughts. "Yeah? So what?" he said. "This is 1960. Nobody matters except us, the Russians, and the Chinks."

Scowling, the elder Pilcher replied, "The ambassador is the only serious challenger to Nixon for the nomination at the moment. Forget Goldwater...too loony for even the mouth-breathing wing of the Republican Party. We can take care of Cabot Lodge. We'll publish a couple of those photos of him hugging Khrushchev...that should do the trick. We tag him as too soft, too liberal. He's making it easy...he's even been sucking up to the coloreds lately. Finish him off and we can focus all our resources on knocking out Nixon and getting you nominated. It'll be simpler...and cheaper...than fighting them both at once."

Max Pilcher paused a moment, trying to gauge if his comments were making the proper impression on his vacant son. As usual, it appeared they were not. Looking for reinforcement, he turned to Tad Matthews and said, "Hell...even Ike thinks Nixon's a fucking idiot."

With a flutter of his smooth, manicured hands, Tad Matthews began to speak. "So true, sir. President Eisenhower has stated several times in public that he is unable to think of a single thing Nixon has accomplished as vice president. Even though he pretends to be joking, the meaning is very clear."

"See? How hard could it be to knock that bum out of the race?" Max Pilcher asked of his son, whose thoughts still seemed to be elsewhere.

"Hey, Matthews," Leonard Pilcher said with a smirk, "how come you always smell like some French whore? That shit in your hair..."

Matthews responded only with a thinly disguised look of revulsion, well practiced. Leonard Pilcher was not improving with age or experience. It had been hard enough getting the idiot elected to Congress, where contests were narrow affairs, quickly and simply decided by finding the lie that would somehow stick to your opponent and sink him while dodging the lies hurled at you. And now he was working to make this ignorant, uncouth man President of the United States. A far more daunting task.

It was almost more than Matthews could stomach. But, if nothing else, he was loyal. He owed a great deal to Max Pilcher. He would serve him in whatever capacity required, whether it involved covering the tracks of his son's frequent drunken sprees and extra-marital liaisons. Or worse.

Max Pilcher tried to steer the conversation back on topic, asking, "Do you even appreciate what's being offered to you, Lenny?"

Leonard Pilcher just smirked. Of course he appreciated what was being offered, what it meant to be president—it meant calling the shots. All of them. And being able to piss on anyone who would not kiss the ring. "Sure I do," he replied, all the while thinking, *Do I deserve any less?*

Tad Matthews jumped into the uneasy lull that followed. "Marketing you is going to be a real challenge, Len. It's not like you've got a bushel basket full of accomplishments to point to..."

"What the hell are you talking about, numbnuts? I've been a congressman almost four years now..."

"With not one piece of legislation to your name," his father interjected. "Hardly even show up, most days."

"I do what I've gotta do, Pop. You get your fucking government contracts."

The elder Pilcher fumed. "Is that so, Lenny? Just like the Randolph bid?"

"Hey, that was a lost cause."

"Only because you fucked it up, son. All you had to do was smile, shake some hands, and keep your mouth shut...and you couldn't even get that right."

Matthews could not bear to listen to another father-son mud-slinging contest. He had witnessed too many of them over the years. He desperately tried to steer the conversation back on track with this question: "So, sir...what kind of image would you like Leonard's campaign to present?"

A few thoughts raced through Max Pilcher's mind. None of them would have contributed anything of worth to the conversation. Somehow, the slogan *Elect Leonard Pilcher, the dumbshit puppet* did not fit the tone. Instead, he offered a caustic response: "That's what I pay you for, Matthews."

"Of course, sir...of course," Matthews stammered, wishing he had never uttered that naïve-sounding question. "We'll want to create an image of wisdom, strength, and good judgment, in contrast to the public perception of Nixon as someone devious, untrustworthy, and weak. Take that picture of him poking his finger in Khrushchev's chest and tell the *whole* story of that *kitchen conference* fiasco…that Khrushchev was wiping the floor with him and that finger-poking was nothing more than Nixon's ineffectual, pathetic response. We'll hold up Leonard as one who will *never* be bested by Khrushchev…or any other Russian."

Tad paused for a moment before continuing. "Unfortunately, we have little in the way of actual examples on which to base this. Perhaps his wartime exploits can be reworked into a tale of courage and heroism…although that's quite a tall order. It's going to be difficult to make much out of only three missions…and then ending up in Sweden."

"Doesn't matter worth a shit," Max Pilcher proclaimed. "The public only needs to know what we tell the papers to print. One man's fuck-up is another man's heroics. What do you think Joe Kennedy's doing for his kid? The Japs cut his goddamn boat in half, for cryin' out loud!"

"True, sir…but Kennedy, or any other Democrat, is not our immediate concern. We've got to get the nomination first."

Max Pilcher harrumphed and impatiently signaled for Matthews to continue.

"Policy toward Latin America will be a prominent…perhaps *the* prominent issue. Especially Cuba. One must project that he will confront and thwart Soviet influence in this hemisphere…and without raising the specter of nuclear war."

Max Pilcher glowered. "*That's* your political assessment? Worrying about atom bombs over some shitheel spic? I've got news for you, Matthews…Castro doesn't want the Russians' help. *He* wants to be the big cheese in Latin America, not just Moscow's flunky. But he doesn't realize yet that he hasn't got the *pesos* for that."

Leonard Pilcher decided it was time to jump back into the discussion. "That cigar-chomping clown, Castro? I'm glad we weren't doing any business with that shit-hole of an island when he kicked out the other little spic...what's his name?"

"Battista," Matthews mumbled. "Fulgencio Battista." It could be torturous, dealing with this willfully ignorant yet obscenely rich fool. "And actually," Matthews added, "Cuba was a lovely place to visit...hardly a shithole."

Leonard Pilcher had no reply, other than his usual, arrogant smirk.

Max Pilcher had a reply, though. "Yeah...you and your *little pal* liked going down there," he said, wielding the power of intimate knowledge like a club. But the elder Pilcher would have loved to phrase *little pal* another way: *Your queer boyfriend. Asshole buddy. The love that dare not speak its name. Or as they like to say in polite circles, "confirmed bachelor." You make it so damned easy to keep you in line, Matthews.*

Tad Matthews absorbed the spoken barb quietly, stoically. Like he always did. But it was time to get back to business.

"Nixon will try to position himself as the foreign policy expert," Matthews said. "Cabot Lodge will have trouble overcoming that he appears to be too friendly with Khrushchev. Having to play nursemaid to the Premier on his trip around the US hurt the Ambassador's image badly. He had to kiss that fat Russkie's ass on a daily basis. Nobody will ever believe that he can be tough with the Russians now. He'll just be seen as another soft, upper crust New England aristocrat, out of touch with real Americans."

"And who's going to believe that Nixon can be a tough guy?" Max Pilcher said with a laugh. "He looks like someone who runs and cries to his momma at the first hint of trouble."

"Exactly my point, sir. Ike has already helped us out by putting a few nails in his coffin. Now, we need to create the image that Leonard is the strong man the public really wants."

"Then make it happen," Max Pilcher said, the dismissive wave of his hand signaling the conversation was closed.

Chapter Twenty-Seven

Joe Gelardi's marriage to Mary had begun to crumble, no doubt, while he was still away at war, or *your little vacation in Sweden,* as she had come to refer to his internment in their last days together. His wartime affair with Pola MacLeish was not the reason. Mary Catherine McSweeney Gelardi could not have known about it. Of that, Joe was certain, and he was right. Mary did not know. Her disillusionment with him and with their life together had different origins.

There had been some talk in town during the war—whispers mostly—that some, if not all, of the aircrews interned in Sweden and Switzerland were actually opportunists who had used the freedom of flight to sit out the war in safety. But the internee issue was a tiny, little known corner of a gigantic world war, and the talk remained muted. That did not stop the occasional blowhard from proclaiming that the internees were *deserters, plain and simple...traitors that should all be shot!* At first, Mary ignored the talk; her husband was neither a deserter nor a traitor. She was sure of that. The blowhards could go to hell.

One morning while riding a Boston trolleybus, she had overheard a wild-eyed airman in uniform talking in hushed tones to an older man. His words carried much farther, perhaps, than he intended. He claimed to be a tail gunner on leave who had survived his required number of missions and made it back home alive, never to fight again. If he had it to do over again, he said, he would have promptly teamed up with a crew who planned to take their plane to a neutral country and be interned. "It happened all the time," the airman said. "The officers would get to talking real secret like...one way or another they'd get rid of the guys on their crew who didn't want to play ball and replace them with guys who did. Next mission...they're gone. Relaxing for the duration in one of them yellow countries that don't have the balls to fight Hitler. Why get your ass shot off? The brass couldn't do a damned thing about it...They couldn't prove nothing."

Mary McSweeney Gelardi had known her husband since they were kids in elementary school. She wanted desperately to believe his military service was honorable—just like it said on his discharge papers—and that he would never be party to desertion. But doubt began to fester. Joe possessed that keen, analytical mind; he was a thinker, not a fighter. It did not take a mathematician to figure the dismal odds of survival in the skies over Europe; even an English teacher like herself could understand what battle statistics really meant. Could she really blame him for conspiring to take the safe way out and come home to her in one piece?

Joe had been home exactly one day when she asked him. His story sounded plausible at first; the plane was shot up, it had been the aircraft commander's decision, and nobody else had a say in the matter. He chose to follow his commander's orders and not join the "mutiny" of the three who parachuted. But his answers to her questions about his life in Sweden had been guarded and vague; he seemed to be making it up as he went along.

He was hiding something, she was sure. After a few more sessions of increasingly pointed questions, he became defensive and refused to discuss it anymore.

Mary really needed the truth. She was even willing to risk that the truth might be that he had been consorting with Swedish women. But she doubted that.

He was not the roving sort—never had been—and had returned home with a tidy sum of money: his airman's pay, intact almost to the penny. Surely a man indulging in wine, women, and song would have found a way to part with a fair amount of that cash, if not all.

"I just want to know the truth," she begged. "I'll understand, Joey...I swear. Whatever it is."

He remained silent.

The blowhards must be right after all, her mind concluded.

She tried desperately to put it behind her. At least she had gotten her husband back alive, she told herself. Others had not been so lucky. But her disappointment would always descend like a dark curtain across their relationship. She would attack herself for the irrationality of her feelings: *What's wrong with me? Why should I be ashamed of my husband if he chose not to get himself killed?*

But the stench of suspicion pervaded her every waking moment. She could not shake the feeling that he had participated in an act of cowardice, a dereliction of duty. She had always believed that grown men faced their fears. Only petulant children ran away.

And why was he so defensive, so secretive about it?

She had no choice but to keep those poisonous notions bottled within her. There was no one with whom it could be discussed. Joe's tight-knit Italian family— mother, father, and adoring sisters—thanked the Lord Jesus and a host of patron saints daily for the safe return of their brilliant, beautiful boy, for all the prayers they had expended for his safe return had been answered. *Their Joey* was home. Mary's two brothers had both served in the Navy and seen no combat. They never questioned Joe's telling of his strange odyssey aboard

The Lady M. The Brothers McSweeney, never the sharpest tools in the drawer, remained in awe of the whiz kid math scholar their big sister had married. Her closest friend at the Catholic high school where she taught had lost a fiancé at Okinawa and was beyond caring about anyone else's postwar burdens.

In May 1945, Joe received his discharge and resumed graduate school. As his studies claimed his every waking moment, Mary could feel their marriage dying. The tender love of childhood sweethearts, which had blossomed into a symbiotic, yet passionless bond that blended academic achievements with young married life, had soured in a cauldron of doubt and mistrust. What was once the joyful adventure of life together was now nothing but the tedium of subsistence. Their infrequent attempts at sex were mechanical and impersonal, mere release that was more embarrassing than satisfying.

Then Joe became *weird* in bed. It had seemed like playfulness at first, a pinning of her wrists above her head that seemed to inspire his lovemaking to a new, robust level. It was different—even exciting—and it startled her, but she did not mind. It inspired the hope in Mary that perhaps through passionate sex they might find their way back to the closeness they had lost.

But he had gone too far. One night, as they lay naked and about to make love, he grabbed the satin sash from her robe and started to bind her hands above her head. There was something in his eyes—something *maniacal*—that upset her. Before he could complete one encirclement of her wrists with the sash, she jerked her hands free.

All hint of sexual arousal had drained from her voice. "What do you think you're doing, Joe?"

His arousal had not drained at all. "C'mon...this'll be fun," he replied, the sash still at the ready in his hands.

Unimpressed, she said, "Maybe for you." Annoyance crept into her voice as she continued, "Why would you think I'd want to do that?"

He seemed genuinely surprised by her refusal. "Ahh, come on, Mary…Let's just try it," he pleaded.

She rolled away and pulled the covers to her chin. "No, Joe," she said. "I do not want to be tied up. Ever. Just forget it and go to sleep."

In an attempt to gently roll her back into his arms, he touched her shoulder. Her hand flew in his direction wildly, slapping him squarely in the ear.

Joe recoiled to the edge of the bed, his ear ringing like a church bell. "OW! WHAT THE HELL DID YOU DO THAT FOR?"

"Serves you right, *pervert.* Maybe you should go sleep with your thesis."

Unable to think of a single word that would make things right, he skulked to the living room couch.

In the weeks that followed, he rarely bothered coming to their bed anymore. When he did, it was just to sleep, perched precariously at the edge of the mattress so their bodies had no chance of touching. Most nights, he would work on his doctoral thesis at the desk in the living room of their tiny Cambridge apartment until the early morning hours, then crash on the couch for a few hours before heading off to campus.

There was not much left of the Gelardi's marriage save a common address and bank account. Divorce was out of the question. They were simply too Catholic, burdened by the holy mandate to preserve the marriage bond, yet devoid of ideas—and the energy—to accomplish that mandate. They descended to that limbo of married couples living separate lives under the same roof. If Joe Gelardi was married to anything, it was the doctoral thesis he was struggling to complete.

They managed to conceal their diseased marriage from almost everyone. Mary's Aunt Milly was a clever old girl, though, and figured it out quickly. At a family picnic, she had pulled Mary aside and said, "You two never touch. Young married couples touch all the time...just look around." And she was right. At this assembly of the large and prolific McSweeney clan, there were at least a dozen newlywed couples, the marriages made possible by the mass release from service of European campaign veterans. As they mingled, their hands would unconsciously reach for each other, touching arms, shoulders, buttocks; Cousin Eddie, the family's inveterate joker, stole a caress of his wife's breast. She twirled away from his grasp with mock annoyance, after which they snuck away to make rambunctious love in the back seat of their battered Plymouth.

Joe and Mary had not come within 10 feet of each other since their arrival.

Mary had felt close to Aunt Milly her whole life, even though the rest of her family—and her father, Milly's younger brother, especially—shunned her as "odd" and "a queer duck." Aunt Milly *was* different from the workaday McSweeneys. She was an artist, a painter. Until Mary, she had been the only McSweeney to attend college. She never married and lived with a succession of women. One uncle described Aunt Milly most succinctly: dyke.

Alone on an outdoor bench, Mary had broken down and spilled out her marital woes to Aunt Milly. The old woman listened impassively, then took her niece's hand in hers and uttered one word: annulment.

Mary had no idea what her aunt was talking about. Catholic marriages were forever, were they not?

What God has put together, let no man put asunder?
Sure, you could get a civil divorce, but you were going
straight to hell. *I'm in hell right now,* Mary thought.
That's all I have to look forward to for eternity?

The old woman threw back her head as she took
another drag on her Pall Mall. She uncrossed her trouser-
clad legs. The oxfords she wore on her feet reminded
Mary of another expression her father had used to
illustrate his sister's lesbianism: *she wears comfortable
shoes.*

"Annulment...that's Catholic divorce, Mary
Catherine," Aunt Milly said. "The diocese here in Boston
will grant an annulment with a minimum of fuss,
provided both spouses are agreeable and no child has
been conceived of the marriage. If there's a kid, it gets a
bit sticky, but not impossible. You do a couple of
interviews with the priest, attest to a bunch of crap in
writing, like *you didn't enter into the marriage with the
full intent to honor the sacrament* and hokum like that. A
couple of months, and *voila,* you're no longer married in
the eyes of the Church. Then you can get a civil
divorce...and you'll have to find another way to get
yourself into hell, young lady."

It all sounded like an ironic answer to Mary's
prayers. She scheduled an interview with a priest from a
parish across Boston, away from Cambridge and her
family's neighborhood. The ball was rolling. All she had
to do was summon the courage to broach the topic with
Joe.

But before she could do that, as if on cue, Mary
found out she was pregnant.

Chapter Twenty-Eight

Since picking up the phone several minutes ago, Lou DiNapoli had uttered little more than *hello*. The caller at the other end, Fred O'Hara, had announced himself only as "your brother," then talked non-stop. But Lou sat and listened patiently, absorbing Fred's frustration, for they were closer than brothers. The war had seen to that. The passing of years since release from the Stalag Luft had not weakened that bond.

Fred had finally ventured into some dangerous verbal territory, something no ears but Lou's should be hearing, and he was forced to interrupt. "Man, this ain't the place. How about we go fishing?"

Go fishing. The code words for a face-to-face meeting, away from prying ears. Away from government wiretaps.

Lou's phone could very well be tapped by NYPD or J. Edgar Hoover and his pistol-packing college boys. Maybe even Eisenhower himself. It would not be the first time. This was the reality of life for an organized crime boss.

Lou DiNapoli, once the 18-year-old ball turret gunner of *The Lady M,* was now a captain—or *caporegime*—for the Montemaro crime family, the youngest man to ever hold that lofty position. His nickname—*The Gunner*—was as much for his wartime exploits as his civilian career. The crew he headed worked the Bronx, controlling prostitution, bootleg cigarettes, and booze for that borough of New York City.

"Let's say we meet in Jersey, okay?" Lou said, then waited for Fred's reply. "Good. Take care, brother,"

Lou said, and hung up the phone.

Jersey: code word for Friday. The meeting would be at the usual place—a little resort in the mountains north of Harrisburg, Pennsylvania—a mid-point between Pittsburgh and New York City. *Resort* was probably giving it too much credit. It was really just a few tiny, run-down cabins in the woods near a small lake made unnavigable by fallen trees and submerged stumps. Not exactly a fisherman's paradise, but the fish probably loved it, as did the locals who needed an out-of-the-way hot-sheet motel for their illicit liaisons. The owner was a retired Bronx merchant who owed the fact that he was still breathing and upright to The Gunner's intervention on his behalf in a local feud a few years back. His silence was assured. Fred O'Hara, union official, and Lou DiNapoli, crime boss, had met there, alone, many times. If any snooping lawmen had ever tried to follow them, they never succeeded in finding this secret haven.

Business was good for Lou and his crew. It was hard *not* to make money running girls. There seemed to be no end to the supply of women desperate enough to join the game or the demand of men willing to pay for their services. Keeping the girls off drugs was a constant concern, though; the Montemaro family did not traffic in drugs. Any member of the family caught dealing would be severely punished. So far, only a couple of family underlings had been stupid enough to defy that edict. *Dim-bulbs,* Lou called them. The Gunner had dealt with one of them personally. That man's body was never found.

The Gunner prided himself on keeping a clean house. Of course, on occasion a john would offer a girl drugs, sometimes marijuana but more often narcotics—morphine, cocaine, barbiturates, heroin. And she would take them. That earned her a good beating, and the same for the john, if he was in reach. If it was a second offense, bones were broken. If it was a third, the bodies would never be found. A Montemaro prostitute could not live long enough to become a dope addict. That was a great selling point for the droves of cops, judges, and city officials who patronized them.

Making a bundle on bootleg cigarettes was even easier. The family would buy up vast lots of cigarettes at their source that were slated to be sold in the American South and therefore subject to those states' dirt cheap taxes. These cigarettes would then be trucked to high tax states in the North and the Midwest and sold on the black market for pennies below local retail. Since the wholesale price paid by the family reflected only the lower Southern state tax, the profits were astronomical. The product was stored in dozens of locations around the Northeast, so damages from the loss of one raided warehouse were minimal. And the raids were infrequent; the local cops and politicians could be bought and did not care, unless some bigwig got a temporary bug up his ass. The federal revenue agents did not want to admit that their occasional busts were little more effective than scooping a cupful of water from the ocean. The raids were just a cost of doing business to the family. A very small cost.

Friday was a cold January day in central Pennsylvania, but clear skies and no snow on the roads had made it a pleasant drive. Lou DiNapoli slid the borrowed Ford Fairlane next to Fred O'Hara's Hudson Hornet in the gravel-covered parking area. Fred was standing on the cabin's porch, already halfway through a bottle of Rolling Rock. The crunch of Lou's tires on gravel as they slowly navigated the winding path had heralded his approach a long way off.

"Where did you find that piece of shit?" Fred

asked in greeting, pointing to the dingy Fairlane, his words floating away in clouds of wispy condensation. "Traveling incognito is one thing, but still...a beat-up Ford?"

Lou pulled his ever-increasing girth from the driver's seat. Several chocolate bar wrappers fell from the car as he exited. He laughed and pointed to the ponderous Hudson. "Anybody who drives a lump like that should keep his fucking mouth shut."

"My God, Louie...you must've gained another twenty pounds! How the hell did you ever fit into the ball turret?"

And in another moment, they were in a bear hug that ended quickly with playful punches to ensure the proper level of masculinity was demonstrated. Even though they were sure no one was watching.

"Good to see you, Louie." Fred rubbed the butt of the pistol in Lou's waistband, under the heavy car coat. "Use this lately?"

Lou guffawed and pretended to frisk Fred. "You packing? I figure you'd need to...all this Pilcher talk of yours has got me worried."

"I keep my word, Lou. I vowed I'd kill the scumbag."

"So what took you so long? I figured you forgot about it."

With an uneasy smile, Fred replied, "Not fucking likely."

They entered the cabin and settled around a small table loaded with a big platter of sandwiches and chips. The old wood-burning stove was pumping plenty of heat.

"Courtesy of our host," Fred said, raising his beer bottle.

Fred related his discussion with Tom Houlihan. How the old man had announced the Amalgamated

Steelworkers would throw their support to Leonard Pilcher for president.

"Sounds like the old guy's gone soft in the head...or fat in the wallet. Maybe both," Lou said between bites of ham and cheese. "You think Pilcher bought him?"

"Yep...no other explanation that I can see. Just between you, me, and the lamppost, ol' Tom's got some big gambling debts. You'd think an old guy wouldn't care that he's into the Caputo family for big bucks...I mean, it's like 'what are they going to do, kill me? I've got one foot in the fucking grave anyway.'" Fred paused and took a big draw on his beer. "But the old prick thinks he's gonna live forever."

"But you told him you're not going to do the Pilcher endorsement, right?"

Fred squirmed in his chair. "I ain't told him shit yet."

"Why? What's he gonna do when you tell him? Shoot you?"

"Maybe," Fred replied. "Or just get up a recall vote and get me thrown out as union president."

"You think he's got that kind of clout?"

"He might."

"You ready to bet your ass he won't go for the first option, Freddy?"

"You mean shooting me?"

"Yeah. It's a lot easier, ain't it?"

Fred slumped in his chair. The look of resignation on his face spoke louder than any words.

"And killing Pilcher makes your problem go away?"

"It makes two problems go away, Lou... two birds with one stone." Fred paused, gazing into space. "You gonna help out me here?"

Lou knew that question was coming, ever since the phone call that prompted this meeting. He rose from the table, letting out a big sigh in the process. He began to stroll around the cabin, as if searching for an escape that did not exist. Finally, the words came.

"I ain't got no dog in this fight, Freddy. I wasn't the one who vowed to kill Pilcher. I never cared about that rich cocksucker then and I don't now. I've got a business to look after." There was a short pause before Lou added: "So do you."

That was not the answer Fred wanted. "We're brothers, Lou, ain't we?"

Lou was annoyed his loyalty was being questioned. "You're damn right we're brothers! I've got your back on this Houlihan business. You and your family are covered, Freddy. I guarantee it."

Lou offered his hand to seal the deal. Fred took it gratefully.

Lou had one more question. "If Houlihan does come after you, you want to hit him back, right?"

Fred pondered that for a moment. Then his face broke into a knowing smile.

"Louie, I think the Caputo family will take care of that for us."

Lou beamed a smile of his own. "You're learning, my friend. You're learning."

Chapter Twenty-Nine

Joe Gelardi smiled as he watched his daughter fly up the steps of the junior high school, a plaid blur beneath a lustrous mane of auburn hair, racing eagerly through stagnant pools of students in no hurry to go anywhere. She excelled at all things academic, the perfect blend of her father's analytical abilities and her mother's love of the arts and literature. As she approached the tender age of 14, it was obvious to all that Diane Gelardi was destined for great things. She seemed completely comfortable holding the world by the tail, and yet she was completely unspoiled and untouched by hubris. To Joe, his daughter was pure joy.

She had chattered non-stop on the short drive from home to school, about algebra tests (which would be a cinch!), student council meetings (she was president), a volleyball game that afternoon, a certain ninth-grade boy she was sure would ask her to the dance, and maybe, since this was Mrs. Riley's night off, they could have pizza for dinner tonight?

Diane's birth in April 1946 had been the event that had temporarily saved the marriage of Joseph and Mary Catherine McSweeney Gelardi. After Mary's clandestine first step toward annulment had been tripped up by the pregnancy, her maternal instincts took over. She relished the thought of motherhood. Both she and Joe came from large families; the thought of creating a family of their own just seemed so *natural*. As the months passed, concepts like internment, desertion, and dishonor were flushed from her mind by the flood of love and joy for this wondrous creature growing within her.

She began to take a more academic and sympathetic view of Joe's sexual proclivities, as well. *Maybe that's what going to war does to men*, she reasoned. *Releases primal urges that are usually suppressed in the normal, peaceful world.* Her cousin Katy thought so, too, as she spoke of sex with her husband in a less refined, whisky-fueled manner: *He fucks me like a goddamn animal since he's been home...I kinda like it.*

Joe had never physically hurt her, and she was sure now it was never his intention. Maybe after the baby was born, they would be able to make a fresh start at *normal* sex, without the *sicko bondage stuff*. After all, they were parents now. Grown-ups.

As her belly grew, Joe, too, became captivated by the magic they had caused. He would disengage from his murky world of equations and stacks of dissertation pages to press his ear, in wonder, to her swelling midriff. And when he did, she would set down the book she was reading or the notebook in which she composed her poetry, run her fingers through his wavy hair, and smile contentedly. Their life was back on track. They had been through a rough patch—a *very* rough patch—but he was still her Joey.

The months after Diane's birth seemed a crazy whirl of sleepless nights, baby formula, diaper pails, and a thesis that hovered frustratingly close to completion. With both their large families in close proximity, babysitting was never an issue. Mary was able to return to teaching and provide the lion's share of income for their young family so work on Joe's dissertation could progress, uninterrupted by the need for cash from temporary teaching jobs. On a grand and glorious day in 1947, with the Gelardi and McSweeney broods in proud attendance, Joseph Gelardi donned colorful doctoral robes for the first time and became Joseph Gelardi, Ph.D. He quickly accepted the junior, tenure-track faculty position offered him by MIT.

Later that year, Joe and Mary traded their Cambridge apartment for the little Cape Cod house in Brookline and a G.I. mortgage. Young Diane blossomed, her fertile imagination turning the small backyard into her own fantasy kingdom. The white picket fence was fortress walls; the swing set a parachute jump; trees were rocket ships; the dilapidated, one-car garage nestled in the far corner was a *magic mountain,* full of mystery and treasure; a rusty monkey wrench hanging on its wall was a *key to heaven.* Leaf rakes were stood upside down to become *secret radio aerials.* To compensate for the lack of flowers in the yard, Diane had convinced her parents to allow her to decorate the garage's barren sides with a finger-painted garden.

The time was right, Joe and Mary thought, to conceive another child. But events in Mary's career would derail that plan before it bore fruit.

In 1949, when Diane was three, several of Mary's poems about childbirth and child-rearing appeared in a New England literary journal. These poems became the core of a collection entitled *A Mother's Joy,* which was published the following year. Sales of the book were encouraging; the publisher pressed Mary for another volume. *A Mother's Joy* became the foundation for a master's degree in literature, granted by Boston University in 1953. Mary said goodbye, with no regrets, to high school teaching and joined the faculty of Simmons College in the fall of that year.

1953 became the last good year of their marriage.

The change in her was subtle, gradual. She became more certain of herself—stronger—more convinced that the things she said were of great importance. The way she dressed changed, too. She pushed the frilly dresses and crinolines that marked her as *a good wife and prim schoolteacher* to the back of the closet, pulled back her fiery red hair, and began dressing in the sleek tweed suits worn by women of position and power. And Joe liked that very much; she had become a whole new Mary, incredibly attractive and desirable. He wanted her like never before.

But to Mary, it meant something quite the opposite: a pulling away—a repulsion—from the conventional life they had had before, a desire for something new and stimulating. Something *intellectual.* Joe was blind to this, until one day, as he waxed nostalgic about his abilities as navigator on the big bomber, she retorted, "Those vaunted abilities of yours didn't prevent that little vacation in Sweden."

The cancer of his internment had not been cured; it had merely been in remission.

He was startled, as if the words had physically struck him. She was defiant, issuing a challenge without an ounce of hesitation or remorse. He needed no words to ask the question; his face spoke it eloquently: *Why? Why now?*

"War is a ridiculous game, Joe…a deadly farce played on a broad stage. Why do you think they call areas of combat *theaters?* It's not to be taken seriously…or glorified. Only prevented."

She sounded exactly like that clique of pacifist faculty at Simmons, led by the notorious Professor Jeffrey Dawkins.

"I'm confused," Joe said, and he clearly was. "Are you ridiculing me specifically or just the institution I couldn't help but be part of?"

"Oh, you could have helped it, all right. You could have had that deferment…you had the papers in your hand. But, no, you just had to go play the great American hero."

"You sound just like that imbecile Dawkins. Didn't that phony bastard discover he was a c.o. only *after* he got his draft notice?"

"Being a conscientious objector is an honorable thing, Joe. Jeffrey Dawkins is a great man. A genius."

"Oh, Christ! He's a commie son of a bitch whose greatest achievement is the number of co-eds he's screwed...and God knows who else! Don't tell me you're palling around with his little fan club?"

"Now you're going to decide who I can associate with, Joe?" Her voice was even, calm, and still defiant.

At that exact moment, Joe Gelardi knew his wife was sleeping with Jeffrey Dawkins.

He should have realized it sooner, the moment he read the foreword Dawkins had written for her second book, *In Love's Wake.* The way he spoke of *her unique sensitivity, her brilliance, her fiery passion (to match her fucking red hair, no doubt!)...Shit! The title alone was a dead giveaway our marriage was finished. I should have actually read a few more of the goddamn poems...at least I might have gotten a chronicle of my failings!*

One poem he had failed to read was entitled *The Honorable Guest.* Now, upon close inspection, he realized it was a malignant account of his time in Sweden, which used forms of the word *intern* as a noun, a verb, and even a phonetic substitute for *in turn:*

> *To cross the frontier that separates*
> *Warrior from internee*
> *His honor he must too intern*
> *And intern...the truth so none could see*

But the final line summarized her feelings most

concisely: *An oath betrayed...a trust denied.*

He did nothing. He listened to the hope deep within him that somehow they were still a unit, inseparable, with a child. No matter what had happened, no matter how painful, they could not be driven apart.

There were other clues he should have caught. Like the name change—suddenly, she had insisted on being called *Maeve.*

"I've known you my whole life, Mary...I married *Mary*...our daughter's mother's name is *Mary,*" Joe said. "Where does *Maeve* come from, anyway, *Mary*?"

"The Celtic goddess-queen," she replied. "Legend has it that she was intoxicating."

More likely, intoxicated, Joe thought.

"And how did you come by this particular gem...no wait! Let me guess! *Jeffrey* thinks it suits you?"

She used no words to respond, just that look she had become so adept at wielding, that cold admission of unpleasant truth that contained not a hint of remorse or apology.

Something within Joe broke at that moment, a spring stretched beyond its limit. He was plummeting without falling, caving into an emptiness that could only mean irretrievable loss. Defeated at last, he said, "I can't take any more of this."

"You won't have to, Joe. I'll be the one...I'm leaving."

"What? How can you leave? How can you do this to our daughter?"

"I'm not doing anything to our daughter, Joe. She'll stay with you."

Joe could not believe what he was hearing. "You're rejecting your daughter? Your seven-year-old daughter?"

"No, Joe, I'm not rejecting her. She's better off with you...better off without having to endure this silent war between us. She's more *like* you...more analytical. She prefers puzzles to poetry. She prefers *you*...or haven't you noticed?"

"But we've been married by God! We can't just turn our backs..."

"Oh, bullshit, Joe...we were married by some priest, not God. And if there really was a God, he wouldn't want us to live together like two strangers, would he? Can't you see how destructive that is for Diane?"

Joe sank into a chair at the kitchen table. He struggled to imagine the future Mary—*Maeve*—had just ordained. She was so different; he was so blind. *How could I have not seen this coming?*

"Besides," she added, "Jeffrey detests children...and Diane detests him."

Joe felt the blood rise to his face.

"When the hell has *my* daughter been around that son of a bitch? You had no right..."

"*Our* daughter, Joe. *Ours.* That makes her mine, too. I have every right." Her tone softened. "Look...it's not like you to be combative. I know you're not going to be an asshole over custody."

Custody. That word sounded alien to Joe. It was something that involved criminals, not children.

The next morning, Mary coldly explained to a quiescent Diane that *Mommy would not be living here anymore*, but they would still do all those important things together that they had always done. Everything would be fine...better, in fact.

And then, suitcase in hand, she walked out the door to Jeffrey Dawkins's waiting sports car: an Austin Healy. Incongruously, Joe's mind began to ruminate on just how impractical and typically British such vehicles were. Cramped and noisy, their occupants froze in winter and were windblown all year round. In the States, they were owned by pretentious, aging assholes who were convinced the cars made them appear more adventurous, more sexually attractive, with those stupid, flat English driving caps hiding their receding hairlines.

Then the bastard smiled and waved to Joe and Diane as he hoisted the suitcase into the boot. Like everything was hunky-dory, *perfectly fucking normal.*

Mary did not look back.

Four months later, she collapsed while teaching a poetry class at Simmons College. She died before the ambulance reached the hospital. The cause of death was listed as cerebral hemorrhage.

They had not even begun divorce proceedings. Joe had been determined to avoid the issue for as long as possible; he had not even retained a lawyer. For Mary, it was a minor administrative detail, something she would get to eventually. There was no rush; Jeffrey's first two marriages had been disasters, drawn out and messy in their dissolution. He did not believe in marriage anymore. The concept insulted him intellectually.

The funeral was a tumultuous outpouring of sorrow, a melting pot of Irish and Italian mourning, one camp fueled by whisky, the other by enough food and wine to nourish an army. Many of Mary's colleagues from the college—neither Irish, Italian, nor Catholic—were startled and not a little intimidated by the noisy spectacle. There was loud sobbing, grief-stricken outbursts, and oaths, with some old women in black trying to throw themselves onto the casket while others formed a wailing cordon around bewildered little Diane, as if to protect her from the clutches of death itself. Surely, all the noise they were making could scare away the devil.

Those colleagues wondered *Had these people no sense of propriety—or dignity?* After stiffly enduring the church and graveside ceremonies, they had had enough and declined the invitation to the McSweeney home for more eating, drinking, and loud commiseration.

Little Diane did not understand all the theatrical fuss. Did they not realize that her mother had actually departed four months ago? She had done her crying then, in private. All this ceremony—and silly talk of *life after death*—seemed a bit after the fact.

One colleague who was not in attendance was Jeffrey Dawkins. The day after Mary's death, he had phoned Joe and announced he would be delivering the eulogy. Joe told him, politely, to go fuck himself. He was free to attend the service if he so chose, but he would not have a speaking role.

So, in an apparent snit for being denied this chance to pontificate for an audience, Jeffrey Dawkins had absented himself entirely. Or, perhaps, he was not too vain to realize that if he appeared, the *peasant factions* of the Gelardi and McSweeney family—a term he had frequently used, to Mary's muted annoyance—would join together to beat the living shit out of him, and Joe would not have stopped them.

Chapter Thirty

"And this just in…"

The grandfatherly newsman launched into the final story of the evening's broadcast. When he first received the copy for this story—mere moments before he was to read it on camera—he was taken aback, even shocked, that the producer had deemed it worthy of airing on a network evening news program. *His* network evening news program. He almost began the reading with a humorous tone, as though this piece might have been intended as a lighthearted, closing punch line. But then he thought the better of it and delivered the piece with the gravitas and concern for which he was famous. After all, he was *the most trusted man in America*. There would be no jokes.

"A man disrupted an Ash Wednesday church service in Philadelphia today," the newsman spoke. "Police detained the man, identified as Anthony Moscone, after he stormed the altar during the mass and began screaming that congressman and presidential hopeful Leonard Pilcher was a murderer, insisting he was an eyewitness to this supposed murder…reportedly in Sweden…during the Second World War. According to witnesses, Mr. Moscone made no mention of who the alleged victim might be during his tirade. Several people, including the priest conducting the mass, were injured during the attempt to subdue the deranged man, none seriously. A police spokesman was quoted as saying that the police are familiar with Mr. Moscone, a veteran known to have suffered psychological trauma during the war and, to quote the spokesman, 'was not right in the head.'"

The newsman paused—a brief but dramatic lull—and removed his dark-rimmed eyeglasses. Then he locked the camera in his omniscient gaze one last time and offered a spontaneous editorial comment. "A sad reminder, ladies and gentlemen, of the terrible price many of our gallant veterans paid to keep this great nation of ours free...And that's the way it is."

As soon as the director signaled *Clear*, the newsman stormed off the set and accosted his producer. "This crap doesn't belong on the news, Sid!" he shouted, waving the copy for that last piece in the producer's scowling face. "Since when do we do reports from the loony bin?"

In his best soothing tones, the producer said, "You know, Wally, this is exactly the type stuff that keeps people tuning in."

"Since when?" the newsman exploded. "This is a *news* organization! We don't do tabloid pieces."

"So you're convinced this man's claim is untrue?"

"I don't know and I don't care! Don't ever hand something like this to me again, Sid. Is that clear?"

The producer paused for a moment, the smile on his face masking the lie he was about to speak. "Anything you say, Wally."

But Sid's true thoughts were something quite different. He did not get to where he was by yielding to every ultimatum of some self-important, smooth-voiced news reader. Even one with serious, unimpeachable credentials as a journalist, like Wally. *Every now and then,* Sid thought, *one of these legends of the airwaves has to get all puffed-up and take a stand for journalistic excellence or some such shit.*

That may have worked with the fossils that used to run broadcasting. But there's a new breed now. I'm part of that new breed...one that recognizes that news isn't a public service or a public trust. It's show business, with business underlined. The bottom line, expressed in dollars, is all that matters. The more people who watch, the more the sponsors open their wallets. Tell them the lies they want to hear...and they won't touch that dial. Wally will get over his little tantrum...and read whatever the hell he's told to read.

Chapter Thirty-One

Joe Gelardi stepped from the chilly Saturday morning into the warm, chlorine-tainted air of the MIT pool house. An hour ago, he had dropped Diane off here—the site of her team's swim meet—and retreated to his office for a few administrative tasks which were only supposed to take a few minutes. But those tasks had taken far too long. As he clambered up the wooden bleachers, half-filled with eager parents, chattering friends, and bored-almost-to-tears siblings of the swimmers and divers, Joe hoped that he was not too late for his daughter's events.

He spotted Diane doing warm-up exercises on the other side of the pool with her teammates; their turn in the water would come shortly. He was not too late, after all. She spotted him, too, offering a brief, clandestine wave of hello that could have been mistaken for just a conversational hand gesture by the others in attendance. Joe smiled and sat down on the hard wooden bench. He would settle for that little wave of hello. A young teenage girl would *simply die* if she was caught affectionately acknowledging a parent in public. He had heard the asides of *Oh, disgust!* that Diane and her friends issued whenever such a transgression was observed. But he knew full well how upset Diane would have been if he had missed her swimming.

The boys' diving events were still in full swing. Joe watched as the young competitors queued at the bottom of the ladder for the high diving platform. Their muscular yet slim, glistening bodies looked like perfect sculptures, smoothly chiseled in flesh-colored stone. One by one they scaled the ladder, paused in stillness and total concentration at the edge of the platform, then plummeted downward in a brief aerial ballet that hopefully ended with the minimal splash of a perfectly executed water entry.

As Joe watched, the diving display took on a very different and sinister appearance. Despite the divers' artistry, the aerial ballet had transformed itself into a horrific montage of boys falling—over and over—just like David Linker had fallen from that building in Malmö all those years ago. To his death. Murdered by Leonard Pilcher.

Joe's head began to spin. He could feel himself growing nauseous. He had to get outside to cool, fresh air. He hoped his daughter would not notice this hasty, anxious exit. His feet stumbled down the bleachers, not quite sure of their next landing despite the predictable symmetry of the wooden steps.

Outside the pool house, seated with head thrown back, eyes closed, on a bench he had never noticed before, Joe gulped the healing air and struggled to clear the sights and sounds of David Linker's death from his mind. He noticed something odd, something changed now, in that awful memory: Pola's face was just a blur. No longer distinguishable—just a hazy oval in a halo of white-blonde hair. His mind, scrambling to protect itself from further distress, had switched its focus to the newly discovered bench on which he sat. *Strange...How long has this been here? Why would anyone put a bench right outside the pool house, so far from the street and the bus stop? What need did it serve?*

His mental meanderings were interrupted by a female voice. "Doctor Gelardi? Are you okay?"

It was Meredith Salinger, with an armload of books and a very worried expression on her face. Joe straightened up and tried to regain the requisite professorial look. Meredith plopped down next to him on the bench.

"Yes. I'm fine," he replied.

"Are you sure? You're all flushed...I thought you were having a stroke or something."

"No. I'm fine, Miss Salinger...Really."

Meredith did not bother to mask her disbelief. It would have been courteous—perhaps proper—to simply smile, move on, and leave the good professor alone. But she was genuinely worried. Joe Gelardi was her favorite teacher, ever. While she had had crushes on older men before—*they had so much more gravity than boys my age*—he had the distinction of being her one and only teacher crush. At 18, she was more than old enough now to act out the physical fantasy of *Meredith and the Professor,* and she did so without shyness or shame when alone in her room. Doctor Gelardi was as wonderful an imaginary lover as he was a real teacher. To this point in her young, scholarly life, her imagination had been the only source of lovers.

She placed her formidable pile of books on the bench, heady works on Physics, Boolean Algebra, and the oddly discordant novel, *Tropic of Cancer,* partially concealed in the middle of the stack. She put her hand against his forehead. *Now I can be his nurse, too! This must be what it's like to be a character in a Hemingway story,* she thought. *Love, lust, and compassion combining to take you soaring beyond ordinary life!*

Joe found her gentle touch consoling, sweet, and a bit melodramatic. But he humored her attempt to play Florence Nightingale.

"I thought so. You're a bit warm," Meredith said. "You look flushed."

"I'm fine, Miss Salinger...Meredith. Really, I am.

I'll bet I just got a little winded climbing the bleachers inside."

Meredith pulled her hand away. She still did not look convinced. "I don't know," she said, shaking her head. "What are you doing around here, anyway, Doctor Gelardi? It's Saturday. Don't you see enough of this place during the week?"

"The swim meet. My daughter is competing."

"Oh! Is your wife here, too?"

"Miss Salinger, I'm a widower. My wife died almost seven years ago."

"Oh my gosh! I'm so sorry, Professor. I just assumed…"

For a brief moment, Meredith Salinger felt ashamed and foolish: *The poor man! And here I am, pretending like I'm some little hussy, schtupping his brains out on a regular basis!* But her feeling of shame vanished, as if she had accidentally opened the wrong door and quickly slammed it shut. She slid closer to him on the bench—just an offer of comfort to someone in distress—but knocked her stack of books to the ground in the process.

She could not help but nervously laugh at her own awkwardness. "I'm such a klutz," she said.

Joe helped her pick up the books. *Tropic of Cancer* ended up in his hands.

"Where did you get this one?" he asked.

"A friend…She picked it up in Europe last summer."

Joe thought of the last time he had seen that title. It had been on the bookshelf in that apartment in Malmö where he and Pola had spent so many nights in lovemaking every bit as turgid as Henry Miller's prose. They would thumb through the sexual passages and exult that they had plumbed the depths of their sexuality as thoroughly, if not more so, than Miller's characters. For a delicious moment, he was back in 1944, in the surreal refuge that tiny flat provided in a world otherwise at war, the feel of Pola's warm body nestled against his, the look of serenity on her face.

Her face! I can see Pola's face again!

"Have you read it yet?" he asked Meredith.

"Some," she said. A teenager's nervous shyness was still in her voice. Now, Meredith's face was flushed, too.

The bending to the ground to collect the books had unsettled Joe's head once again. He slumped back onto the bench, grabbing it for support with trembling hands.

"Miss Salinger, I don't...feel so good."

Meredith Salinger drove slowly off the MIT campus, onto the streets of Cambridge. She had not driven a car since Christmas break, back home in California. Joe Gelardi's Ford sedan was not proving very difficult to master, however.

"Are you sure you don't want to go to a hospital, Doctor Gelardi?" Meredith asked.

"No, Miss Salinger. No hospital. Just take me home. I'll be fine."

Diane Gelardi seemed as skeptical as Meredith Salinger of her father's assurances. She leaned forward from the back seat and placed her arms around his shoulders. Her forehead rested on the nape of Joe's neck. "I'm really worried about you, Daddy."

"I'm okay, pumpkin. Everything's going to be all right. I just got a little woozy back there."

From the corner of her eye, Meredith saw how Diane's embrace of her father had tightened, how her head was pressing tightly against his neck.

"Easy, Diane…let him breathe," Meredith said.

For a brief moment, Diane deeply resented Meredith's—*this stranger's*—intrusion. But she stopped herself. This nice young lady was going well out of her way to help her and her father. She deserved to be treated kindly for that alone. *And she's a girl going to MIT!*

Meredith Salinger was the walking, talking realization of Diane Gelardi's personal dream: being an MIT co-ed. But this girl, this student of her father's who she had not even met until a short while ago, was somebody Diane desperately wanted to know better. She lightened up on her father's neck.

"Oops! Sorry, Daddy," Diane said.

"Do I turn here?" Meredith asked.

"Yeah…make a left on Vassar Street," Diane answered. She had beaten her father to the punch; he was left with a finger in the air, vaguely pointing left, and feeling suddenly irrelevant.

Meredith downshifted, slowed, and gingerly guided the car through the turn. As the steering wheel spun back to the straight-ahead position, she applied the accelerator with newfound confidence.

"You know, until now, I've never driven anything bigger than a Volkswagen," Meredith said. "That's my brother's car. My dad never lets me drive his big Mercury."

"It looks like you're doing just fine to me," Joe said. "You know, Meredith, Diane plans to study math at the Institute, just like you."

"Yup. In five more years," Diane added.

The atmosphere in the car changed at that moment. It was no longer one of dread, of a horrific event unfolding in slow motion before your eyes. The future— and by association, the present—suddenly looked bright and very assured. They all felt it.

Diane reached into her bag of swim gear and pulled out a medal on a bright red ribbon. She thrust it in her outstretched hand to the front seat.

"Daddy, I almost forgot! You didn't see it, did you? We won our event...The 400 meter!"

Joe held the medal in his hand and admired it. "Good job, pumpkin," he said with genuine pride. Meredith gave the medal a quick, approving glance, too.

"Hey, Meredith," Diane said, "when we get to our house, do you want to listen to some Elvis Presley records?"

"Sure! I'm crazy about Elvis!"

Chapter Thirty-Two

The business day was only half over and her feet were already killing her. Why had she worn those shiny new pumps? Sure, they looked spectacular and had cost a small fortune. For the moment they sat, empty, under her desk. In a few minutes, the brief respite would be over, and she would have to slip them back on, trek down the hall to the story line-up meeting—that daily competition that determined the course of a television news writer's career—and argue for the placement of her pieces in the evening's network newscast. Then, it was back to her desk to pound out the chosen story assignment, a mere 100 words that must somehow condense and encapsulate some event of towering importance to be read on the air by "the most trusted man in America."

She wondered, *Who am I trying to impress with these damn shoes, anyway?* After all, she was still an attractive woman, honey-blonde, tall, shapely, and in her mid-thirties, the age when a woman's beauty transcends well-sculpted body parts and attains an aura of grace and ripened sexuality. But it was not about attracting men. There had never been a man in the news division Allegra Wise would consider taking to bed, much less marrying. Besides, office romances always ended badly, strewn with emotional baggage and leaving another enemy stalking the place who knew too much about you. She had seen it happen to too many other women over her 10 years at the network. And it was all so pointless. This was broadcast news. Sleeping around might get a girl ahead in some businesses, but here it just assured you a perpetual seat in the back row. Allegra Wise certainly wanted to move up, but that staircase remained impossible to find if you were unfortunate enough to be a woman. No matter how clever your analysis or brilliant your writing. A pair of stylish shoes was certainly not going to help. This was an old boys' club, plain and simple. Women were to be subjugated, penetrated, and ignored. Never respected.

Still, a voice called out from deep within her: *But it never hurts to look good, does it?* Outside this office there were still plenty of men, if she only had the time.

If there was a "most trusted man in America" riding the airwaves, why could there not be a "most trusted *woman* in America?" Allegra Wise craved that title more than anything on God's green earth. It was easy enough for a woman to be a journalist and toil on the back pages of some newspaper all her days. She had done that for a while, fresh out of Hunter College and back in her native Pittsburgh as World War II came to a close. But the seductive quality of voices—calm, authoritative—spilling into living rooms across a city, across a nation, could not be denied. Those voices had spoken to anxious families huddled around their radios each night, telling them of the world at war, spreading joy when the news was good and comfort when it was bad. Edward R. Murrow, Gabriel Heatter, H.V. Kaltenborn, Eric Sevareid—men such as these were her first idols; there were no women from which to choose.

She had campaigned for—and won—the police beat at that Pittsburgh paper, an unlikely place for a woman. But she did not shirk from the challenge; as her boss had said, "She did real good...for a woman." She almost married a cop, too—a detective—but the erratic hours their respective careers demanded kept them apart more often than not. Despite its fiery promise, the unnourished relationship withered and died.

Her unwieldy name—Allegra Wyznicki, the

product of a Polish father and an overly romantic Italian mother—posed no obstacle in the print medium. But when she was given a shot to write for a local radio station and then a network station in New York City, her name proved incompatible with on-air aspirations. Allegra Wyznicki was a mouthful to spit out on the air and even harder for listeners to comprehend. Allegra Wise was born.

She grimaced as she eased her size 11 feet back into the gleaming black pumps, thinking *patent leather takes forever to break in, too!* She stood, smoothing the skirt of her Chanel suit, picked up her notebook, and headed down the hall. She ignored the complaints of her sore, blistered feet. It was time for business.

The news staff shuffled through the piles of photographs on the conference table, searching for their lead story. Most of the photos had to do with Cuba. Fidel Castro continued to nationalize American-owned businesses on the island nation; President Eisenhower's response to the nationalizations, a great reduction in the amount of Cuban sugar purchased, was looking more ineffective and counterproductive by the day. The Russians had been more than delighted to buy up the difference.

Sid, the producer, glanced at a photo depicting a Cuban peasant loading sugar cane on a truck and then slid it to a man across the table. "Harry," the producer began as the smoke from his cigarette floated slowly and crazily upward like windblown skywriting, already indecipherable. "Give me a piece from the sugar companies' point of view...you know, how much they've done for Cuba, how long they've been there...how Ike looks on this as unlawful seizure. Mention the fruit companies, too. You know the drill."

A man at the far end of the table, another writer, spoke up. "I guess you don't want to mention how they've been bleeding Cuba...and a whole bunch of other countries...dry for years, do you?"

The producer took a long drag on his cigarette, his menacing glare providing the answer in advance of the words that spewed in a cloud of smoke, as if a dragon was actually speaking. "You're damn right we don't."

It was time to move on to other topics. Allegra Wise had not paid much attention to the Cuba discussion; international relations were not her strong suit. National politics was, however, and the photo before her looked like her winning lottery ticket. That do-nothing congressman from her home state—Leonard Pilcher— was getting serious about a run at the Republican presidential nomination. Here he was in that photo, at some podium, with his steel baron father and some staffer standing behind him. And that staffer—that skinny, dapper guy—she knew him! Well, knew of him, anyway. Thaddeus Matusik was his name. Her older brother had been in the same high school class with him. She had had a prepubescent crush on him. He seemed so physically perfect, all smooth skin with sleek, rippling muscles underneath; that shock of beautiful, slicked-back hair, always a little too long. That fine face, like a Greek god—*Okay, maybe a Polish god.* She and her girlfriends had clandestinely followed him all around the lake that summer, giggling madly when they thought they had been found out, all the while hoping they would be.

But that was the summer that something *bad* had happened. It was all rumors, spoken in hushed tones in that upscale little suburb, but the story went like this: 15- year-old Thaddeus—Tad to his friends—had been caught in the bathhouse at the lake with a vacationing boy from a faraway town. They were both naked, but they were not showering—they were lying on a bench, one on top of the other. "*Doin' things*," her brother had said, with that asinine grin that meant he had no earthly idea exactly what they had been doing or what it might signify, but he took delight in knowing they were in really big trouble for doing it. Thaddeus Matusik never returned to the local high school; the gossips whispered that he had been shipped off to some private academy, maybe even a military school. It sounded plausible; his dad owned a successful business and was well-connected in local politics. He could afford the money but not the constant reminder of scandal his son's presence would represent.

Oh, that's him, all right, Allegra told herself. And to cap it off, they had something besides a home town in common: he had changed his name, too. According to the caption at the bottom of the photo, Thaddeus Matusik was now Tad Matthews.

When the producer gruffly asked for the next story, Allegra's hand shot up.

"I want to cover this Pilcher candidacy, Sid," she said. "I think I've got an *in* with his staff."

Chapter Thirty-Three

An atmosphere of confusion hung in the half-filled auditorium. Obviously, something was not quite right, not going according to plan. The opening ceremonies were over. The VFW color guard had done their parading. The pledge of allegiance to the flag had been fervently recited by all present. A Catholic priest had beseeched God to bestow his blessing upon them. The winner of the county high school poetry contest had recited her piece—a simplistic ode to the natural forces that had constructed the rippling, parallel bastions of earth and rock that were the Allegheny Mountains—to tepid applause. The main event was well past due.

Yet, the stage remained empty except for the occasional appearance of that thin, anxious staffer who approached the podium, announced himself as Tad Matthews, senior aide to Congressman Pilcher, and told the murmuring crowd, "It'll just be a few minutes more...Please bear with us. The Congressman will be here momentarily."

Despite Matthews's assurances, the crowd was becoming increasingly restive. Men shifted uncomfortably in their seats. Ladies with faces and hair that seemed to be set in stone fanned themselves lazily, more out of annoyance than stuffy air, for it was anything but warm in the auditorium on this January day. In anticipation of a large crowd, the heat had been turned down. Those few who had bothered to come expected to witness Congressman Leonard Pilcher announce his intention to seek the Republican nomination for President of the United States. A few were diehard supporters—a very few. The rest just wanted to witness the launch of a campaign that would surely devolve into a train wreck fairly quickly.

It was rumored that Fred O'Hara, the new president of the Amalgamated Steelworkers Union, was slated to appear, in all likelihood to introduce the Congressman. That would amount to an endorsement of Pilcher's candidacy by the ASW, an event as dubious as the Pilcher candidacy itself.

"Freddy's probably gonna tell us *not* to vote for the son of a bitch," a burly man in an ASW jacket said, loud enough for all in the auditorium to hear. Anxious, volatile men in matching union jackets seated around him began to chuckle. The outnumbered Pilcher supporters in earshot scowled in silence and checked once again to ensure that an ample number of police were, in fact, present to protect them from union thuggery.

Local newsmen in the back of the hall, cynical to a fault, scribbled idly in their notebooks as they exchanged wisecracks. Annoyed photographers milled about. No newspaper would pay for pictures of some congressman's aide stalling for time or a schoolgirl reading her guileless verse.

The source of all this confusion was nestled backstage, behind closed doors. Congressman Leonard Pilcher was not en route to the assembly; he had arrived some time ago. Tad Matthews had personally seen to the uncharacteristic punctuality. Fred O'Hara, however, was nowhere to be seen, and the Congressman was enraged. Max Pilcher sat quietly in a corner, fuming, as his son ranted.

"Is O'Hara in the bag or not?" the Congressman yelled at his senior aide.

Tad Matthews felt like he was about to be pushed over a cliff. He was scrambling for a handhold.

"Look…he's supposed to be here. We have Houlihan's assurances…"

Leonard Pilcher pounced. "Houlihan ain't the fucking union president anymore! He's just another retired crook now! *His* endorsement don't mean shit!"

Matthews was still grasping for some salvation. "Look, maybe he's been in an accident or something."

"Accident, my ass! This is the son of a bitch's way of crapping in my face…and old Houlihan's face at the same time! Me and O'Hara ain't exactly war buddies, remember?"

Max Pilcher held up his hand. Leonard and Tad stopped talking immediately.

"I'm sure it's no accident O'Hara's not here," the elder Pilcher began. "If he thinks he's got the balls to defy Houlihan, God bless him. We haven't forked over any cash yet. If O'Hara doesn't play ball, Houlihan'll find somebody who will…if he wants his goddamn money. In the meantime, let's cut our losses here and get on with the show."

Max Pilcher paused to relight his cigar. "Now, Matthews," he said, the first puff floating from his lips, "you go out there and introduce my boy."

Within moments, as news cameras flashed, Leonard Pilcher stood onstage, announcing he was a candidate for the Republican nomination for President. His platform would be *Strength and Leadership for America*. He reminded the small crowd, and the empty chairs in their midst, that they lived in dangerous times: "The Russians, the Red Chinese, and their friends around the globe will do all they can to destroy our nation, our freedoms, and our way of life. But with the help of God, WE WILL PREVAIL!"

The applause was anemic, barely polite. Pilcher then sought to state his qualifications for that high office.

"I have served you in the House of Representatives for nearly four years..."

A voice rose from the ASW faction: "You've been serving your daddy, that's all, rich boy." The union men were in a boisterous mood now. The fear that had brought them here, that their leader would betray their union by endorsing some mill owner's pampered offspring, had been set aside.

It was obvious right away that Leonard Pilcher was angered by the remark or perhaps just by the temerity that allowed an unspoken truth to be uttered aloud. A better politician might have easily parried that comment with a humorous aside or ignored it completely, without missing a beat. Instead, Leonard Pilcher became strident and condescending:

"I've been to war...I faced the enemy in the sky over Europe...I've cheated death. The wisdom I've gained...the courage I've demonstrated...will lead this great nation to greater things. God Bless America!"

And then he fled the stage, leaving a flustered Tad Matthews to face a barrage of flashing cameras and shouted questions from the newsmen, now driven to a frenzy by the whiff of freshly-spilled political blood.

Stomping about his father's office in a blind rage, Leonard Pilcher looked ready to chew the carpeting. Tad Matthews was doing his best to ignore him. So was Max Pilcher. But the younger Pilcher was putting up quite a fuss. "I'll kill that son-of-a-bitch O'Hara!" he said, kicking a plush armchair's leg for emphasis.

"Oh, calm down, Lenny," the elder Pilcher said. "The ASW endorsement would have been a nice little coup, but it's not that important. O'Hara will be out on his ass in no time. Houlihan will see to that...if he wants his money, that is."

"Fuck that," Leonard replied. "He's a dead man. *I'll* see to that."

Max Pilcher shook his head in disappointment, thinking: *How could any son of mine be so terminally stupid?* He tried to reason with Leonard. "Oh, that would be just great, wouldn't it? Turn O'Hara into a martyr! Don't I have enough trouble with those fucking union monkeys as it is?"

Leonard took those words like a petulant child, defiant chin jutting out, arms tightly folded across his chest. Tad Matthews found the vision amusing and not at all surprising. He had known Leonard Pilcher too well and far too long.

The elder Pilcher was not finished. "So you'll do no such thing. It's not necessary this time." There was a short, ominous pause before he concluded, "Not like it was with Blanding."

For a brief moment, Tad Matthews could not comprehend what the old man had just implied. Then it hit him full force: Leonard Pilcher had once before conspired to murder. So had his father.

It was only four years ago, during the congressional race for the 14th district seat. It was Leonard Pilcher's first time vying for elected office, and the Republican nomination was not going his way. The opponent, Kent Blanding, had a sizeable, seemingly insurmountable lead.

Blanding owed his popularity to sheer visibility. He was an active pilot, with his own aircraft: a pretty blue and white Bonanza with the distinctive V-tail, which he named *Kent's Komet.* He put the plane to good use, constantly commuting between his district and Washington, D.C. It enabled Kent Blanding to always seem to be in two places at once.

But Blanding had been making furtive overtures

to the unions; the steel industry bosses that owned Pittsburgh were not pleased. That was all they needed—a congressman who catered to the hired help rather than the bosses, those gracious overlords who allowed bread on the tables of the rabble. If Kent Blanding could not be stopped at the ballot box, they would have to employ other means.

On a clear spring evening in 1956, *Kent's Komet* nosedived into the hills of southern Pennsylvania on the westward leg of her usual commute. The small plane disintegrated on impact; there was little left of any appreciable size except the engine crankcase, buried eight feet deep in the hard, rocky ground. Not much to work with in a forensic investigation.

While the federal accident investigators hypothesized, throwing around terms like *pilot error, spatial disorientation, structural failure,* and *improper maintenance,* father and son Pilcher knew what really had happened. Blanding's death was no accident. They had paid two shady characters to sabotage the intricate control mechanism that blended the pilot's elevator and rudder commands into a unified input at the V-tail control surfaces. It had all been Leonard's idea. He had not flown a plane since the war, but he still knew how to turn one into a deadly weapon.

In the final seconds of his life, Kent Blanding found himself suddenly unable to control his aircraft. And, as uncontrolled aircraft are prone to do, it began a brisk descent, for planes in trouble rarely go up. Lacking corrective input, the descent progressed to a full-fledged nose dive from which there was no recovery.

Tad Matthews could hardly find his voice. "You mean...he was...*killed?*"

Both father and son Pilcher seemed so unconcerned, so casual. Leonard smirked as he said,

"That would have been quite a convenient *accident* for us, don't you think?"

Just above a whisper, Matthews said, "But you attended his funeral, Leonard."

The smirk stayed on Leonard Pilcher's face. "Yeah. So? Wouldn't it have looked ungracious if I didn't?"

Tad Matthews had always believed that Max Pilcher was capable of anything. In all Tad's years in his employ, though, the topic of murder had never surfaced. Now, here he was, admitting it without shame, without remorse, without fear of consequences. There must have been more murders, Tad thought—people who just vanished; *moved on*, they would say, never to be seen or heard from again. Now, Tad Matthews knew Leonard was just as willing and able to murder as a matter of course.

The Pilchers found the shell-shocked state of their legal advisor most amusing. Clearly, he found the concept of expedient murder a distressing revelation, but they had no fear of him running to the authorities. Surely, Tad Matthews realized he could end up just as missing—just as *moved on*—as any other adversary. But Leonard could not resist adding this one final tidbit of incriminating information: "Who do you think paid the guys who did it, Tad? Who hires all the private investigators we use around here?"

The answer to that question rang in Tad's head like an alarm gong: *I do…I do…I do.* How many times had he posted the expense as *private investigators* in the checkbook ledger for any one of a number of shadow accounts, just as he had been instructed and just as he had believed? They frequently hired investigators—some legitimate and established, others fly-by-night—to snoop on people against whom they needed leverage. Now, he realized, leverage can involve more than information; it could mean death.

Yes, the Pilchers had committed murder as if it was just a normal part of business, Tad Matthews thought, still horrified by the mere suggestion. Even worse, he was complicit. An accessory to murder.

But the Pilchers seemed so matter-of-fact, so comfortable with it. Suddenly, Tad saw the whole Moscone situation in a new light: *Maybe Kent Blanding wasn't Leonard Pilcher's first victim? Could he have really committed a murder in Sweden?*

Tad could feel the saliva gushing to his mouth. Then a spasm in his abdomen. He was seconds from throwing up. *Not here! Not in this office!* He could not remember if he asked to be excused as he raced to the bathroom down the hallway.

Back in Max Pilcher's office, Leonard seemed confused. "What the hell is wrong with him?" he asked, pointing in the direction of Tad's hasty exit.

The elder Pilcher leaned back in his chair and pivoted toward the tall windows. His gaze focused well beyond the clouds of smoke being belched from the smokestacks of Pittsburgh, far into a future only he seemed to be able to envision. How would he ever get there with this idiot for an heir and the squeamish Tad Matthews for legal counsel?

He answered his son's question without bothering to look at him. "What you've just seen, my boy, is the reason why people like Matthews can never be leaders. They just don't have the stomach to do what's necessary."

Chapter Thirty-Four

Allegra Wise was still kicking herself for missing the Pilcher publicity event that had devolved into the ASW endorsement fiasco. She had found out about it too late; there was no time to get to Pittsburgh. She was determined not to miss the press conference that followed two days later, but the plane trip from New York had been brutal. The "puddle-jumper"—a dingy, twin-engined prop airliner that dripped a variety of fluids all over the ramp, smelled like a musty cellar, and administered limb-numbing vibration in plentiful doses—had buzzed around and through the late winter storms, treating the passengers to a rough ride that left many nauseous. A scheduled 20-minute stop in Scranton turned into a 2-hour ordeal, as a grizzled mechanic in filthy coveralls, chomping a wisely unlit cigar, ministered to an engine that belched clouds of grayish smoke and spit unburned gasoline while refusing to start. By the time that engine finally came to life, allowing the plane to reach Pittsburgh, Allegra was exhausted, frazzled, and seriously contemplating a return trip to New York City by bus.

And it all seemed for nothing. The press conference was in its waning moments as Allegra Wise made her way into the hotel's ballroom. Tad Matthews was now standing in for Leonard Pilcher, fielding the last few questions. The congressman and Republican presidential hopeful, after apologizing for being expected elsewhere, had already made his exit.

When Matthews asked for a final question, Allegra was shouting it before he could finish speaking.

She might have been late to the press conference, *but damn it, I'm not going to be shut out.* Annoyed faces, overwhelmingly male, turned their glaring eyes to the tall, well-dressed woman shouting her question from the back of the room.

"Allegra Wise, CBS News," she bellowed. "Does the Congressman have a comment regarding the man…as reported by CBS…who accused the Congressman of committing a murder in Sweden during the war?"

A murmur of amusement rippled through the room. Somewhere in the throng a male voice offered a derisive sigh: "Oh, Jesus!"

Tad Matthews's face screwed up as if he had just smelled something putrid before shifting to a condescending smile. With a dismissive wave of the hand, he said, "That ridiculous accusation was answered long ago, miss. We won't dignify it with any further comments."

A smattering of supportive applause greeted Tad's answer. Allegra felt herself sinking into a hole. She needed to throw herself a rope; nobody else in the room seemed interested in helping her. So she yelled, "But does the Congressman know Mr. Moscone? Did they actually serve together in the war?"

His face did not lose the smile. He raised a hand in a tidy wave of goodbye and spoke once more into the microphone. "Thank you all for coming, ladies and gentlemen." He stepped down from the podium and made his way across the ballroom.

A hand touched Allegra's shoulder. She was not surprised. She had seen it before—goons planted in a crowd to intimidate and silence those who might try to embarrass the speaker. She wheeled to face the intruder, her voice gathering all the menace it could muster as she said, "Take your goddamn hands off me!"

Her assailant was merely a waitress who had been manning the nearby refreshment table. The waitress fought the urge to spout something equally harsh to this pushy, ungrateful Amazon with the fresh mouth. But trading barbs with the guests would only get her fired. This crappy hotel job had been hard enough to find. She had mouths to feed.

"No disrespect, ma'am," the waitress said, "but your change purse fell out of your bag. Didn't know if you'd noticed."

Feeling relieved—and a bit foolish—Allegra retrieved the purse from the floor. As she stood, she removed a dollar bill from the purse and extended it toward the waitress—an apology wrapped as a gratuity. But the waitress was gone, returned to her station at the refreshment table. Allegra did not pursue her. She pursued Tad Matthews instead.

She caught him at the doors at the far side of the ballroom. Matthews was chatting with a small knot of local newsmen, his eagerness to break away becoming more obvious by the second. This was usually the moment a staff member would come to the rescue, claiming *an urgent phone call* or some other convenient untruth. But Tad Matthews was working alone. There were no staff members to extricate him.

He could not help but notice the tall woman approaching, the one who had asked that irritating final question. But he pretended not to see her as he traded clipped remarks with the newsmen, repeating several times, "Okay, that's it, boys. Gotta go."

When he had finally pushed through the doors and began striding down the hall to the hotel's lobby, he found himself face to face with the roadblock that was Allegra Wise. He flashed a smile more insolent than friendly and tried to skirt around her. She sidestepped, blocking his path and bringing him to an annoyed halt.

"If you don't mind, miss…"

"Why, Thaddeus Matusik! Is that any way to greet an old friend?"

He truly thought that he was being confronted by the rudest woman on earth. Or maybe the craziest. "Pardon me?" he asked, at the limit of his patience.

"Oh, come on, Tad…it's me! Ally! Ally Wyznicki."

He stood silently for a moment, processing memories long suppressed. Finally, the cogs fell together.

"Tommy Wyznicki's little sister? Really? I could have sworn in there that you said your name was *Wise.*"

"See? We've got something else in common…We've both dumped our Polack names."

"And you work for CBS?"

Allegra Wise nodded proudly.

He could not help but be amused by the coincidence of their new names, but he grew more wary by the minute of her intrusion—and its implications: *Knowledge is power…and she certainly knows me. A reporter who knows things about you is the worst enemy you can have.*

He danced about uncomfortably in a losing attempt to hold down the panic rising within him. "Holy smoke! Tommy's little sister…How is old Tommy, anyway?"

"Just great! Got a law practice in Baltimore…great wife, two swell kids."

"I'm…I'm glad for him," he stammered. "Look, Ally, I've got to go. We've got a big meeting…"

She did not let him finish. Grabbing his arm, she pulled him toward the lobby bar. He complied without resistance; he did not want to make a scene with half the press in Western Pennsylvania in attendance. As he had witnessed back in the ballroom, she could get loud. Better just to ride this one out and escape as soon as possible.

"I won't keep you long," she said. "We've got some catching up to do, *Thaddeus.*"

He did not mind the table she selected. It was in a quiet corner, far from the boisterous, fresh-from-the-office heavy drinkers that bellied up to the bar at 4:05 in the afternoon. When the waitress arrived, Tad Matthews ordered a Coca-Cola. Allegra Wise's drink request was, "Scotch. Rocks."

She got right to the point. "I really want to talk about this Moscone guy, Tad."

"And as I have already told you, Ally...there's nothing to talk about. The man is mentally disturbed. Probably schizophrenic. The congressman has no relationship with him. Never did."

"The police talked to some people at the VA hospital, you know. Mr. Moscone was definitely a bomber crewman who was interned in Sweden. A radio operator, they said... that would make him some kind of enlisted man, no?"

Matthews nodded warily.

"And the Congressman was a bomber pilot...An officer, right?"

Tad feigned boredom. "Of course. This is all public record."

"And by the way, Tad, Mr. Moscone is not mentally disturbed. Or schizophrenic. He suffered from combat fatigue. You can recover from that, you know, with your mental faculties and memory pretty much intact."

"Is that so? I have it on good authority that he didn't fly nearly enough missions to get combat fatigue."

"Oh? How many missions does it take, Tad?"

"More than *three*, that's for sure." Instantly, Tad wished he had not given away that piece of information. He dodged for cover: "That's what they said on the news, right?"

She had him. Tad had screwed up, badly. *That was almost too easy,* Allegra thought, struggling to suppress a satisfied grin. *We didn't even know how many missions Moscone flew...until now!*

Allegra knew full well that individual service records were not a matter of public record. Even congressmen did not have access without the written approval of the serviceman, his next of kin, or a court order. Tad Matthews knew too much about Anthony Moscone, certainly more than Allegra knew at this point. And that information probably did not come from any government archive. If a judge had authorized release of Moscone's records to Pilcher, that would be easy to determine, but *I have it on good authority* somehow did not sound like the product of a court order.

"How many missions did the congressman fly, Tad? Was he interned in Sweden at any time?"

"You'd have to check with the congressman on that."

You can bet I'm going to check, honey, flashed through Allegra's mind. She took a deep pull on her scotch. *Mission accomplished. There's a definite connection between Leonard Pilcher and Anthony Moscone.*

She glanced at her watch. She still had plenty of time to get to the airport, but she launched into a fluttery, apologetic goodbye and quickly made her escape.

Just before boarding the evening flight to LaGuardia, she put in a collect call to Sid, the producer. "Boss," she yelled into the phone, "I need a sit-down first thing tomorrow morning with you and Wally. It looks like we've got a major scoop on the story of the year, maybe the decade."

Much to her surprise, the producer agreed without the cross-examination to which such pitches were usually subjected. "Scoop of the decade, eh? That's just great. But you realize, Ally, that this is only the first year of the decade, right?"

He laughed. The producer never laughed.

"We'll talk more in the morning," he said. "Have a nice flight."

"Don't you want to hear the details?"

But he had already hung up.

That's weird, Allegra thought. *And here I was, figuring Sid would piss in my corn flakes, like he always does.* She rushed to the airplane, its far-side engine already coughing to life. She could not have known the reason for Sid's agreeableness. When she called, the secretary who had answered at that late hour was, in fact, straddling the producer as they had sex in his plush executive's chair.

Chapter Thirty-Five

The flight back to New York was mercifully uneventful. Allegra was in her Manhattan apartment by 11:00 p.m., plenty of time to get a good night's sleep before that all-important 8:00 a.m. meeting. But she slept hardly at all. Her brain would not stop churning.

Up at 6:00, dressed and made-up by 7:30, and in the office by 7:55. Five minutes to spare. She dropped her pillbox hat and gloves at her desk, made a quick stop at the ladies' room to recheck her hair and makeup, smooth the lines of her new blue suit, and make sure there were no smudges on her matching pumps. Satisfied that all was in order, she took a deep breath and strode off to the conference room.

Already seated were Sid, the producer, Wally—the most trusted man in America—and two researchers. Allegra breezed in, grabbed a cup of coffee from the serving table, and eased into a chair at the big table.

"So, are you ready to lead with *Presidential candidate is a murderer,* Ally?" Wally asked, with a big smile. "Do we have any idea who he supposedly killed?"

"No, but I'm working on it," Allegra said.

She gave them the whole rundown. How Tad had said too much—and how he must know too much. What he let slip had probably come from someone's personal knowledge of Moscone's internment. Pilcher must be hiding something, at the very least the fact that he, too, had been interned in Sweden. There was something fishy about the three-mission thing; the standard combat tour for an Eighth Air Force bomber crew in late 1944 was 35 missions.

Wally sat back and puffed his pipe. He was deeply interested. This had the smell of a blockbuster scoop. Catching a politician in an omission, an outright lie, or a crime before anyone else was a newsman's wet dream.

"But the internment story won't cut much ice unless we've got a body to go with it," Wally said.

The producer pointed to Charlie, the senior of the two researchers, and said, "Check for subpoenas of Moscone's military records. See if Pilcher's been snooping around." Charlie nodded while tearing a page on which he had just scribbled from his notebook.

"Shouldn't take more than a day or two, provided the subpoena was in either the D.C. or Western PA Federal Court," Charlie replied, passing the torn-out page to the young female researcher seated beside him. "Give these guys a call. See what they've got," he told her.

Charlie turned back to the producer and said, "If they filed someplace else, that may take a while to find."

"Bomber crewmen didn't end up in Sweden by themselves," Allegra added. "They arrived by the planeload. Ten men per plane. If Moscone was there, there were others from his crew. If we could get confirmation from another source...a believable source...that Moscone and Pilcher were actually interned in Sweden..."

The producer interrupted. "Is that right, Charlie? Ten in a crew?"

"Yeah, she's right," Charlie replied. "But it still won't prove Pilcher killed anyone."

"Of course not," Wally said, "but that's where we start." He took a big puff on his pipe, then added, "The little lady knows how to do her homework."

If the producer was enthusiastic about any of this, you could not tell from his expression. "I want this story growing legs real quick," he said. "I like the feel of this one...but if it starts to fuck the dog, I'll kill it in a heartbeat. I don't need to make us a target of some big money hot-shots when all we've got is an empty gun."

Wally frowned. "I think we can be a little braver than that, Sid."

The producer paused to light another cigarette before continuing. "Let's see how brave we are when our budget gets slashed to nothing. Ally...you're going to find this Moscone guy, right?"

"Uh-huh. That's first on my list."

"And what about interviewing Pilcher himself?" Wally added. "Is your contact still going to open doors for you?"

Allegra tried her best to sound confident: "Oh, I think he might."

Wally had no reply, verbal or otherwise. He just kept smoking that pipe, looking content and all-knowing. The white clouds from his pipe that rose in puffs and the thick, dark-rimmed glasses, like a windshield, reminded Allegra of *the little engine that could.*

"Let's go over what we already know about the good congressman," the producer said. "The general impression is that he's a lightweight, propped up by Daddy's money, right?"

"Actually, boss, *lightweight* is being pretty generous," Charlie began. "*Useless* is how most describe him. We've got a lot of archive material from his two congressional runs. Despite all Daddy's money, he got in the first time only because the incumbent, Kent Blanding, conveniently killed himself in a plane crash. Pilcher never would have gotten the nomination otherwise. The steelworkers' unions were dead set against him. Seems young Leonard has always been quite the problem child...drunk driving, messing around with women even after he got married. There are some fairly credible rumors that he got a few of these ladies in the family way…and Daddy paid for the abortions. All hushed up, of course."

Wally could not help but chuckle. He had heard this story before and many others like it. What would politics be without a whole lot of sin?

Charlie continued, "We've still got a lot of stuff on deep cover that never aired. He's the only son…the male heir. Apparently, Daddy has this dream of putting his kid in the White House. Been groomed all his life, despite the fact the kid is a total fuck-up…"

"Ah-hem!" Allegra interrupted, with mock seriousness. "Again with the dirty mouth! A little respect, gentlemen! There are ladies in the fucking room!"

Wally chuckled. Nobody else did.

Charlie rolled on without missing a beat. "He managed to graduate from Pitt on the strength of the endowments Daddy made, went for the glory with the Air Corps in the war, although nobody seems to know much of anything about his war record…yet. Could be one of those instant heroes in uniform whose tune changes after he realizes you might actually get killed doing this shit."

Wally, the old war correspondent, chuckled again and said, "His achievements in Congress have been nothing short of dismal…practically nonexistent. He's sponsored zero bills…and apparently caused his father's company to lose a big government contract…"

"The Randolph deal, right?" the producer asked.

"Yeah, that's right," Charlie continued. "He didn't show for some big, important meet-and-greet…looks like he was on a bender and shacked up with some tootsie…must have just slipped his mind."

None of this was news to the producer. "So," he said, "who thinks this clown is presidential material?"

Wally set down his pipe. He spoke in that serious tone he used on the air, the one that made you trust him. "His Daddy's wallet, that's who."

The producer had one more question. "Do we know how many American airmen were interned in Sweden during the war?"

Charlie had the answer to that one, too. "About one thousand, boss. Roughly one hundred airplanes' worth."

"A pretty small haystack, people," The producer said. "Let's figure out who Pilcher supposedly killed...and who else knows about it."

Chapter Thirty-Six

Tad Matthews had no choice but to tell Max Pilcher of his encounter with Allegra Wise. The old man was less than thrilled by the news. He would have been far less thrilled if Tad had told him the whole story, including how he had let the comment about *only three missions* slip out. Tad may have been foolish with Allegra, but he was not suicidal. He would cover his mistake somehow. He would fix it before it did permanent damage.

"So how much does this woman know about you, Matthews?" The subtext of that question was: *Does she know you're a faggot?*

"I was in the same class as her older brother. She was just a kid...I think she had a crush on me," Tad replied.

Max Pilcher found the *crush* part amusing—and strangely reassuring. Maybe Matthews's peculiarities were well concealed back then, too.

Tad then spoke words he knew were almost certainly a lie. "Aside from knowing that I've changed my name, she doesn't know much of anything."

"So we've got to make sure she can't connect the dots about Lenny's war record," the old man said.

"Yes, sir. Anything that Moscone says is already discredited. Everybody knows he's crazy." Matthews said, beginning to feel confident, convinced he had dodged the bullet. "We just need to make sure that no part of Leonard's military record sees the light of day. That whole Swedish adventure must remain concealed. Forever."

Max Pilcher nodded in agreement, then leaned back in his huge leather chair. He looked troubled. Another question was deep on his mind: "You don't suppose that idiot son of mine actually did kill someone in Sweden, do you? I mean, everybody approves of murder in concept. Whether they've got the balls to pull the trigger themselves, though..."

"I'm not sure *everybody* approves, sir," Matthews interjected.

"Oh, don't give me that holier-than-thou crap! People kill when it's necessary. It's that simple," Max Pilcher stated flatly. That patrician certainty in his voice was unmistakable: *only fools question such obvious truth.*

At that moment, Leonard Pilcher entered the office without so much as a knock, bypassing the secretary guarding the door and leaving the flustered woman in his wake.

"Give me and my son a moment, Matthews," Max Pilcher said.

Tad Matthews shut the door behind him on his way out. Leonard Pilcher strolled about his father's office like he owned it, even laying hands on some of the prized ornaments with which his father had decorated the place. Max Pilcher was having a difficult time concealing his irritation with this impudent, supposed adult he called his son.

"Sit down, Lenny," Max Pilcher said. "We've got to have a little talk."

Leonard claimed a comfortable chair. Exuding boredom, he draped his leg over one of its arms.

"You don't know this Moscone character, do you?" Max Pilcher asked. "Did he fly with you?"

Without batting an eye, Leonard Pilcher replied, "Never saw the son of a bitch in my life, Dad."

"So it's all bullshit?"

"Of course it's bullshit," the younger Pilcher said. "He's either out of his mind...or he's part of some other campaign's hatchet job, that's all."

The father looked skeptical. "My sources haven't found any evidence of that, son. The other candidates aren't taking you seriously enough to bother running a hatchet job...not yet, anyway."

Leonard shrugged. "Okay...so he's crazy! Don't worry, Pop. This'll die all by itself."

Max considered his son's analysis for a moment. Then he shrugged, too, and rose from his chair, signaling this brief engagement closed. "Fine," he said. "Send the faggot back in here."

Leonard remained seated, motionless. He looked confused.

"The faggot...the queer. Get him in here, Lenny."

Leonard's face still registered no understanding of his father's order. Max Pilcher was incredulous.

Finally, Max shouted, "Matthews, you idiot! Matthews! What's the matter? You didn't know he was a nancy-boy?"

Leonard Pilcher looked more confused than ever. His father shook his head, perhaps in disbelief or perhaps in regret for siring this dullard sitting before him. His words escaped his mouth like a sigh of deep regret. "Son, you are dumber than a box of rocks. How do you think I keep Matthews in line so easily? Knowledge is power, my boy...Knowledge is power."

Chapter Thirty-Seven

Joe Gelardi sat nervously in the reception area, wondering why he had bothered to arrive on time. The chairman of the math department was notorious for keeping visitors waiting, absorbed as he was with the demands and politics of running a prestigious academic unit at MIT. The secretary had reminded the chairman twice: *Doctor Gelardi is here, sir.* All she had received in return was a perfunctory wave of acknowledgement as he continued with one pressing phone call after another.

Joe knew exactly why the chairman wanted to see him. A few days ago, while leading a class in Boolean algebra, he had observed two male students on the rooftop below his upper floor classroom's window. They were engaged in horseplay that made them appear to be fighting, just like Leonard Pilcher and David Linker had been on that rooftop in Sweden. But Joe could not see or hear that these young men were exchanging laughs and boyish grins rather than angry looks and hateful words. His smooth and orderly presentation to the class became halting and incoherent.

The boys on the roof made their way to the ledge, still engaged in the good-natured pushing and shoving that looked like something altogether different—and frighteningly familiar—to Joe Gelardi. As they leaned over the edge to yell to colleagues in the courtyard below, Joe Gelardi, pressed against the classroom window, began to tremble. Bewildered students rushed to his side and asked what was wrong.

"HE WAS KILLED THAT WAY," Joe blurted, then collapsed to a seated position on the floor. Almost a fetal position. Those close enough could hear him whispering through his sobs, *Oh God, he killed him...That bastard killed him...*

Help was summoned. A faculty member gave Joe a glass of water as another helped him to a chair. A campus policeman arrived. An ambulance was called.

The term *nervous breakdown* was uttered by a few of the pitying onlookers. Most, however, just looked on and shook their heads sadly, finding nothing else appropriate to do or say.

Within a few minutes, Joe regained his composure. Those who had come to his aid hesitantly retreated, not quite convinced that he was *fine... just fine*, no matter how many times he reassured them.

Stifling the humiliation that raged within him, he resumed the class.

It was 15 minutes past the appointment time, and the chairman was still on the phone. Joe pulled a folded document from the inside pocket of his sport jacket. He unfolded it like a poker player arranging his hand, taking care the secretary could not read it.

It was an offer of employment from IBM. The space for the accepting signature—Joe's signature—was blank. He stared at the paper, deep in troubled thought.

"The chairman will see you now, Doctor Gelardi," the receptionist finally said.

Joe carefully folded the job offer and returned it to his jacket pocket. As he entered the office, he was surprised to find the chairman seemingly relaxed and unhurried. He had expected to find an impatient man, harried by the pressures of his lofty position. Instead, he found what appeared to be a sympathetic friend.

"Hold my calls, Sally," he said to his secretary. He stood and offered a handshake and a warm smile to

Joe. As they settled into chairs, there was a moment of awkward silence before the chairman spoke.

"We're very worried about you, Joe."

Joe did not feel the need to say very much. The chairman's tactfully worded attempts to stimulate dialogue boiled down to one simple question, which he finally came right out and asked: "Are you happy here, Joe?"

The words Joe would have liked to say coursed through his mind: *What does he expect me to say? No, sir...I'm miserably unhappy with the never-ending politics of this place and seriously considering leaving?*

"You're a wonderful teacher, Joe. Your students adore you."

Great...so why have I been getting the runaround over promotion and tenure? Doesn't everybody act a little strange around here from time to time? And Forbes Nash is out of his ever-loving mind, but you never had the nerve to kick him out...

"But there's something troubling you, Joe. I wish I knew what it was. Quite frankly, this could have a major impact on your career at the Institute."

"You mean on my application for tenure?" Joe asked.

There was a long pause. "That...and more," the chairman finally replied.

Joe struggled to keep down the anger that was rising inside him. The urge to announce his resignation right then and there—and accept the offer from IBM in his pocket—was very strong.

I should sign this job offer right now...right on his desk! How's that for a resignation?

But that would not help anything.

Must stay calm...analytical...Make a decision based only on facts, not emotion.

Most importantly, Joe had to do what was best for his daughter. Without an answer to that question, the job offer would remain unsigned for yet another day.

The chairman's look of sympathy faded. The playing at Dutch uncle was over. The cold efficiency and formality of an administrator appeared.

"Perhaps it would be best if you took a leave of absence, Doctor Gelardi. I'll arrange it with the provost. Take as long as you need. You'll be paid as usual."

There was no mistaking it—he was being suspended. Unofficially, of course. A prelude to dismissal disguised as some sort of sabbatical. No black mark in his CV. At least not yet. The job offer in his pocket buoyed him like a life raft in a troubled sea.

Joe rose to leave. He knew escaping that office would feel like a rush of sweet freedom.

The chairman's tone softened once again, and he offered one last piece of advice: "Get some help, Joe. Then we'll see what we can do about your position here."

Chapter Thirty-Eight

Philadelphia: Allegra Wise wished she knew this city better. Even though she was a Pennsylvania native from the affluent Pittsburgh suburbs, she had only managed the requisite school trips to view the historic landmarks of the City of Brotherly Love. She had certainly never spent a second in its rundown neighborhoods, one of which she was now walking through, searching for the house where Tony Moscone lived.

She looked painfully out of place here, a well-dressed businesswoman strolling through a concrete purgatory of dilapidated row houses, the late afternoon sun casting long shadows on their cracked and crumbling brickwork. Their life-scarred occupants—women probably in their 30s but looking 50—eyed her through tattered curtains with great suspicion. Noisy children, bundled against the late winter cold in faded, often-patched hand-me-downs, interrupted their street games to gawk at her, surprised and amused by this tall woman who might as well be a visitor from another planet. Allegra certainly felt like one.

She had witnessed the seamy side of life before as a reporter on the police beat in her native Pittsburgh. The detective she met and took as her lover during that gig had been circumspect when discussing the horrors he saw doing his job amidst the city's lower strata. One warm summer night, as they lay still, entwined and damp after making love, he had said to her out of the blue, *Ally, I wish you'd get some other job. I don't want you to see the things I have to see.*

It was not that well-off people did not kill and maim each other; she knew better than that. But on streets like the one she was currently walking, the threat of violence and random death just seemed so much more real. More likely. Her cop lover had given her a piece of advice, and she was employing it now: *Always walk down the street like you own it...less chance somebody will fuck with you.*

That advice seemed to be working. The tallest among a group of boys lounging on a stoop—maybe 12 years old—took a deep drag on his cigarette, then called out in a menacing tone, "Hey, lady! You lost or somethin'?"

Mustering all the confidence she could gather, Allegra replied, "No, young man. I know exactly where I'm going, thank you."

There was some mumbling among the boys. A little snickering, too. The tallest one spoke again, just loud enough for Allegra to hear. "Nah, she ain't no social worker, dipshit. She's dressed too good."

Allegra walked on, unmolested. *Maybe they do think I own the street,* she hoped, fighting the urge to quicken her stride. She regretted not having the cab from the train station drop her off right at Moscone's address, but she wanted to walk these streets. She needed a feel for the place to better understand who Tony Moscone was. But that sociology class bullshit was feeling pretty weak right now. *What a dope I am,* she thought. *The place is a shithole! I could've figured that out still safely inside the cab.*

She stopped and checked her notebook. The house number was crudely applied to the brick in freehand brush strokes of white paint. *Yep, this is it...723.* She climbed the steps. There was no doorbell. She knocked.

Nothing. She knocked again.

There was activity behind the door. The click of a deadbolt. The door opened a crack, as far as the safety chain would allow. An unfriendly female face—plain, pasty, not a hint of makeup—peered through the slim opening.

Harshly, the face behind the door asked, "Whaddaya want?"

"Miss Moscone? I'm Allegra Wise from WCBS TV, New York. I'd like to talk to Anthony..."

She was interrupted by a string of curses from the face behind the door. Much to Allegra's surprise, the door almost closed, then flew wide open—and standing in the threshold was a small, frail, but agitated woman, probably 40 but looking much older. Face flushed, eyes bulging, her frizzy black hair looked like it was ravaged by an electric shock. Her bony body swam about in a baggy housedress and tattered sweater, quaking in foreplay to the rage she was about to unleash. Ninety pounds of dynamite with a very short fuse, standing on sinewy feet in fuzzy bunny slippers.

"I TOLD YOU SONS OF BITCHES TO LEAVE MY BROTHER ALONE! AIN'T HE BEEN THROUGH ENOUGH?"

Allegra was certain this crazy little woman had just sprayed spit all over her, but she stayed calm and tried to be reassuring. "I'm only trying to get Anthony's side of the story, Miss Moscone..."

But Theresa Moscone was in no mood for reassurances.

"GET THE GODDAMN HELL OUT OF HERE, LADY!"

Then the door slammed in Allegra's face. Had she looked up, she might have seen a face at an upstairs window, just watching. Tony Moscone's face.

Despite the background din of city noise, Allegra

felt she was in a bubble of silence. She considered knocking again. *No point,* she rationalized. *No telling what that crazy little bitch might do next.* She would have to find some other way to interview Tony Moscone. She jammed her business card through the mail slot in the door. *Couldn't hurt,* she rationalized again.

Only then did it dawn on her that she would have to run the same gauntlet on the way out of this neighborhood as she had on the way in. It was a few blocks to the nearest phone booth; she would have to call for a cab from there. None seemed to cruise these mean streets in search of fares.

Much to Allegra's surprise, the streets were practically deserted as she retraced her steps. The children were gone, probably called in to supper by their world-weary mothers. But she continued to walk as if she owned the street, even though there was no one else laying claim to it at the moment.

Once at the phone booth, she decided to first check in with her office in New York. She was startled to find that there was a phone message from Tony Moscone, received just a few minutes ago. "The ink on the message slip isn't even dry yet," the secretary on the other end of the line said.

The message was brief: *If you want to talk to me, meet me at Monty's Deli on Kensington at 6 p.m. Any cabbie will know it.*

Tony was right—the cabbie knew Monty's like he knew Independence Hall or the Liberty Bell. Allegra arrived at the crowded deli well before 6 p.m. She took a table near the back, ordered a sandwich and coffee, and waited. Everyone was staring at her. She looked out of place here, too. "Some high-class broad slumming with the working stiffs," a patron muttered, intentionally loud enough for Allegra to hear.

She ignored them. This day had shaped up to be much longer and far more tiring than she imagined. Her feet, in their expensive pumps, were killing her. *At least it's not my time of the month,* she thought. *That would be the perfect capper.*

Allegra would have known Tony Moscone even if she had not seen his mug shot. She picked him out the moment he walked in. A small, wiry man—a build much like his sister's. *These Moscones sure don't come from a line of giants,* Allegra thought. He was jittery, with eyes that constantly darted but never seemed to be looking at anything. His hands were jammed tightly into the pockets of his well-worn pea coat, shoulders hunched forward. He seemed to be trying to fold up into himself, to disappear. She waved at him; he started her way. She towered over him as she stood in greeting.

"I had to wait until I left for work. Otherwise, she would've known something was up," Tony said.

"She...being your sister?" Allegra asked.

"Yeah, who else? I heard the browbeating she gave you...Theresa means well, I guess. But I don't need no more of her shit. Don't need no big sister looking out for me."

Allegra ordered him coffee. Beneath his pea coat, Moscone wore the white uniform of a kitchen worker. He was sure she was making mental notes, sizing him up without asking him a damn thing. He held open his coat to reveal the stenciled logo *Hotel Cornwall* on his uniform shirt.

Deadpan, he said, "So you don't think I'm some *doctor* or something. I work at the hotel up the street. The VA got me a job there. I guess they got tired of babysitting me."

"What do you mean by babysitting?" Allegra

asked.

He looked straight at her for the first time, his dark eyes boring into her with a sad yet fierce intensity that she did not expect and found unsettling. "Lady...I lost my frigging mind in that airplane. I've spent years in and out of that VA...just so I can be a goddamn dishwasher. I knew all about radio, you know...and I still do, damn it! I could have been an engineer or something..."

Allegra found herself moved by Tony Moscone's words. *He just encapsulated sixteen years of hell in three sentences. Brilliant.* They both took a sip of coffee before continuing.

"Mr. Moscone, who did you see Captain Pilcher murder?"

He paused before answering. "Davey. Davey Linker. That bastard pilot threw him off the roof."

Allegra leaned closer. "Who was Davey Linker? A friend of yours?"

"One of our gunners on *The Lady M.* And yeah...he was a good friend. A real swell guy. Smart as a whip, too.*"

"You were both in Pilcher's crew?"

"Uh-huh."

Allegra jotted feverishly in her notebook. She took a deep breath before speaking again.

"Mr. Moscone, did anybody else witness Linker's murder?"

"I don't know...I just know what I saw." He paused. In an instant, he was agitated.

"Look, I know what you're gonna say...what they're all saying. Moscone's out of his fucking mind! He's crazy! Don't listen to him!"

He was nearly in tears now. "Even that guy on the TV said I'm a nutcase!"

Now it was Allegra's turn to look Tony straight in the eye. "If I believed that, Mr. Moscone, I wouldn't be here."

That calmed Tony a bit. Allegra leaned forward and asked, "What else can you tell me about your time in Sweden?"

Shaking his head sadly, he said, "Not much. I just remember us guys from the crew walking around in civvies all the time...like we was on vacation or something." After a long pause, he added: "And that nice blonde lady who took care of us."

"Do you remember the blonde lady's name, Mr. Moscone?"

"No. Sorry...and call me Tony."

"Do you remember the names of the other crew members, Tony?"

"Of course I do!" he replied. He proceeded to reel off—with great precision—the full names, ranks, and hometowns of the other four members of *The Lady M's* crew in Sweden: Joe Gelardi, Ed Morris, Frank Hughes, and David Linker. "And Hughes hung himself over there."

"Hughes committed suicide?"

"Yeah," he said, then added with a tight-lipped smile, "and they still call me the crazy one. Ain't that something?"

Allegra did the math. "That makes only six," she said. "Weren't there ten men in a bomber crew?"

"Yeah...four guys weren't there," Tony replied.

"What happened to them?"

Another long pause. "Don't know that either, lady."

"But can you tell me their names, too?" Allegra asked.

"Sure," he replied, and then reeled off the names,

ranks, and hometowns of the remaining four: Harry Lapinski, Lou DiNapoli, Larry Harkin...and Fred O'Hara.

Allegra stopped writing at the mention of that last name: Fred O'Hara. Something clicked in her memory. The Philadelphia Inquirer she had picked up at the train station earlier was still jutting from her bag. She grabbed it and scanned the front page, searching to see if her memory served her correctly. Sure enough, at the bottom of the page, there was an article titled *ASW No-Show for Pilcher Endorsement.* She felt her pulse quicken: *Could this be another obscure link that no one else has uncovered, falling from the heavens right into my lap?*

Breathlessly, she repeated Tony's last bit of information. "Fred O'Hara? From Pittsburgh?"

"Yeah, that's what I said."

Pointing to the article, she said, "A man named Fred O'Hara just happens to be president of the ASW. Wouldn't that be a fascinating coincidence?" She tried to control the urge to sprint to a phone.

Tony Moscone just stared back at her blankly. He had no idea what she was implying.

Chapter Thirty-Nine

The telephone receiver dropped from Tom Houlihan's hand, bounced off its cradle, and came to rest on the table. Lying on its side, the receiver became a visual representation of unfinished business. That's exactly what the phone call had been about: unfinished business. The ASW's endorsement of Leonard Pilcher had not happened.

And the payment Houlihan was due for said endorsement—that had not happened, either. The Bahamian bank account set up to collect it languished at the same minimum required balance since its inception.

The telephone receiver began the harsh claxon that signaled it was off the hook. It took a few moments before Houlihan, still in shock from that phone conversation, became aware of the annoying sound and summoned up the energy to silence it—not by hanging up, but by seizing the cradle, jerking it from the table and its cord from the wall in the process, then flinging the entire apparatus across the room. One of his wife's precious porcelain lamps had the misfortune to be in the trajectory. It disintegrated to a thousand clattering shards, punctuated by the flash of the shattered light bulb and the *thud-thud* of the cradle and receiver striking the wall beyond, a split-second apart.

Mercifully, the chaos in the living room had not awakened Tom's wife, still a sound sleeper in her late 70s. She would wake eventually, though, and when she did, recriminations for the broken lamp would be loud and lengthy.

Her and her shitty lamp are the least of my

worries, Tom imagined. He made his way outside to the back porch. It was a beautiful night on the Gulf Coast of South Florida—a bright moon, a gentle breeze off the water. Across the yard, his Chris Craft cabin cruiser— *Union Maid*—bobbed silently at its dock, like so many others in this cove-side community, populated mainly by retirees from the frozen North.

This is heaven, Tom thought, *but I ain't got a penny to pay for it. That gambling money...the vig the Caputos are laying on it's gonna kill me! The forty grand I owe doubles if I don't pay by the end of the month. After that, I'm screwed. The endorsement money from Pilcher would have covered the forty grand...with ten grand left over.*

But that ungrateful son-of-a-bitch O'Hara has the balls to go against me? Who the fuck does he think he is? I made *him...he'd be nothing without me. Can't the little prick see that?*

Houlihan sagged into a wooden deck chair and considered his options. Time was running out. O'Hara had to go. He was sure he could fix a recall election and put a more compliant lackey into the union presidency, but there was no way that could happen before the end of the month.

Gotta be sooner than that, Houlihan resolved. He sat completely still for a few more moments, letting the enormity and finality of his decision wash over him. Then, he rose and shuffled back into the house.

He needed a phone. The one in the living room lay in a useless heap, its severed wires coiled around it. But there was another phone in the bedroom where his wife slept.

Good thing she sleeps like the dead.

Gently, silently, he lifted the receiver and dialed "O."

In a voice barely above a whisper, Houlihan said, "Operator, I'm calling long distance…"

His wife stirred but did not wake. Tom waited and listened as a series of female operators with Southern accents announced their city—*Jacksonville, Atlanta, Knoxville, Richmond*—making their innocent contribution to Tom Houlihan's dirty work by connecting his call farther down the line. Finally, a decidedly non-Southern female voice that seemed to be at the other end of a long tunnel announced, "Pittsburgh."

A moment later, as a phone in that steel-making town rang at the home of his most trusted henchman, Tom Houlihan mentally composed his message: *We're gonna get O'Hara out of office…with a bullet.*

Chapter Forty

Fred O'Hara threw the newspaper down on his desk in disgust. It landed with a *plop*, the photo on the front page still staring up at him with that mocking grin. The headline of the article that accompanied the photo blared: *PILCHER CANDIDACY PICKS UP STEAM.*

As O'Hara fumed in silence, his secretary stuck her head in the door.

"There's some TV reporter from CBS on the phone for you," she said.

"Tell him *no comment.*"

"It's a she," the secretary replied. With a puzzled expression on her face, she added, "Says she wants to ask about *The Lady M?*"

Fred sank into his chair as if the weight of the world was pressing down on him. "Okay, put her through," he mumbled.

He stared uncomfortably at the phone for a few moments, as if mesmerized by the blinking light on the incoming line button, before he took the call.

Chapter Forty-One

Charlie, the head researcher for the news team, sat impatiently behind a desk cluttered with documents, publications, and photos. Allegra Wise paced before him. He did not even look up at her as he began to rattle off the information his staff had uncovered. "The tail gunner, Hughes, is dead, Ally...hung himself while interned."

Allegra frowned. "I already know that, Charlie. And Harkin, the bombardier, is dead...Lapinski, too, according to O'Hara."

"Ooo, there's no fooling you, is there? But wait...you're gonna love this. DiNapoli...he's a *mobster* right here in New York City. Runs the Bronx for the Montemaro Family."

She rolled her eyes. "I figured that one out, too...O'Hara talked about him a little. They were POWs together. It was pretty obvious."

"Well, goodie for you, Ally! I suppose you didn't actually get to talk to Mr. DiNapoli?"

"You suppose correctly. The phone number turned out to be a delicatessen on Fordham Road. O'Hara and DiNapoli aren't much help, though. They weren't in Sweden."

Charlie laughed. "Yeah, I know," he said. "Now this Morris guy...he's still in the Air Force, but good luck finding him. Wherever he is, it's classified. It would take an act of the Pentagon to unearth him. But this Joseph Gelardi...he sounds like a real egghead. You shouldn't have any trouble finding him...and the Boston area is *simply lovely* this time of year."

Allegra checked her open notebook, tapped her

pencil against the page, tallying its contents. "That just leaves our alleged murder victim, David Linker," she said, slamming the notebook shut.

Chapter Forty-Two

PILCHER FOR PRESIDENT signs seemed to be plastered everywhere across this city. As Allegra Wise made her way across the University of Pittsburgh campus, they lined every thoroughfare like guideposts, funneling the crowds to the campus auditorium where Leonard Pilcher was to speak.

There must be two thousand people stuffed into this crappy little hall, Allegra thought as she muscled her way toward the front seats, utilizing sweet but hollow words of apology and elbow leverage to clear her path. The crowd was mostly college kids, with some faculty, a few local bigwigs, reporters, and photographers, all wanting a good look at this unlikely presidential candidate. The press flyer stated that the congressman would entertain questions after his speech. She would not be the only reporter chomping at the bit to ask the congressman a question or two. One would have to be assertive to get a word in. Allegra was determined to make her question *entertaining.*

Allegra wondered if the large number of students were present merely because professors had been requested to cancel classes during the congressman's appearance. Empty chairs in the auditorium would reflect poorly on the university, an institution that benefited much from the Pilcher family's largesse. Failure to appear supportive of that family's endeavors might have a negative impact on future endowments.

Allegra finally located an unoccupied seat near the front. It had not been an easy search; she bulled her way to it, settled in, and caught her breath. Several bookish young men to her left spoke with great seriousness of the US role in Central and South America and what the continued presence of a Republican in the White House might mean for that role. The sorority girls sitting to Allegra's right were busily comparing the contents of some fashion magazines.

The university president strolled onto the stage, said a few words of thanks to those in attendance, and moved quickly to the main event. "Ladies and gentlemen," he said with the oily grace of a carnival barker, "I give you the next president of the United States, Congressman Leonard Pilcher, from the great state of Pennsylvania!"

He had failed to whip the crowd into the desired frenzy. The applause was tepid, at best, but Leonard Pilcher seemed not to notice. He stood with arms raised high, acknowledging the weak applause as if he was some conquering hero soaking up the accolades of the adoring masses.

One of the sorority girls to Allegra's right said, a little too loudly, "Look at him! You'd think they just crowned him king of the world or something!" Then all the girls dissolved into derisive giggles. Allegra wondered if Pilcher would put his arms down before the anemic clapping died out completely or if he would keep them up, leaving him looking even more ridiculous. He put them down just as the clapping ceased.

Pilcher then launched into a droning, boilerplate political speech that had the already disinterested audience shifting impatiently in their seats. After 10 minutes of speaking that seemed like hours, Pilcher, attempting to punctuate some mundane point with a grand physical gesture, accidentally swept the water glass from the podium with his arm and sent it crashing to the stage.

The audience snickered, but Pilcher seemed unaffected by the gaffe. With a wide grin, he kept right on speaking. "A little water over the dam, eh? But no matter...As I was saying, diplomacy not rooted in strength is a fool's game." He paused for dramatic effect. "I've been to war. I know about strength. I was one of *those crazy heroes* who bombed Germany!"

There was no response from the audience—none at all. Surely that was a guaranteed applause line, was it not? But they sat as one monolithic mind, craving intellectual nourishment but being fed nothing. The few murmured comments that rose in that awkward stillness, though unintelligible, possessed the unmistakable tone of mockery. In the shadows of the last rows, several audience members decided they were finished with this charade and slipped out the doors.

In the wings, Tad Matthews watched in horror. Had he not beaten into Leonard's foolish head *don't mention the war...especially your war record!* Yet there Leonard was, uttering two blatant falsehoods in one sentence: *hero* and *bombed Germany.* An argument could have been made that Pilcher had been truthful about the *crazy* part, at least.

Immediate damage control was necessary. Matthews hurried onto the stage and whispered something in Pilcher's ear. The words left Pilcher disoriented and fumbling. It appeared to Allegra that Matthews was actually trying to nudge Pilcher from the stage with a subtle but undeniably urgent motion of hips and shoulders.

If I'm going to say anything, it'd better be now, Allegra thought. She sprang to her feet.

"Congressman," Allegra called out, "it was rumored that you would receive the surprising endorsement of the ASW. Did you and that union's president, Mr. O'Hara, serve together in the war?"

The question blindsided Leonard Pilcher. Startled, he attempted to approach the podium, speaking words that were nothing but an unintelligible stammer. Before any meaningful sound escaped Pilcher's mouth, Tad Matthews grabbed the Congressman's arm.

With a look that could only be described as one of annoyance and disgust, Pilcher violently shucked Matthew's grasp. Then, Pilcher turned back to the stunned audience. Allegra searched her brain to find just the right words to describe the look now adorning Pilcher's face as he glared at her: *It's a smirk,* she decided, *but I've never seen someone so drenched in superiority! It's nothing but raw contempt! Unbelievable!*

She had asked uncomfortable questions of politicians many times before. The usual response was some fancy dance around her query, a vaguely worded denial that could deflect the truth long enough for the denier to make his getaway.

But Pilcher's response was something totally different: a silence that defiantly screamed *Fuck you. Even the truth can't hurt me.*

Her eyes remained locked on Pilcher's for another moment. Matthews whispered to Pilcher again, with more urgency this time. Pilcher's look of raw contempt turned from Allegra and was now focusing itself on Matthews.

Allegra shouted her follow-up: "WERE YOU AND MR. O'HARA CREWMATES? WAS MR. MOSCONE?"

The audience buzzed with excitement. This mundane political event had suddenly gotten interesting.

In what looked to the onlookers like two grown men dancing an awkward two-step, Pilcher and Matthews exchanged places so that Matthews was now before the microphone. His gaze swept the auditorium, then focused on Allegra. Matthews began to speak; his tone could only be described as *offended.* "Miss Wise, as I told you once before, we will not be dignifying that nonsense with further explanations."

Tad Matthews paused, relishing the fact that he had regained control—however briefly—of what could very easily become a hostile mob. It was time to make a hasty exit, before some other troublemaker picked up Allegra Wise's line of questioning. He raised his hand in a wave of goodbye; Pilcher took the cue and did the same. Matthews spoke one more time: "That's all we have time for, ladies and gentlemen. Thank you."

And then the stage was empty. Suddenly, everyone in the audience was talking to their neighbor at once, all voicing the same thought in 2000 different ways: *What the hell just happened?*

The only one not speaking was Allegra. She settled back into her seat, a satisfied smile on her face. A triumphant thought filled her head: *This story's going to get me on camera...or win me a Pulitzer...or both!*

Chapter Forty-Three

Fred O'Hara was awake at the first sound. The dull *thump*—someone bumping into furniture on the first floor of the darkened house, nudging it out of place just a bit. Someone unfamiliar with the layout—an intruder. He jostled his sleeping wife awake, and clamped a hand over her mouth to silence the inevitable, irritated, *What? What?*

In an urgent whisper, Fred commanded, "Stay up here with the kids. Keep everyone quiet. Take the phone into the closet and call the cops, quick!"

Her terrified eyes pleaded a question above the hand still clamped to her face: *Why? What's the matter?*

"We've got company downstairs," he said.

Fred slid to the floor and reached beneath the bed. When he stood, he was holding the pump-action shotgun he kept there. A gift from Lou DiNapoli. Fred chambered a shell. The action made a soft *clack-clack* sound. He felt sure that whoever was downstairs would never hear it.

More shuffling sounds from the lower floor. Closer to the staircase that led upstairs. Heavy footsteps trying to be stealthy but failing. Fred peered from the bedroom into the dark hallway, the shotgun's barrel leading the way. He could just make out the staircase, its lower end lit dimly by street light that filtered in though a downstairs window.

He could hear the muffled ratcheting of the phone's dial as his wife called the police from behind the closet's closed door. He stepped into the hallway and crouched low at the upper landing of this narrow, walled staircase. To get to him and his family, an intruder would have to climb it—and walk into a perfect killing zone for Fred's shotgun.

Probably a couple of them, Fred thought. *Get them all on the stairs, then let them have it.*

The heavy footsteps were very close to the lower landing. Fred still could not see the intruders. He tightened his grip on the shotgun. Nestled his finger firmly against the trigger. Held his breath. He could feel his pounding heartbeat.

Any second now...

A moment of silence that seemed to last an eternity. A darkened emptiness that was crowded with invisible assailants somewhere below, their breathing so heavy that he could feel but not quite hear it.

Wait for it...

And wait he did. But no shadowy figures materialized. Suddenly, there were scuffling sounds. A sharp *thump* by the base of the stairs, quickly followed by another. Two loud *thuds* as heavy objects hit the floor, like sacks of potatoes—or bodies. A few seconds later, the sound of things being dragged toward the back door. Men's voices speaking low, the words unclear but the accent of the New York City streets unmistakable. The sound of the back door closing, then stillness in the house. A car's wheels crunched to a stop on the gravel driveway.

Still cradling the shotgun, Fred made his way downstairs. Nobody was there, nothing was out of place. From a window, he saw the shadowy silhouettes of four men stuffing two slack human forms into the trunk of the idling car. The trunk lid was slammed shut. The shadowy figures retrieved what appeared to be baseball bats from the ground and tossed them into the car. One figure turned toward the house and saw Fred in the window. The figure made a slight, downward-pushing motion with his open hands that meant *Take it easy,* followed by a "thumbs-up" signal: *Everything's under control.*

Then they were gone.

An hour later, after Fred's shotgun had long been returned to its hiding place, a police car arrived. The lone officer took Fred's report with eyes that were heavy from sleep and disinterest. The steel mills owned the cops, too. From the chief of police down to the lowest flatfoot, the unspoken rule of thumb was *let the union scum and the niggers kill each other all they like.*

"No blood, nothing taken," the officer noted as he stifled a yawn.

Then he was gone, too.

Later that day, it all made more sense to Fred O'Hara. The afternoon newspaper reported that the bodies of two local thugs had been found by the banks of the Ohio River. *An obvious example of union violence,* a police official stated. Their skulls had been shattered by blows from a blunt object, plus three bullets were added to each skull for insurance.

Fred recognized the victim's names. Tom Houlihan had used them many times before for the union's dirty work.

A telegram sat on Fred's desk at the union hall. Its message was brief: *I've got your back.* Its signature: *Your Brother.* Fred smiled as he folded the telegram and stuffed it into the pocket of his suit jacket.

Chapter Forty-Four

It became clear to Allegra Wise very quickly that this was not going to be an easy interview. The modest Chicago home of Isaac and Sarah Linker, David Linker's parents, had an air of melancholy and pain about it. Like a shrine to a lost son, pictures of David—a few in uniform, most not—were everywhere. It was obvious that Allegra's visit was tearing at the 16-year-old wound of their son's strange death once again. A wound that would not heal.

Sarah Linker, a plump woman in her mid-50s, sat on the living room sofa, dabbing at her moist, reddened eyes with a handkerchief. Isaac Linker, still lean and spry despite his advancing years, sat next to his wife and held her hand tenderly in his, the weathered hands of a working man. What Allegra had just told the Linkers had stunned them to silence for a moment.

Allegra was riveted by Isaac's piercing eyes. She was a bit intimidated by them, too.

"David was wise beyond his years," Isaac said in a low and gravelly voice, as he clutched his wife's hand tighter. "He wanted to be a lawyer, you know."

"He was accepted at the University of Chicago," Sarah Linker added, her soft voice beginning to tremble, "but he enlisted…" Her voice trailed off. She buried her face in her hands. "My only child! Buried across the ocean! We can't even afford to visit his grave." No more words would come, only the mournful sounds of a mother still grieving for her son.

Now Isaac was fighting back the tears. "A moment, please, Miss?" he asked of Allegra. It was a respectful demand, not a question. He took his wife in his arms.

Allegra took a sip of the tea she had been offered and tried to shake the feeling that she, too, was on the verge of tears. She had interviewed many people touched by tragedy, but the Linkers were different. With quiet dignity, they left no doubt that they had suffered not only a loss but an injustice that would never be explained or corrected.

And I'm going to bust my ass to get that explanation, Allegra vowed silently.

Her eyes scanned the living room, stopping on each picture of David. No matter the age of the boy in the photo—from toddler to 18-year-old airman—the look on his face was the same. It was one that you'd see in the portrait of a monarch, a great statesman, or a judge: confident, commanding, unafraid. The look of someone who had it all figured out, not someone who could be so beaten by life that he would choose to end it.

But pictures can fool you, Allegra thought. *I've got to stay objective here. But these poor people…I feel so bad for them.*

Isaac Linker turned back to Allegra. "Somebody is telling a terrible lie, Miss Wise. The army…the Swedes…who knows?" He paused, shaking his head. "But know this…we will never believe our David committed suicide. Never."

Sarah softly reinforced her husband's words. "A lie. A terrible lie."

Isaac Linker was not finished. "Now you tell us some *meshugenah,* some crazyman, says that this *politician* killed our David? Do you have proof?"

"Not yet, Mr. Linker. I only have Mr. Moscone's account."

Isaac threw up his hands in frustration. "What

good will that do? The army closed the book on our David a long time ago. No *meshugenah* is going to make them reopen it."

"Mr. Linker, I came all this way to Chicago to just speak with you. And I'm going to keep traveling until I've tracked down the whole crew of that airplane. Somebody else has got to know something."

The hardened despair written on the Linkers' faces cracked just a bit. They had lived so long without hope—perhaps the tiniest ray was now shining through. Were they no longer alone in the fight to rescue their son's integrity? If this *shiksa* who towered over them was their only hope, so be it.

"Then Godspeed, Miss Wise," Isaac said.

Chapter Forty-Five

Tom Houlihan drummed his fingers with nervous impatience as the bank teller counted out the cash. Four hundred and fifty-six dollars—all that was left in his account. He did not even bother to count it himself. He hurried from the bank, hopped in his station wagon, and started driving.

As he drove south along Highway 41, the swamps of South Florida had never seemed so empty, so worthless, so endless. A road passing through nowhere, going nowhere. A barren reminder of the collapse of his grand scheme.

That fucking O'Hara's protected! Go figure! He's got some big friends...God knows who they are...and now I've got maybe two mobs trying to kill me.

The only thing on Tom Houlihan's mind now was survival. He would get no money from the Pilchers to pay off his debt to the Caputo family. He had to run for his life.

He would try to lay low for a while at a little bar on Marathon Key that an old friend owned. Ditch the car. Stay out of sight. Get off a letter to the wife telling her to extend her visit with the relatives in Ireland indefinitely. *Sorry, babe,* the letter would say, *but there ain't nothing to come back to, anyway.*

Maybe the Caputos will forget about the money...or maybe I can catch a boat to Mexico.

Maybe Hell could freeze over, too. How could I have played this thing so damned wrong?

Chapter Forty-Six

The beginning of Joe Gelardi's *leave of absence* from MIT was only a few days away; the tying up of administrative loose ends that would make the leave possible was almost complete. The exhilaration he had felt after escaping the meeting with the chairman last week had faded quickly, though. The real weight of the issues he faced quickly began to crush back down on him.

It was not just the money. He would make a better salary as a staff mathematician at IBM, one that he could only dream of at MIT. He felt fairly sure he had made peace with IBM's proprietary claims on his work, yet the job offer remained unsigned. Two other obstacles continued to block the path to decision and wrench his very soul.

First, he loved to teach. There was nothing quite like seeing the already brilliant students grow under his tutelage, as the bright academic light that shone within each of them burned with ever-increasing intensity. As intellectually rewarding as pure mathematical research would be to him, he doubted it would ever fill the void that ceasing to teach these bright young minds would create.

But if I ever expect to teach at this place again, I've got to conquer these panic attacks. I can't undo David Linker's death. Let it go. It's over. Done.

But that was the same lie he had told himself countless times before.

Second, Diane did not want to leave Boston. She was quite emphatic when she cried, "Armonk? Where on earth is that? And what's going to happen to me there? I belong *here*, Daddy!"

Joe tried to make her see that moving would hardly be an end to anything. There would be new schools, new friends—not a cessation but an enhancement of an already rich and exciting existence. But their visit to IBM's headquarters at Armonk, New York, complete with a tour of the community, had driven Diane into a silent funk that lasted the long drive back to Brookline.

At the breakfast table the following morning, Diane made her proclamation. "I won't live there, Daddy. I *have* to stay here. I can't leave my school and my friends. *You* have to stay here, too."

Mrs. Riley, their housekeeper, decided this might be a very good time to go to the basement and start some laundry. She did not want to be seen as hovering over this discussion, despite having a vested interest. She had been with the Gelardis for almost seven years, ever since Mary had walked out. If Joe and Diane moved away, she would need another job. Well into her 50s, she was not eager to be back on the job market. The years with the Gelardis had been good, for the most part. She had hoped to drag this job out until she hit Social Security.

Joe did his best to keep this discussion with Diane open, civil, and logical. "And why would *I* have to stay here, sweetheart?" he asked.

"Because you're loyal to MIT and you love your job."

"Of course I'm loyal to MIT. I've spent my whole academic and professional life there. But maybe it's time for me...for *us*...to move on."

The look of pain on Diane's face was proof that she did not agree. "I *have* to stay here, Daddy," she repeated.

"Okay, fine. Let's say, for argument's sake, that you stayed. Where would you live, sweetheart? You're thirteen."

With the myopic optimism that young people often mistake for wisdom, she replied, "I'll live with Meredith! And I'm nearly fourteen!"

Joe wished he had not let out that little laugh, for that was all it took to drive his daughter to indignation and tears. She stormed from the table.

"Diane...honey, wait."

She stopped in her tracks, but she would not turn to face him.

"Sweetheart, you've got to be realistic about this. Sure, you and Meredith have hit it off...you do homework together..."

Diane interrupted. "We do lots of other good stuff, too."

"I'm sure you do, honey...I'm sure you do. But she's almost nineteen. She's got her hands full with her own life. I've told you a hundred times how hard it is to be a young woman at MIT."

"So? She can handle it. So can I."

"I know you can, honey...and your time will come. Sooner than you think."

"It's still five years away. That's forever, Daddy."

"No, it's not, Diane. Don't rush yourself. Just take things as they come. Now come back and finish your breakfast."

Diane trudged back to the table and toyed with her food. Twice she started to say something but then changed her mind.

"What? What do you want to say?" Joe asked.

Without looking up from her plate, Diane asked, "What about Mrs. Riley?"

"Oh, honey...don't worry. I'll help her find

another position. Somebody at the Institute is always looking for good help."

But Mrs. Riley was not the only thing still on Diane's mind. Hesitantly, she said, "It's just that... I'm afraid..."

"Afraid of what, honey?"

She sighed. She might as well just spit it out. "I'm afraid that if you're not on the faculty, Daddy, I'll have much less of a chance of getting into MIT."

Joe sat motionless at the table, dumbfounded. As Diane gathered her schoolbooks, Mrs. Riley reappeared in the kitchen.

"Hurry, child, or you'll miss your bus," the housekeeper said.

"I'm going...I'm going," Diane replied. She gave Mrs. Riley a peck on the cheek and headed out the door. She was careful not to slam it. She did not want her father to think she was still mad. Once she had gotten *that* off her chest, her anger had quickly drained.

There. I said it. All I can do now is wait and see, Diane thought as she hurried to the bus stop.

Mrs. Riley stared silently at Joe for a moment, arms crossed. Joe knew that look on her weathered face very well. When it was flashed his way, it could mean only one thing: *For a big genius, you can be a real dumbshit sometimes.*

Finally, Mrs. Riley broke the uncomfortable silence. "She's right, isn't she, Professor?"

Joe nodded, but he knew what she asked was not really a question. It was just a statement of the obvious from a woman who had spent her life observing the mechanism of society from beneath. It was no secret that his daughter was academically brilliant. But he had never realized just how astute she had become in the ways of the world until that moment.

As Joe scanned his small, cluttered MIT office, pondering what to take home and what to leave during the *leave of absence,* the math department secretary appeared in his doorway. She nodded toward the reception area—there was a tall, well-dressed woman standing there. The secretary said, "Doctor Gelardi, you have a visitor...that reporter who phoned yesterday."

The tall woman rose to meet Joe as he entered the reception area. "Allegra Wise, CBS News," she announced, flashing press credentials. "Can I steal a few minutes of your time, Doctor Gelardi?"

They settled into Joe's office. Allegra marveled that it was crammed full of books on mathematics; *I didn't think there were this many math books in the whole world.* One wall was covered by a blackboard, full of equations. There were many photos scattered about the office of a cute, auburn-haired girl, spanning the ages from toddler to teenager.

"Your daughter?" Allegra asked.

"Yes, my daughter Diane."

Allegra also noticed there were no photos of a wife; the man she faced across the desk did not wear a wedding ring. *I've heard these academic types can be tough to live with. He does seem to be in another world at the moment...really ill at ease...in some kind of rush. His eyes are darting around like he's taking inventory. This might be a little tougher than I thought.*

"So what can I do you out of, Miss Wise? It is *Miss* Wise?"

Ahh, that's interesting...an attempt at humor yet without the flirtatious tone. He's nervous. Great! Nervous guys can be very talkative.

"Yeah, it's *miss.* But please call me Ally."

"All right, Ally...Now what would CBS News want with me? I'm very pressed for time."

"I'll be brief. You were an airman during the war, correct?"

"Yes. I was a navigator in the Eighth Air Force."

"I've done some checking. You served with Congressman Leonard Pilcher."

Allegra was stunned by the sudden change in Joe's demeanor. *Whoa! He didn't like the sound of that one bit. He turned away like I slapped him or something. I'm hitting a nerve somewhere...Tread carefully now, Ally.*

Joe turned to the window; his eyes became fixed on something far in the distance. He paused a few moments before answering. "Yes, I was in Pilcher's crew."

"On *The Lady M?*" she asked.

Joe nodded.

"You're aware he's seeking the Republican nomination for president?"

"Of course. I read the papers."

"Would you vote for him?"

"This is Massachusetts. We tend to vote for Democrats."

Allegra laughed. *Should have seen that one coming.*

"Were you and the congressman interned together in Sweden?"

Joe's face flushed. He seemed irritated now.

Oh boy, Allegra thought, *talk about hitting a nerve!*

"Unfortunately, yes...we were," he replied.

"And Anthony Moscone was there, too?"

"Well, he was there in body, anyway...if you know what I mean."

Allegra nodded as she checked her notebook.

"Doctor Gelardi, perhaps you'd care to comment on the Congressman's remark that he was 'one of those crazy heroes who bombed Germany?'"

Joe became incredulous, asking, "He said that? He actually had the nerve to say that?"

Allegra patted her notebook like it was the source of all wisdom. "Yep. Heard it with my own two ears."

There was a long pause before Joe began to speak again. "Well, Miss Wise...Ally...that's simply not true. We bombed France on two milk runs. Then we dropped our last load on some fish in the Baltic on our way to Sweden. Nothing heroic about any of that...not in the least."

Allegra was writing furiously in her notebook. Without looking up, she asked, "That's very interesting. Fred O'Hara told me pretty much the same thing...minus the fish part. May I quote you on that?"

His answer was abrupt. "I prefer you do not, Miss Wise."

Allegra took his refusal with a poker face. *No matter...anonymous sources work fine if they're all saying the same thing.*

Joe now seemed a bit startled. "You've spoken to Fred? I haven't seen or spoken to him since...that day."

She paused to recalibrate her questioning.

"So, Pilcher, his crew, and that plane flew a total of three missions?"

"That's correct."

This is so fine, she thought as she tried not to smile. *He flies only three missions and high-tails it to Sweden...and it's confirmed! War hero, my ass!*

Allegra turned a page in her notebook with what seemed to be a grand flourish. She did not mean it to be a dramatic prelude to her next question. She was simply on a roll at the moment and needed a blank page in a hurry.

"What can you tell me about the death of David Linker, Doctor Gelardi?"

She swore she could detect the slightest tremor in Joe as he heard the question. *Did he just tremble? A little hard to tell...He's been so damned twitchy the whole time.*

He gestured with his hands before speaking—both raised, open, palms up, signifying *Who knows?* "Can't tell you much of anything, I'm afraid," he said.

Allegra winced. She struggled to keep a pleading tone from her voice. "The people I've talked to so far...your fellow crewmen, Mr. Moscone and Mr. O'Hara, plus David Linker's parents...all refuse to believe David Linker committed suicide. Mr. Moscone's mental state is, of course, in question...and O'Hara wasn't even in Sweden. But you were, Doctor Gelardi. Do *you* think it was a suicide?"

"I'm not a psychiatrist or a policeman, Miss Wise. I can't help you any more than that. Now, if you'll excuse me, I must be going."

"Wait! Can I buy you lunch, perhaps?"

"No time. I'm in quite a hurry, Miss Wise."

"Maybe we can finish this later? Tonight, perhaps?"

"We're already finished, Miss Wise. I have nothing to add."

She handed him her business card. He stuffed it into his briefcase along with some papers from his desk.

Allegra added one more request: "If you think of anything...anything at all...please call me."

Outside the building where she had just met with Joe Gelardi, the taxicab was waiting for Allegra.

"Dispatcher says you wanna go to the Greyhound

station, right?" the driver asked as he threw her bulky suitcase into the trunk.

"Yeah. And step on it...I'm running late."

"Ooookay, lady...anything you say. Where're you headed?"

"Nashua, New Hampshire."

"That ain't much of a drive," the cabbie said. "How about I take you there?"

Allegra crooked an eyebrow and opened the negotiation with a demand: "Off the meter."

After a few moments of haggling, they agreed on a price.

Allegra had no idea that at that same moment, Joe Gelardi was hunched over a toilet. So shaken was he by her visit, his body convulsed with dry heaves which persisted long after the stomach had emptied its contents.

Chapter Forty-Seven

It had not been such a great day for flying. By the time Fred O'Hara had set down his twin-engined Piper at Teterboro, he was physically and mentally exhausted. The line of storms, bringing March snow to the inland areas and a cold, harsh rain to the East Coast, had proved an almost impossible challenge for an airman to get around or through. But he had found his way, bumped and battered by turbulence and the ever-present danger of airframe icing. He now sat in an office in a small warehouse in the Bronx, sipping coffee with Lou DiNapoli.

"Shitty flight, eh?" Lou asked as he took another bite of his chocolate bar.

"You know it, brother," Fred replied. "Thought I was going to have to turn back for sure."

"It's gotta be really bad for you to think about turning back, Freddy."

Lou picked up a snub-nosed revolver from the table and began idly spinning the cylinder. He turned to the large window that looked out on the warehouse floor. A ring of cars—expensive, flashy sedans—were parked there. A dozen tough-looking characters—Lou's men—lounged against the cars. A few had baseball bats in their hands.

In the center of the ring, suspended from a ceiling-mounted hoist, was a man—upside down, bound, and blindfolded—his head swaying a few feet off the floor. Lou's men took turns taunting their suspended captive with invectives and jabs from the fat end of a baseball bat. Blood began to drip from the captive's face, forming a small pool on the floor below.

Behind the glass window of the office, Lou and Fred could not hear the taunts, but every jab with the bat caused a moan they could hear softly but clearly. The spectacle was making Fred a bit squeamish. Lou noticed Fred's discomfort and began to laugh.

"What's the matter with you? You've done worse yourself," Lou said, placing the pistol into a holster on his belt.

Fred shrugged. "Yeah, I have, haven't I?"

"No shit, killer," Lou replied, popping another piece of chocolate into his mouth.

"What did that poor fucker do, anyway?" Fred asked.

Lou popped the last piece of the chocolate bar into his mouth before answering. "Let's just say that he *disappointed* me."

"Hmm...You guys sure like your baseball bats," Fred said. "Couldn't help but notice them that night at my place."

"Let's just say that they're very effective weapons in certain circumstances...affordable yet versatile." Lou turned serious. "But speaking of disappointments, can you believe the shit that scumbag Pilcher's putting out? Like he's some kind of fucking war hero?"

Fred let out a derisive laugh. "What did you expect?" Then he, too, turned serious. "Did that skirt reporter get ahold of you?"

Shaking his head, Lou let out a derisive laugh of his own. "Freddy, Freddy, Freddy...Of course not. We don't talk to the press in this line of work." After a brief pause, he added, "Neither should you."

"I didn't tell her shit, Louie...aside from the fact that Picher is a lying scumbag. And what do we know about what happened in Sweden, anyway? We had our own fucking problems, remember?"

Lou's face took on a pensive look. He remembered all too well.

Fred stood and began to pace the room. "That son-of-a-bitch Pilcher needs to get dead, Louie. Right now."

Lou moaned. "You gonna start with this shit again?"

"You've gotta help me with this thing, Louie..."

Lou jumped to his feet. "Listen to me! I told you before...this ain't my fight. I ain't getting involved with pushing the button on no politician. Not for that."

"We spent almost a year in the Stalag Luft because of that chickenshit coward, Lou!"

"We made a choice, remember? Besides, what took you so fucking long?" Lou mimicked Fred's words with a mocking, whiny tone. "I'm gonna kill him, Louie...I'm gonna kill him!" His voice turned serious again. "Gimme a break, Freddy. It's been sixteen fucking years. Just forget about this shit, OK?"

Dejected, Fred slumped into a chair. This was not what he wanted to hear. Lou put a comforting hand on Fred's shoulder.

"But I'll tell you what I will do," Lou said. "All you little chatterboxes are gonna need someone watching your asses now. You and Tony, at least...that's for damn sure. You screw with the Pilcher family and you just might be the ones getting dead. You didn't really expect to crap in their faces with that endorsement bullshit and walk away clean, did you? Houlihan coming after you was small potatoes compared to the shit storm that kind of money can bring."

"I've been fighting the Pilcher family for years, Louie. It ain't nothing new."

On the warehouse floor, Lou's men cut down the

hostage. He crashed to the floor, whimpering and struggling against his bonds.

Lou surveyed the scene out the window. "See? We didn't hurt him so bad. We ain't fucking barbarians...we're businessmen."

Chapter Forty-Eight

The New Hampshire primary, the kickoff event to the presidential election season, was just two days away. Nashua was a forest of campaign signs and banners. Everywhere Allegra Wise looked, the work of the small army that made up Leonard Pilcher's campaign staff had managed to outdo that of the other candidates by at least two to one. PILCHER FOR PRESIDENT, the campaign signs screamed in bold letters. Some signs added the message AN AMERICAN HERO. Others added COURAGE YOU CAN COUNT ON.

Pilcher's daddy sure is pumping a ton of money into this race, Allegra thought as she wolfed down a sandwich and coffee. The quaint Main Street restaurant in which she was dining had red, white, and blue bunting draped across its facade. The CBS sound truck was parked on the street outside. The unit director held up five fingers to the restaurant window for her to see. That gesture meant she would be on the air—live—in five minutes, for the first time in her career.

She pulled the compact from her purse and checked her face. *Good thing this is just a voice-over without video...I look like shit.*

After the semi-successful interview with Joe Gelardi, the cab trip from Boston to Nashua had been quick and relatively relaxing. It had given her enough time and solitude to perfect her 30-second report on the Pilcher campaign for an evening news TV broadcast. She was ready to throw some stones at Pilcher's *hero* nonsense, coast to coast. She had enough solid information to go on now. Allegra had held her breath while the producer read the proposed on-air report she had just dictated from the restaurant's phone booth. After an agonizing silence, the producer said, "So now we've got two sources...*sane* sources...confirming the three missions and the internment angle..."

But the alleged murder angle would have to remain on ice for the time being.

After one last sip of coffee, Allegra Wise stepped out to the street and approached the microphone that had been set up on the sidewalk. She smoothed her skirt, trying to keep her knees completely covered, hopefully hiding that they were knocking together from nervousness.

The unit director began the countdown to air by raising his hands, all fingers extended. One by one, those fingers folded into the palm until the last remaining finger was transformed from the tick of a second to a pointer—one that was pointing straight at Allegra. She was amazed how composed she felt as her words started to flow.

"As we approach the beginning of the presidential primary season here in New Hampshire," Allegra began, "this reporter has uncovered new information concerning underdog candidate Leonard Pilcher. The congressman's claim of *being a hero that bombed Germany* may well be something of an exaggeration. Informed sources say that Mr. Pilcher spent a considerable portion of his time overseas as an internee in Sweden, safely out of combat after only three missions, and never actually dropped a bomb on German soil..."

The unit director's hand was up again, its fingers counting down the last five seconds of the voice-over segment. Allegra was pleased when she spoke the final word of her report just as the last finger retracted and his hand became a closed fist.

"And we're out," the director said. "Good job, Allegra."

Yeah! It was a good job, she thought, clearly pleased with herself. *Keep this up and I might even get my mug on camera soon.*

Chapter Forty-Nine

Tony Moscone pulled the collar of his pea coat tight around his neck against the late night chill. Stuffing his hands into the coat's pockets, he made his way quickly down the deserted Philadelphia street. The white pants of his kitchen worker's uniform, still sporting the splatters from a day's work at the hotel, seemed to give off an eerie glow in the light from the street lamps.

A noise: a car's engine started, then settled into a hum that sounded barely above idle speed. Tony glanced over his shoulder to see a dark, nondescript sedan rounding the corner, a car just like the ones police detectives drove. It fell in behind him, keeping pace. He walked a little faster. It was only two more blocks to his house.

The car's engine suddenly revved faster. The dark vehicle sped past him a car length, then lurched to a stop as the front doors flew open and two men jumped out. They wore suits, ties, overcoats, and fedoras—just like Dick Tracy.

The beefier of the two stepped in front of Tony, blocking his path. The other, tall and lean, circled behind him to prevent an escape back up the street.

"You're going to have to come with us," the beefy one said.

Tony's reply was loud and full of panic. "WHAT? WHAT THE HELL DID I DO?"

The men in suits closed in.

"GET THE FUCK AWAY FROM ME! HELP! HELP! POLICE!"

The lean one laughed. "We *are* the police,

numbnuts."

They grabbed Tony and dragged him toward the car. The lean cop held one of Tony's wrists in a hammerlock. He slapped a handcuff on it and grabbed for the other wrist, which was flailing wildly.

"Settle down, shithead," the beefy one said as he slammed Tony's head against the car.

Two more cars rounded the corner with a squeal of tires—but these were much too flashy to be carrying policemen. They squealed to a stop, bracketing the police car. Half a dozen men—silent men holding their unbuttoned overcoats closed—spilled from the cars and advanced toward Tony's assailants.

The two cops arrogantly stood their ground and flashed their badges, hands resting on pistols still not drawn. The silent men produced baseball bats from beneath their coats and deftly swatted the badges from the cops' hands.

The cops tried to pull their pistols. They were swatted away, too—with much more force this time. The two cops crumpled to the pavement, clutching their shattered hands to their chests. For good measure, they pummeled the cops with body blows from their bats for a few moments before the silent men climbed back into their flashy cars and sped off. The groaning cops were left sprawled in the gutter.

Tony Moscone might have enjoyed seeing his assailants beaten to a pulp, but he was long gone. As soon as the first blow from a bat had been struck, he had fled up the street to his house, a set of handcuffs still dangling from one wrist. He had never seen the faces of the silent men who saved him.

It had been several days since the attack, and Tony Moscone still refused to leave the house. He hid behind the locked door of his second-floor bedroom, only stealing out to grab some food from the kitchen or use the toilet when he felt sure that his sister was sleeping or out shopping. He had managed, with great difficulty, to remove the handcuff by sawing through it with a hacksaw, an arduous process that had dulled several blades and taken the better part of a day. During all this, his sister periodically stood outside his door, screaming obscenities and warning, "You'd better get your ass to work, Anthony!"

He had already missed three shifts at the hotel kitchen. No doubt, they had fired him.

Tony's dingy, cluttered room looked more like an electronics repair shop than a proper sleeping space. A battered wooden table against a wall served as the main workbench, its top surface scorched by soldering irons like some wood burning craft project gone awry. In his self-imprisonment, he had kept himself busy fixing the old radios and television sets others had left at curbs and in alleys for the trash man. They were stacked everywhere, in various states of disassembly. Some had taken temporary residence on the narrow bed, so he slept on the floor that night. It was easier than making room someplace else for them or trying to sleep among the sharp metal edges and fragile glass vacuum tubes that bristled from the exposed chassis.

The next morning, as he put the finishing touches on a TV that he had just brought back to life, he heard a car pull up to the curb. He peeked out the window.

It's one of them flashy jobs...like those guys who saved my ass drove.

A knock on the door. There was none of the usual tirade his sister hurled at unwelcome visitors, which included practically everyone on the planet. *I guess she ain't home,* Tony surmised.

Another knock. Tony peeked out the window again. There were two guys in suits—one leaning on the Cadillac, the other on the doorstep. Tony tried to duck away from the window, but the guy leaning on the car spotted him and called out, "HEY, MR. MOSCONE...WE'VE GOT A MESSAGE FROM YOUR OLD WAR BUDDY, LOU DINAPOLI."

Louie DiNapoli...from The Lady! If these guys are doing his bidding, he sure must be doing okay for himself.

Tony went downstairs and opened the door.

The guy on the steps said, "Too bad you didn't stick around the other night...we gave them two scumbag cops a good beating for you. Them dirty bastards won't be bothering you no more. Anyway, Mr. DiNapoli has a deal he'd like to offer you..."

Chapter Fifty

The after-dinner coffee in his cup had long turned cold. Joe Gelardi rose from the kitchen table and walked to the stove. The percolator Mrs. Riley had left was still hot. He poured himself a fresh cup.

Mrs. Riley had left the old table-top radio on, too. Joe had paid it no attention as he was staring pensively at the document on the table, but now the excited male voice from the radio, spitting words in machine-gun patter, seized his attention. Joe stopped in his tracks. He could not believe what this voice was saying:

With 95 percent of the vote counted, Congressman Leonard Pilcher has received a totally unexpected 46 percent to the vice president's 48 percent. Here at Richard Nixon's New Hampshire headquarters, what should be an air of jubilation is instead one of deep concern. To the vice president and his campaign staff, this most narrow of victories in what should have been a cakewalk is as good as a loss. This primary changes the complexion of the Republican race completely...

In the Gelardi dining room, Meredith Salinger watched as Diane struggled with a problem in the Calculus. Diane fussed; the radio in the kitchen was disturbing her concentration.

"Daddy, could you *please* turn that down?"

But Joe did not seem to hear her. He was motionless. *Shell-shocked,* Meredith thought.

The radio voice feverishly continued: *What seemed like a sideshow last month has turned into a Cinderella story. This race may have just begun, but Leonard Pilcher could indeed end up winning his party's nomination for president. We now take you to Pilcher Campaign Headquarters...*

Both girls were startled as Joe's coffee cup slipped from his hands and crashed to the table. The hot coffee splattered all over the document on the table—the still-unsigned employment offer from IBM.

"Daddy, are you okay? Daddy?"

Joe did not answer. He did not even look his daughter's way.

Fred O'Hara was anything but motionless. In his living room, he had been listening to the same radio broadcast as Joe Gelardi—and flinging anything he could get his hands on in a drunken rage. The whiskey bottle he had just drained was only the latest missile.

His hands seized a heavy metal paperweight—embossed with military aviator's wings—from the desk. In an instant, it, too, was flying. It struck a wall full of framed family photos, some of which clattered to the hardwood floor, leaving a minefield of broken glass and crumbled plaster.

Fred slumped back against the sofa, awaiting the remorse he knew would set in shortly. Remorse for the drinking, remorse for the destruction to his home—and remorse that Leonard Pilcher still drew breath.

Allegra Wise gathered the collar of her stylish spring coat tightly around her neck as she shivered in the cold March night. She cursed her choice of outer garments: *Dammit! Screw fashion...it's still winter up here.* The streets of downtown Nashua, New Hampshire, were still teeming with people on this primary night, many of them abuzz about the amazing showing of Leonard Pilcher at the ballot box. She corralled a middle-aged couple, their practical but obviously inexpensive clothes marking them as working class locals. She thrust the microphone of her miniature reel-to-reel tape recorder toward them and asked, "How do you feel about those who say Leonard Pilcher is too young, too inexperienced to be president?"

The man responded with typical New England skepticism. "Hell, what did all of Eisenhower's experience get us? Got us pushed around by them commies, that's all. That Pilcher boy's proved himself a leader...he's a damn war hero, for crying out loud! A real *fighting* war hero."

His wife chimed in with great enthusiasm. "He seems like such an upstanding young man, from a fine family." She paused, a scowl crossing her face. "And he won't be taking no orders from the Pope of Rome, neither...not like that Kennedy boy."

The couple turned and bustled off down the street before Allegra could ask another question. Exasperated, she scanned up and down the sidewalk for another interviewee. She did not notice Tad Matthews in a doorway across the street, pointing her out to an unsmiling man in a trench coat—a *Hard-Boiled Man* with an air of quiet violence about him.

Chapter Fifty-One

The air was still and deadly quiet in Max Pilcher's office, like the eye of a hurricane or the sudden lull just before the tornado swirls in and lays waste to everything in its path. Max felt his anger surging as he took in the sight of his insolent son, lounging in an armchair, pouting; Leonard Pilcher was never one to take criticism well.

"I'm going to say it again, Lenny...maybe it will get through your thick skull this time. That *war hero* crack was an asinine move, son."

Leonard continued to study his fingernails as he replied, "Aren't you the one who always says *tell them the lie they want to hear?*"

With those words, the storm front had finally arrived. Max had had quite enough of this imbecilic lout.

"YEAH...AS LONG AS IT WON'T COME BACK AND BITE YOU IN THE ASS, YOU IDIOT. I HATE TO BREAK THIS TO YOU, LENNY, BUT YOU AIN'T NO FUCKING WAR HERO. THE PRESS IS GOING TO HAVE A FIELD DAY ON YOUR STUPID ASS."

The younger Pilcher remained slouched in the chair, unmoved by his father's tirade. He answered only with a shrug.

Tad Matthews picked this inopportune moment to enter the office. He immediately sensed the familiar tension in the air, stopped in his tracks, and turned to exit. "Oh...I'll come back," Matthews said.

But Max Pilcher waved Matthews into the office impatiently. "No, no, Matthews. Get in here. We've got to get the spotlight off this Sweden bullshit."

The elder Pilcher put his hand on his chin, deep in thought. Tad Matthews stood and waited. He had no idea what Max had in mind.

Leonard Pilcher puffed his cheeks and forced out the breath through pursed lips. It made a sound like a wet fart. His father took no notice.

A moment later, with his mental calculations complete, Max Pilcher turned to Matthews and said, "Get the Pentagon on the phone...I need to talk with General Brown."

Chapter Fifty-Two

The bright lighting of the television studio complimented the suntanned face of the man in the blue military uniform. He was led by a stagehand to one of two comfortable-looking chairs that faced the TV cameras. The cameras were bulky, standing as tall as a man on their pedestals, and appeared to weigh a great deal as their operators rolled them across the studio floor. To the man in the blue uniform, they looked intimidating, like one-eyed robots closing in for the kill. A small circular table separated the chairs. Another stagehand placed two mugs of water on the table. The cups bore the TV station's logo: a large number 7, surrounded by its call sign, KLAX, Los Angeles.

Senior Master Sergeant Ed Morris, US Air Force, picked up one of the cups and took a sip. The chair proved very comfortable, but he found it hard to relax. He had been traveling for over 36 hours, all the way across the Pacific from a place called Saigon, Vietnam. It had been just him and the flight crew on the mammoth C-124 transport plane. The aircraft commander, a major who was an old-timer like Morris, had said, "You're either some kind of hero, Sarge, or you're in real deep shit to have a big bird like this sent just for you."

Ed Morris was very tired from the journey. Usually he could sleep like a baby on any airplane on which he was not a crew member. But this time, the droning of the four big piston engines had not had their usual, sleep-inducing effect. There was much on his mind. He felt more like a prisoner being brought to trial than a career military man with a chest full of decorations. Since being *The Lady M's* flight engineer all those years ago, he had done and learned much. Once released from internment in Sweden, he had gone to the Pacific and flown against Japan on B-29s. When the Korean War broke out, he was among the first bomber crews in the fight. He had learned the workings of US military aircraft inside and out. His knowledge and experience were much valued in the Air Force.

This unplanned odyssey had begun two days ago. He was summoned from the air base where he was serving as team leader of a small group of American aircraft maintenance advisors to the fledgling South Vietnamese Air Force. Their mission was clandestine; the United States had no official military presence in this little-known Southeast Asian country locked in conflict with its Communist brothers to the north. Morris and his men were teaching the South Vietnamese how to care for the aging but still-capable combat aircraft the American government had provided in the hope of keeping the South from becoming another toppled Asian domino.

The man he had been summoned to see was Colonel Johnson, the commander of the support squadron. While technically Morris's boss, the two hardly knew each other. They had only come face-to-face twice before.

The colonel had seemed congenial at first, like an old buddy to the senior NCO standing at parade rest before him. "Got a message here from General Brown," he began in a slow drawl.

Morris was startled. "The chief of staff, sir?"

"Yeah, *that* General Brown. He'd like you, *Sergeant* Morris, to do him a little bitty favor."

Ed Morris felt his insides tighten into a knot. This could not be good.

The colonel picked up a dispatch from his desk and casually flipped it to Morris. "Take your time reading it, Sergeant. Make sure it sinks in real good."

Ed Morris's face dropped as he read. When he was finished, he placed the dispatch on the colonel's desk and returned to the parade rest brace before speaking.

"With all due respect, sir...I'm afraid I ain't got nothing good to say about Congressman Pilcher...then or now."

The congeniality vanished from Johnson's manner. "Well then, *Sergeant* Morris, that's just a damn shame...a real damn shame. You see, I haven't forgotten about those shenanigans at your warehouse last year...Neither has the general."

The colonel paused, making a *tsk-tsk* sound with his tongue as he shook his head with mock sadness. "A fine record like yours, Ed...a year from retirement and your pension...all wiped away by some *silly little oversight.*"

So there it was—blackmail. The *silly little oversight* of which the colonel spoke, when viewed in the harsh light of day-to-day reality, had been merely business as usual in this God-forsaken place. A number of aircraft parts meant for the Vietnamese—several truckloads' worth—had left Morris's warehouse at Tan Son Nhut airbase without any signed documentation indicating who had received them. That was not an unusual occurrence in the bizarre world of Vietnam, where urgency and apathy happily coexisted. In the supposed rush to get grounded planes back into the air, repair parts often vanished from the shelves without a paper trail. Sometimes an overworked supply clerk meant to get to the paperwork later but got sidetracked and forgot. Or the Vietnamese mechanics took the part from the shelf without bothering to go through proper channels.

But most likely, those parts had simply been stolen by South Vietnamese officers and sold on the black market. Genuine American components fetched a high price in the developing world. These officers had spent their entire lives in a country at war with one oppressor after another: the French, the Japanese, the French again, and now their brothers to the north. Conflict was the norm; there was no reason for them to expect it would ever end, so one must learn to profit from it. Now the Americans were here, with their massive affluence, foolish optimism, and naïve misunderstanding of the workings of the world. Profiteering had suddenly become very easy. Theft was endemic. Locks only stopped honest men.

Usually, such losses were just written off the balance sheets, provided that you knew it was missing in the first place. To discover what was missing at any given time, however, you had to be constantly taking inventory, and nobody—certainly not Ed Morris's little team—had the time or manpower for that.

This particular loss would have escaped without consequence but for a surprise visit by some inspector general and his team. This IG was bucking for his first star and needed to make a name for himself. His auditors did their usual thorough scouring of the logistical records and uncovered over two-hundred thousand US dollars' worth of replacement parts unaccounted for. That was enough money to send the responsible party to federal prison for 20 years. Senior Master Sergeant Edwin Morris was that responsible party.

It had looked really bad for Morris at first. He would be found guilty no matter how they looked at it. If the stuff was deemed stolen, the poor security and inventory control that had allowed the theft to occur and remain undetected made him guilty of negligence and inattention to duty. Or, if he colluded in the undocumented transactions, he was guilty of conspiracy and theft from the US government. Either way, he was going to Leavenworth, stripped of rank and benefits. A statement of charges was prepared. Court martial proceedings were scheduled. The new commander of the support squadron—Colonel Johnson, fresh from the States—had confined him to quarters pending trial. That was the first time Morris had met his new boss.

Then, in keeping with the bizarre character of life in Southeast Asia, the political winds shifted. Two State Department types—sweating buckets in their tropical worsted suits, custom made in Hong Kong—had paid Colonel Johnson a visit. Behind closed doors, the men from State said, "To proceed with a court martial, there would need to be a detailed investigation...and the findings of such an investigation might prove embarrassing to our Vietnamese allies. Therefore, Washington has mandated that this matter be dropped immediately."

What was a few dollars in aircraft parts between friends, anyway?

Shortly thereafter, Morris was released from confinement to quarters and summoned to Colonel Johnson, who breezily informed him, "Certain parties above my pay grade have decided to put this little matter on hold. But be advised, Sergeant Morris...this matter will not be forgotten."

Still braced at parade rest, Ed Morris's eyes drifted to the dispatch on the colonel's desk. *He was certainly right about the "not being forgotten" part,* Morris thought. *I'm screwed...I either do this PR stunt for the big brass or I lose everything and rot in Leavenworth.*

That fucking Pilcher!

The congeniality had returned to the colonel's face. "Now I'm not trying to play the bad guy here, Ed. I think we can work this out *real* easy..."

So here Ed Morris was, *working it out* in a television studio in Los Angeles. The interviewer who now sat across from him seemed as robotic as the cameras they faced but far less intimidating. In his heavy stage makeup and expensive, tailored clothes, he struck Morris as resembling a woman dressed as a man. Or perhaps a circus clown. The questions the interviewer posed were read straight off a teleprompter, carefully worded to yield the answers that Morris had been told to give by those people *above his pay grade.*

As General Brown, the Air Force Chief of Staff had told Max Pilcher: *What could be better for your boy than a glowing testimonial from a former crew member? And I happen to have just such a crew member readily available."*

It was getting hotter than midday in Saigon under the TV studio lights. The interviewer leaned in for the closing questions.

"So, Sergeant Morris, as you've said in your own words, Leonard Pilcher actually *saved* your life and the rest of his crew's as well. Do you regard that as an act of heroism?"

"Yessir, I do," Morris replied. "Captain Pilcher made the tough decision...the *right* decision." His throat had gone completely dry. Clumsily, he reached for his cup of water. It toppled slightly before he caught hold of it. Some of its contents had landed on the interviewer's trousers.

The interviewer never flinched. Morris was aware

of the cameras moving, readjusting their aim. *Kinda looks like the clown pissed himself,* Morris thought. *I guess they don't want that in the shot.*

"One more question, Sergeant...isn't it against regulations for a member of the military to endorse political candidates?"

Morris smiled, not from happiness but the amusing irony this question provoked. Those *above his pay grade* had said it would be asked *to keep us all honest.* Even though Ed Morris would be lying through his teeth.

"Affirmative, sir," Morris replied. "But I'm not endorsing anyone. I'm just setting the record straight."

The interviewer extended his hand. "Thank you, Sergeant Edwin Morris, for your candor...and your service to your country." Then he turned to the camera and said, "We'll be right back after these words."

Morris rose and walked to the studio exit. The Air Force officer monitoring the interview—a young captain without aviator's wings on his chest—was waiting for him by the door with a smug smile on his face.

What does that pencil-pushing desk jockey think he's grinning at? Morris thought as he returned a look that was anything but a smile. With a tone that flirted with disrespect without crossing that line, he asked the groundling captain, "Am I free to go now, sir?"

The captain nodded and held open the heavy studio door for Morris. As the senior master sergeant made his way down the hall with great purpose, the captain's face still wore that same smug grin.

Still in his dress uniform, Ed Morris sat on a stool in the Los Angeles airport bar and nursed his beer. He still had an hour before his commercial flight to Honolulu departed. From there, he would have to catch a ride on a military transport back to Saigon.

Thank God that bullshit is over, he thought as he took another sip. He felt disgusted and dirty, soiled once again by association with Leonard Pilcher.

Across the bar, a middle-aged man admired the many ribbons adorning Morris's uniform blouse. He caught the sergeant's eye.

"I was in the big one, too," the middle-aged man said. "Twelfth Air Force...North Africa, Italy, France. All that fruit salad you've got...you must be some kind of hero, Sarge."

Morris took a moment before mumbling, "Nah. I ain't rich enough to be no hero."

Chapter Fifty-Three

Tad Matthews knocked on the Manhattan hotel room door for the third time. The first two knocks had been soft and polite, respectful of the early hour. This third knock bordered on an impatient pounding. It did the trick—there was a click as the door unlocked from inside and swung open to reveal a groggy Leonard Pilcher, clad only in boxer shorts.

Inside the dimly lit room, empty liquor bottles and glasses littered the floor. The silhouette of a woman rose from the bed, draped herself with a sheet in one fluid motion, and vanished into the bathroom. Tad could discern enough, even in the darkness, to know the woman was not Mrs. Leonard Pilcher.

Slurring his words, Pilcher asked, "What the hell time is it?"

"Seven-o-five. We need to be at the studio in forty minutes."

Pilcher grumbled and walked back into the room, leaving the door wide open. Tad remained in the hallway.

"Should I call the lady a cab?" Matthews asked, his voice barely above a whisper.

Pilcher gave a dismissive wave of his hand and did not bother to keep his voice down. "Nah. The bitch can call her own goddamn cab."

"We'll be waiting downstairs, Congressman," Matthews said as he pulled the door shut. Alone in the hallway, he did not bother hiding the look of disgust on his face.

Allegra Wise, still in her pajamas, juggled her

cereal bowl in one hand as she fiddled with the rabbit ears of her TV set. Even though it was Sunday morning, she had set an alarm. She had no intention of missing *Meet The Press*. Leonard Pilcher was to be the featured guest.

She plopped onto the couch just as the first question was hurled his way. "Congressman, the story of your internment in Sweden during the war is largely unexplored..."

Pilcher interrupted the panelist. "That's because there's not much to explore, I'm afraid."

The screen image shifted back to the panelist in time to display his look of annoyance at being interrupted. With an even tone, he continued his questioning. "Recently it has come to light that two of your crew died while in Sweden, both reported as suicides. Surely you must feel some regret...and some responsibility...that young men under your command took their own lives in those circumstances?"

Allegra was conflicted at the sound of those words. She was proud to think: *Yeah, recently it has come to light because I'm the one who dragged it into the light.* But at the same time, she was annoyed: *Don't suppose I'll be getting much credit for that, here or anyplace else. Perhaps I've been a little too free with sharing my information around the newsroom.*

Pilcher shifted uneasily in his chair. Affecting a glassy-eyed gaze into the distance, he said, "Well...the simple fact is, those boys who killed themselves, and their buddy, the one who said those outrageous lies about me in a house of God...they were all very troubled boys. I was very concerned about them." Pilcher choked up as he continued. "My only regret is that I didn't have the wisdom back then to take them off flying status before that fateful mission."

If he was faking the emotion, he was doing one hell of a job selling it.

Allegra was furious and wide-eyed with disbelief. Milk and cereal dribbled down her chin as she shrieked at the television, "THAT'S NOT WHAT I HEARD, YOU LYING SACK OF SHIT! THEY MIGHT AS WILL HAND YOU THE OSCAR NOW."

She grabbed her notebook, madly flipping pages until she found where she had recorded Joe Gelardi's unlisted home telephone number, a product of Charlie's diligent research. She dialed the operator. "I'm calling long distance," she said into the phone. "Brookline, Massachusetts…"

Chapter Fifty-Four

Triumphant and cocky from his *Meet The Press* performance, Leonard Pilcher sauntered into his father's office. "I laid it on pretty thick for those TV news clowns, don't you think, Pop?"

Max rose from his desk and stepped toward his son. Leonard smiled, expecting a warm handshake, maybe a proud embrace. Instead, the old man punched him squarely in the mouth. The younger Pilcher staggered backwards, a look of shock on his face. There was a trickle of blood down his chin, but Leonard was not combative. He began to cry.

His voice quavering, Leonard asked, "What did you do that for?"

The elder Pilcher rubbed his punching hand, stoically handling the pain. "You lied to me, Lenny." With a mocking tone, he continued, *"Never saw the son of a bitch in my life,* you said." The mocking tone vanished. It was time to berate. "Now you go and tell the whole world that fucking lunatic Moscone was in your crew! You pissed right in my face!"

Leonard whined like a child. "It doesn't matter anymore! It never did! I'm going to win this thing!"

Max looked skeptically at his son. In measured tones, he said, "Do you understand what I'm trying to achieve here…for the both of us?"

Leonard did not answer. He just sulked.

"DO YOU?" his father roared.

The younger Pilcher nodded sullenly.

"I hope so, Lenny, because winning or not, I'll have you beaten to within an inch of your fool life if you ever lie to me again."

Leonard mustered up some defiance. "I'm glad Mom's not alive to hear you talk to me like this."

The elder Pilcher found that amusing. "Son, your mother was the most vicious creature I ever knew. She would have snuffed out your sorry life a long time ago…and not lost a minute's sleep over it."

Chapter Fifty-Five

Viewed through the glass doors of the phone booth, Allegra Wise was obviously fired-up. She seemed to be shouting into the mouthpiece, although none of her words penetrated the thick glass to the bustling lobby of Boston's Logan Airport. The throngs passing by paid her no attention. She was nothing special, just another anonymous traveler acting out her life.

One person was watching her intently, though. In a nearby phone booth, the Hard-Boiled Man, who Tad Matthews dispatched to follow her on that cold night in Nashua, had his eyes glued to Allegra. He was in the middle of a phone call, too.

"Yeah, that's right," the Hard-Boiled Man said into the phone. "That skirt reporter had a sit-down with Gelardi…Right, that's him. The college teacher."

An impatient traveler paced outside the booths, waiting for one to be free. He had already tapped on a few of the closed glass doors, wordlessly beseeching the callers within to *hurry up!* while frantically checking his wristwatch. He came to the Hard-Boiled Man's booth. In response to his pantomimed plea, he received a raised middle finger and a badge pressed against the glass. The badge read *Detective, Boston PD*. The impatient traveler scurried off. His call could wait; his flight would not.

Allegra was pitching her story to the producer with everything she had. "Listen, Sid! Gelardi finally gave me some good dirt! He said they caught Pilcher consorting with Germans in Sweden! Linker accused him of being a traitor! To his face!" She paused and listened. What the producer was saying puzzled her.

"Oh, *come on,* boss! Linker! You remember…the Jewish kid who might have gotten murdered? And now I find out Pilcher made *lots* of anti-Semitic remarks." These new details were not getting the enthusiastic reception she had hoped for—but she kept pushing. "Well, no…he still won't say Linker's death wasn't a suicide. But couple everything else with Moscone's story…"

A look of horror crossed her face. "WHAT DO YOU MEAN, MOSCONE DOESN'T COUNT? WE REPORTED IT, DIDN'T WE?" The producer's response did nothing to calm her. "HE'S NOT INSANE, SID! I'M SURE HE'S TELLING IT STRAIGHT!"

She slumped against the booth's wall as she listened. Dejection began to set in, making her next words a plea. "Look, boss, I'm pretty sure Gelardi's still holding back…"

But her argument was making no headway. "Okay, okay," she said. "I hear you. I still need verification on the murder angle."

Allegra slammed the receiver onto its hook. She tried to compose herself but not before kicking the wall of the booth a few times. Finally, she calmed down, took a deep breath, and mumbled to no one in particular, "Verification…from God only knows where." In a second, she was out of the booth and striding across the lobby.

Tracking her progress, the Hard-Boiled Man briskly snapped to his feet and said into the phone, "Gotta go. She's on the move." He listened to the voice on the line for a brief moment more, then said, "Sure. I know what to do."

Chapter Fifty-Six

Joe Gelardi felt quite out of his element in this posh New York City restaurant. This was obviously a place where high-powered people decked out in fine clothes did their business. The food was ridiculously expensive, with portions so small they seemed like mere punctuation on the fine china. Though dressed in a suit and tie like all the other men in the room, Joe felt his well-worn outfit clearly labeled him as the typical shabby professor. *Thank God I didn't wear the jacket with the elbow patches,* he thought as he picked at his little cube of broiled halibut.

The young, sharply dressed IBM personnel executive sitting across the table seemed quite at home as he attacked his microscopic serving of coq au vin. Joe was sure he had seen him slip the maitre d' a $20 bill to secure this window table. Joe wondered, *Do mathematicians get an expense account like that at IBM?* He strongly suspected they did not. *And cocktails with lunch! Are these people working or not?*

The IBM man pushed his plate aside. It was time to get down to business. "I can't tell you how pleased we are you'll be joining the company, Doctor Gelardi." He pulled a fresh copy of the employment offer from his leather portfolio and slid it across the table to Joe.

Joe signed it quickly. "I'm a bit embarrassed about what happened to the original letter." He capped it with a white lie. "Kids! What can I say?" Immediately, he felt deeply ashamed. It was his fault coffee spilled all over the original document. Indicting his innocent daughter to save face with this stranger was nothing short of cowardly. *Maybe I should have blamed Pilcher instead.*

The IBM man smiled. "I know what you mean. I have two of my own. Quite a bit younger than your daughter, though."

Joe took one last, lingering look at the document before handing it back. He expected to feel some degree of regret, perhaps even melancholia, to go along with this first step of a major life change. But there was none. At least not yet. He actually felt light-hearted and sure he was doing the right thing.

"So, Doctor Gelardi, we'll plan on you starting in three months?"

"Yes, absolutely. That should give me ample time to wrap things up in Cambridge."

"Excellent. I'll have legal draw up the contract for your signature. It should be in your hands in a few weeks. Welcome aboard, Joe…May I call you Joe, Doctor Gelardi?"

"Of course," he replied, not knowing or caring in the least what corporate protocol dictated at this moment. He was simply relieved and content to savor the heady exultation that this bridge was finally being crossed.

Outside the restaurant, as Joe and the IBM man shook hands in farewell, their eyes fell on PILCHER FOR PRESIDENT campaign posters plastering a wall across the street. With bubbly enthusiasm, the IBM man said, "You know, Joe, the company is very high on Congressman Pilcher. We think he'll make one hell of a president. Don't you?"

Joe's stomach lurched; he felt as if the wind had been knocked out of him. The irony that his first step into the corporate world would involve endorsing a murderer had struck him a sharp blow. Fighting the urge to vomit right there on the street, he forced a shaky smile and replied, "I'm sure he will."

"Shall we share a cab?" the IBM man asked.

"No, thanks. I need to take care of a few things first."

When he finally regained a grip on himself, Joe Gelardi had no idea how many blocks he had aimlessly walked across Manhattan. Thirty-five minutes had elapsed, though, since he left the IBM man outside the restaurant. The train would not get him back to Boston before nightfall; he needed to check his messages at MIT. Some matters, he was sure, would need his immediate attention. Despite the leave of absence, his responsibilities to his students would not be finished until a resignation was tendered and took effect at the end of the semester.

The math department secretary thought nothing was odd when she first answered Professor Gelardi's call. "And you have one other message," she said. "From a colleague at NYU."

The operator broke in. "Please deposit fifty cents for five more minutes."

Joe fumbled for the change as the secretary's confused voice crackled in his ear. "Is this long distance? Where are you, anyway, Doctor Gelardi?"

"Oh, I'm just out doing some research," he replied. He could tell she was not convinced. The harder he tried not to sound evasive, the more evasive he sounded. His only hope was to change the topic. "You were saying I had a call from someone at NYU?" he asked.

He could hear her shuffling message slips. "Oh, here it is. A Doctor MacLeish called. Pola Nilsson-MacLeish."

The receiver dropped from Joe's hand and swung like a pendulum at the end of its cord. He was oblivious to the secretary's muted voice squawking from the earpiece, "Doctor Gelardi, are you there? Hello? Hello?"

Through the ambient noise of the telephone line, the secretary thought she could make out a few mumbled words, words like *Why now?* and *Can't be!*

Poor Professor Gelardi! He must really be losing his mind, the secretary thought.

She was just about to hang up when Joe returned to the line. But his voice was very different. She had never heard him quite like this. He sounded *positively anxious.*

"Okay, Give me the number for Doctor MacLeish," he said, his voice shaking. "I'm ready to copy."

Chapter Fifty-Seven

Late afternoon rush hour in lower Manhattan. Joe Gelardi had already missed his train back to Boston. He suspected he would miss the later one, too. Impatient people hurried by, anxious to get to someplace else, be it home, a dinner engagement, a lover's warm embrace—but they were nothing to Joe but multi-colored blurs.

There must have been sounds, too. Loud sounds: car horns, motors revving, the whistles of traffic cops, the roar of subways below the sidewalk grating—the rumble and whoosh that was the background music of city life. But all Joe Gelardi heard was that voice—that wonderful, lilting, accented English—of the woman for whom he had once given up his soul. The woman who was once again walking beside him.

The years had done nothing to mar Pola Nilsson-MacLeish. She was flawless in her early 40s: polished and fit, her white-blonde hair made even more striking by some strands of silvery gray now weaved through it. At the top of her field, she looked every inch the accomplished academic. Joe could not help but share the cordiality she offered. But they both treaded carefully; their tragic history could not be cast aside lightly.

"So you told that reporter nothing about David's death?" Pola asked. She made it sound like an innocuous question, just a part of light conversation.

"That's right," Joe replied. "Not a word. Now, why don't you tell me exactly what you're doing here." Immediately, he winced. He wished that had not come across like he was giving her the third degree.

"It's a wee bit of a long story, Joseph. Stockholm

can be so…well, bleak."

"Yeah, I know. You banished me there, remember?" In an instant, he was berating himself. *Again with the snide tone! Give her a break, for crying out loud! This can't be easy for her, either.*

She let his remark slide as if she never heard it. "So I took this visiting professor's post at NYU for a while."

As they crossed Washington Square, they navigated through a flock of pigeons scavenging the sidewalk. They were startled as the birds took flight en masse. She grabbed his arm for balance and did not let go.

"Really, Joseph…I'm very sorry to hear about your wife. I'm a widow myself. Four years now."

"Oh, I'm sorry. What happened?"

Pola gripped his arm tighter. "Reginald crashed his sports car. Bloody fool fancied himself James Dean. Roddy took it very hard."

Joe was surprised by the mention of this new name. "Roddy?" he asked.

"My son."

"Your son? How old is he?"

"Roddy will be fifteen this July. He's at boarding school in Switzerland."

Joe rapidly did the math in his head. His feet stopped cold in their tracks. Pola found the startled, deer-in-the-headlights look on his face most amusing. "No, silly, he's not yours! Blood types, you know. Rh factor problems and all that." She paused for a moment, her smile broadening. "And we were so careful."

"How would you know my blood type, Pola?"

She laughed out loud. "It's on your dog tag, Joseph!"

"You kept my dog tag?"

She began to walk again, their linked arms pulling him with her. "Of course I still have it," she replied. "Now let's get back to why I called you." She paused, gathering strength, waiting for the noisy city bus to pass so she would not have to shout. "It's time, Joseph. Time to tell the world what we know about Leonard Pilcher."

Joe dragged them to a stop again, dismayed by what she had just said. He jerked away from her angrily. They squared off right there on the sidewalk, frozen in confrontation, oblivious to the annoyed pedestrians swerving around them.

"NO! YOU'VE GOT TO BE KIDDING, POLA! WHY NOW? HE'S RUNNING FOR GODDAMN PRESIDENT!"

"All the more reason to stop him. It's time, Joseph...Time to do what we should have done years ago."

A burly man in workman's clothing passed hurriedly between them, roughly brushing against them both. "You own the fucking sidewalk, pal?" the burly man yelled as he continued briskly on his way. Joe guided Pola to the relative safety of a vestibule, out of the pedestrian traffic flow.

His next words were thick with sarcasm. "Oh, I see, Pola...It's still *your* decision." He paused, his eyes darting about, searching the city streets for wisdom as he tried to come to grips with her demand.

"Joseph, it's the right thing to do."

"NO! I can't be part of this. Not now!"

Pola took a step back and eyed him curiously. "Oh, isn't this interesting! Now *you're* the one who thinks he has something at stake!"

"Damn right! I don't need to lose this job before it even starts. IBM thinks Pilcher is the cat's ass."

Shaking her head sadly, Pola said, "You don't

belong at IBM, Joseph. You're too brilliant to be a *yes man*. I've read your publications, you know. All of them."

Joe was genuinely surprised to hear that.

"And Pilcher is still a murderer," Pola continued. "No matter what anyone thinks."

There was a tense silence between them for a few moments until a seething Joe went back on the offensive. "You've got some damn nerve, Pola. I did what you wanted, then you threw me out on my ass. Now, out of the blue, you want me to ruin my life for you...again!"

His words stung Pola deeply. But she was determined not to shed tears. "Joseph, I still see that boy falling...Every day for the last 16 years."

"Join the club, lady. Join the damn club."

She lost her battle with the tears; they began to flow down her cheeks. "And it's my fault his killer still walks free."

The one foot of distance that separated them in that vestibule might as well have been the distance from New York City to Malmö. Joe's anger softened; his eyes were cast down, studying their shoes. But she knew full well he was refusing to yield.

"Fine," she said. "If you won't help me get Pilcher, I'll bloody well do it myself."

She turned and walked away with a determined stride. Joe took a step after her but stopped himself. He could not—no, he *would not*—muster the words that would make her turn back.

"Sorry I wasted your time, Joseph," she called without breaking step, then added, "You don't have to worry...I'll leave you out of it."

The pigeons had followed them. As they swirled overhead, a solitary feather fluttered to the ground past Joe's face. He picked up the feather and stared at it. *In*

Malmö, he thought, *when David died...in the bell tower...there was a pigeon feather. Or am I just imagining it?*

Gently, he put the feather in his coat pocket.

Chapter Fifty-Eight

Allegra Wise was perplexed: the other reporters seemed to be avoiding her as she arrived in the newsroom. Her greetings were met with glacial smiles and awkward silences; their eyes would not meet hers. *Gee, am I suddenly a leper?* she wondered. *Something's up...and it can't be good.*

She was not surprised in the least when the producer shouted her name from his office door, unceremoniously summoning her to a private audience. *Okay. This must be the moment of truth. Let's see what the hell I did wrong now. He probably wants to nickel and dime my expense account for the New England trip.*

"Close the door," he said. Those ominous words sent chills down Allegra's spine.

The producer got right to the point. "We're pulling you off the Pilcher campaign, Ally."

She was stunned. That was the last thing she expected to hear. "Come on, Sid," she pleaded. "This is just getting good!"

The producer scoffed. "It ain't *getting good*, honey. You've had your chance, but you've come up with *squat*. Pilcher's a big story now. The network wants a bigger name covering him." Finished with her, he shuffled some papers on his desk and said, "See the editor for your new assignments."

The brutal finality of his words stung worse than a slap in the face. In a few seconds, Allegra Wise was back at her desk, an isolated, defeated woman with nothing to do, adrift in a sea of very busy male colleagues.

Chapter Fifty-Nine

Mrs. Riley put the last of the supper dishes away. Diane and Meredith had helped with clearing the table and started to wash the dishes, but Mrs. Riley shooed them out of the kitchen. "You girls go do your schoolwork. This is my job," the housekeeper said.

She knew it would not be her job for much longer, though. Professor Gelardi was going to take that job in New York; she was sure of it and had already made her peace with the thought of moving on. *I ain't got no choice,* she reasoned. *I can't be moving to no Armonk.*

Still, Professor Gelardi's sudden change of plans for tonight seemed so out of character. *Those IBM hot-shots must be sparing no expense wining and dining him,* Mrs. Riley thought. *Why else would a day trip turn into an overnighter on such short notice? Unless they've rolled out the call girls? Just as well...God knows that man could use a righteous screwing. Good thing I packed him a change of drawers.*

Edna Riley would miss this house. She would miss Diane. She would even miss Joe Gelardi a little.

In the dining room, she found Diane and Meredith intently working with slide rules, deep into some math. "I made you fresh cookies for your little pajama party, girls. They're in the pantry," she said as she put on her coat.

Diane looked up from her calculations. "Gee, thanks, Mrs. Riley! See you tomorrow!"

The two girls sighed with relief as the door closed behind the housekeeper. "She can be a little stern, can't she?" Meredith asked.

"Oh, she's all right," Diane replied. "Sure, she's

not a bundle of laughs...and she can be a little *territorial..."*

Meredith laughed out loud. "Yeah, I can't believe she threw us out of the kitchen. We were just trying to help."

"But she takes care of me and Daddy really well." Turning serious, Diane said, "And thanks for staying over tonight. This is just like having a really smart big sister."

Meredith smiled; she liked the sound of that. Always wanting a sister, her parents had managed to curse her with nothing but annoying younger brothers. She laid her slide rule down on the table. "You said your dad sounded so secretive when he called...I'll bet he's seeing some lady."

Diane scowled and stomped off to the refrigerator. "Who cares? I wish he wouldn't take that stupid job."

A voice in Meredith's head whispered *you and me both, little girl...*

Diane rummaged in the refrigerator for a moment; her head popped up from behind its open door. "Darn it, Meredith! We're out of root beer. I had my heart set on root beer floats."

"I can run down to the corner and get some," Meredith said. "Will you be okay for a few minutes?"

"Of course I'll be okay...I'm almost fourteen, for Pete's sake!"

Grabbing her coat, Meredith headed for the door. "Be back in a jif. Finish up those problems while I'm gone, little sister."

Chapter Sixty

Tad Matthews had barely picked at the main course, a delicate soufflé. He could not muster any interest in the crepe suzette his lover now prepared for dessert. Watching the delicate pancakes, soaked with liqueur, being set alight only reminded him of the flames of Hell, flames in which he was sure he would soon be roasting.

Brad—the cook, his roommate and lover—was a bit put out that Tad was not enjoying this special feast he had slaved to prepare. "Come on, baby...lighten up, for crying out loud. At least loosen your tie a little," Brad said as he snuffed the flames with the lid of the chafing dish. "Nobody can pin anything on you. You're just their employee."

Angrily, Tad pushed back from the table and walked to the picture window of their big apartment. How could he expect Brad to understand anything about how this business—how politics—worked? *He's just a kid of twenty-five. A full fourteen years younger than me. What does he know of the world?*

Suddenly, Brad was nestled against his back, arms wrapped tightly around his waist. Tad broke his grip and turned to face him.

"You don't understand, Brad. I set up the payment for Blanding's murder..."

"But you didn't know what you were doing!"

"It doesn't matter! I'm an accessory, Brad...an accessory to murder!"

Brad backed away, the body language and facial expression unmistakable: complete rejection of Tad's pronouncement. Tad hesitated, unsure of the grounds for this rejection. Was Brad refusing to accept an inconvenient fact, as a child would? Or was he daring to challenge its legal basis?

Brad quickly resolved the puzzle. With deep conviction, he said, "No court in the world would convict you."

The reply exploded from Tad's mouth. "AND JUST WHAT FUCKING LAW SCHOOL DID YOU GO TO, YOU STUPID LITTLE SHIT?"

Immediately, he wished he could take those words back. He had never spoken to Brad like that in their two years together. Oddly enough, Brad might be legally correct, but it did not matter. The Pilchers were above justice. The law did not apply to them, and they had no trouble setting up other people to take the fall when it suited them. Insulting the man he loved was not going to make his involvement in the Blanding murder go away.

The hurt look on Brad's face had been most deceptive, however. Before Tad could make a gesture of amends, Brad hauled off and punched him—hard—in the stomach. The strength of the blow startled Tad Matthews, who found himself sitting on the floor, arms protecting his midsection, gasping for breath.

Brad squatted beside him; now it was his turn to make amends. "I'm sorry, baby, but you had that coming. Now listen to me...we've got to get you far away from those people. Let's pack the car. We'll leave tonight. How does San Francisco sound to you?"

Tad shook his head violently. He was surprised to find he had the wind to speak. "No. You don't understand. Nothing will ever happen to them. But they'll find me and they'll ruin me...They'll ruin us."

Brad really did not understand. The law still seemed black and white to him; he could not fathom these shades of gray. Before he could say a word, the phone rang. He turned to answer it.

"Don't touch it," Tad said. "Let me get it."

Brad did as he was told. Tad struggled to his feet and lifted the receiver.

"Hello?"

There was a long pause as Tad listened to the caller. With each passing second, his face fell deeper into a look of grim resignation. Finally, he said, "Yes, I'll take care of it. I'm on my way, Leonard."

Brad watched wordlessly as Tad pulled on his coat, then stopped at the dining room table. In an attempt at conciliation, he took a hasty bite of the crepe suzette. For a brief moment, Tad's grim countenance softened. "Hey, that's really good," he said. "Can you save some for when I get back?"

Sullenly shaking his head, Brad replied, "It can't be saved."

Chapter Sixty-One

It was nighttime in Manhattan, and Joe Gelardi roamed the streets aimlessly. He was still reeling from the momentous events that marked this roller coaster of a day: the thrill of a new job, the thrill of old love, a painful wound ripped open and rubbed with salt.

It was wonderful to see Pola again...at least at first. So exciting to be together again, even if it was just for a stroll! I'm sure she felt it, too...but why did she have to ruin it? Why does she want to go after Pilcher now, after all these years?

Those words she said when he refused to help her: *now you're the one who thinks he has something at stake!* They were true—and they meant only one thing: he had failed David Linker all over again.

He paused before an electronics store. A television in the window blared a news program. The talking head on camera was reading a political story:

Now the Pilcher juggernaut rolls into Wisconsin. A win in that state's primary will give the congressman a considerable boost over Vice President Nixon for the Republican nomination. We asked the congressman what he thought about his chances in Wisconsin...

The image on the screen cut to the smiling face of Leonard Pilcher. He was being interviewed; his words were confident:

I know the fine, hard-working folks of Wisconsin appreciate our message of strength, courage, and integrity. I believe we'll do just fine here.

Joe recoiled in disgust and turned away from that face on the screen. He wished he had never made that call to Pola, never missed that train. He just wanted to be home.

His hands were jammed in his coat pockets. One hand found the feather he had put there as Pola walked away. He pulled the feather out and stared at it, thinking *Pola, Pilcher, pigeon shit...that pretty much sums up my sorry state. I'll bet my late wife could have whipped that up into one hell of a poem.*

Gently, he returned the feather to his pocket and walked on.

Carrying a sack full of root beer bottles, Meredith approached the front door of the Gelardi house. She smiled as she saw Diane waving from the window. She would have waved back, but her hands were full.

A dark sedan lurched to the curb, stopping with a loud *screech.* Shadowy figures of two men leapt out. They grabbed Meredith; one clamped a hand over her mouth as a needless precaution—she was too startled to scream.

Now the damsel in distress in this streetlight theater, Meredith made a vain attempt at struggling, but it was no use. In an instant she was in the car. The sack lay on the sidewalk; sparkling shards of glass from broken pop bottles crunched under the men's shoes. The root beer flowed to the gutter in a half dozen shimmering rivulets.

Inside the house, Diane watched in disbelief. She grabbed the telephone and, with a trembling finger, dialed. "Operator, get me the police!" she said, surprised at the calmness and command in her voice.

Sitting in the back seat of the sedan, sandwiched between the two men who abducted her, Meredith had no idea where they were driving. She was sure a long time had gone by—*maybe an hour,* she thought, *but it's really hard to tell time when you're blindfolded. Why did they bother, anyway? I guess they don't realize I'm blind as a bat without my glasses.*

The only thing anyone had said to her, right as they sped away from the Gelardi house, was *sit still and we won't have to use the cuffs.* A few times early in the drive, they pushed her head down to her knees and held it there, probably because they were in a place where she might be seen. That had not happened for quite a while, though. To her relief, no one had otherwise laid a finger on her. At least, so far.

She was surprised to find herself only angry and not terrified. *This has to be some kind of fraternity prank or something...Maybe this is Mitch Grayson and some buddies getting even for how I demolished his work in Linear Algebra class. I wish I could hear more of their voices...but from the little I've heard, they don't really sound like boys I know. They're not acting like them, either.*

Now she was scared. *These guys are too calm, too organized...like they've done this lots of times before. These aren't boys...these are men.*

A gruff voice from the front seat said, "Tell your father that he'd better stop talking to reporters, kid."

She could not help it—the first thing out of her mouth was a laugh. They had obviously made some kind of mistake.

"My father?" she said. "What are you talking about? My father *is* a reporter...and he lives three thousand miles from here, in Sacramento, California."

The car *screeched* to a halt. If Meredith had not been blindfolded, she would have seen the driver pivoting toward the back seat. His angry face would have emerged from shadow as he flicked on the dome light. She would have seen the Hard-Boiled Man.

The back door flew open and Meredith, still blindfolded, was roughly ejected from the car. She heard a soft *thump* as some object landed at her feet. The car sped off. She pulled off the blindfold. It was already too far away to read its tag number, even if she could see.

The object at her feet was her purse. Its contents appeared intact; even her eyeglasses had been placed inside. She put them on, hoping the dark, myopic blur around her would turn into some form of civilization.

No such luck. She was in the middle of nowhere: a two-lane hilly road in woods devoid of man-made light. She started walking in the direction from which her kidnappers' car had come.

It was near midnight when Joe Gelardi, exhausted and emotionally drained, finally entered the deserted lobby of his Manhattan hotel. The sleepy desk clerk looked up from his crossword puzzle. "Oh, yeah...Doctor Gelardi...you'll be with us for another night?" the clerk asked as he retrieved the room key from its slot. A slip of paper came out of the slot, as well. "Oh, and you have a message," the clerk said.

Although numb from the battering he had taken this day, a jolt of fear awakened Joe's mind and body as he read the message: CALL HOME IMMEDIATELY. URGENT. DIANE.

Chapter Sixty-Two

As he drove home, all Tad Matthews could think of were the flames of Hell he had seen in that flambé crepe suzette earlier in the evening. What he had just done made it no less likely he would roast in those flames.

He had written a check for $5000, drawn on a Pilcher shadow account, to a firm called AMO Investigations. He had delivered that check through the mail slot of a darkened office in a shabby and deserted downtown building. The firm's name was written on a crude cardboard sign, held to the door with a single nail. That sign, and any record of that firm's existence, would be gone by the close of business tomorrow, Matthews was sure. Just as soon as the check was cashed—and as soon as someone ended up dead, probably.

These guys don't have much imagination, Matthews thought. *AMO Investigations...That has to stand for Allegheny, Monongahela, and Ohio, the three rivers that converge here in Pittsburgh. Surely, it wasn't from the Latin for 'I love.'*

He lingered on the word *love* as his thoughts shifted to Brad. Would that lovely boy still be waiting for him when he returned? Tad Matthews hoped with all his heart that he would be.

At a small airport on the outskirts of Pittsburgh, two men, each carrying a satchel, wandered through the parked aircraft in the late night darkness. They did not belong here, but the chain link fence around the airport's perimeter only stopped honest people. It was no deterrent to these dark-clad saboteurs. Despite the light burning in the field operations office, they saw no other soul around.

They approached Fred O'Hara's airplane. The fat one asked, "Is this the one? Tricycle gear, twin engines. N9184K...that's the tail number, right?"

Using a penlight, the thin one checked a notebook. "Yeah. This is the one, all right," he replied.

It only took a few moments for the fat one to pick the lock on the plane's cabin door. *Easier than boosting a car,* he thought, as he jumped back to the ramp and hurried to the tail of the plane. Bending over, hands on knees, the fat one propped his back against the lower fuselage to lend support.

The thin one had entered the cabin, pulled down the back seat and climbed into the aft fuselage. He crawled from frame to frame until he reached the tail. "You're under there, right?" he called to the fat one.

The fat one grunted from the strain. "Yeah, I'm here," he answered. "You weigh more than I thought for a scrawny little shit."

"Well, don't fucking move until I'm back out," the thin one said. "We don't want this son of a bitch to stand on its tail. That'll leave marks. They'll know somebody was screwing with the airplane for sure."

The thin one removed a device from his satchel. It was made up of two objects taped together. One was a green canister with the word *THERMITE* in yellow lettering. The other was a barometric altimeter. He set the altimeter to 5000 feet, then clamped the device to the plane's structure, adjacent to the control cables.

Crawling back out of the aft fuselage, the thin one smiled. *That thermite is some hot shit,* he thought. *In a heartbeat, it'll burn through that aluminum and stainless steel like butter. Turn this crate into a flying brick...*

He reinstalled the back seat and exited the cabin,

finding the fat one trying to stretch his tired legs and back. "Hey, slim," the thin one said, "it's a little late for you to start getting in shape, don't you think? Now lock this thing up like we were never here."

The fat one flipped him an extended middle finger and quickly finished his assigned task. Then they vanished into the night.

Chapter Sixty-Three

He had dreaded making this call all night. Now it was morning, and amidst the bustling crowds of New York City commuters at Pennsylvania Station, Joe Gelardi found himself calm and full of purpose as he dialed the number at a phone booth. Diane was safe; Meredith was shaken but unharmed by her ordeal. Mrs. Riley and her grown sons were watching over both of them. The Massachusetts State Police were involved. It was time to warn Pola.

He waited as the dispassionate NYU operator put him on hold and took her sweet time connecting to Pola's extension. *Hurry up, dammit! They're calling my train already. I can't miss this one.*

Finally, a ring replaced the crackling, telephonic void, and then Pola was on the line. "It's Joe," he said in a rush. "Listen carefully, I don't have much time…"

He frowned as she interrupted. "No, Pola, I haven't changed my mind. But you've got to be more careful. I believe Pilcher's goons tried to kidnap my daughter." He paused again as she spoke. "No," he continued, "they got one of my students instead. She's safe and unharmed, though."

He found her next comment bordering on the ridiculously obvious. Irritated and more impatient by the moment, Joe responded, "OF COURSE IT WAS MEANT AS A WARNING!"

The station announcer's voice boomed from the PA. It was the final call for the 8:35 to Boston.

"Pola, I've got to catch my train. Look…if you're really going to do this, protect yourself and your son...Please!"

Pola sat alone in her office, lost in troubled thought as she turned the thin metal object in her hand over and over again. The phone call from Joe had yielded a double surprise. First, after their encounter yesterday, she had been convinced she would never hear from him again. Second, it took a lot less than she had thought to trigger Pilcher's violent instincts.

Joe hadn't even let the cat out of the bag about the murder and yet that ruthless bastard came after him. Obviously, somebody was watching Joe...or that reporter...or both of them. And somebody will be watching me very soon, too. But I was daft not to consider the danger in all this to my son.

Her resolve had not slackened, however. The metal object she caressed in her hand comforted her and gave her strength. Even if there was no hope of a rekindled friendship with Joe Gelardi, at least he still cared enough to watch out for her.

Thank you for the warning, my old love...Was I a fool to think that horrible man who drove us apart could somehow bring us together now? It was so nice to think we could be close again, even for just a little while...But I must go ahead and do this, with or without you, Joseph. David Linker deserves justice. I owe it to him.

With a determined smile tinged by melancholy, she gazed at the shiny metal in her hand. Raising it to her lips, she kissed it. Then she returned Joe Gelardi's dog tag to her purse.

She had made plans to ensure her safety; this turn of events only demanded she employ those plans sooner than she had thought. Plus, they now needed to include her son, Roddy. *Better to be safe than sorry.*

The irony of those words shook her for a moment.

Better to be safe than sorry...That sentiment, turned on its head in Malmö 16 years ago, is what caused all this mess in the first place, you silly girl.

She reached into her purse and removed an address book. Finding the number for the Swedish Embassy, New York City, she dialed it. When she got the consul on the line, the conversation was in Swedish, its tone friendly but businesslike. "Bjorn," she began, "it's Pola. It's time I called in those favors we discussed."

Chapter Sixty-Four

Allegra Wise never dreamed she could be this bored. *Writing obits was more exciting than this,* she thought, as she strolled aimlessly around the Spring Garden Show at New York Botanical Gardens. Notebook in hand, photographer in tow, she searched for something—anything—that would yield a story with a touch of uniqueness.

In a remote corner of the show, she stopped at a display booth filled with stunningly beautiful flowers of all types. A display table sat front and center. Eyeing the press pass dangling from her neck, the exhibitor launched excitedly into his pitch. He was a short man, bald on top of his head, with tufts of thinning hair sticking straight out from the sides. His voice was shrill, like nails on a blackboard.

Allegra could not help but be amused. *This guy looks like one of those cartoon mad professor types...Sounds like one, too.*

"My process has revolutionized the home fertilizer industry," he said. Drawing her attention to a large display board, he got to the heart of this revolutionary process with great enthusiasm. His presentation quickly became a rant on the evils of commercially available fertilizers. Allegra struggled to understand the apparatus he displayed before her: a pail with a large crank handle protruding from the top.

This thing looks like a butter churn...and it churns...OH, GOD! DON'T TELL ME!

Like a magician presenting his prized illusion, he unsealed a small, waxed carton to reveal the fetid source of his revolution in home fertilizers. He dumped the contents of the carton into his churning machine.

As she covered her nose, Allegra was not sure whether to laugh or cry. "Let me get this straight," she said. "You make this fertilizer yourself, entirely from human feces?"

Beaming with pride, the exhibitor crowed, "Yes! Isn't that brilliant? Abundant and totally free! Of course, you can also add animal droppings and plant compost..." He grabbed the pail and crank device from the table, but his motion was too eager. It slipped from his hands and fell, making a loud *clunk* as it hit the ground. Mercifully, the contents remained inside.

That clunk...from a pail of shit, Allegra thought. *That's the sound of my career hitting bottom.*

Chapter Sixty-Five

The train from New York City to Boston seemed to take forever, but Joe Gelardi still walked through his front door a bit after 2 p.m., just as he had figured. Diane, Meredith, and Mrs. Riley were waiting for him.

"You're right on time, Professor," Mrs. Riley said as she took his coat. "The cops should be here any minute."

She had nearly spit when she said the word *cops,* for Edna Riley was not fond of the police. *Got me a family full of them thieving sons of bitches,* she had been known to say. *Ain't much difference between a crook and a cop...sometimes, none at all.* When Detectives McGinty and Fallon, from the Massachusetts State Police, flashed their badges at the front door, she ushered them inside with a cold, sarcastic greeting: "Well, Jesus, Mary, and Joseph...we're all saved. The state boys are here."

It was a state police case for now. Although Meredith had been snatched in Brookline, she had been dumped 25 miles away, in a state forest in Middlesex County. She had walked almost five miles in the dark, finally stumbling across a pay phone on the outskirts of Carlisle. The one car that had passed her on that desolate road sped by the frantically waving young woman without even slowing down. The state police would be more than glad to hand the case off to the FBI if they determined it really was kidnapping and not just false imprisonment, malicious mischief, or lord-knows-what.

They settled into the living room. Detective McGinty handed a piece of paper to Meredith. "Here's the report filed by the Middlesex County Sheriff's office," McGinty said. "Is all the information correct, to the best of your knowledge?"

Meredith studied it for a moment. "Yes, as near as I can tell. The times are all approximate, you realize."

McGinty snatched back the report. As the detectives continued their questioning, Joe sensed a disturbing trend: *They don't seem very interested in getting to the bottom of this. They're trying to shift the blame to Meredith...like this is somehow all her fault...like she had caused her own abduction.*

It was Mrs. Riley, though, who quickly screamed foul. When Detective McGinty demanded a list from both girls of all the boys they were seeing, Edna Riley was fearlessly in his face, her words snarling. "I'd change that tone right now, paddy. Show these young ladies some respect. They're good girls...smart girls...not some little tarts who go slutting themselves around. The little one here is only thirteen, for crying out loud."

Her outburst left Joe, Diane, and Meredith startled and speechless. Having had little experience with police in their lives, they never expected to be regarded as anything other than upright citizens. These cops were treating them like suspects, though. The *upright citizens* were becoming irritated and indignant.

His housekeeper was a bit wiser about how the wheels turned in the minds of law enforcement officers and did not mind saying so. Joe fully expected the cops to slap handcuffs on Mrs. Riley and drag her to their car. Instead, McGinty and Fallon were locked in a fierce stare-down with Edna Riley, a battle of wills which the cops were fast losing. They could see in her eyes a woman who would not be bluffed.

Desperate to restore calm and reason, Joe addressed the detectives. "Gentlemen, perhaps we can get back to what exactly happened last night?" He breathed a sigh of relief as the detectives backed down and continued their questioning with a softer, more conciliatory tone. Mrs. Riley relaxed in her chair, savoring her victory.

"That's all they said, Detective," Meredith replied to McGinty's next question. "Tell your father he'd better stop talking to reporters."

Scribbling in his notebook, Detective McGinty did not look up as he asked, "Does your father have any enemies who might want to silence him?"

"He's a reporter!" Meredith said, rapidly losing her patience. "Of course he has enemies! But he certainly wouldn't need to be talking to other reporters about them. He would just write it himself. You can see the logic in that, can't you, Detective?"

A bit flustered, McGinty continued, "And you never saw their faces?"

"I told you...I was blindfolded. But I could peek out the bottom a little. I did notice one thing."

"What's that, miss?"

"When they turned the light on, the two in the back with me were wearing white socks, like you'd wear with sneakers. But they had on dress shoes."

Detective Fallon was wearing white socks. His partner pretended not to notice. Everyone else in the room did.

"You mean sweat socks, like teenaged boys would wear?" McGinty asks.

Meredith could not help but stare at Fallon's socks as she replied, "No, Detective. These weren't boys. These were men. Four of them, I'm pretty sure."

Joe had become impatient, too. "Detectives, isn't it obvious that the target of the kidnappers was *my* daughter?"

The detectives frowned. McGinty shook his head, saying, "No, Doctor Gelardi, nothing here is obvious at all. There's no ransom demand...and they let her go real quick. Can't make much of a kidnapping charge out of that."

"Only because they grabbed the wrong girl, Detective," Joe said.

McGinty did not miss a beat, asking, "By the way, Doctor...you haven't been talking to any reporters, have you?"

"Actually, yes. I have."

"About what, Doctor?"

"I was asked by CBS News to relate some of my war experiences."

Joe noticed that both detectives had stopped taking notes. The looks on their faces could only be described as skeptical.

"That doesn't seem to be much of a motive for abduction and terroristic threats, does it?" Detective Fallon asked.

Diane enthusiastically raised her hand as if she knew the answer to a question in class. "I know the license plate started with a *P*. I saw it through the window," she said, pointing to the living room's bay window.

The detectives exchanged amused glances. "Miss, I'm afraid that's not much help," Fallon said. "We could turn up a thousand dark-colored sedans with a plate like that. Could have even been an out-of-state plate." Both detectives closed their notebooks.

Fallon turned from the crestfallen Diane to Meredith. "Perhaps, Miss Salinger, you should go home to California for a while. Take some time off to put this ordeal behind you."

Meredith jumped from her chair like she had just

received an electric shock. She began to berate the detectives. "NO! I'm not leaving school! I'm perfectly all right, and I've already discussed this with my parents. Do you have any idea how hard it is for a girl to get into MIT in the first place?"

From the dull looks on their faces, the detectives obviously did not know or care. Rising to leave, McGinty said, "Unless there's something else any of you want to add…"

He was interrupted by Mrs. Riley's guffaw. She turned to the professor and the girls and said, "Save your breath. They ain't interested in doing anything. I could tell the second they walked in the door."

McGinty handed his business card to Joe. In the authoritative voice all cops must master, the voice that subverted grammar and turned any question into a command, the detective said, "Doctor, could we have a word? In private?"

Joe led McGinty and Fallon to the front yard. Standing on the walkway, McGinty said to his partner, "Start the car. I'll be right with you."

McGinty fixed a stern gaze on Joe. "You know, Doctor, all your people here got some friggin' attitude. That housekeeper, especially. I'm gonna let it slide…this time."

Joe felt his indignation rising once again, but he said nothing. *I'm not going to let this incompetent asshole goad me.*

Suddenly, a look came over Detective McGinty that caught Joe completely by surprise. It was a smug, superior smile—with a scolding turn of the head and a raised eyebrow that meant *I've got you all figured out, chum…I know your secrets.*

"You know, Doctor…if you really care about your little girl…you should think about keeping a real low profile for a while. Maybe running your mouth to reporters ain't such a hot idea, is it?"

McGinty turned and strolled to the waiting car, calling casually over his shoulder, "You enjoy what's left of this fine day, now."

The chill that coursed through Joe Gelardi's body had nothing to do with the cool temperature. His knees nearly buckled. He scanned up and down the street lined with still-bare trees but sensed nothing out of the ordinary. There was nothing but boisterous children coming home from school, zigzagging down the street on bicycles, laundry flapping gently on backyard clotheslines in the steady breeze, the faint, tinkling discord of a neighbor practicing on an out-of-tune piano.

Somebody is watching me...watching my every move. How else would they know?

The state policemen's car was well down the street before it snapped back into Joe's perception. *This is paranoid, I know...It's too far away to read, but I could swear that license plate starts with a P...*

No...I must be going crazy.

He did not remember going back into the house, but suddenly he was in the hallway, face to face with Edna Riley. She put a calming hand on his shoulder and led him to the living room and his easy chair.

"Where are the girls, Mrs. Riley?" he asked.

"They're in Diane's room. You and me have to have a little talk, Professor. Ain't none of my business what shenanigans you've got going on, but we need to protect Diane."

"Meredith, too," Joe adds.

"Come on, Professor...they weren't looking for Meredith. That was a mistake. She'll be okay. But God-knows-who is looking to hurt you. Worry about Diane now."

"Protect? But…how?"

"Not with them useless cops, that's for damn sure. But my two youngest, Sean and Patrick…they're both laid-off right now. They've got plenty of time to play bodyguard…and they'd be glad to help you out."

Mrs. Riley gave Joe a reassuring pinch on the cheek. "You can take care of whatever crap you're in without having to worry about her. Now, I've got to start cooking dinner. Go upstairs and tell your daughter everything's going to be okay. She's worried sick about you."

McGinty and Fallon walked into Boston Police Headquarters and headed to a detectives' squad room upstairs. They went straight to a desk in the back of the room; the detective seated there had his back to them.

After checking that no one else was in earshot, McGinty said to the seated detective, "Looks like the good professor got the message, wrong girl or not."

He swiveled his chair to face them, the slightest of smiles on his weathered face. It was the same face of the man Meredith Salinger might have seen driving the car that night—if she had not been blindfolded. It was the same face Allegra Wise might have noticed following her—if she had had the time to notice. It was the face of the Hard-Boiled Man.

His smile faded quickly. He nodded and uttered just one word: "Good."

Chapter Sixty-Six

Fred O'Hara had hoped for better weather. If he got off the ground in the next 30 minutes, though, he could beat the storm front that was threatening to make this flight from Pittsburgh to Teterboro, New Jersey, a dangerous proposition. He took the weather reports from the operations office counter and stashed them in his flight bag.

This was his home airfield. His airplane was parked outside, visible through the large window. Fred had already finished her preflight inspection. All she needed now was some fuel.

From his desk behind the counter, the flight dispatcher asked, "You want to file your usual, Mr. O'Hara? IFR at 8000 feet?"

"Yeah, sure. Go ahead."

The dispatcher glanced at the weather map pinned to the wall and asked, "Is 80 gallons going to be enough?"

"Hell, yeah. I'm just going to Teterboro."

The dispatcher decided to make friendly conversation. "Business or pleasure?"

With a frosty glare, Fred replied, "Is that any of your business?"

The dispatcher cringed, wishing he had never asked that innocuous question. *Jesus! What's wrong with me? These big union guys are no different from gangsters...Mind your own business and don't piss them off!* Flustered and intimidated, he dialed the phone to file Fred O'Hara's flight plan.

There was a news program playing softly on the

radio. Something the announcer was saying caught Fred's ear:

With the Wisconsin primary just days away, a shocking development from across the sea. The Swedish Ministry of Justice has announced that they are investigating the allegation by former American airman Anthony Moscone that presidential hopeful Leonard Pilcher committed murder while in Sweden during World War Two. A second witness, a Swedish national whose identity is being withheld for the present, has come forward to support the charge that Congressman Pilcher killed a fellow interned airman, Sergeant David Linker...

Fred O'Hara found himself not surprised at all by what he had just heard.

Climbing toward 5000 feet, Fred realized he had been too optimistic about the weather forecast. Dark, towering clouds were building in his flight path. His plane bumped along in worsening turbulence. *I'll never get over that stuff. I've got to stay low and pick my speed up. If I can't outrun it that way, I'll have to turn back.*

He eased the control column forward and readjusted the throttles for fast cruise. The altimeter on his instrument panel reversed its increasing trend at 4900 feet and began to creep slowly downward. Hidden in the aft fuselage, the altimeter on the saboteurs' thermite bomb started to wind down, too. The detonator contacts, which had been set to make their deadly connection at 5000 feet, had been only a millimeter apart before beginning to separate again.

Keep the nose down for a bit...pick up all the speed I can get.

Grabbing the microphone, Fred briefed Air Traffic Control on his new plan. "It's looking pretty crummy up ahead. How about I stay at 4000 feet and deviate around it?"

"9184 Kilo from Center...you don't want 8000 anymore?" the voice in Air Traffic Control asked.

"That's affirmative, Center. 9184 Kilo is looking for 4000."

"9184 Kilo from Center...that's approved."

Chapter Sixty-Seven

The scene at Leonard Pilcher's Wisconsin Primary headquarters was sheer chaos. The press conference was to begin in five minutes. Campaign staffers scurried about in panic.

Tad Matthews was no less panicked. He was trying desperately to brief an indifferent Leonard Pilcher. "Remember, Leonard...Wisconsin is loaded with Swedes. Say nothing, and I mean *nothing* detrimental about them, or you can kiss this state goodbye. And remember...you're not much of a comedian. Don't even try to make any jokes. Just stick to the script...like glue!"

A disdainful look on his face, Pilcher said, "Keep your drawers on. I know what I'm doing."

A few minutes later, in front of the reporters, things were going fairly well. Leonard Pilcher had not gone off script once. He was delivering his lines with conviction and just the right touch of righteous indignation. On the new Swedish murder allegations, he said, "This is an example of campaign lies and distortions of the lowest, most outrageous form. The allegation is completely false and no doubt instigated by my opponents."

He paused and surveyed the crowd, trying his best to look presidential. Then, launching into his closing remarks, it all fell apart. "I know the good people of Sweden and King...umm...King... ahh...*Adolph* will quickly put an end to these ridiculous allegations."

A sea of hands shot up as the reporters, like sharks to prey, smelled blood. "King WHO?" several shouted, without waiting for the invitation to speak. A horrified Tad Matthews rushed to the podium—his only hope at this point was damage control. "That's all we have time for, ladies and gentlemen," Matthews said, nudging Pilcher away from the microphones. As he escorted Pilcher from the stage, Matthews hissed, "It's *King Gustav,* you fucking idiot!"

Outside the auditorium, a large, enthusiastic crowd had gathered. Many were carrying PILCHER FOR PRESIDENT signs. A male reporter for a radio network approached the crowd and picked out one man not carrying a sign to interview. He asked the man one question. The response was emphatic: "Of course I believe Congressman Pilcher! Hell, them Swedes wouldn't even fight Hitler! Where do they get the balls to screw with a real live American hero?"

On the telephone in his Pittsburgh office, Max Pilcher was trying desperately to get a word in edgewise; the secretary of state was doing all the talking. When Pilcher finally got to blurt out a complete sentence, it was rife with petulance and disappointment. "Christian, I was expecting a little support from this administration."

Secretary of State Christian Herter was not moved to be conciliatory. "Let me spell it out, Max. Sweden has no love for you, Ike, your son, or the Republican Party at the moment. There's nothing we can do."

As soon as the feigned cordiality of goodbye was complete, Max Pilcher slammed the phone onto its cradle, shouting the parting insult no one would hear: "Goodbye, you useless son of a bitch!"

Quickly, he placed another call. This one also brought him no pleasure. In seconds, he was bellowing into the telephone: "I DON'T GIVE A SHIT ABOUT SOME BITCH REPORTER! IT'S THE WITNESSES

THAT NEED TO BE SHUT UP. NOW, JUST WHO
THE HELL IS THIS *SWEDISH NATIONAL?*"

He scowled as he listened to the reply.

"WELL, FIND OUT, GODDAMMIT! WHAT
THE HELL AM I PAYING YOU FOR?" the elder
Pilcher said, before slamming his beleaguered phone onto
its cradle once again.

A classroom full of chattering NYU students fell
silent as their professor entered the room. Today,
however, she was accompanied by a man: tall, blond,
well-built, a stern expression enhanced by piercing blue
eyes.

Pola Nilsson-MacLeish introduced the tall blond
man to her class. "Mr. Andersson is an associate who will
be observing for a few weeks," she said.

As Lars Andersson settled into a seat at the back
of the class, something became obvious to the students
who turned to sneak a look: the man wore a shoulder
holster beneath his suit jacket.

Chapter Sixty-Eight

The black limo was waiting on the Teterboro Airport ramp as Fred O'Hara shut his plane's engines down. He had made it around the storms unscathed. It had added flight time, but he still got there with plenty of reserve fuel.

Fred emerged from the cabin door and stood on the wing's walkway, stretching the cramped discomfort of the flight from his body. The limo pulled up alongside. A rear window rolled down to reveal Lou DiNapoli's smiling face.

"Where've you been, brother? We're late for lunch," Lou said.

Fred climbed into the limo and found Lou munching on a chocolate bar. With a laugh, he asked, "You couldn't make it a couple more minutes without a snack?"

"Hey, I'm fucking starving here, Freddy. You took forever."

"Sorry, man. Weather. You remember what that's like."

Lou squeezed the chocolate bar wrapper into a brown and silver ball and tossed it to the foot well, where it joined several others. "Yeah, I remember all that shit…getting bounced around in that ball turret like some kid's toy. Good times, eh, brother?"

In a private area of the Italian restaurant reserved for VIPs, Lou DiNapoli chowed down heartily as Fred picked sparingly at his food. They had already waded through three courses: antipasto, calamari, spaghetti.

Now the indulgent waiters were plopping plates of veal scaloppini before them. This was the type of food that put you to sleep, and Fred needed to be wide awake for the flight back to Pittsburgh later. He pushed his plate of veal away.

The waiters rolled their eyes. Diners who did not gorge themselves at this establishment were a rarity. *Some people just don't know what good is* was the only explanation that made sense to them. *Now, Mr. DiNapoli...he knows how to eat!*

A waiter made another of his many attempts to fill Fred's wine glass. He covered the mouth of the glass with his hand and said, "Hey, pal, I told you...none for me. I'm driving."

Undeterred, the waiter topped off Lou's glass.

"Alfredo," Lou said to the waiter, "you and the boys want to take a smoke break or something for a few minutes?"

Alfredo got the message; Mr. DiNapoli and his guest wished to speak privately.

Once the waiters scurried away, Lou asked, "So, you're thinking Pilcher really killed Davey Linker?"

"I don't know, Louie. I wasn't there, remember?"

Lou took another bite of the veal. He seemed lost for a moment.

"But what about Joey the Professor?" Lou asked. "He was there. What do you think he knows?"

"Good question, Louie. Maybe we'd better ask him."

"He's in Beantown, right?"

Fred nodded.

"And if he knows anything, he wouldn't bullshit us," Lou said.

Fred nodded again, then asked, "Maybe we give him a call?"

"Nah, Freddy...this is too important. We've got to do it face-to-face. Can that flying piece of shit of yours handle two people?"

Fred was half-serious as he replied, "Not if you keep eating like that."

Chapter Sixty-Nine

In another part of New York City, miles to the south, the hallways of academic buildings all around Washington Square were crowded with NYU students and faculty hurrying to be someplace else. Doctor Pola Nilsson-MacLeish was in this throng, with Lars Andersson close behind. They made their way to a down staircase.

Across the hall, a woman in a floppy hat leaned against the wall, holding an open textbook as if studying. Concealed in the book's pages was a photo of Pola. The brim of the hat concealed the woman's face; if it did not, it would have been obvious that she was far too old to be a co-ed.

As Pola reached the staircase, the woman dropped the textbook and raced at her from behind. Unseen by Pola, the woman's arms reached out with palms open; she was intent on shoving the professor down that long, steep flight of stairs.

But she was not unseen by Lars Andersson. He blocked her path just before she reached Pola. There was a struggle; the floppy hat fell off, revealing a face contorted not in fear, but in the grim determination of one used to conflict, locked in a life-or-death battle. She was tough, but no physical match for the tall, muscular bodyguard. He held her thrashing form fast with one arm around the throat; with his other arm, he pushed Pola MacLeish away from the staircase to safety. Bystanders who just a moment ago were lost in their own preoccupations frantically gave the melee some space while trying to make sense of this strange chaos before them.

Lars Andersson never saw the woman produce the switchblade knife. She slashed at his restraining arm and was able to jerk away, prepared to strike at him again. He was startled for a moment but not hurt; the knife had only sliced into the sleeve of his thick woolen overcoat and not his arm. But now, the blade pointed straight at his midsection, made vulnerable by the unbuttoned overcoat.

She lunged with the knife but never made contact. The force of the bullet from Lars Andersson's .45-caliber pistol caught her in mid-lunge and at such close range it knocked her backward with great force. It was the would-be assassin, not her intended target, who tumbled down the staircase. The switchblade knife clattered after her. As the now-screaming bystanders clawed their way over each other to get to safety, the woman in the floppy hat lay dead at the base of the stairs. Her blood pooled slowly beneath her, its deep red in sharp contrast to the white stone steps on which it flowed.

The uniformed NYPD cops who responded to the shooting at NYU were startled to find two homicide detectives already working the scene. The detectives were in a very foul mood and seemed to be going about their tasks in a great rush. "Just keep the gawkers back," one of the detectives told the uniforms. "We've got this all covered."

"You've got the shooter?" one of the uniforms asked.

"Yeah," the detective replied, rolling his eyes. "Get this...he's a fucking *diplomat.*"

The detective's partner had already searched the pockets of the dead woman at the base of the staircase. They were empty, just as they were supposed to be. But he got a surprise when he rifled her bulky handbag. Even though there was no identification to be found, a crumpled business card—*his* business card—was stuck in the bottom of a compartment. As he removed the card and palmed it like a gambler concealing a trump card, he mumbled to himself, "Damn sloppy of that stupid broad." A few minutes later, that business card became just another scrap of trash in a Washington Square refuse basket.

Later, in the coffee houses and taverns around Washington Square, still-excited students recounted tales of their brush with mortality on that staircase. One overwrought co-ed swore she heard the assailant shriek *I'll teach you to give me an F, you bitch,* but it was all fantasy. The excitement those fantasies buoyed, coupled with the prodigious amounts of alcohol consumed, ensured that many more collegians than usual would get laid that night.

Chapter Seventy

It was a gorgeous afternoon for flying. The air over Long Island Sound was smooth; the only clouds were some patchy cumulus floating peacefully above 6000 feet. The storm front Fred O'Hara skirted earlier this day over central Pennsylvania had stalled in its journey to the northeast, leaving a sunny day along the Atlantic seaboard.

Fred was relaxed at the controls, happy to be in the air again. Lou DiNapoli filled the front seat to his right, enjoying the sights and munching on a chocolate bar. As Lou took the last bite, Fred pointed to a trash bag between their seats and played the scolding elder: "Put the wrapper in there, Louie, not on the floor. I don't want any crap getting into the rudder pedal linkage. This girl ain't your fucking limo."

Lou balled up the wrapper and pretended to toss it at Fred. "Keep your shirt on, *Lieutenant,*" Lou said, with all the theatrical insolence he could muster. "I was aircrew, too, remember? I know the drill." He placed the wrapper in the trash bag with an exaggerated flourish of his arm.

The altimeter on Fred's instrument panel wound upward through 4000 feet and kept climbing. In the aft fuselage, the altimeter on the hidden thermite bomb did the same.

"We're headed for 8000, right?" Lou asked.

Fred nodded, adding, "We'd climb faster if you weighed a little less." Lou responded only with a raised middle finger.

After a few moments of amiable silence, Fred

asked, "So what if Joey says that Pilcher really did kill Davey Linker?"

Lou broke into a smile. He patted Fred on the shoulder as he replied, "If that's what Joey says, my friend, I just might have to help you out with that little promise you made to Pilcher."

"You mean you'd help me kill him?"

"Absolutely, Freddy. Absolutely. That would change everything."

It was time to report to Air Traffic Control once again. Fred picked up the microphone and began the position report: "9814 Kilo to Center, we're through 5000, going for 8..."

His words were cut off by a blinding flash. The cabin became oppressively hot and filled with acrid smoke that burned their eyes.

"I CAN'T SEE A FUCKING THING, LOUIE! POP THE DOOR...WE GOTTA GET RID OF THIS SMOKE!"

Without having to leave his seat, Lou heaved his considerable girth against the cabin door, overcoming the force of the slipstream pinning it closed. The door opened a crack, adding the deafening roar of engines and wind to the chaos. The cabin began to clear as the smoke was sucked out through the thin opening and joined the slipstream.

Watching the path of the smoke as it exited, it became obvious to Fred and Lou that something behind the rear cabin seat was burning.

"WHAT THE FUCK, LOUIE! THERE'S NOTHING BACK THERE TO BURN! IT'S NOTHING BUT METAL!"

Despite this implausible calamity, the plane was still flying normally. Fred scanned the instruments: *Everything looks normal...*

With a *SPRONG* that was more felt than heard, the control yoke went limp in Fred's hands—its fore-and-aft tension was gone. The plane's nose began to drop with a stomach-wrenching lurch. What had been a steady climb rapidly decayed to a brisk descent. Fred instinctively pulled back on the yoke, but something was desperately wrong. It came all the way back into his lap with no effort at all.

Something's broke bad here, Fred told himself, belaboring the obvious in his confusion. *That much elevator should stand her on her tail! But nothing's happening! I can't stop her...We're still going down!*

Not believing his own eyes, Fred moved the yoke back and forth through its full range of travel. There was no response from the airplane. They had dropped to 3000 feet already.

Another *SPRONG*—and the rudder pedals kicked, then went limp beneath Fred's feet. Fred and Lou exchanged bewildered, frightened glances.

"LOUIE...WE'VE GOT TO PUT OUT WHATEVER'S BURNING, THEN SORT THIS SHIT WITH THE CONTROLS OUT! TAKE THE EXTINGUISHER...GO BACK THERE!"

Lou was already out of his seat, fire extinguisher in hand, and moving aft before Fred could finish speaking. He yanked down the backrest of the rear seat and stared in disbelief at the sight that greeted him in the aft fuselage: intense, compact flames—like a 4th of July sparkler but 100 times brighter, so bright you could not look directly at them—were burning away the tail of the airplane.

They had dropped to 2000 feet.

Shielding his eyes, Lou blasted away with the fire extinguisher—but the flames did not subside. "I CAN'T PUT IT OUT, FREDDY! IT'S LIKE THAT THERMITE

SHIT WE HAD IN THE SERVICE!"

Tossing the empty extinguisher aside, Lou grabbed his overcoat and began to wedge his bulky frame into the aft fuselage, a space so confined that a man of normal dimensions could only fit on hands and knees. Lou's barrel-like physique made entry a most daunting task.

The holes that had burned through the fuselage skin were now acting as vents to clear the smoke, giving Lou a clearer view of what had happened. There was a tangle of severed control cables—tough, stainless steel cables, thick as a child's crayon—burned clean through by the thermite.

The plane's nose started to come up; they were no longer descending quite so fast. Fred called out, "HEY, THAT'S GOOD! YOU'RE SHIFTING THE C-G AFT!"

"I'M DOING WHAT?"

"YOU'RE SHIFTING THE C-G...THE CENTER OF GRAVITY. GO BACK A LITTLE FARTHER, LOUIE."

But Lou was nearly face-to-face with the flames. "I WOULD IF I COULD, BROTHER." Using his overcoat as insulation from the intense brightness and heat of the flames, he tried to break away pieces of the burning, weakened metal and jettison them through the scorched holes in the skin.

It was a losing proposition; the overcoat was burning up, too. Lou's hands and face were being blistered and worse by the heat. If he looked directly into the white-hot flames, he was sure he would go blind. With the charred remnants of his overcoat, Lou managed to snuff out the smoldering ends of the severed control cables.

"THE CABLES ARE BURNED THROUGH, FREDDY."

Fred's mind reached into its bag of emergency procedures. *OK...Loss of elevator control: use power and move the C-G to maintain pitch control.*

They were at 1000 feet. The descent had slowed to barely 100 feet per minute.

Lou was no stranger to the workings of an airplane; the war had seen to that. He could tell by looking at the control quadrants in the tail which of the red-hot cables worked the elevators and which the rudders. The elevators were far more critical at the moment, the *up* elevator especially. Ignoring the searing pain, he grabbed the aft end of the severed *up* elevator cable with one hand.

Now he needed to sort out the forward cable runs, the four that went to the control yoke and rudder pedals. He grabbed and pulled those cables with his other hand. "FREDDY, I'VE GOT SOMETHING HERE...REAL GENTLE LIKE, PULL BACK ON THE YOKE." Sensing which of the cables was tightening, he said, "OK...THAT'S GOOD."

It was sorted out—Lou DiNapoli had become a human link in the airplane's control system. He knew he would pay the price in third-degree burns, but that price was still cheaper than death.

"GO AHEAD, FREDDY...FLY THE UP ELEVATOR."

Gingerly, Fred pulled back on the yoke. Feeling the pull on the cable in his right hand, Lou pulled on the cable in his left—and the plane's nose began to rise.

"HEY! YOU'VE GOT IT, LOUIE! CAN YOU GET DOWN ELEVATOR? AND RUDDERS, TOO?"

"I'VE ONLY GOT TWO FUCKING HANDS, FREDDY. GOING UP'S THE PROBLEM. WHEN YOU PULL, I PULL. WE CAN ALWAYS GET HER TO GO DOWN, RIGHT?"

Fred had to admit it: Louie was right. It was easy to get an airplane to go down: just chop the power and down she went. Going up was always the hard part—you needed the elevators for that. They could live without the rudder, too, as long as both engines kept running. *The turns won't be so pretty, that's all.*

Fred relaxed a little. They were flying straight and level. He had the barest semblance of control. *Just got to get ourselves to the nearest airport...* He ran his finger across the map clipped to the sidewall. *Stamford...maybe Bridgeport.*

Lou's frantic cry broke Fred's deliberations. "FREDDY...I CAN'T HOLD THIS SHIT MUCH LONGER. AND WE'VE STILL GOT A FIRE BACK HERE...THE FUCKING TAIL'S GONNA BURN OFF PRETTY SOON!"

Tension gripped Fred once again. *So much for that "nearest airport" shit...We're going in the drink.*

"LOUIE, WE'VE GOT TO DITCH!"

"NO SHIT!"

"I'M GOING TO CUT THE THROTTLES AND EASE HER DOWN...WE'RE GONNA NEED A LOT OF ELEVATOR TO FLARE JUST BEFORE HITTING THE WATER."

"COUNT ME IN, BROTHER. JUST HURRY THE FUCK UP."

There was just not enough time to do everything you should do before ditching. But there was one thing Fred knew he *must* do. He grabbed the microphone.

"MAYDAY MAYDAY. THIS IS PIPER 9814 KILO. POSITION OVER THE SOUND, SIX MILES SOUTH-SOUTHEAST STAMFORD. WE'RE GOING IN THE WATER."

Fred had no idea if anyone answered; he was too busy to listen. They were 100 feet off the water and dropping fast.

"OK, LOUIE...THIS IS IT!" Fred pulled back hard on the control yoke.

Lou could not help but scream as his grip tightened to relay Fred's input to the elevator; the pain was that intense. But he hung on—he did the job. The nose rose sharply. The descent slowed...

And then the tail snapped off. Everything that kept the plane pointed where you wanted it to go was gone in an instant. The plane nosed over violently, slammed into the water, and ripped apart. The wreckage sank in seconds.

Nothing but air bubbles and a slick of aviation gasoline rose to the surface.

Chapter Seventy-One

Take as long as you need, the mathematics department chairman had said while pushing the leave of absence on Joe Gelardi. After the events of the last few weeks, Joe was certain: he did not need to absent himself from the Institute any longer. He needed to busy himself as he always had, with teaching. He owed it to his students to guide them through the completion of the semester before heading for Armonk.

Hell, there's no hurry tendering my resignation...I haven't even seen the IBM contract yet. The wheels of corporate bureaucracy must grind even slower than those of a university. If I don't return to the classroom, I'll dwell on this Pilcher-Pola-pigeonshit business...and slowly go out of my mind.

The chairman was wholeheartedly in favor of Joe's return. The strange abduction of a student from outside the Gelardi home had brought a new, unforeseen element to the equation of his absence. The Institute could be cast in a very bad light if the unfounded, but inevitable, talk of an "unstable" professor's possible involvement in this bizarre episode made the news. Fortunately, the police did not seem to be very interested in Meredith Salinger's brief ordeal. Consequently, the press was not interested, either.

More importantly, the Institute had gotten wind of some really fortuitous news: the official police report did not even mention anything about Joe Gelardi, other than the sidewalk outside his home was the site of the abduction and his home was the location of Meredith's follow-up interview by state police detectives. Nothing wrong there: students frequently visited faculty homes. But if the police were to change their mind and decide to probe deeper, it would be most important for everything to appear perfectly normal at the Institute. A leave of absence would cause questions to be raised.

The chairman had become far more concerned with another facet of Joe's absence: the senior faculty had been far too busy with their own courses and research to assume a colleague's classes in mid-semester. The graduate teaching assistant the chairman had selected as Joe's replacement came from a miniscule pool of possible substitutes. This teaching assistant, a young man named S.P. Hagedorn, had quickly proven himself not up to the task. To be more precise, Joe Gelardi's brilliant students—especially the superlative Miss Salinger—were eating the incompetent Mr. Hagedorn for lunch, consistently indicating a better grasp of the subject matter than their new teacher. The rapidly spreading joke throughout the department was that *S.P.* stood for *sleeping pill,* uninspiring and sleep-inducing as Hagedorn's classroom presence was. The chairman could not allow the academic standards of the Institute to appear compromised, and it was too late in the semester to replace Mr. Hagedorn with yet another novice teacher.

The mathematics department would, therefore, welcome Joe back from his brief absence with open arms, as if he had suffered nothing more serious than an appendectomy. In the shadow of new events, the emotional disturbances that triggered Joe's leave of absence remained unexplained, unresolved, and nearly forgotten in the Institute's collective memory.

Now he was back. In his first class, Number Theory, the students were relieved and delighted to have him. Joe watched with joy and pride as student after student paraded to the blackboard to expand on the numerical progression exercise he had proposed at the beginning of the class. He gave the students center stage, retreating to a window ledge seat at the back of the classroom, interjecting infrequently and only when necessary to guide the discussion or propose a new twist.

It was Meredith's turn at the blackboard. As usual, she found the work child's play, neatly tying up a challenging equation effortlessly. When she turned to ask Professor Gelardi if it was okay to propose a corollary to her solution, she stopped in mid-sentence; the professor seemed to be in a trance as he stared out the window, not responding to her question.

Oh, no! she thought. *Please don't tell me he's doing it again!*

The look of alarm on her face made the class turn as one to Joe at the back of the room. Many had seen this crazed look of his before, and his frightening collapse that followed, when those boys had engaged in horseplay on the roof of the adjacent building. They had all felt the sting of the words *nervous breakdown,* for they had seen it with their own eyes. Now, that sting was back, and this time, they feared, it would take him from them for good.

They could not hear the voice in Joe's head: *He fell...he died. We did nothing about it. Could Pola be right? Is this the time to tell what we know?*

And then, just as quickly as he had slipped away, he snapped out of it. "I'm sorry...did I miss something?" he asked, an inquisitive smile on his face. "Miss Salinger, I believe the floor is still yours. Keep it rolling." Signaling for her to proceed, he whirled an outstretched finger playfully above his head—the signal to start aircraft engines. As he walked confidently to the blackboard, that finger still whirling in the air, the room shuddered with a collective sigh of relief.

Chapter Seventy-Two

Allegra Wise took one look around the room and thought, *Welcome to hack heaven.*

She was the only female among a dozen reporters prowling New York City Police Headquarters. Most of the others were older, wizened, and rumpled. Though one or two actually loved working the police blotter, most long ago accepted that they were stuck in a lackluster niche for the rest of their working days. Then there was the starry-eyed kid, sure that this was just the first rung in his meteoric rise up the ladder of success.

Allegra suddenly felt old and wizened, too. *I felt like that kid once, when I first got put on the blotter in Pittsburgh. Boy, was I stupid. All you get here is small stories about small crimes...Maybe I should think about changing careers.*

One of the old reporters welcomed her with the good-natured camaraderie of a fellow slogger. "Hey, Ally...how'd you get stuck here? I thought you were a real comer."

Drearily, she replied, "Just lucky, I guess."

As long as I'm here, she figured, *I might as well try to do some work.* Unlike the others present, she was not much for killing time with crossword puzzles, pinochle, or Mickey Spillane paperbacks. A rotund sergeant had just waddled through and dropped the latest summary of today's police reports on the table. Allegra got her hands on it first.

Same shit, different day, she thought as she flipped through the summary. On the very last page, something finally caught her eye. It was the report of an attack on an NYU professor and the killing of the assailant by a private security guard. It went on to mention both the professor and the security guard were Swedish citizens. The assailant's identity had not yet been determined.

Boy! Someone's hushing this up pretty good...Can't believe this didn't make the Daily News already..And why would a professor need a private security guard, unless...Whoa! Wait a minute! Swedish citizens? Just days after Sweden's announcement about the Pilcher investigation? Could there be a connection? Or am I just dreaming?

Allegra jotted down the name of the professor and hurried to a phone. Pacing nervously as far as the phone's cord would allow, she got the NYU switchboard on the line. "Operator, I need the number for Pola Nilsson-MacLeish...That's correct, she's faculty."

Chapter Seventy-Three

The hulking blond man guarding the hotel room door had taken quite a while to check her bag and scrutinize her press credentials. *Is smiling against this guy's religion or something?* Allegra Wise thought, her impatience boiling over and becoming obvious. Yet, the guard remained expressionless and unhurried. He spoke English slowly, with a thick Swedish accent that lacked inflection. "We cannot be too careful," he said, "after the attempt on the professor's life."

Looks like they've got the careful part covered, that's for sure. This guy's obviously packing...That's one hell of a bulge under his jacket. She did not dare complain when he asked her to remove her coat and gave her a polite frisking.

"I understand, sir, believe me," Allegra said, hoping agreeableness might hurry this process along. She just might be the first reporter to get Pola Nilsson-MacLeish's incredible story. For all she knew, though, some bigwig like Edward R. Murrow could stroll out of the elevator any second, leaving Allegra Wise out in the cold and out of luck.

Finally, the guard returned her press credentials. "Everything seems in order," he said as he opened the door to the suite and allowed Allegra to enter. The opulence of the suite surprised Allegra. *Pretty fancy digs! Some of these professors must really rake it in.*

At the far end of the sitting room, near the curtained windows, Pola Nilsson-MacLeish rose from a plush easy chair to greet her. The professor was dignified, relaxed, and smiling, everything Allegra was not at the moment. She clasped Allegra's offered hand with both of her own.

"Thank you for seeing me on such short notice, Professor MacLeish."

"Please, dear, call me Pola. May I call you Allegra? Such a beautiful name."

Allegra felt her tension begin to drain away. "Why so formal? Call me Ally," she said, punctuating her words with a buoyant laugh. Pola's unlikely Scottish accent, that had so surprised her when they spoke on the phone just a few hours ago, now charmed and soothed Allegra like a warm ocean breeze. They settled into comfortable armchairs.

"Tell me, Pola, am I really the only reporter you've spoken to?"

"Yes, you are. I had every intention of offering my story to any American newspaper or broadcast network who would listen, but you connected the dots first and found me before I was fully ready to come forward." Pola picked up a tall stack of handwritten pages on the table between them. "You've forced me to get my notes in order a little sooner than I planned. I don't want to end up looking as bonkers as Anthony Moscone did in the American media."

The serene smile faded from Pola's face. "That doesn't explain your eagerness, though, does it, Ally? I've already checked...You're not here on behalf of your network."

Allegra swallowed hard. She felt like a kid caught with her hand in the cookie jar. *Shit! If she checked with CBS, Sid already knows what I'm doing. That blows my element of surprise with him.* But she bluffed with some hard-nosed self-confidence. "I'm a reporter, Pola. If I smell a good story..."

Pola's smile returned as she cut Allegra off. "No

need to be defensive, Ally. You're just what I need at the moment...a reporter genuinely willing to listen."

Lady, you're just what I need at the moment, too, Allegra thought. She relaxed and flipped open her notebook.

"That gentleman at the door," Allegra said. "Is he the one who shot and killed your assailant?"

"Oh, no, dear. Although Mr. Andersson enjoyed diplomatic immunity as an embassy official, it was far better for all concerned if he left the country immediately." Pola smiled reassuringly before continuing. "Don't worry...I'm still very well protected. I trust you found Mr. Bjorkman quite thorough?"

Allegra tried her best not to sound sarcastic as she recalled the frisking. "Yes. Very thorough."

The interview began in earnest. The sordid story unfolded: Malmö, Pilcher, Linker, the murder she saw. When Allegra asked, Pola recited the roster of Pilcher's crew in Sweden. "There was David Linker, of course, Edwin Morris, and the poor lad who hung himself, Frank Hughes. Then there was Anthony Moscone. And Joseph Gelardi."

"Did you get to know any of them well?"

"Morris and Hughes, not at all...Linker, a bit...And Moscone? No. His condition made things very difficult. But Joseph and I were friends. Good friends. In fact, we met recently for the first time since the war, here in New York City."

The excitement those words triggered in Allegra's body caused a tingling that was almost sexual. *I knew it! I knew Gelardi was holding something back. They were friends, she says. Don't bullshit a bullshitter, honey...That sparkle in your eyes when you said his name...I'll bet dollars to donuts you two were fucking. And lovers share secrets...*

But Allegra's mental victory dance was short. Even if she was right about Joe and Pola being lovers, it still netted her exactly zero. Gelardi could continue to stonewall her questions until she was blue in the face. All she had gained was one—and only one—potentially credible witness to Leonard Pilcher's crime in Pola MacLeish. The confirmation of another credible witness still eluded her—*and this MacLeish woman seems fully aware of how easily the media—or a politician—could destroy a witness if they so desired. Just like with Moscone, Pilcher could skate away from her allegations, too.*

It was time for Allegra to go for broke. "Do you think anyone else, besides you and Tony Moscone, could have witnessed this murder?"

Pola smiled coyly. Her serenity was not about to be shattered. "That's unknowable, my dear."

That was not the answer Allegra was hoping for. *She either really doesn't know...or Professor MacLeish is the greatest poker player in the world.*

"Will you be seeing Professor Gelardi again?" Allegra asked.

"I don't know, Ally. We both live very busy lives in different cities."

"If I can get Professor Gelardi to agree, could I interview the two of you together...maybe even on the air?"

Pola considered that for a moment before nodding in agreement. "Yes, Ally, I'd be very happy to do that. Very happy, indeed."

Chapter Seventy-Four

Clouds of soot belched from the smokestacks of Pittsburgh's steel mills, darkening the dull daytime sky. Max Pilcher stood at his office window and searched in vain for a ray of sunlight, but none leaked through to lift his spirits. There was nothing uplifting in the news Tad Matthews had just delivered in person, either.

"So this Swedish woman in New York," Max said. "She's still alive?"

"I'm afraid so, sir," Tad Matthews replied.

Max muttered to himself, mimicking Tad's words with exaggerated, lispy inflection: *I'm afraid so, sir...I'm afraid so.*

After a frustrated pause, Max said, "This was all 16 years ago. Isn't there some statute of limitations in Sweden?"

"Yes, sir...but it's 25 years for murder."

The sky outside the window only seemed to be getting darker. "Shit," Max said. "So what do we do if the Swedes indict?"

"We ignore it."

"Excuse me? Ignore it?"

"Yes, sir." Matthews said, his eyes scanning an open file folder. "There is no extradition treaty in force between the US and Sweden...probably won't be one for years. They can't touch him, even if they could manage to cobble together an indictment. Of course, there is another possibility to consider."

"And that is?"

"If Leonard was suspected of a crime while in uniform, it could be argued that American military law applies to internees, and there is no statute of limitations on murder in the UCMJ."

"What the fuck is the UCMJ?"

"The Uniform Code of Military Justice...the law of the armed forces."

That stunned Max Pilcher. Suddenly, he seemed more than an older man—he had become an aged man, bewildered and unsteady. He seemed lost as he tottered to his desk and dropped awkwardly into his chair. After a moment, the aged man reverted to the powerful older man Tad Matthews had always known. The look of bewilderment had vanished.

"You mean the Army would try to court martial my son?" the elder Pilcher asked.

Tad replied, "Yes...and the penalty could be death."

The roar of laughter that escaped from Max Pilcher was something Tad Matthews had never heard from any human being before. It was not an expression of mirth; it was a sonic assault, an acoustic threat. The laughter subsided quickly. The malevolent atmosphere it created did not.

"The Army will do no such thing, not to my boy," Max Pilcher said with absolute certainty. "Let's get back to the question of a Swedish indictment. We should just ignore it, you say? And then we go into a presidential election with a candidate under indictment for murder in a foreign country?"

"That's right, sir. It hasn't mattered so far...the polls in Wisconsin show it."

Tad could feel the explosion coming. He could not imagine what he had done to provoke it; he had said nothing but the truth. He braced himself as Max Pilcher's verbal onslaught began.

"SURE! AND ALL THAT HAPPENS IS I'M

OUT THE ONE HUNDRED MILLION DOLLARS IN BUSINESS I DO WITH THE SWEDES EVERY GODDAMN YEAR! DID YOU THINK OF THAT POSSIBILITY?"

The force of those words rolled over Tad like a shock wave, pinning him to his chair. His voice strained as he tried to offer a defense. "But surely, sir, with Leonard in the White House, we can easily make up the lost business..."

Tad had to duck quickly to dodge the heavy paperweight Max Pilcher flung at him. It barely missed his head, then dropped to the carpeted floor beyond and rolled a few turns with a muted *thump...thump...thump*—like a severed head bouncing from the guillotine—before coming to a stop. He almost wished the paperweight had done him in. The physical blow might have provided welcome relief from Max Pilcher's tirade, which was obviously not finished.

"IS THAT SO? I DON'T NEED BUSINESS ADVICE FROM SOME FAGGOT LAWYER! NOW GET OUT OF MY SIGHT...AND GET YOUR CANDY ASS BACK TO WISCONSIN AND DO YOUR DAMN JOB!"

Tad Matthews was too mortified to utter a word as he fled the office.

Chapter Seventy-Five

The cab ride from lower Manhattan to midtown was taking forever in the thick midday traffic. *I could have walked faster than this,* Allegra thought while fuming in the cab's back seat. *Who am I kidding? I should be running!*

At 50th Street and Madison Avenue, seven blocks from her destination, she could take no more. "Let me out here," she said to the cabbie, throwing a five-dollar bill into the front seat for the $1.30 fare. "Keep the change."

Before the cabbie could offer a word of thanks, Allegra was barreling up Madison Avenue on foot. *Shit! I just gave away my lunch money! But hey...if this meeting goes as it should, this girl won't be eating lunch at the Automat ever again.*

Once inside the network building, she made a quick stop at the ladies' room to freshen up. Then she barged right past the producer's secretary, straight into his office. Breathlessly, she said, "Sid, I've got the scoop on the Swedish national. I just interviewed her."

He sat, saying nothing, arms tightly folded, his look of annoyance made more ominous by the clouds of cigarette smoke that floated before it every time he exhaled. She tried to catch her breath, waiting for his disapproving glare to crack into a smile of approval. That smile never came.

"I told you, Ally...you're off the Pilcher story."

"Didn't you hear me, Sid? This is the scoop that's going to blow Pilcher right off the map!"

Scowling, Sid shook his head dismissively. "Are you sure about that? Did you bother to do any background on this woman?"

"Not yet, but I can tell you she's the real thing."

"Let me guess...some broad with a Swedish accent feeds you a line of bullshit and you swallow it whole?"

"Actually, boss, she speaks with a Scottish accent." Instantly, she felt foolish to have offered more ammunition for his suspicions.

Sid threw up his hands in exasperation. "Ahh, for crying out loud! Now I'm telling you for the last time, Ally...touch this story again and you're canned. Fired. Terminated. Understood?"

"YOU DON'T EVEN WANT TO HEAR IT? THIS'LL WIN THE GODDAMN PULITZER, SID!"

"Keep your voice down, lady. And no...I don't want to hear it. Not from you."

That was Allegra Wise's breaking point. All the years of being disrespected, passed over, and shunted to scut work coalesced and erupted into a display of defiance and determination that surprised even her.

"Then fuck you, Sid. I'll just take it someplace else. Any network would kill to put this on the air."

She turned to storm out of the office but collided with a well-dressed older man who had just entered. She recognized him instantly; the likeness to the portrait in the building's entry hall was unmistakable. He was so much shorter than she imagined; Allegra found herself staring down into the inquisitive eyes of the chairman and president of the network, T. Homer Paulsen.

Standing by Mr. Paulsen's side was Wally, the most trusted man in America, happily puffing on his ever-present pipe.

"Any network would kill to put *what* on the air, my dear?" Mr. Paulsen asked.

Sid stepped from behind his desk. "This isn't

worth your time, Mr. Paulsen. I was just…"

A glare from T. Homer Paulsen was all it took to silence Sid.

"No, I think I'd be very interested to hear this young lady's story," Mr. Paulsen said. "As will you, Sidney."

Mr. Paulsen held a chair for Allegra. "Have a seat, miss…I'm sorry, I didn't catch your name."

Before the astonished Allegra could say a word, Wally provided the introduction. "Homer, I'd like you to meet Allegra Wise, one of the brighter lights in our newsroom."

"Shut the door, Sidney," Mr. Paulsen said as he and Wally settled onto the plush sofa. "Now, my dear Allegra…tell us exactly how we're going to win this Pulitzer."

Chapter Seventy-Six

They thought they would never make it to the surface.

Escaping from an airplane that had crashed in deep water and was rapidly sinking took every ounce of your mental and physical abilities. Although the adrenaline had made their minds razor sharp, Fred O'Hara and Lou DiNapoli were both badly injured. Fred's leg, braced for the plane's impact with the water, had its shinbone fractured when that impact crushed the plane's nose. Lou's hands and face were burned from his struggle with the thermite fire and severed control cables.

They were not sure exactly how they escaped the broken, submerged airplane. At first, they only remembered the searing pain in their lungs as they struggled upward from some murky depth for what seemed like an eternity. Once they broke the surface and took that first sweet gulp of air, the pain of their injuries returned and took center stage. In a few moments, that stage would be shared with the imminent prospect of death by exposure in the frigid water. Miraculously, a nearby Coast Guard vessel had heard Fred's SOS.

Now, a day later, they rested in a Connecticut hospital room. Two of Lou's men had driven up from the Bronx and stood guard in the hallway. Fred was in traction for his broken leg. Lou's hands were swathed in bandages, his face badly blistered. The reason for the doomed flight to Massachusetts dominated their thoughts.

Fred O'Hara dropped the telephone receiver into its cradle. From his chair by the window, Lou asked him, "So what did Joey the Professor have to say?"

"He said he's on his way. Should be here in about four or five hours."

Lou pondered those words for a moment, then rose from his chair. "I can't wait that fucking long, brother."

"Where're you going, Louie? What's the big rush?"

Fred had never before seen the look that came into his friend's eyes, not even when they had stared down the muzzle of some German's submachine gun. Usually sparkling and impish, they were now narrowed and lifeless. *Like snake eyes,* Fred thought. His facial burns made the look all the more sinister.

The coldness in Lou's voice was startling, too. "Unless you've got some more enemies you're not telling me about, that son-of-a-bitch Pilcher just tried to kill you. How he got at your airplane beats the shit out of me…but he almost got me, too, so now I've got a score to settle…and I ain't waiting no sixteen fucking years to do it, Freddy." Pointing to the huge bodyguard in the doorway, Lou said, "Tiny'll stay with you until your people get here. And Freddy…tell Joey I'm sorry I couldn't hang around for him."

Lou summoned the other bodyguard. "Ralphie, help me get dressed. We're getting out of here."

The phone call from Fred O'Hara had badly shaken Joe Gelardi. Just hearing from his old war buddy, whom he had not spoken to since that fateful day in the skies over Germany, was startling enough. To find out that Fred—and by coincidence, Lou DiNapoli—had nearly died while traveling to talk with him about a matter *that could not be discussed over the phone* had Joe in his car and driving toward Connecticut within an hour.

Now, standing beside Fred's hospital bed, their

conversation flowed easily. They still felt the strong bond of warriors, even after all the years. Joe pointed to the adjacent, empty bed and asked, "Where's Louie?"

"I'm not real sure," Fred replied. "He left this morning...just checked himself out, third-degree burns to the hands and all." His voice dropped. "Just between you, me, and the lamppost, though, I know what he's doing."

"Yeah? What's that?"

"He's going to pay *a little visit* to our mutual friend, Congressman Pilcher."

Joe did not get the implied threat in those words. Puzzled, he asked, "*Little visit*? What on earth for?"

Fred found Joe's bewilderment amusing. He made a hand motion like an airplane diving straight down, then pointed to his leg, hanging in its traction device. "Who do you think did this, Joey?"

"Wait a minute...if Pilcher did that to you and your plane, can't you go to the police? The federal authorities?"

Fred found that amusing, too. "They ain't on our side, Joey."

Joe's mind flashed back to the encounter at his home with the state police. Detective McGinty's words rang in his head: *You know, Doctor...if you really care about your little girl...you should think about keeping a real low profile for a while. Maybe running your mouth to reporters ain't such a hot idea, is it?*

From that moment on, Joe Gelardi was convinced beyond a shadow of a doubt. There could only be one person behind all this deadly mayhem: Leonard Pilcher. And Leonard Pilcher must be stopped. By any means possible.

And if IBM doesn't like it, the hell with them.

"Yeah...I'll bet you're right, Freddy, I'll bet you're right," Joe said, then paused to bask for a moment in the exhilaration his newfound wisdom brought. An awkward silence ensued; Joe clumsily sought to fill it by asking, "What kind of business did you say Louie was in?"

"I didn't...but you know what a cop is, right?"

"Of course."

"Then let's just say he's the opposite, Joey."

There was another awkward silence as those words sank into Joe's mind. Fred finally broke it by addressing the bodyguard at the door. "Hey, Tiny...give us a minute, will you?"

With Tiny gone, Fred asked, "So tell me, Joey...how did Davey Linker really die?"

Joe was surprised at the sweet relief that began to flow through his body, for the time had finally come to unburden his soul of the awful secret. He pulled up a chair and started to tell Fred O'Hara the story of what happened in Sweden.

An hour later, after the telling was done, Fred looked relieved, too. He nodded with satisfaction as he said, "Guess I had that lousy son-of-a-bitch Pilcher figured out all along. You know he tried to put a hit on Tony Moscone, too? Got some lowlife dirty cops to try and do him in."

"No...I didn't know that, Fred. Is he okay?"

"He's fine. Louie's got him covered. He even set him up in a TV and radio repair shop up in the Bronx, real close, so he can keep right on covering him." Fred scribbled something on the notepad by his side. He tore off the page and handed it to Joe. "You're going to be in New York City, right? Look Tony up...there's the address of his shop. He'd love to see you."

As Joe rose to leave, Fred snapped a crisp, military salute and said, "You watch out for yourself now, Joey. Do you and that lady friend of yours need some help from Louie, too?"

"No, I think we've got it covered," Joe replied, proudly returning the salute.

Chapter Seventy-Seven

She was not listening to the crooner on the morning wake-up radio show lamenting his lost love. Clad only in bra and panties, Allegra Wise was too busy rummaging through her bedroom closet, searching for just the right outfit for today's important business. Nervously, she selected—then rejected—one suit or dress after another.

Finally, she came to the sky blue suit. The plain white blouse she usually wore with it hung alongside. She lifted the garments from the closet rod and laid them on the bed.

I always thought this get-up made me look like a stewardess...But maybe that's not such a bad thing today. Men always cotton up to stews right away...It's that perception of the easy lay.

Quickly, she struggled into the girdle, slid into stockings, donned the white blouse, and slipped into the tight skirt. She stood before the full-length mirror as she pulled on the jacket and stepped into smart black pumps. As she pivoted back and forth for the quarter and side views, she was not unhappy with what she saw.

All I need now is a set of wings and a matching cap...I could be flying for Pan Am.

Allegra made her way to the kitchen, shut off the stove burner beneath the chattering percolator, and poured herself a steaming cup of coffee. As she sipped it, the music on the wake-up radio show ended. It was time for the morning news; a male voice boomed from the speaker:

Tomorrow's Wisconsin Primary is shaping up as

a showdown between Vice President Nixon and Congressman Leonard Pilcher. A victory for Mr. Pilcher could make him unstoppable in his bid for the Republican nomination...

Allegra clicked off the radio. "Unstoppable, my sweet ass," she muttered. She sorted the stacks of handwritten pages from yellow legal pads scattered across the kitchen table. Most of the pages were transcriptions of previous interviews. She sorted them into piles bound with paper clips, their top pages labeled in bold letters *MATTHEWS, MOSCONE, O'HARA,* and *MACLEISH.* The files were then placed into a folder labeled *PILCHER/WWII.*

The yellow pages that remained on the table were a fresh list of interview questions. She shuffled through the pages, stopping to cross out something here or add something there, until her furrowed brow relaxed and a contented smile crossed her face. She savored the sweetness this day had finally brought. The top page of this last pile was labeled *GELARDI.* Joe Gelardi had—at long last—agreed to be interviewed about that murder in Sweden.

What a difference a day can make, Allegra thought, as she clipped the pages of questions for the Gelardi interview together. *Here I was, calling his office, calling his home...and he's never there. I'm thinking the guy's ducking me...and out of the blue, he calls me! From just up the road in Connecticut, yet! Tells me he's on his way to Manhattan...and now he wants to talk. What changed his mind? His lady friend, I'll bet...Doctor Pola Nilsson-MacLeish.*

The radio announcer reported the time. Allegra checked her wristwatch against the radio time and her kitchen clock. All were in agreement: 8:05 a.m. In one hour and fifty-five minutes, she would meet with Joe

Gelardi at CBS headquarters in midtown Manhattan. Pola MacLeish would be there, too. *With her bodyguard, Mr. Happy Hands, no doubt.*

Once that meeting was over, Allegra would have the scoop on a story that could completely rewrite the presidential race. With any luck at all, she would be the one breaking that story on the air.

Chapter Seventy-Eight

The pouring rain had slowed the heavy traffic on the Connecticut Turnpike to a bumper-to-bumper crawl, but Joe Gelardi did not care—even if it meant his arrival back home in Brookline would be much delayed. He appreciated the solitude behind the wheel, the lulling hum of the car's engine, barely above an idle, the insistent patter of the rain on the car's body, the rhythmic *swish-thump—swish-thump* of the wipers as they danced back and forth across the windshield, keeping the beat to a song only they knew. This rain-soaked traffic jam gave him time and peace of mind to reflect on everything that had transpired yesterday in New York City and what would happen next.

He had been amazed how easily the story of David Linker's death had flowed from his mouth, guided by questions from Allegra Wise. He had to admit that at first she had intimidated him, just like she had when she tried to interview him at MIT: *I thought it was going to be the attack of the 50-foot newswoman all over again! She is sooo tall! She could be really menacing if she wanted to be! Once we all sat down, though, and she gave those endless legs of hers a rest, things went pretty smoothly...Hell, she already knew what happened in Malmö. She's just looking for corroboration...*

Pola had said little during his interview, finding it necessary only to fill in the blanks for the names of Swedish officials and some locations—names he had long forgotten or never knew.

One thing he was sure of: *Having Pola there made all the difference. It made everything right again.*

Joe and Pola had been startled when the anchorman, *the most trusted man in America—Wally, they all called him, in a way that could only be described as reverence*—strolled into the room to greet them, happily puffing on his pipe. He did not linger; this interview was clearly Allegra Wise's show. They could not help but notice the encouraging way Wally patted Allegra's shoulder before leaving: *It was like he was giving his blessing.*

Then there was that final question from the newswoman: "Why has it taken you so long to come forward? Everyone will want to know that."

There were a few moments of anxious silence before Joe began to speak. "We were young," he said. "Sometimes, it takes a long time to fully realize what a terrible mistake you've made..."

Pola finished his sentence. "And even longer to correct it."

"That's great. Perfect," Allegra Wise said. "Say it exactly like that when we're on the air."

For the first time in 16 years, Joe Gelardi did not feel he had failed David Linker.

Something else happened yesterday, also for the first time in 16 years. Joe Gelardi and Pola Nilsson-MacLeish had slept together. His mind eagerly retraced their steps after the interview concluded. There was the ride to the lobby in that crowded elevator, all eyes locked forward and unseeing, no words spoken; the two of them pressed tightly shoulder to shoulder, neither interested in lessening the pressure of that contact.

She squeezed my hand. She didn't turn to look at me, but I could tell she was smiling. She's still such a tease...

There was that awkward moment in the lobby when Pola's bodyguard—*that sullen Mr. Bjorkman—*

joined them. Yet, just as quickly as he appeared, he seemed to melt away, though he was never more than a few feet away from them at any time. As they lunched, he was seated by himself at a table against the wall—*you have no blind spots when you're against a wall.*

Afterwards, as they strolled around Washington Square, with Bjorkman a few paces behind, Joe asked, "Aren't you a little uneasy to be out in public like this? After what happened?"

Taking his arm, she replied, with the honesty of a child, "No, Joseph. I know you'll protect me." Turning and nodding toward her bodyguard, she continued, "Besides, Mr. Bjorkman is with us."

As they relaxed with coffee in her office before her 3:00 p.m. Developing Economies seminar, Bjorkman took up his post in the hallway.

I enjoyed sitting in on that seminar, Joe reflected. *Watching her engage those students was so refreshing...I almost forgot how brilliant she is! And what classroom technique! How gently she slapped that glib know-it-all kid down after he botched that Harrod-Domar Growth Theory presentation. How encouraging she was of those who seemed less sure of themselves. That bodyguard, though...the Bjorkman fellow...he certainly does stay focused on his job. That's a good thing...But he never smiles, not even a hint of one. Oh, well...I guess that goes with the grim territory.*

Over a sumptuous dinner in Little Italy, the talk turned serious. Their live on-air interview was in two nights' time. Leonard Pilcher's cat would really be out of the bag then.

"Will you get a bodyguard, Joseph?" Pola asked, her face beginning to show the glow from her second glass of Chianti.

"No. I can't afford that." With a flippant grin, he

nodded toward Bjorkman, seated at a corner table. "And I'm not quite the national treasure in my country you seem to be in yours. Don't worry. I'll be fine. Just so my daughter is protected."

"I wish you'd reconsider."

"Pola, once we've been on television Pilcher wouldn't dare touch us. It would be too late...and too obvious."

She emptied her wine glass and set it on the checkered tablecloth, never taking her eyes off him. Picking up a breadstick, she wielded it like a pointer, a teacher tapping an imaginary blackboard. "I hope you're right," she said. Turning to glance toward Bjorkman, she repeated, "I hope you're right."

The cab ride back to her hotel, with Bjorkman in the front seat with the driver, was made in contented silence. The giddy buzz of the Chianti had faded, leaving a pleasant glow that foreshadowed the sex Joe felt sure they were about to have. They were holding hands like teenagers, not caring if anyone else noticed.

I'll bet she's remembering how good all our times together were. Lord knows I am. Look at her face, gazing at the city lights. She seems so happy, like she's off in some fantasy world...

They ceased holding hands the moment they left the cab, submitting in autonomic unison to some unwritten rule of decorum for people their age. She took his arm instead, as Joe wondered whether it was *more for support than affection after all the Chianti?* As they made their way across the lobby of Pola's hotel, Joe hesitated, then stopped in front of the reception desk. He felt awkward, out of place. He feared he might be overstepping some boundary the wine had erased.

"What's wrong, Joseph?"

He stammered his reply. "I guess...I should check

in."

Her arm still tightly clutching his, she began to usher him toward the elevators. "Are you out of your bloody mind?" she asked, the glow lighting her smiling face once again.

Joe could not be sure, but he thought—just for a moment—he had finally seen Bjorkman break into a smile, too.

Still stuck in the rainy traffic jam, Joe was lost in the memory of last night with Pola.

The sex. What can I say about the sex? Except that it was all—no, it was more, than I hoped. It was tender, yet passionate. Totally uninhibited, without reservation. Completely satisfying, just like it was in Sweden...well, except maybe for that last time.

His mind's eye could see their sweat-glistened bodies locked together in that sweet movement, each thrust erasing a little bit more of the 16-year emptiness in their souls. The hotel bed had rocked noisily with their motion, providing a percussive beat as the headboard struck the wall rhythmically: *swish-thump—swish-thump...*

A horn began to overlay the beat. Quickly, more horns joined into an insistent cacophony. They were not being played by some crazed musicians in his subconscious. They were car horns: the traffic had finally picked up its pace. Joe's car had not; there was a good 10-car length between it and the vehicle in front. That distance was growing by the second. The rhythm of lovemaking's memory was now played by the windshield wipers, the song they had been performing all along finally clear: *swish-thump...swish-thump...*

Ahh...the rain has slowed up. Now we're making decent speed again. It's a shame I've got to drive all the way home, just to return to New York for the interview tomorrow. But what the hell...CBS is springing for the airline ticket.

But I need to go home. Diane must hear the whole story before it's broadcast to the world...and she must hear it from me, face to face.

Chapter Seventy-Nine

Once the traffic jam in Connecticut eased, Joe made it back to Brookline in record time. He pulled into his driveway just as Diane was finishing supper. She sat at the kitchen table with Sean Riley, her protector for the day, as Sean's mother plied them with fresh-baked apple cobbler.

His mouth full of dessert, Sean managed to say, "The professor's back."

Diane jumped into Joe's arms the instant he walked through the door. "Daddy! I missed you so much!"

"Missed you, too, pumpkin." Sniffing the air, Joe added, "Umm...that cobbler smells great! Can I get some of that, too?"

"Don't you go spoiling your dinner, now," Mrs. Riley said. "I've made your favorite...chicken pot pie."

By the time Joe had finished his supper and sorted through the accumulated mail, it was after 8:00 p.m. Diane was in her room doing homework. Sean Riley had departed, his duties for the day long concluded. Joe approached Mrs. Riley, who was busy putting the kitchen in order. "Edna," he said, "I need to talk privately with Diane. I'll fill you in later, okay?"

There always seemed to be a look of furrowed concern on Edna Riley's face, but, strangely, his words shocked her and deepened that look into something approaching abject fear. Joe had no intention of upsetting her; quite the contrary, he hoped his news would come as a great relief to all concerned.

Seeking to calm her, Joe added, "No, this is a

good thing. Really! For all of us!"

The fear washed from his housekeeper's face; the usual concerned look returned. Her voice heavy with skepticism, she said, "Oh, so it's *good* news. You scared the life out of me, Professor. Seven years I've worked in this house, and you've never once called me *Edna* before. I was fearing something dreadful." She hoisted the last of the supper dishes from the sink and placed them in the drainer. "Where do you want to chat with little missy?"

"The living room," Joe replied. "There's something on television I'd like her to see."

When Diane entered the living room, Joe was seated before the small black and white television set, watching news coverage of the Wisconsin primary. She twirled a single feather between the fingers of one hand.

"Where'd you get that feather?" Joe asked.

"When I hung up your coat before, it fell out," Diane replied. "I guess it was in your pocket."

Joe welcomed her discovery. *Yes...the pigeon feather. I had forgotten all about it.* "May I see it?" he asked.

"Sure." She handed him the feather.

Joe took it and twirled it happily between his fingers, just as his daughter had a moment before. As if on cue, a smiling Leonard Pilcher appeared on the television screen, standing before an election tally board and a happy crowd of supporters. The chalk-etched figures on the board were being updated to show the Wisconsin primary now tied: based on early returns, Pilcher and Richard Nixon were neck-and-neck. A news announcer shouted confirmation of the results over an outburst of wild cheering. Joe placed the feather on the coffee table, reached to the television set and turned the volume control all the way down.

Pointing to Pilcher on the screen, Joe said, "Diane, honey...it's time I told you a story about me and that man."

As he told his story, Diane seemed confused at first. She was not following the relevance of the war and her father's bomber crew and their internment with life as they knew it today. Then he told her about his *friend* from Sweden, a woman named Pola, and how Pola had come back into his life after all these years. His daughter began to comprehend the meaning of all this, and she found that meaning troubling and threatening. *A betrayal.*

"Is she your girlfriend?" Diane asked, her voice trembling.

"We're very good friends, sweetheart."

She stammered her next question: "Do you...love her?"

"Yes, I think I do, Diane." He paused, not quite sure how to handle her reaction, one he had failed to consider. "I was hoping you'd be happy for me."

Her stony silence was all the answer he needed. "But there is so much more I have to tell you," he said.

Diane was not sure she could take much more. What she had heard so far was distressing enough. She was already weeping softly. Joe could tell she was pulling away, emotionally if not physically, as his story continued.

With the exultant face of Leonard Pilcher on the screen for a backdrop, Joe told his daughter about the death of David Linker. As he mimed with his hands the motion of something falling, Diane's expression changed from petulant to horror-stricken. Her soft weeping turned to unabashed sobs as she buried her face into her father's shoulder.

Seen only to Joe, Mrs. Riley's face peeked in from the kitchen. He read her accusing look with certainty: *You lying bastard! Good news, my foot!*

Speaking softly into Diane's ear, Joe finished his story. When he was done, she lifted her head from his shoulder and composed herself. After dabbing at her eyes with a handkerchief, she turned to glower at the face of Leonard Pilcher on the television screen. It was a look of hatred, something Joe had never seen from his young daughter.

Her manner was distant, yet her voice was purposeful. "Of course you have to tell, Daddy. You can't let that man be president. He's a killer."

Joe Gelardi found himself overwhelmed by that simple logic—*the wisdom of a child.* The news announcer's lips moved frantically on the muted television, shouting a silent confirmation of the tally board's latest figures: *a two-point lead for Pilcher over Vice President Nixon.*

Diane's eyes did not meet his as she asked, "Can I go now?"

Chapter Eighty

For a moment, Joe Gelardi thought they had never left Boston's Logan Airport. As he stepped through the airliner's doorway and onto the boarding stairs, the airfield's ramp looked, sounded, and smelled just like the ramp at Logan. The blinding reflection of sunlight on polished aluminum fuselages, the roar of aircraft piston engines, the aroma of the salt water that formed a good share of the airfield's curved border, the reek of aviation fuel and engine exhaust—it was all the same. The past 90 minutes of rumbling and lurching through the sky had all seemed to be for nothing; they were back where they started. If it were not for the words *LaGuardia Airport* spelled in bold letters across the terminal building's façade and a glance to the west that revealed the smog-veiled Manhattan skyline just a few miles away, Joe could have been fooled. He had been so distracted by his own concerns during the flight that he had paid no attention to the landmarks that had drifted past his window.

Hell…who could miss the rivers? The bridges? The Empire State Building? And to think Uncle Sam trained me to be an aircraft navigator…

It was near noon. In six short hours, he and Pola would be on television, telling the world the true story of Leonard Pilcher. He was already queasy with nervousness.

God…what if I sound like some blithering idiot on the air?

Then, there was the problem of his daughter. *I should have anticipated how threatening the prospect of a woman in my life—our life—would be to Diane. How stupid I am!*

He was halfway to the gate before he noticed the smiling Pola, waving to get his attention from behind the chain link fence that separated terminal from ramp. Mr. Bjorkman was close by her, standing watch.

Look at her! She doesn't look nervous at all, Joe thought.

"Didn't you see me waving like a bloody fool?" she asked, before pulling Joe close for a welcoming kiss.

"I was...let's say, preoccupied," Joe replied when the kiss was done. He exchanged barely perceptible nods of greeting with Bjorkman.

"No matter," Pola said as they head into the terminal. "Let's get into Manhattan and have some lunch."

"I'm not very hungry, Pola. My stomach's a little upset."

"What? A big flyboy like you can't take a little plane ride anymore?"

"It's not the plane ride."

Her smile faded. There was no mistaking it now. Something was on Joe's mind.

"Are you having second thoughts about the interview?" she asked.

"No. Not at all."

Pola sighed deeply. "Then you've told Diane about us, haven't you?"

"Yes, I've told her everything. She understands about Pilcher just fine..."

"But she doesn't fancy another woman in your life, does she?"

Joe's silence was all the reply she needed.

"Oh, that poor, dear child," she said, grasping his arm tightly with both hands. "I was afraid she might take it badly."

The limousine slowly plied its way through the thick midday traffic of Manhattan. In its back seat, Tad Matthews was trying to brief Leonard Pilcher, who was more interested in browsing the newspaper's sports page. The paper's headline screamed PILCHER JUGGERNAUT WINS WISCONSIN.

"We really should have talked about this on the plane, but you insisted on napping," Matthews said.

Without looking up from the newspaper, Pilcher replied, "A man needs his sleep, you know."

Tad Matthews knew full well why Leonard needed that nap on the plane from Wisconsin to New York City. The congressman had not slept at all last night. The victory celebration had turned into another excuse to bed at least one woman from his campaign staff. Two was quite probable.

Undeterred, Matthews plowed ahead. "You're going to make the rounds of the newspapers and TV shows. People need to see you unconcerned about this Sweden nonsense, talking about real issues."

Leonard's attention remained fixed on the newspaper.

"Are you even listening to me, Leonard?"

Pilcher let the paper drop to his lap. "What does it matter?" he asked. "They've shot their wad on this Sweden thing already. It'll die all by itself...real soon."

Frustrated, Tad replied, "I'm glad you think so...You barely won Wisconsin, Leonard."

Pilcher shrugged off the comment and went back to the newspaper. As he turned the page, an article's title caught his eye: STEEL UNION BOSS SURVIVES PLANE CRASH. For a moment, he seemed stunned by the words he was reading. But the familiar smirk soon returned to his face.

"Gee, ain't that a shame?" Leonard said. "O'Hara had himself a little accident."

Now it was Tad's turn to smirk as he thought, *I wasn't going to mention this, Congressman...but since you've graciously provided the set-up, I've just got to pull the trigger.*

"By the way, Leonard, your father knows it was you who tried to get rid of Fred O'Hara. And he's not very happy about that."

Tad Matthews watched with quiet amusement as Leonard's face lost the smirk and froze into a look of panic. Tad understood; he knew well how uncomfortable life could be when you have displeased Max Pilcher. *And yet his idiot son never seems to learn.*

At last, the cab carrying Joe, Pola, and Bjorkman arrived at Pola's hotel. The ride from LaGuardia to downtown Manhattan had taken forever in the dense midday traffic. The sidewalk at the hotel's entrance was buzzing with reporters and photographers. A shiny black limousine was parked at the curb, its driver lounging against one of its prominent tail fins. Pedestrians gawked as they passed, wondering what famous person might be drawing all this media attention. That question remained unanswered as the pedestrians hurried on their way.

Several hotel security guards—silent, unsmiling men in matching blazers—manned the entrance, intent on keeping the newsmen out. As Joe and Pola passed through the revolving doors into the hotel, Joe laughed and said, "For a moment, I thought those reporters might have been waiting for us."

Pola was relieved: *Finally, he laughs! In the cab, I couldn't get him out of that funk no matter what I said.* But the prospect of being besieged by reporters dampened her spirits. Soberly, she said, "Tomorrow, Joseph. They'll be all over us tomorrow."

They passed through the lobby bar on their way to the restaurant. The bar reverberated with boisterous voices and laughter, crowded with those for whom lunchtime cocktails were a normal part of the business day. A man rose from a secluded corner table and made his way toward Joe and Pola. He parted the clouds of cigarette smoke as he walked, like a magician making his stage entrance through some mysterious mist. He wore an expensive suit and a smug smile on his face. His arms were spread wide in greeting.

"Well, well, well," Leonard Pilcher said, "fancy meeting you here! I couldn't believe my eyes! If it isn't my two favorite lovebirds! What brings you to the Big Apple, *Joseph?* Does she still call you that?"

With menacing swiftness, Bjorkman moved to step between Pilcher and the woman it was his duty to protect. Pola stopped him with an outstretched arm. "It's all right, Mr. Bjorkman," she said.

Three men materialized from the corner table. One was Tad Matthews. The other two were tall and burly: Pilcher's bodyguards. The congressman raised a hand to stop them as they approached. His voice loaded with sarcasm, Pilcher said, "That's okay, guys. These are some old friends of mine."

The bodyguards on both sides retreated a few steps, hands discreetly at the ready to reach for the pistols under their jackets. As Joe and Pola shot nothing but daggers with their eyes at Pilcher, the patrons closest to the confrontation took notice. They became transfixed by one of the adversaries: *Didn't I just see him on television or something? That couldn't be...Is it really him? What's his name...that guy running for president?*

The other patrons sucked down their cocktails,

oblivious to any distraction.

Pilcher seemed to be enjoying this face-off. "No...let me guess," he said. "A little tryst, perhaps? A brief respite from the old ball and chain?" Focusing his leering gaze on Pola, he added, "I'm telling you, MacLeish...You must be some hot piece of ass if he still wants to bang you after all these years."

Pola grasped Joe's arm, trying to pull him toward the door, but he stood firm, training a feral glare on Pilcher. "Still every inch the gentleman, aren't you, Pilcher. Apologize to the lady."

In a voice dripping with insincerity, Pilcher replied, "Oh, I'm soooo sorry." But his manner quickly turned huffy. "But how about showing *me* a little respect? Shouldn't that be Captain Pilcher to you...or Congressman Pilcher? Hell, soon you'll have to call me Mr. President."

"Not if we have anything to say about it," Joe said.

Pola's fair, alabaster features turned even whiter with shock at Joe's words. "No, Joseph! Not now!" she pleaded.

Pilcher erupted in anger. "What? Are you two planning on spreading more bullshit about me? I'd think twice about that, if I were you."

Pola's grip on Joe had not slackened throughout the exchange. He finally gave up his ground and allowed her steady pull to lead him to the door. An enraged Leonard Pilcher followed, just a step behind them.

"Did you hear me?" Pilcher said. "I'm not playing games here. Try to shit on me and you're going to need bodyguards the rest of your miserable lives."

A voice from the onlookers murmured, "Oh my God...that's Congressman Pilcher!"

Tad Matthews streaked in and grabbed Leonard

Pilcher, trying to pull him away from his quarry. Hissing in a stage whisper, Matthews said, "Shut the fuck up, Leonard! What is wrong with you? There are people..."

His words were cut short by Pilcher's fist striking him squarely in the jaw. Matthews sank to his knees as Pilcher bellowed, "KEEP YOUR FILTHY HANDS OFF ME, FAGGOT!"

The Congressman's bodyguards swooped in, shielding the assailant from the assailed, as bar patrons hastily scattered to the periphery of the room. Safe behind his protectors, Pilcher turned his taunts to his campaign manager: "Get up, you fairy. I didn't hit you that hard."

Slowly, Tad Matthews stood. Rubbing his sore jaw, he glared hatefully at Leonard Pilcher.

"Check us out of here, Matthews," Pilcher said. "I ain't staying in this shithole."

Tad shook his aching head. "Do you suppose we could wait until after the interview with the Times? It's scheduled for 2:00 p.m...in your hotel suite." He glanced at his watch; it said 1:20 p.m. "A little late to change venue, wouldn't you say?"

Leonard scowled, as if the duties of this election business were nothing but nuisances. "Yeah, fine," he said. "But right after that, we're gone."

Moments later, Joe and Pola were waiting for the hotel's elevator. A tense and vigilant Bjorkman stood nearby, repeatedly scanning the lobby for any further threat. His hand remained where it had been ever since the scene in the bar, inches from the pistol on his waist.

Joe was still fired by adrenaline. "Maybe we shouldn't be staying here," he said, his eyes darting about just like Bjorkman's.

"Don't be ridiculous, Joseph," she replied, her manner calm and collected. "This is where I live. Nobody is running me off...especially not *that* man."

A single chime—the elevator doors opened and the three stepped on board. Another couple hurried to catch it but was dissuaded by Bjorkman's menacing gaze and hulking frame blocking the threshold.

"Sorry," Bjorkman said to the couple as the doors slid closed. The tone of his voice was not in the least bit apologetic.

As the elevator raced skyward, Joe asked Pola, "Do you still have an appetite?"

With an incredulous smile, she replied, "Of course I do! Let's just order room service. We'll still have time to pay that visit to Tony Moscone before going to the studio."

Chapter Eighty-One

Double-parked on a lower Manhattan street, the big black Cadillac idled. Lou DiNapoli sat in the back seat, growing more frustrated by the second with his heavily bandaged hands. His attempts to remove the wrapper from a chocolate bar had all resulted in failure; it had slipped from his encumbered grasp for the third time. The henchman sitting next to him, fully aware of his boss's fierce independence and mercurial temperament, had been reluctant to intercede. But he could sit and watch no longer. Reaching for the chocolate bar on the seat, he said, "Let me help, boss. Them hands must hurt like a bastard."

Giving in to the offer of help, Lou replied, "I've had worse." His desire for the sweet chocolate had overridden whatever do-it-myself determination he had left. The henchman unwrapped the chocolate and offered a piece, like a priest presenting the host at communion.

Before Lou took the offered treat, he called to his driver, "What time is it, Dino?"

"Three minutes past the last time you asked, boss," the driver replied.

Lou grimaced. *This is taking too fucking long.*

On a rooftop a block away, the sniper squinted into the scope of his high-powered rifle. He counted to himself for what seemed like the hundredth time *two, three, four, five, six, seven, eight floors up...From the southeast corner, I count one, two, three, four, five windows. Come on, already! Where are you, asshole! I know you're in there...Step into my crosshairs, please.*

His arms were growing tired. He had been holding the heavy weapon at the ready for too long; the long silencer screwed onto the muzzle made it even heavier and harder to balance. He had seen several people move past that fifth window on the eight floor, but the face that matched the photo he carried had never come into view. He changed position, moving a few feet to his right so he could rest the non-firing hand that gripped the rifle's forestock against a rooftop ventilator. It increased the angle of the shot, but it was still well within his expert capabilities. Now, it was time to count all over again: *one, two, three, four, five windows...*

Chapter Eighty-Two

The lunch from room service was finished in short order. Pola devoured her sandwich; Joe hardly touched his. By 2:20 p.m., they were in a cab heading north from downtown Manhattan to the Bronx.

"Fordham Road, eh?" the cabbie said in the thick accent of a native New Yorker. "You want me to step on it, pal? Or do you got all frigging day?"

"As quickly as possible, please. We're expected at three," Joe replied.

With those instructions, the ride became something akin to a Monte Carlo rally. The cab snaked with alarming speed through the thick traffic of lower Manhattan, not even bothering to slow down for the traffic lights that had clearly turned red in time for it to stop. Once on East River Drive, its rapid progress northward mocked the speed limit signs posted at frequent intervals. In less than 15 minutes since Joe, Pola, and Bjorkman boarded, it had crossed the Harlem River into the Bronx. Less than five minutes later, the cab screeched to a stop before Fordham TV and Radio Repair. Its passengers finally released their death grips on the safety straps hanging from the door posts.

The hotel concierge had advised them the trip to the Bronx by cab would take *about 40 minutes, provided there were no unusual traffic delays.*

"You want I should wait?" the cabbie asked.

"Yes, we'd appreciate that," Joe replied. "Mr. Bjorkman will wait with you."

"It's your dime, pal…The meter's running," the cabbie said, settling in to pass the time with a girlie magazine while totally ignoring the imposing Swede beside him in the front seat.

Chapter Eighty-Three

Tad Matthews was going through the motions of his job mechanically, like a robot that made phone calls, signed invoices, and cleaned up his master's messes. If he allowed himself to think about the lunacy of working for the Pilchers all these years, he would probably scream, right there at the hotel's front desk. He had made up his mind. Fortune be damned, this was his last day in their service.

Ever since that scene in the bar a few hours ago, where Leonard had punched him and called him a *faggot* right there in public, right in front of potential voters, Tad Matthews had finally had enough. He admitted to himself, for the first time, that he had been toiling in a lost cause. Leonard Pilcher could not—*no, should not*—be president. He would no longer have anything to do with the megalomaniacal dreams of that father and his incompetent son. They would have to find themselves another lawyer-turned-errand boy. While Leonard, puffed up by his narrow Wisconsin victory, had swaggered his way through the interview with The New York Times—never managing to coherently answer one of the reporter's questions—Tad Matthews had been preparing his letter of resignation. He would deliver it to Leonard at the end of business today, backing it up with a special delivery letter to the old man in Pittsburgh. Then he would make his escape. Even if it meant hiding forever from their deadly tentacles for the rest of his life. It would be worth it. All that was left to do was check Leonard out of this hotel and into another uptown, then see that he got through the day's remaining news interviews without making a compete ass of himself.

Across the hotel lobby, an elevator door slid open and Leonard Pilcher strutted out, his bodyguards close behind. His smug smile had faded by the time he reached Matthews at the front desk, for no one in that bustling lobby had given him as much as a nod of recognition. Only the desk clerk greeted him, with a less-than-reverent "Good afternoon, Congressman." To the others, he was just another businessman—another well-heeled asshole in a suit and tie—among tens of thousands in this city. Certainly not a candidate for some party's presidential nomination.

"Matthews, do you have my briefcase?" Pilcher asked.

Not bothering to look up from the papers he was signing, Matthews replied, "Since when do you have a briefcase?"

"Since now. I must've left it in the room. Go get it."

Tad motioned toward the two bodyguards. "Why can't one of the gorillas go back and get your goddamn briefcase?"

"Because they work as a team...and I told *you* to do it, that's why. Is the limo out front?"

"Of course it is," Matthews replied, sliding the signed paperwork across the desk to the clerk. "But wait for me here until I fetch your briefcase. I don't want you wading through those reporters out on the sidewalk alone."

"Fine with me. I'll be in the bar. Make it quick, Matthews."

As Tad made his way to the elevators, Leonard Pilcher mumbled something under his breath. The bodyguards were fairly sure he said *fucking smartass faggot.*

A thrill passed through the sniper's body. The crosshairs in the rifle's scope were zeroed on the back of a man's head. *Finally! I can't see the son of a bitch's face...but he's alone, sitting right in front of the window, the fifth window...and he's talking on the phone. It's got to be him.* He checked the telltale signs of wind one last time—the steam rising from pavement grates, flags flapping, chimneys spewing their smoke. *Speed and direction are still the same. Don't touch the sight settings.*

His finger caressed the trigger, slowly but smoothly increasing the pressure, almost ready for the final, delicate squeeze. *Still can't see his face...but it's got to be him.*

It's got to be.

It had taken Tad Matthews a minute to find the briefcase. It was under the bed, hidden, as if put there by some child not wanting his parents to find it. When Tad pulled it from under the bed and opened it, his jaw dropped in disbelief; it contained nothing but a few trashy paperback novels and an almost-empty bottle of whiskey.

He had to laugh. If he needed any further reinforcement for his decision to resign, this was it. Any sense of urgency to retrieve Leonard from the lobby bar and finish the business of the day dissolved. He settled into the chair by the window to make a phone call, one he had thought he would not be making until later that evening.

"Brad," he said to the phone, "it's me. Listen carefully. Pack a bag...There will be an open ticket to Mexico for you at the airport...yes, of course, Brad. I mean Greater Pittsburgh Airport. Now stop interrupting me. I don't have much time...Yes, of course I'm going, too. I'll be meeting you there…No, this is not a vacation. This is freedom…"

After that gentle squeeze of the trigger, it had taken the sniper's bullet slightly less than one second to shatter the fifth window, a millisecond more to shatter Tad Matthews's skull. As the sniper quickly tore down his weapon and placed it into its carrying case, a nagging doubt clutched at the pit of his stomach: *I never saw the face…but it had to be him.*

In seconds, he was on the stairs leading from the roof. His mind offered one further rationalization: *And Louie DiNapoli don't pay if there ain't no body.*

Chapter Eighty-Four

Tony Moscone's shop was one of several comprising the ground floor of a five-story tenement on busy Fordham Road. Beyond the front counter, two long workbenches lined the walls in the bright fluorescent light. They were crowded with radios and television sets undergoing repair and the equipment needed to troubleshoot them: meters, oscilloscopes, signal generators. More radios and television sets were scattered on shelves and the floor. It looked like there were at least 50 units in various states of assembly. Boxes of spare parts were crammed into any available space under the benches.

In the middle of all this sat one smiling man, perched on a high stool, engulfed in the wavy ribbon of smoke rising from the soldering iron in his hand. Tony Moscone was busily bringing a recalcitrant television set back to life.

A bell rang as the shop's door shut behind Joe and Pola. Tony looked up from his work. His smile broadened as he bounded from the stool.

"You're early, Professor," Tony said, surprising Joe with the ferocity of his hug.

"Let's just say our cabbie was inspired," Joe replied. "It's good to see you, Tony. You look terrific."

With a good-natured laugh, Tony said, "Yeah, I'll bet you were expecting the same old Section Eight basket case." Proudly, he swept his arms across the panorama of his shop. "Things are better for me now. Did you see Louie?"

"No, he was gone from the hospital by the time I

got there."

"Too bad. Louie's a real good friend to have."

Joe eyed the premises skeptically. "Can Louie really protect you here?" he asked.

Tony replied with a confident smile. "Professor, you don't know Louie. He *owns* the Bronx. Not even the cops bother me here." He fixed a benign, inquisitive gaze on Pola.

"You don't remember me, do you?" Pola asked.

"Even if I don't, I sure know *of* you, Doctor MacLeish." Tony gave her a hug, too—gentler this time, but no less heartfelt. "I guess the two of you are going to show the world that old Tony Moscone ain't so crazy after all."

They settled into a reminiscence both painful and liberating. Soon, tears were rolling down all their cheeks. They found it difficult to utter the name *David Linker* without choking up. They avoided saying the name *Pilcher*, as if saying it would invoke some evil entity. They referred to Pilcher only as *him,* except for the one time that Tony, talking of when he was assaulted on that Philadelphia street, used the term *piece of shit.*

"Pardon my French, ma'am," Tony said immediately after letting that oath slip.

"That's all right, Tony," Pola answered. "I speak fluent French. I understand completely."

When the telling was finished, they all felt drained and winded, like they had completed a marathon. Tony sat quietly, his gaze troubled and distant, as if trying to look beyond the horizon to a world that might have been. It took a few anxious moments before he could voice what was on his mind. It was not said as a condemnation or accusation, just a statement of fact. "Looks like all these years we've been in the same boat. I feel like I let Davey down, too. First, I couldn't say nothing, even if I wanted to. Then, when I could, they thought I was nuts."

Placing a comforting hand on Tony's shoulder, Joe said, "There's nothing more you could have done, Tony."

Tony's face was that of a lost and frightened child, desperately clinging to the hope that his salvation might be at hand. As he looked to Joe and Pola, he voiced a plea: "But *you're* going to do more, aren't you?"

"Yes, Tony, we are," Joe said, checking his wristwatch. "In less than two hours, in fact."

A news flash interrupted the programming on at least a dozen TV sets in Tony's shop. A talking head reported the shooting at the hotel as a *possible* assassination attempt on Leonard Pilcher. Tony broke the stunned silence: "I guess we ain't the only ones looking to put the screws to the congressman."

Joe's mind flashed back to his reunion with Fred O'Hara at the hospital and Fred's mention of Lou DiNapoli's *little visit* to Pilcher. With grim certainty, Joe said, "Perhaps we're not, Tony...Perhaps we're not."

Chapter Eighty-Five

It did not take long for confusion and chaos to engulf the hotel. A chambermaid preparing a room across the hall heard the shattering glass. When her knock went unanswered, she let herself into the suite. For a brief moment, she was not sure what to make of the scene that confronted her in the sitting room. Curtains billowed, propelled by wind from the man-made canyons of Manhattan blowing through a window without its glass. Unmuffled traffic noise from the street below assaulted her ears. There were gooey droplets of pink matter sprayed on the walls and furniture. She looked down to see the body of the thin, well-dressed man, the back of his head hideously misshapen and matted with dark, fresh blood, sprawled face down on a carpet saturated with more blood and strewn with glass shards.

A hotel guest in the suite next door surmised out loud that the chambermaid's screams could be heard across the river in New Jersey.

In minutes, there seemed to be a battalion of police in and around the hotel. A lockdown was imposed; no one was allowed to enter or leave. An irate Leonard Pilcher informed the pot-bellied veteran police officer holding him, his bodyguards, and the other patrons in the bar captive that he was, in fact, *Congressman Leonard Pilcher...and I could leave whenever the hell I wanted.* The unimpressed cop deftly blocked Pilcher's path, stared him down and said, with the certainty of experience, "And I'm the Queen of England. Sit the fuck down, my friend. Have yourself another cocktail. Nobody's going no place until the scene commander says so."

Information leaked from the hotel with the inaccuracy typical of chaos. Before long, the reporters queuing outside, waiting hours for Pilcher to emerge, were hearing *a man was found dead in some congressman's room*. Like in a game of telephone, that factoid was unwittingly revised as it passed from reporter to reporter, quickly becoming *a man was murdered in the congressman's room,* and finally *the congressman was murdered in his room!* Reporters clawed over each other to get at the nearby payphones and call in their stories. If it was true, this was news worthy of a two-inch headline: *Presidential Candidate Murdered!* If it turned out to be bullshit, at least their editors knew they had their ears to the rumor mill.

It took almost an hour for detectives to determine the congressman was not lying dead on the floor but being interrogated in the bar by one of their squad. The scene commander, a nervous captain who seemed uncomfortable under the weight of the gold bars on his shoulders, could feel the disappointment rippling through the reporter ranks as he provided that update. Returning to the hotel bar, the captain apologized profusely for the detention and assured Leonard Pilcher that the mayor had authorized around-the-clock police protection while the congressman was in their fair city. In fact, the mayor was on his way to the scene at this very moment to offer his personal apology.

Despite Leonard Pilcher's wishes, a press conference was hastily scheduled at his New York City campaign headquarters. He had no interest in talking to anyone, least of all the press. He was certain the bullet that killed Tad Matthews had been meant for him. That certainty made him want to cower in his limo as it drove straight to the airport so his plane could whisk him safely back to Pittsburgh. It had taken a phone conversation with his father to get him in front of the microphones. The elder Pilcher had spoken only two sentences during that brief conversation. After listening to his son blubber *Someone is trying to kill me, Daddy,* Max Pilcher said, "Get your ass back out there in front of the cameras where it belongs. Try acting like a man, you imbecile."

The crowd of reporters was loud and surly, each clamoring for his turn to speak. The hostile tone of the first reporter's question startled Pilcher. "A new poll just out today," the reporter said, "shows your support dropping sharply, despite your narrow win in Wisconsin. Your comment?"

Pilcher bristled. "I don't believe in polls," he said, "and even if I did, I'd say they were nonsense. You members of the press need to stick to your job and ask relevant questions."

A second reporter shouted above the din. "Do you believe you were the intended victim of the shot that killed Mr. Matthews?"

An incredulous Pilcher replied, "Of course I was! There're lots of evildoers who'd like me dead…who don't want to see a strong, vigilant America in this dangerous world."

"Like who?" the reporter countered.

Campaign staffers at the periphery of the room cringed. Pilcher was once again dangling one foot over the edge of the political cliff. This was where Tad Matthews used to step in and prevent Pilcher from falling head first into the abyss of idiocy—but Tad Matthews was no longer among them.

"A decisive leader makes enemies," Pilcher offered in reply. "That's what happens when you make the hard choices a leader has to make. Next question."

Reporters' hands shot up, but a tall woman

pushed forward and seized the floor. "Allegra Wise, CBS Television…"

All heads turned. There was murmuring—*CBS TV? Who the hell is she?*

Allegra shouted her question. "Congressman, there seems to be an atmosphere of foul play surrounding your campaign. Two murders, several assaults, a kidnapping…and a mysterious plane crash that…"

A furious Leonard Pilcher interrupted. "I'LL REMIND YOU, MISS, THAT THIS IS AMERICA, WHERE WE DON'T STAND FOR LIES AND INNUENDOES! ALL THOSE PEOPLE MAKING ALLEGATIONS AGAINST ME DON'T HAVE THE NERVE TO MAKE THEM TO MY FACE!"

Cool and unintimidated, Allegra replied, "I believe I just did, Congressman."

There was stunned silence in the room. The campaign staffers squirmed in discomfort, praying vainly that one of their number would summon the courage to yank their candidate from the stage.

"NEXT QUESTION," the red-faced Pilcher shouted, but he was unheard as the murmurs in the room strengthened to a tumult.

Chapter Eighty-Six

Joe found himself amazed how bright the lights in the television studio were. *No wonder they told me to wear a light blue shirt under a dark suit jacket. With all these spotlights blazing, white makes a terrible glare on a TV screen, they say. And what it must take to cool this place! How do they muffle the sound of all the fans running, drawing all that hot air out and pumping the cool air in? What a marvel of acoustics! It's quiet as a tomb in here.*

It was good that his scientific mind was captivated by those technical issues. If he thought about what he and Pola were about to set in motion, he would be far more on edge than he already was. They sat close together at an oval coffee table in a corner of the sound stage, an empty chair to their left. A stagehand placed a pitcher of ice water and three glasses on the table. The clock on the studio wall read three minutes until 6:00 p.m.

Allegra Wise walked onto the sound stage with the grandfatherly anchorman Joe and Pola had met the day before. As they diverged to their respective places on stage, the anchorman smiled warmly and said, "You'll do just fine, Ally." He then took his seat behind the desk at center stage, cleaned his thick-framed glasses with a tissue, and slipped effortlessly into his guise as *the most trusted man in America.*

The tall newswoman offered a nervous smile as she settled into the third chair at the coffee table. "Are you ready?" Allegra asked Joe and Pola, as she shuffled the pages of notes before her over and over again with unsteady hands.

Pola was, by far, the calmest of the three at the coffee table. With a serene smile, she replied, "Ready if you are, luv."

Joe felt the cool dampness of sweat at his collar, in his armpits, and on his forehead. *Good God! And it's not even warm in here! I hope I don't get the shakes, too.*

A make-up lady swooped in, dabbed at his forehead and applied a touch more powder to his face. She was in no great hurry as she worked; the cameras would not be aimed their way quite yet. Stepping back to judge her efforts, she nodded approvingly, then exited the stage as the newscast began.

"Good evening from New York," the anchorman said. "Alarming allegations continue to rise about congressman and presidential hopeful Leonard Pilcher. The Swedish Ministry of Justice announced today that it has brought forth an indictment for murder against Mr. Pilcher. Yet, the congressman remains defiant."

The monitors in the studio switched to a taped confrontation between Leonard Pilcher and reporters. Pilcher's face filled the screen as he ranted, "As I've said many times before, the charges against me are complete and utter nonsense! I'm no quitter! I have no intention of withdrawing."

Pilcher's face disappeared from the monitors, replaced by the face of the anchorman. Removing his glasses for dramatic emphasis, he continued: "CBS News has uncovered startling new information on the Swedish murder allegation. Here with a remarkable, exclusive report is the newest member of our CBS news team, Allegra Wise."

The little red light atop the camera facing Allegra began to glow. Another camera rolled silently into position to capture the three at the coffee table from another angle. Its red light came on, too, as the director pointed to Allegra like a cop directing traffic.

In that instant, Joe felt his fear and nervousness swept away by a rush of exhilaration. *This must be what it feels like to go over Niagara Falls in a barrel.* He stole a glance at Pola and was thrilled by what he saw: *Look how calm, how beautiful she looks. She is completely ready to do this...and so am I.*

He had not realized until that moment he was squeezing her hand—and she was squeezing back. Their hands were not visible in the monitor; they were being shot from the shoulders up. Neither felt the desire to let go.

Allegra Wise was completely ready for her moment, too. She took a deep breath and began to speak. "I'm here with Professor Pola Nilsson-MacLeish of the University of Stockholm and Professor Joseph Gelardi of MIT. They have a most shocking story to share with us..."

At the Gelardi house in Brookline, Diane and Meredith were glued to the television. Diane was wary. Meredith was enthralled.

Her face screwed into a sneer, Diane said, "So *that's* Pola..."

"Yeah! She's so great!" Meredith added. "So incredibly poised and well spoken! How hard that must be, with the story they're telling."

"What about my dad? He's doing great, too, don't you think?"

"Of course," Meredith replied, "but I already know how great he is."

Diane remained unimpressed. "I don't know...I think she's icky."

Meredith gave her a good-natured poke in the arm. "Don't be such a retard, Diane. Give the lady a break. She's a professor, for Pete's sake."

The stage director glanced at his stopwatch and signaled Allegra with a twirling forefinger, held above his head: *One minute left. Wrap it up.* The timing was perfect. Allegra was down to her final question.

In a businesslike tone that lacked any hint of accusation, she asked, "The question on everyone's mind is, of course, *why did you wait so long?"*

There was a pause before Pola began to answer. Her smooth, professional veneer cracked just a bit. It was difficult enough admitting a mistake, but doing it in front of a million or more people took every ounce of inner strength a person might possess. Slowly, solemnly, she began to speak. "Sometimes, it takes years to fully know just how terrible a mistake you've made…"

As she paused again to compose herself, Joe, with a calmness and certainty that seemed to come out of nowhere, finished her sentence: "…and years more to correct it."

Chapter Eighty-Seven

The secretary thought a saboteur's bomb had killed Max Pilcher. When she heard the *bang,* she raced in from her desk in the outer office, expecting to find the old man blown to smithereens—*those filthy union animals will stop at nothing!* Instead, she was surprised to find him sitting quietly at his desk, blankly staring at what was left of the television, its chassis still smoking, the phosphorous dust from the shattered, imploded picture tube still swirling in the air.

She did not need to ask what had happened. His heavy desk set—pens, inkwells, and nameplate set in a highly polished, replica steel girder—was now sitting inside the television's cabinet, among shards of shattered glass that used to be the picture tube. It did not take a genius to figure out how it got there.

"Are you hurt, Mr. Pilcher?" the secretary asked, although he seemed at least physically intact.

He replied only with a grunt and dismissive wave of his hand. Then he mumbled something to himself. Although it made no sense to her, she was fairly sure he had said, "Reporters and college teachers! What is this fucking world coming to?"

"I'll call the custodians to clean this up," she said. "Can I get you anything else? I was hoping you wouldn't be needing me anymore today…It *is* after 6 p.m."

His clarity and command returned as if a switch had been thrown. "Get the New York people on the phone," he said. "Right now!"

As she hurried to her phone console in the outer office, Max Pilcher's unsmiling eyes settled on Leonard's photo hanging on the wall. He picked up a paperweight from his desk—a globe of the world cast in steel—and flung it at the photo, scoring another direct hit. As the paperweight and photo crashed to the floor, he knew what he must do: *Got to get that idiot son of mine back here, pronto...and keep him away from those fucking news people.*

Chapter Eighty-Eight

They had hardly touched their suppers. The feeling of relief after their television interview was all-consuming and satisfying. Eating seemed an unnecessary ritual in the completeness of their world at that moment. So did talking. They had hardly uttered a word since returning to the hotel suite.

Joe topped off Pola's half-empty cup of coffee from the pot on the room service cart. She sipped it slowly. Relaxed in a plush armchair, her trim legs were tucked beneath her. The ribbon that tied back her white-blonde hair had been long discarded. The luminous strands fell past her shoulders and seemed to light her contented face.

The Swedish Embassy had insisted they stay out of the public eye once the on-air interview was done. Being constantly besieged by reporters was the biggest concern now; already, the hotel switchboard had been deluged with calls asking for interviews with the suddenly notorious professors. Joe had instructed Mrs. Riley to leave the phone at his house off the hook once their conversation ended. The housekeeper's two sons, reinforced by a few burly friends for around-the-clock coverage, would have no trouble keeping the media out of the yard and away from Diane.

It was Pola who finally broke the silence. Her words escaped like a reluctant sigh: "It's over, Joseph."

The pleasant bubble he inhabited to that moment seemed to shatter around him. *What does she mean, "It's over?" The way she said it... Is she talking about this whole Pilcher ordeal...or is she talking about us? But the way she said it! Oh shit...here we go again!*

When he found the words to speak, their tone surprised him. His deepest fears had hedged their bets—and those words came out sounding flippant: "You're not banishing me again, are you?" He found it impossible to breathe as he awaited her answer.

She set down the coffee cup, rose from the chair and approached him on stocking feet. With one hand, she caressed his face. With the other, she began to unbutton her blouse.

"No, you silly laddie. That's not what I mean at all," she said, leading him to the bedroom.

There was nothing wrong with the sniper's appetite. In a quiet corner booth of a New Jersey diner just across the Hudson from Manhattan, he was downing his second cheeseburger with all the trimmings. Work always left him ravenously hungry. Now, it was time to find work someplace else, far away, where Lou DiNapoli could not find him. *Louie ain't got no use for fuck-ups.*

The waitress tried to strike up a conversation as she placed another milkshake before him. "Did you hear? Some lunatic tried to kill that guy running for president. What's his name? Pilfer, or something like that?"

"Pilcher," the sniper said, without looking up. "Yeah. I heard."

"The news is saying he shot the wrong guy...campaign manager or something like that."

"Heard that, too."

He had not looked at her, not even once. He went right back to eating, wolfing down the rest of the cheeseburger without saying another word. The waitress took the hint and moved on to another booth, but not before sending an ugly glance his way. *That bastard better not be as stingy with the tip as he is with them words.*

In a few moments, his plate was clean. He threw a 10-dollar bill on the table and made his way outside, into the diner's dimly-lit parking lot, which was crowded with cars. The evening air had turned frigid and bracing; the sniper raised the collar of his coat and held it tight to his neck against the cold. *It won't be this nippy in Tucson,* he thought as his big Buick rumbled to life.

Foot still on the brake, he put the gearshift into reverse. There was a *tap-tap-tap* on his window. Even in the shadows of night, he recognized the face of Dino, Lou DiNapoli's driver—and the muzzle of a pistol's silencer resting against the glass.

The sniper's foot slammed the accelerator to the floor, but not before the *pop-pop* of two silenced gunshots shattered the window and tore paths through the sniper's skull. The big Buick raced backward at the command of a dead man's foot. It came to rest only after smashing into two cars parked across the way.

Dino was back behind the wheel of Lou DiNapoli's Cadillac as it cruised the New Jersey Palisades. Manhattan was aglow across the river. They would be over the George Washington Bridge and back in the Bronx in no time.

In the back seat, Lou's bandaged hands rested in his lap. The henchman seated by his side fed him a chocolate bar, one bite-sized piece at a time. Pensively gazing on the lights of the city across the Hudson, Lou said, "What a shame. That guy was such a good shot. Too bad he shoots the wrong son of a bitch."

From the driver's seat, Dino asked, "So how do you wanna handle this Pilcher thing now, boss?"

Lou savored the piece of chocolate in his mouth before answering. "Gonna bide my time. We'll get ourselves another chance…real soon."

Chapter Eighty-Nine

It was Diane's last swim meet of the season. Joe had made it a point to be back from New York in time. If he had not, he knew his daughter would see it as choosing Pola over her. Pola knew it, too: she was the one who had taken pains to make sure he was on that first morning flight back to Boston. When she shook him awake at the ungodly hour of 4:35 a.m., he found his bag already packed, his clothes laid out, his airline reservation rearranged, and a taxi waiting to whisk him to LaGuardia Airport.

As the late afternoon sun cast its horizontal rays through the pool house's high windows, Joe climbed to his usual seat at the top of the bleachers. He was uneasy—he could not shake the memory of what had happened the last time he was here; the light-headedness, the nausea he felt as young boy after young boy plunged from the high diving platform toward the water—each dive a replica of David Linker's death plunge. *I don't remember how, but I managed to flee this place...only to be rescued by Meredith Salinger.*

Now it was time for the boys to dive again. As the first climbed the ladder to the top of the high platform, Joe braced himself. The young man prepared himself for his leap; Joe took a deep breath and held it.

The diver launched himself into the air, arms extended, and arched backward. Head and feet exchanged positions; he plunged downward—gracefully downward—and entered the water like a needle, leaving only a small splash to mark his impact. In a moment, he popped to the surface and swam to the ladder, applause ringing in his ears.

Joe let the deep breath out. Another boy left the platform and flew gracefully to the water's surface. There was more applause, and Joe realized he was among those clapping. He felt no hint of nausea, no danger of blacking out. His breathing was perfectly normal.

On the other side of the pool, Diane's team had emerged from the locker room, ready to swim. She was smiling and looking his way. When she was sure he had seen her, she waved energetically, both hands high above her head. He returned the wave with his own hopeful smile. *When I spoke to her on the phone last night, she was so upbeat...She didn't even seem negative about Pola's coming to visit us.*

Joe relaxed against the bleacher seat behind him. The high-diving event was finished. No more boys would be falling through the sky—not in this pool house, not in Joe Gelardi's mind.

The sound of Pola's voice filled his head. The words she said last night that had left him so confused at first now had a meaning that was crystal clear: *It's over, Joseph.*

The telegram from IBM was waiting for Joe when he and Diane returned home from the swim meet. Mrs. Riley had conspicuously placed it on top of today's mail pile; she pretended to ignore Joe as he stared at the Western Union envelope in his hand, as if debating whether to open it or not. Diane and Mrs. Riley exchanged an anxious glance that kindled fear in the young girl's heart. The job at IBM—and the unwelcome move to Armonk it entailed—had been the elephant in the room nobody mentioned, shoved into a corner by the more pressing events of the past few weeks. But here was that elephant—front and center—suddenly demanding all their attention. Diane's penny loafers felt glued to the floor as she watched her father slowly open the envelope.

Joe unfolded the telegram within. It contained a single terse paragraph:

Certain political activities have called into question suitability of your employment offer -(Stop)- Corporate policy prohibits active political campaigning by employees -(Stop)- At direction of senior management offer of employment to you is hereby rescinded -(Stop)- Good luck in your future endeavors -(Stop)-

Diane and Mrs. Riley had slowly drifted toward each other as Joe read, their collective dread pulling them together like some magnetic attraction. Joe was expressionless as his eyes scanned the telegram once, twice, then a third time. Slowly and carefully, he folded the sheet of yellow paper back to envelope size as his expression brightened to a broad grin. Then, eyes twinkling with fiendish delight, he tore the telegram over and over, the pieces floating to the floor like so much confetti.

When the last scraps of torn paper had settled, he turned, still a very happy man, to Diane and Mrs. Riley and said, "We didn't want to move there, anyway, right?"

It took a second for the good news to be recognized as such. Once the meaning of her father's words sank in, though, Diane broke into a cyclonic dance that propelled her toward him. Her powerful hug when they met nearly knocked him off his feet. She spun away toward the housekeeper, crying for joy as she shouted, "Mrs. Riley! We're staying! We're staying!"

Mrs. Riley was crying for joy, too. "Glory be!" she shrieked, linked in embrace with Diane, joining her whirling dance. "I prayed to the Blessed Mother every night he'd come to his senses!"

As the two danced down the hallway, Joe settled

into his easy chair and breathed a sigh of relief. *It's all finally come together,* he thought. *Boy, it's a damn good thing I had decided not to sign that contract. Otherwise, I'd be pretty pissed off right now, wouldn't I? Hell, I didn't belong there anyway. I'm a teacher, plain and simple.*

Chapter Ninety

In the den of Leonard Pilcher's Pittsburgh mansion, it was deathly quiet. Since his return from New York City late last night, Leonard had hidden from the world, alone in this room. No one else had entered. Slouched in an easy chair, he was inebriated and nauseous, having consumed nothing but copious quantities of Scotch whiskey and mixed nuts. The adjoining bathroom reeked of the splattered vomit that had missed the toilet bowl.

A faint knock on the locked door shattered the silence. "Go away," Pilcher said with a heavy slur.

Another faint knock, followed by the trembling voice of a little girl. "Daddy, I want to talk to you." The voice belonged to his seven-year-old daughter, Daisy. "Can I come in, Daddy?"

His reply stumbled out and hardly sounded convincing. "Not now, baby. Daddy's busy."

There was a click from the door lock. The knob turned. *Shit! My goddamn wife gave the kid a key?* He straightened up in the chair and tried to appear presentable, but it was a vain effort.

The door swung open and young Daisy swept in, wearing a pretty pink dress and pouting lips. She was on the verge of tears. A few steps behind was her older sister, Amanda, wearing her usual expression of disinterest and annoyance. At 10 years of age, Amanda was the picture of her mother in face and mannerisms, right down to the single strand of pearls around her neck.

Daisy's tears started to flow. "Daddy...kids at school say you're a bad man! That you killed somebody!"

Amanda rolled her eyes, an affectation she acquired from her mother at a very early age.

Despite the limitations imposed by the alcohol, Pilcher tried to be comforting. "Oh, baby girl...that's just politics. People will say all kinds of things to win an election."

"So you didn't kill anyone?"

He kissed her forehead. "Of course not, sweetie."

Daisy threw her arms around her father's neck as Amanda rolled her eyes once again. "Just do what I do," the elder sister said. "Tell them when Daddy's president, he's going to throw their stupid parents in jail."

He was not sure when his wife entered the room, but she was standing there now, big as life, in the doorway. As she began to speak, she, too, rolled her eyes. "Leonard, your father's here to see you."

Those words were all it took to make Leonard Pilcher throw up all over his daughter's pretty pink dress.

Once he was alone with his son behind closed doors, it did not take long for Max Pilcher to get right to the point. He was withdrawing financial support for his son's presidential race. There was no point wasting another nickel on this sinking ship. Without that financial support, there would be no presidential campaign for Leonard Pilcher.

Still sporting flecks of his own vomit, Leonard responded by flinging a whiskey bottle against the wall. Bellowing like a wounded animal, he said, "WHY ARE YOU SHITTING ON ME LIKE THIS? IT AIN'T FAIR!"

Max just glowered in disgust at his drunken son.

Now with a pleading tone, Leonard kept right on talking. "You could get me the vice president's slot,

Daddy...Don't need a primary for that." He paused to wait for a response but got only disapproving silence from his father. "Then, once I'm on the ticket," Leonard continued, "maybe something could happen to him..."

Max laughed, shaking his head in disbelief at the same time. "So we just kill a president, too? Is that your answer to everything now, Lenny?"

"Why not, Daddy?"

Max had stopped laughing. His look of disgust returned. "You lied to me, Lenny. I gave you the world and you shit in my face. You could have just told me the truth about everything. I could have fixed it all. But now..."

Max walked away toward the door. "I can't trust you, Lenny. I tried...Believe me, I tried. But I just can't trust you anymore."

As he opened the door, he stopped and turned back to his son. The tone of his voice now dark and ominous, Max said, "You're on your own, son. Best of luck."

The voice in Leonard's head kept repeating his father's last words: *You're on your own, son. Best of luck...You're on your own, son...* With each replay, the message grew more menacing. *I've heard that tone in his voice before, but it was never aimed at me.* His booze-addled mind shuddered to a dismal conclusion: *It can mean only one thing... The old bastard thinks he's going to have me killed.*

There was a strange, warm sensation between Leonard's thighs. It took a moment for him to realize that he had pissed himself.

Before he stepped through the door, Max Pilcher uttered the words that put Leonard's fevered mind at ease. "If you were anyone but my son, Lenny..."

Leonard reveled in the relief those word provided.

In his mind, he finished his father's sentence: *If you were anyone but my son, Lenny...you'd be a dead man.*

The elder Pilcher slammed the door behind him as he exited, leaving his drunken son alone and grinning like an idiot.

Chapter Ninety-One

The weekend had finally arrived. Pola would be on the morning train to Boston, arriving just before lunchtime. Joe fussed with his tie in front of his bedroom mirror. He did not see Diane leaning sullenly against the door frame, watching him.

"Gee, Daddy, I've never seen you wear a tie on Saturday before."

Startled, Joe turned to his daughter in the doorway. She looked lovely in her newest dress and sparkling patent leather shoes. "I just can't seem to get this knot right," he said.

"Here...let me help you." In a moment, she had him looking perfect.

"We'd better hurry, Daddy. You really don't want to be late."

Joe and Diane made the drive to South Station in awkward silence. Joe became increasingly anxious with each passing minute. Finally, as he maneuvered the car into a parking spot near the station, he asked, "You are going to be nice to her, aren't you, honey?"

Diane, arms defiantly crossed, answered with teenage insouciance. "I'll try."

As they hurried through the terminal lobby, Diane asked, "Aren't you forgetting something, Daddy?"

Joe's anxiety climbed a few notches higher. "What? What am I forgetting?"

Diane radiated disapproval as she assumed the role of adult scolding a child. "Flowers, Daddy. You should give her flowers when she steps off the train.

Come on...there's a flower stand right over there."

Pola was just as anxious as Joe as she stepped from the train car to the platform. Like Joe, she, too, desperately wanted this first meeting with Diane to go smoothly. She supposed she checked her tote bag *at least a thousand times* since the train left New York City to make sure the gift box containing the expensive scarf for Diane was still there.

Mostly, she prayed that any attempt to get close to Joe's daughter would not be rebuffed with a chilly *You're not my mother,* spoken or unspoken.

Pola did not see them at first. She looked around apprehensively—and suddenly, there they were, hurrying toward her along the crowded platform. She forced her face into a smile while trying desperately to read the expression on Diane's face, a face to this moment she had only known from the photograph in her father's wallet. She was relieved to find the girl returning a reserved, but pleasant, smile.

Of course, someone could smile while they're sticking the knife in you, too, Pola thought.

The distance between them along the platform rapidly closed. Joe and Pola exchanged a chaste kiss over the spray of flowers he clumsily pushed her way.

"Oh, Joseph, thank you! They're beautiful! And Diane! It's so wonderful to meet you! You look so pretty!"

"Thank you, Doctor MacLeish," Diane said while making a barely perceptible curtsy.

Please tell me this young girl is as sweet as she seems...and not just waiting for a chance to sabotage me.

"Oh, child, please call me Pola."

Perhaps it was just an American teenager's misunderstanding of a foreign figure of speech, very

Scottish and very benign. Or perhaps it was the beginning of the war she feared Joe's daughter would wage against her. Whatever the reason, Diane's reply was swift and razor sharp, "I'm not a child, Doctor MacLeish."

None of them were especially eager for the planned lunch in Cambridge. The drive from the train station had been punctuated only with brief, awkward bursts of small talk between Joe and Pola. Diane stared quietly out the window in the back seat, refusing to participate. She had politely accepted the gift scarf from Pola, glanced at it momentarily, closed the box and pushed it away across the car seat. The prospect of sitting in even more silence around a restaurant table was only making the tension in the car worse.

By chance, Joe had parked the car in front of a Cambridge book store near the Harvard campus. With enthusiasm he hoped would rub off on his two ladies, he said, "You know, there are a few books I need to pick up. Why don't we all browse around a little before lunch?"

He got no argument—and little enthusiasm in return—from Pola or Diane.

The store was crammed wall-to-wall and floor-to-ceiling with books. Narrow aisles of old wooden bookshelves stood like dusty phalanxes in the dim light; the three wandered these aisles separately. Diane was keeping an eye on Pola, catching fleeting glimpses of her father's lover, already with an armful of books for purchase, as she popped in and out of view through the cluttered shelves. Diane prowled, ever searching, although she was not looking for books:

I'll bet she's trying to get Daddy into an empty row so they can make out.

Diane stopped in mid-aisle to spy through the shelves. Something on a book's spine caught her eye—

the author's name: Pola Nilsson-MacLeish. Diane took a step back; every book on that shelf was by the same author. They were college textbooks, at least a dozen different titles. She looked down the aisle to the sign marking the section. It read *Economics.*

"Holy cow!" she muttered as she pulled one of the textbooks from the shelf. As she leafed through it, her eyes opened wide with astonishment. The pages were crammed with mathematical formulas—*and this is no simple algebra, either! I can't even follow this stuff!*

She pulled another book from the shelf and found it, too, was filled with mathematics, most of it far too advanced for her to comprehend.

By the time she had riffled the pages of the third book from the shelf, Diane Gelardi was completely in awe of Doctor Pola Nilsson-MacLeish—so in awe that she did not realize Doctor MacLeish was now standing beside her.

"Well, what do you think?" Pola asked, startling Diane and causing her to drop the book to the floor. "Do you agree with my analysis, Diane?"

Diane could hardly contain her excitement. She scooped the book from the floor and hurriedly scanned page after page as Pola smiled down at her. Finally, Diane's finger fell on a single, complex equation. She looked up at her newest hero, her eyes sincere and bright, and said, "Agree with it? I don't even know what any of it means yet! But you'll teach me, won't you, Pola?"

Neither Pola nor Diane realized that Joe, standing at the end of that same aisle in the rear of the store, was watching them. The midday sun cast its warm light through the sole window at the front of the bookstore. This light formed the backdrop that framed his two ladies, wrapping the vision of their happy, animated conversation in a bright halo.

Something about that book in Diane's hand, I guess. Whatever it is, I think it's done the trick.

He did not want the moment to end. He could go on looking at the two of them like this forever.

Chapter Ninety-Two

The staffer on the ladder struggled to dislodge the PILCHER FOR PRESIDENT banner high on the wall. On the floor of the cavernous room below him, dejected staffers packed up the detritus of a failed presidential run in disillusioned silence. The campaign headquarters, like the campaign itself, was closing down.

With a mighty tug that almost spilled him from the ladder, he finally broke the banner free. It fluttered slowly to the floor, landing silently between a row of desks. Staffers carrying boxes to the trucks outside trod on the banner like it was not even there.

A television still in a corner played the evening news. Allegra Wise was on camera. Several staffers stopped to listen as she spoke.

"Congressman Pilcher announced his withdrawal from the presidential race via letter to the Republican National Committee," Allegra reported. "No plans for a public statement by the former candidate have been announced."

More glum faces gathered to watch the woman on the black and white screen.

"Staffers at his congressional offices in Washington and Pittsburgh responded to this reporter's inquiries with 'no comment.'"

A female staffer began to gently sob. A few more, including some men, dabbed at their moist eyes as Allegra completed her report.

"The congressman has remained out of the public view since eye witnesses, on this network last week, corroborated the Swedish murder allegation against him.

This reporter has been unable to determine the congressman's current whereabouts."

Leonard Pilcher was a bit unsure of his current whereabouts, too. He was alone, driving a *piece of shit* station wagon on a deserted, two-lane road in southern New York State. *Or maybe I'm in northern Pennsylvania...All I know is the sun's setting behind me, so I'm heading east, like I want to be. I may be going a little out of my way, but I can't risk driving through Philly or New York City.* He had not bothered to consult the road map, crumpled in the passenger's foot well, for the past hour.

When the three-day drunk, locked in his den, had finally ended, he decided it was time to hit the road, alone and anonymous. That could be a difficult proposition for a public figure, holed up in a mansion with a small army of reporters waiting at the gate for him to emerge.

Once the booze started to wear off, he had come up with a plan. Reporters, after all, were only human: *they've got to eat, sleep, and shit just like the rest of us.* He could watch them from his den window. Right after sunrise and sundown, their numbers thinned considerably for an hour or so.

More importantly, they had gotten used to the comings and goings of the estate handyman who usually drove this station wagon around the grounds and on errands to town. The reporters did not care much anymore about the comings and goings of this vehicle or the workingman driving it, wearing his rough, wool plaid jacket, baseball cap, and smoking a pipe.

Ol' Henry must have rolled down the window and given them a ration of foul-mouthed shit when they shoved a microphone in his face.

It had been a simple matter to dig out an old plaid

jacket and baseball cap from the outdoor clothes stored in the basement. He even found the never-smoked pipe his oldest daughter had given him a few birthdays back. Now he would be properly disguised to drive off in the beat-up station wagon, unmolested by the news media.

Hell, the car's mine, anyway. They can't exactly report it stolen. Not something I'd normally be caught dead in, though.

He had stuffed a healthy pile of cash from the wall safe in his den into an overnight bag. He did not count it, but he supposed it was more than enough. Buying the necessities of everyday life would be a new experience for Leonard Pilcher. He never had to do it before. He had no idea what those everyday items cost.

But hell...if the peons can afford it, it can't be that much.

The note he left for his wife was a lie. It said he was going to spend a few days by himself at the family hunting lodge in the mountains of central Pennsylvania. He had no intention of going anywhere near it, however.

That should throw them off my scent for a while...like that bitch wife of mine could give a sweet shit, anyway. By the time anybody decides to look for me, I'll already be back.

Then he hit the road, heading east. He needed a little time. He needed freedom—to think, to act.

Like Daddy said, you're on your own, son. Best of luck.

It was well past midnight of that first driving day when the station wagon pulled into a rundown motel outside Albany, New York. Leonard Pilcher was desperate for some sleep. So was the desk clerk who had been jarred from his nap to check him in. Cash was exchanged for a room key with a minimum of fuss.

Pilcher had signed the register *John Taylor, Altoona, PA.* The heavy-lidded clerk did not look capable of recognizing his own mother, let alone this most ordinary-looking man in a ball cap before him who just a few short days ago had been running for president.

As Leonard Pilcher settled into the lumpy mattress, distracted by the rhythmic *thump-thump-thump* of headboard striking wall and the guttural, lustful moans of the couple next door, he tried to keep one thought foremost in his mind: *By this time tomorrow, I'll be there.*

After a fitful sleep, Pilcher awoke with the sunrise. Stumbling to the sink, he splashed cold water on his face; he did not bother to shave. After donning clean underwear and shirt from his overnight bag, he was back in the station wagon, still heading east, searching for a place to eat.

A few miles down the road, he found it—a diner so dilapidated it looked as if a strong wind might blow it over. But the smell of eggs, bacon, and sausage cooking was invitingly strong in the rutted, unpaved parking lot.

Pilcher was stunned as he stepped inside. The clientele was mostly colored; the staff were all colored. There was a moment of silence as everyone glared at the stranger in the door, decided he was no threat, then went back about their business. Spotting an empty seat at the far end of the counter, away from the other customers, Pilcher breathed a sigh of relief: *Oh well...Not much chance any of these jigaboos will recognize me.*

He settled into the seat. The interior of the diner was only slightly less shabby than the exterior, but inside, the aroma of breakfast being fried up was far more intoxicating. A short, portly waitress on the other side of the counter approached and poured him a cup of coffee. She demanded, rather than asked, "What's yours, mister?"

"I'd like to see a menu," Pilcher replied.

"Hey, Clarence," she bellowed to the cook. "Mr. Hoity-Toity here needs to see a menu!"

The diner's occupants erupted in raucous, derisive laughter. As it died down, the waitress pointed to a chalkboard on the wall. "Can you read, man? That there is your menu." With a graceful twirl that belied her considerable girth, she headed to the other end of the counter, saying in a voice that was loud, theatrical, and sarcastic, "Take all the time you need, your highness."

The laughter swelled once again. Red-faced, Pilcher sat and endured it, slowly sipping the coffee. He stared into the cup, pulling the brim of his ball cap down to hide a little more of his face. *Let these monkeys have their fun. They won't lay a hand on you as long as they can keep running their stupid mouths...Just sit still. Let it pass. Don't want to do anything that's going to call more attention to myself...Damn, this coffee is good!*

In another moment, the laughter ceased, and nobody in the diner cared in the least about *that white man without a lick of sense* in their midst. The waitress sauntered back down the counter toward Pilcher. "You ready to order now, mister?"

"I'll take the two eggs, over easy, with hash browns. And more coffee, please."

"Comin' right up."

She placed the order at the kitchen window, then returned with the coffee pot. She studied his face as she poured. "You growin' a beard, sugar?"

After the battering he had just taken, Pilcher welcomed the small talk. "Been thinking about it," he replied. "Makes me look a little like Hemingway, don't you think?"

The waitress let out a hearty yelp of a laugh. "No,

sugar, it don't. He handsome," she said, walking away.

She returned a few minutes later with his eggs. After setting the plate down, she studied his face again. "You know who you do look like?"

Tension rose rapidly in his body as he thought *No! This is all I need...to be recognized in this shithole!* Struggling to remain calm, he replied, "No. Who do you think I look like?"

"That guy...the candidate. That murder in Sweden guy. What's his name?"

Pilcher bluffed a smile and shook his head. "Nah...I don't look anything like him."

The waitress considered his face for another moment, then nodded. "Yeah, you right. He handsome, too. But he must be one stupid motherfucker to get his high and mighty ass locked up in some foreign country."

Pilcher shook his head again, this time in protest. "No, that's not true. Sweden can't touch him."

"Sounds to me like they already did, sugar," the waitress replied.

Chapter Ninety-Three

Joe walked softly down the upstairs hallway, the telephone receiver pressed to his ear, its cradle in hand by his hip. The phone's long cord snaked along the carpet to the small table where the phone usually rested. He peeked into Diane's darkened bedroom.

Softly, Joe said into the phone, "Diane's asleep. Do you want me to wake her?"

"No, don't wake her," Pola replied, her voice echoing in the long-distance lines from New York. "I just wanted to tell her what I have planned for your visit here next weekend."

"She can't wait to come to New York," Joe said. "You know, I've got to say it again, honey…I can't tell you how relieved I am you two hit if off so wonderfully."

With a sigh that sounded both relieved and grateful, Pola replied, "You and me both, laddie!"

Joe shut the hallway light and walked into his bedroom, dragging the phone cord behind. He closed the door gently, then relaxed on the bed to continue their conversation.

"Pola, do you really think there's a chance you could be coming to Harvard?"

"I think so. The new Economics chairman is an old friend. He's been chatting me up about coming on faculty there ever since I left Stockholm. Wouldn't that be brilliant, Joseph?"

"I can't think of anything better."

The conversation drifted happily on into the night, full of hopeful speculation about a life together, with both their careers centered in Cambridge. Neither of them cared one bit at the moment about the long distance charges that were piling up—or anything else, for that matter.

Down the hall, Diane slept soundly. Her school books and trusty slide rule were scattered across the foot of the bed. She was deep in a beautiful dream: *I'm at the top of the Empire State Building...I can see the whole world from up here!*

But suddenly, something was pulling her down from her lofty, imaginary perch. She was not on the Empire State Building anymore—she was back in her bed. A strong hand was clamped over her mouth, pushing her head deep into the pillow. There was the dark shape of a man leaning over her.

I'm not asleep! This is really happening!

The scream that tried to escape from the depths of her soul sounded like nothing more than a muted grunt, stifled by the hand gagging her mouth, inaudible past the walls of her bedroom. There was the glint of a knife's blade before her face. With the powerful kick of a competitive swimmer, she squirted from her attacker's grasp just as the blade slashed the now-unoccupied pillow.

She fell to her knees beside the bed as her attacker whirled to strike again with his knife. The metal slide rule clattered from the bed to the floor beside her. She grabbed the sturdy device, screamed with all the might her lungs would allow, and thrust it at the attacker's face like a bayonet.

It was the attacker's turn to scream as he recoiled in pain and fell from the bed. His hands covered his face—Diane's slide rule had struck him squarely in the eye. His knife had flown from his hand. It slid beneath the dresser and was lost to the darkness.

In his bedroom, Joe heard the screams. He yelled into the phone, "Hang on! Something's wrong!" Dropping the receiver to the bed, he dashed into the hallway.

Pola's frantic voice pleaded to no one: "Joseph? Joseph? What's going on?"

Joe rushed into Diane's bedroom and flipped on the light. He saw his terrified daughter crouched on the floor beside her bed. On the other side of the bed, a man knelt on the floor, hands over his face.

Her voice trembling, Diane shouted, "Daddy, he's got a knife!"

Joe scanned the room for a manic instant but saw no knife. Moving quickly to shield Diane, he searched for something—anything—to use as a weapon, but found nothing. He pulled his daughter to her feet and propelled her toward the door. Then, he savagely pushed the bed into the assailant with an adrenaline-fueled shove of his bare foot, hoping to buy a few milliseconds of time to get Diane to safety.

The assailant was knocked back by the bed but quickly rose to his feet, his face still covered. Then he spoke: "I'm gonna kill you and that little bitch daughter, Gelardi."

The voice was unmistakable. It belonged to Leonard Pilcher.

His hands suddenly clear of his face and balled into fists, Pilcher leapt over the bed, covering the distance so rapidly Joe could not react. But no punches landed. Instead, the two men joined into a relentless, whirling clinch as the bizarre dance of death began once again— just like on that Swedish rooftop so many years ago, when David Linker was Pilcher's ill-fated partner. Locked together, they careened into the narrow hallway.

They were a match in strength; neither could get the upper hand as they spun and bounced off walls—but Pilcher had one advantage: he was wearing shoes. He managed a few kicks against Joe's shins and tried to stomp on his bare feet. But locked together as they were, they were too close. The blows stung, but the short, ineffectual jabs did nothing to deter Joe. Pilcher could not risk the wind-up—the raising of his kicking leg off the floor—that would yield crippling power. Such a move might allow Joe to knock him off balance.

So on they whirled, down the hallway—until they lurched through the door into Joe's bedroom. Joe stumbled—*over my goddamn briefcase!* Suddenly free of Pilcher's grip, Joe fell—and struck his head soundly against the dresser.

He fought for consciousness as Pilcher loomed over him. "I should have put you down like a dog back in Sweden, you guinea bastard," the congressman muttered. "Just like your Jew-boy buddy."

Pola's distressed voice spilled from the phone. "Joseph! What's going on?"

Her Scottish accent was unmistakable. Pilcher picked up the receiver and said, "I'm coming for you next, you fucking bitch."

Pilcher returned to Joe, still supine and groggy on the floor, and grabbed him by the throat. But he made a mistake—his feet straddled Joe, who managed a respectable kick to the congressman's exposed groin. Backpedaling and bellowing in pain once again, Pilcher collided with Diane, who had just reappeared in the doorway. She still held the slide rule—but in her other hand, she wielded a new weapon: a cast-iron frying pan. With a mighty swing, she cracked him across the back of his head with the heavy pan. Pilcher buckled—but recovered almost instantly to backhand her into the hallway. He then slammed the door shut and with a flick of the latch, locked her out...

And then Joe was upon him again. The deadly dance continued—they whirled through the bedroom, leaving a path of objects knocked from the furniture in their wake. Pilcher grabbed a tottering lamp and tried to smash it against Joe's head...

But before the blow could land, the pair stumbled over some unseen obstacle. Pilcher slammed hard, back first, against the bay window. Its weathered wooden framework groaned, then split apart with the *pop* and *clatter* of shattering glass. The lamp slipped from Pilcher's hand and tumbled out, through the void where the window used to be, to the ground below.

Leonard Pilcher found himself dangling in space—his body half-in and half-out of the broken, second-floor window—like a precariously balanced teeter-totter, his head outside, looking up at the stars. The only thing stopping him from plunging to the ground was Joe's tenuous, one-handed grasp on the straining fabric of his jacket's breast pocket. Joe's other hand clung to the wall, the only way to keep himself inside and on his feet.

In a voice that seemed not to recognize he suddenly held the losing hand in this lethal game, Pilcher said, "If I die, my daddy'll put you in the electric chair."

"You and daddy can go straight to hell, Pilcher."

There was a sharp *crack* as the lower sash gave way. The delicate balance was upset—Pilcher's lower body began to slide out of the window opening. His hands grasped for Joe's arm, but managed to clutch only the thin fabric of a pajama sleeve, which immediately tore away, a lifeline secured to nothing. As if in sympathy with Joe's torn sleeve, the breast pocket on Pilcher's jacket—the only anchor left in this roiling storm—popped a thread, then another—and in a swift chain reaction of failed stitching, the pocket tore free of the jacket...

And Leonard Pilcher fell, head first, 20 feet to the ground below. The muted *thud* of impact was masked by the loud, sickening *crack* of his neck breaking.

Then, for a few moments, the street was deathly quiet again.

Lights were coming on in the adjacent, closely-spaced homes. Doors opened, and half a dozen neighbors rushed to the Gelardi front lawn. They stood, silent and open-mouthed, in a circle around this broken, motionless stranger. Their uncomprehending eyes panned back and forth between the wheezing body lying before them and the stark face of their neighbor, Joe, standing in the ragged hole that used to be an upstairs window.

A siren wailed in the distance. It seemed to be getting louder and closer.

Pilcher's body was paralyzed and he found it difficult to speak; his mouth was filling with blood. His glazed eyes cast a final, contemptuous glare at the people looming over him. Then, he closed those eyes and, gurgling like a man underwater, said, "Shit...Witnesses."

Rattling, choking sounds—frightening to listen to—escaped his immobilized body. Congressman Leonard Pilcher was gagging on his own blood. The bystanders stepped back as those sounds quickly rose to a frightening crescendo, then just as quickly diminished in intensity and frequency until they seemed to cease. But there was one last rattle—and when it was finished, Leonard Pilcher was dead.

Chapter Ninety-Four

The golden summer of 1960 would soon be drawing to a close in Malmö. The entire city still seemed to be in vibrant celebration of the warm weather, but any celebration had its boundaries. Within the gates of the Jewish cemetery on Malmö's outskirts, the somber mood knew no season.

Amidst lush shade trees, the headstones in neat rows were all topped with the Star of David. Before one such headstone, a rabbi offered a blessing. The headstone bore the inscription:

DAVID LINKER
SERGEANT, USAAF
FEBRUARY 6, 1926—SEPTEMBER 25, 1944

Standing next to the rabbi were David Linker's parents, Isaac and Sarah Linker. They were finally able to make the trip to their son's grave, courtesy of CBS News. It had been a small price for the network to pay in exchange for the Linker's on-air interview following Leonard Pilcher's exposure and downfall.

Behind Isaac and Sarah, a respectful distance away, stood Joe Gelardi and Pola Nilsson-MacLeish. For them, their coincidental trip to Sweden was a holiday with their children.

Isaac and Sarah clung to each other during the rabbi's prayers, weeping gently. When the rabbi was finished, he whispered a few kind words to the grieving parents, then bid them goodbye. Isaac and Sarah lingered before the grave, still clinging to each other. They stepped forward, each laying a hand on the headstone, speaking soft words to their son Joe and Pola could not hear. Then, still holding her tightly, Isaac Linker escorted his wife from the gravesite.

As they walked—slowly, a bit unsteadily—Isaac turned to give Joe and Pola a harsh look that seemed a silent accusation. Sarah caught him doing it; she pulled him to a stop and said a few words—soft, reproachful words—to her husband. Joe and Pola could only make out one of Sarah Linker's sentences, a simple demand: *Go to them!*

Reluctantly, Isaac released the grasp on his wife and approached Joe and Pola. He stopped a few feet from them, took a moment to compose his thoughts, then directed them to Pola with a stern face. "Back in 1944, you arranged this for my son?"

Neither Pola nor Joe could determine if this question foreshadowed praise or condemnation, but they feared it was the latter. "Yes, Mr. Linker," Pola replied. "I was responsible for arranging the burial."

While Isaac Linker took a few more moments to compose his thoughts, his stern expression began to soften and his eyes moistened. His voice quavered as he spoke. "The rabbi told us that everything was done properly according to Jewish law." He stopped to dab at his eyes. "My wife and I...we want to thank you. Thank you both, very much."

Isaac extended his hand. Joe took it first for a brief handshake. When Pola extended her hand, Isaac took it tenderly in both of his and kissed it.

Chapter Ninety-Five

After the graveside ceremony for David Linker, Joe and Pola wandered lazily back to the heart of Malmö. It had been a quiet and reflective walk through cobblestone streets that Joe had trouble recognizing; much had changed in 16 years. New, modern buildings were now interspersed among the old buildings he remembered. There were just two tasks left to accomplish before returning to the States. The first was to corral their precocious, adventurous teenagers.

Diane and Roddy, Pola's 15-year-old son, had spent the morning at Ribersborg beach, swimming in Öresund Sound. Joe had permitted the outing on the strict condition that they stay away from the bath house, with its nude bathing. Pola had found it hysterically funny when he said to her, "I won't have our kids running around staring at each other's bare asses."

When Pola finally stopped laughing, she said, "Oh, Joseph, that's just so...*American.* Surely you remember the bath house is segregated? And don't you realize Diane and Roddy consider themselves family now? Siblings would rather die than look at each other's bare asses."

The teenagers were right where they promised to be, at the airline ticket office. When their parents arrived at the appointed, mid-afternoon meeting time, they were in animated conversation, leafing through a book on Swedish tourist sites. Diane, full of excitement, blurted an urgent question. "Daddy, can Roddy and I go see a film? Right now?"

Joe answered with a question of his own,

expressing his usual amount of fatherly concern. "What's playing?"

Proud to show off her rapidly growing Swedish vocabulary, Diane replied, "Misen Son Rot."

Joe frowned; he did not understand a word of what she said. Roddy stepped in to translate. "The Mouse That Roared, sir." His flawless English shared his mother's Scottish accent.

Until this moment, Pola had merely watched this scene with an amused smile. She turned to Diane and said, "But honey, it'll be in Swedish, you know."

Diane's enthusiasm was not to be deterred. "That's okay," she replied. "Roddy can translate for me. If I need help, that is."

Roddy chipped in an endorsement of his soon-to-be stepsister. "She's a very fast learner."

Joe and Pola exchanged a parental nod of approval and the teenagers, beaming with delight, streaked for the door. "Be back at the hotel by 1900 hours, you two," Pola called after them. "We have to pack tonight...Early flight tomorrow."

"Doctor Gelardi," the ticket agent called from behind her desk. "We have your tickets all ready."

Joe took the tickets as Pola chatted amiably in Swedish with the ticket agent. Everything seemed to be in order. There were four tickets, one for Joe, Pola, Diane, and Roddy. The itineraries were the same on each ticket: Malmö—London—Boston.

Now there was just one more thing to do before going home.

A beautiful sunset had begun to cast its orange glow across Malmö as Joe and Pola emerged from the staircase. They were at the top of the bell tower once again, the same tower from which they witnessed David

Linker's murder. The few pigeons perched on the deck's railing were unperturbed; they did not fly away as the humans approached the railing.

The lovers were silent for a few minutes, basking in the beautiful view and evening breeze. The city below them seemed to be gilded. "Didn't I tell you it was beautiful?" Pola asked.

Clinging to each other tightly, they turned as one to look down at the police barracks roof. It looked exactly the same as the last time they had seen it, with one big exception. This time, it was devoid of people.

They found no words to say, but they both knew they were sharing the same somber reflection: *we did wrong...we fixed it the best we could.*

Almost in unison, they both took deep breaths and turned to face the sunset once again. Joe's lips found Pola's and they kissed tenderly. He nodded toward the bells hanging motionless and silent, their slack lanyards swaying easily in the breeze. He sounded a bit concerned when he asked, "What time did you say they go off?"

Before Pola could answer, the ropes tightened and jerked—and the bells began to swing. The pigeons took flight; the lovers clamped their hands over their ears, their laughter drowned out by the thunderous pealing.

Joe could read the answer to his question in Pola's lips. *Now!* she was saying, her eyes bright and happy, but her voice stood no chance against the power of the bells. And when the tolling of the bells was finally done, their hands found each other once again. As they embraced, a solitary pigeon feather that had settled on the railing was swept up by the breeze and floated downward, gently downward, to the cobblestone street below.

*****

About The Author

William Peter Grasso's novels explore the concept *change one thing...and watch what happens*. Focusing on the WW2 era, they weave actual people and historical events into a seamless and entertaining narrative with the imagined. His books have spent several years in the Amazon Top 100 for Alternative History and War.

A lifelong student of history, Grasso served in the US Army and is retired from the aircraft maintenance industry. These days, he confines his aviation activities to building and flying radio-controlled aircraft.

Contact the Author Online:
Email: wpgrasso@cox.net

Connect with the Author on Facebook:
https://www.facebook.com/AuthorWilliamPeterGrasso

Follow the Author on Amazon:
https://amazon.com/author/williampetergrasso

More Novels by William Peter Grasso

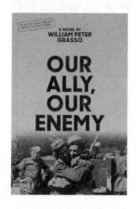

Our Ally, Our Enemy
Moon Brothers WWII Adventure Series
Book 3

Allies can be your worst enemies.

1945. The war may be going badly for the Third Reich, but they continue to develop "super weapons" to throw against the Allies. As the Moon brothers—fighter pilot Tommy and tanker Sean—struggle with the myths and realities of defeating the new technologies, a new threat appears: their Soviet allies are intent on dominating Europe. But a game-changer still looms: in the mountains of Bavaria, the Germans are preparing a super weapon against which there is no defense.

Fortress Falling
Moon Brothers WWII Adventure Series
Book 2

France, October 1944: Fort Driant may be a 19th century anachronism, but it proves itself an impregnable obstacle to Patton's forces as they fight to seize the city of Metz, a gateway to Germany. Another fortress—a *Flying Fortress*—may be the key to the fall of Fort Driant. The Moon brothers are in the thick of the battle as Tommy volunteers for *Operation Aphrodite*, a gambit that turns unmanned heavy bombers into radio-controlled flying bombs of enormous power. But as zero hour for *Aphrodite* approaches, his brother Sean is trapped in the tunnels of Fort Driant, with the Germans just inches away behind armored doors. It's a race against time for the GIs to take Driant—or escape before the *Flying Fortress* falls.

Moon Above, Moon Below
Moon Brothers WWII Adventure Series
Book 1

France, August 1944. In this alternate history WW2 adventure, American and British forces struggle to trap and destroy the still-potent German armies defending Normandy. But the Allies face another formidable obstacle of their own making: a seething rivalry between generals leads to a high-level disregard for orders that puts the entire campaign in the Falaise Pocket at risk of devastating failure—or spectacular success. That campaign unfolds through the eyes of two American brothers—one an idealistic pilot, the other a fatalistic tanker—as they plunge headlong into the confusion and indiscriminant slaughter of war.

Operation Fishwrapper
Book 5
Jock Miles WW2 Adventure Series

June 1944: A recon flight is shot down over the Japanese-held island of Biak, soon to be the next jump in MacArthur's leapfrogging across New Guinea. Major Jock Miles, US Army—the crashed plane's intelligence officer—must lead the handful of survivors to safety. It's a tall order for a man barely recovered from a near-crippling leg wound. Gaining the grudging help of a Dutch planter who has evaded the Japanese since the war began, Jock discovers just how little MacArthur's staff knows about the terrain and defenses of the island they're about to invade.

Operation Blind Spot
Book 4
Jock Miles WW2 Adventure Series

After surviving a deadly plane crash, Jock Miles is handed a new mission: neutralize a mountaintop observation post on Japanese-held Manus Island so MacArthur's invasion fleet en route to Hollandia, New Guinea, can arrive undetected. Jock's team seizes and holds the observation post with the help of a clever deception. But when they learn of a POW camp deep in the island's treacherous jungle, it opens old wounds for Jock and his men: the disappearance—and presumed death—of Jillian Forbes at Buna a year before. There's only one risky way to find out if she's a prisoner there...and doing so puts their entire mission in serious jeopardy.

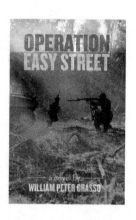

Operation Easy Street
Book 3
Jock Miles WW2 Adventure Series

Port Moresby was bad. Buna was worse.

The WW2 alternative history adventure of Jock Miles continues as MacArthur orders American and Australian forces to seize Buna in Papua New Guinea. Once again, the Allied high command underestimates the Japanese defenders, plunging Jock and his men into a battle they're not equipped to win. Worse, jungle diseases, treacherous terrain, and the tactical fantasies of deluded generals become adversaries every bit as deadly as the Japanese. Sick, exhausted, and outgunned, Jock's battalion is ordered to spearhead an amphibious assault against the well-entrenched enemy. It's a suicide mission—but with ingenious help from an unexpected source, there might be a way to avoid the certain slaughter and take Buna. For Jock, though, victory comes at a dreadful price.

Operation Long Jump
Book 2
Jock Miles WW2 Adventure Series

Alternative history takes center stage as Operation Long Jump, the second book in the Jock Miles World War 2 adventure series, plunges us into the horrors of combat in the rainforests of Papua New Guinea. As a prelude to the Allied invasion, Jock Miles and his men seize the Japanese observation post on the mountain overlooking Port Moresby. The main invasion that follows quickly degenerates to a bloody stalemate, as the inexperienced, demoralized, and poorly led GIs struggle against the stubborn enemy.

Long Walk to the Sun
Book 1
Jock Miles WW2 Adventure Series

In this alternate history adventure set in WW2's early days, a crippled US military struggles to defend vulnerable Australia against the unstoppable Japanese forces. When a Japanese regiment lands on Australia's desolate and undefended Cape York Peninsula, Jock Miles, a US Army captain disgraced despite heroic actions at Pearl Harbor, is ordered to locate the enemy's elusive command post.

Conceived in politics rather than sound tactics, the futile mission is a "show of faith" by the American war leaders meant to do little more than bolster their flagging Australian ally. For Jock Miles and the men of his patrol, it's a death sentence: their enemy is superior in men, material, firepower, and combat experience. Even if the Japanese don't kill them, the vast distances they must cover on foot in the treacherous natural realm of Cape York just might.

Unpunished

Congressman. Presidential candidate. Murderer.
Leonard Pilcher is all of these things.

As an American pilot interned in Sweden during WWII,
he kills one of his own crewmen and gets away with it.
Two people have witnessed the murder—American
airman Joe Gelardi and his secret Swedish lover, Pola
Nilsson-MacLeish—but they cannot speak out without
paying a devastating price. Tormented by their guilt and
separated by a vast ocean after the war, Joe and Pola
maintain the silence that haunts them both...until 1960,
when Congressman Pilcher's campaign for his party's
nomination for president gains momentum. As he dons
the guise of war hero, one female reporter, anxious to
break into the "boy's club" of TV news, fights to
uncover the truth against the far-reaching power of the
Pilcher family's wealth, power that can do any wrong it
chooses—even kill—and remain unpunished.

East Wind Returns

A young but veteran photo recon pilot in WWII finds the fate of the greatest invasion in history--and the life of the nurse he loves--resting perilously on his shoulders.

East Wind Returns is a story of World War II set in July-November 1945 which explores a very different road to that conflict's historic conclusion. The American war leaders grapple with a crippling setback: Their secret atomic bomb does not work. The invasion of Japan seems the only option to bring the war to a close. When those leaders suppress intelligence of a Japanese atomic weapon poised against the invasion forces, it falls to photo reconnaissance pilot John Worth to find the Japanese device. Political intrigue is mixed with passionate romance and exciting aerial action--the terror of enemy fighters, anti-aircraft fire, mechanical malfunctions, deadly weather, and the Kamikaze. When shot down by friendly fire over southern Japan during the American invasion, Worth leads the desperate mission that seeks to deactivate the device.

Shamnel
540-981-7700

Made in the USA
Columbia, SC
17 March 2024